Praise for the w

Terribl

The first in the Redamancy Series, *Terrible Praise* is a highly engrossing story. As noted by the author, the definition of redamancy—an obscure word well suited to Stela—is the act of loving in return. Themes of identity, fulfillment, loss, loyalty, love and redamancy are explored in complex, nuanced ways. The characters draw the reader into the story while the pacing keeps the reader engaged. Hayes' writing is a pleasure to read and provides thoughtful and sensitive observations, especially when it comes to her characters.

-Lambda Literary Review

I LOVE a first person that is written well. A good first person can really pique my curiosity and keep me guessing, and Lara Hayes had me confused (is she really crazy?!) but never lost and always interested. The leading ladies are Stela and Elizabeth, I enjoyed the way they were written especially Elizabeth. Her actions were rational and logical which I can get behind. Stela has a mysterious air to her and I love that sort of thing...Two thumbs up.

-The Lesbian Review

This is another debut book that I never once considered that it was. While this may be the first published book, it's clear that Hayes knows how to write. I'm happy to say I loved the ending and it gave me hope. This is going to be a series so it ends when new things are just beginning. I enjoy different and more cerebral reads on occasion. And I like where the series seems to be headed, so I will be reading more.

-Lex's Reviews, goodreads

ALL TOGETHER STRANGER

BOOK TWO THE REDAMANCY SERIES

Other Bella Books by Lara Hayes

The Redamancy Series
Terrible Praise

ALL TOGETHER STRANGER

BOOK TWO THE REDAMANCY SERIES

LARA HAYES

2020

Bella Books, Inc.
P.O. Box 10543
Tallahassee, FL 32302

Printed in the United States of America on acid-free paper.

First Bella Books Edition 2020

Editor: Cath Walker
Cover Designer: Judith Fellows

ISBN: 978-1-64247-119-9

Acknowledgments

My deepest thanks to everyone at Bella Books for their work on this book and their continued support, especially Linda and Jessica Hill. Thank you to my amazing editor Cath Walker, it was a dream to work with you again.

I would not have completed this second installment without the love and encouragement of my mother and brother. And there would be no sequel without the support of each and every person who purchased *Terrible Praise*.

Thank you to Carolyn, my friend and pre-reader. Thank you to Dana, my friend, mentor, and fellow author. Thank you to my loves Megan and Jackie. Thank you to both Nicks, Robby, Mandy, Seth, Lizzy, Kelly, John, Lorelei, Stephen, and Catherine. Thank you to Veda, Jess, Natasha, and Sue.

“It is very painful, I think, to be told: ‘You enchanted the world for me, you made me feel things I never knew I could, now please be normal at dinner.’”

-Brian Phillips, *Run to the Devil: On The Ghosts and the Grace of Nina Simone*

Redamancy (noun): The act of loving in return.

For Meg.

I

Crepuscule

I'm never tired anymore.

My eyes open of their own accord at sunset, a phenomenon I sense in my marrow, but no longer witness. The sensation is not exhilarating, bearing some resemblance to vertigo.

Falling asleep occurs without my knowledge or consent and is not prefaced by fatigue. No matter where I am or what I'm doing, at precisely five a.m. my vision tunnels, my ears ring and an impenetrable slumber sucks me into oblivion. I don't hear the voices of those around me while incapacitated. I can't discern light from dark and absolutely nothing wakes me until my body registers the descent of the sun.

Stela is the only reason I was able to verify any of this. We tried everything I could think of to postpone my inevitable shutdown, but I will black out mid-sentence when sleep comes. Even standing in the middle of the room or walking. After two rather embarrassing attempts to prolong my coherence through physical exertion—during which I fell asleep on top of and underneath her—I gave up.

The others tell me that they too rose and fell at dusk and dawn in the early years, but that after a time—months or years—they were able to delay this forced repose, though not by very much and not without considerable physical and mental discomfort. For beings with an astounding capacity to retain even the most mundane, the Strigoi have a curiously lax relationship with time. They've also urged me against comparing Stela's sleeping habits and my own. She is unique in that respect, and by her own account she's been largely in control of her sleep patterns for as far back as she can remember.

Fane is another matter entirely. The only thing I know for certain about his chronobiology is that his tolerance for sunlight far exceeds Stela's. In fact, I'm not sure whether he sleeps at all and any question is swiftly rebuffed by everyone, including Stela, who is being either intentionally evasive or honestly does not know.

High overhead the projector switches on and washes the empty window panels in stark white nothing. The bedside lamp follows a few seconds later, precipitated by the clunky tick of an automated timer. The ticking stops and in the gritty illumination that casts a spiderweb of shadows along the floor, her right arm tightens around my waist.

Delicate fingers trace abstract patterns on my abdomen in silent salutation. The gesture has become something of a ritual for us, and I roll over on my back to find her smiling down at me warmly with her elbow propped on her pillow. Stela's pale blond hair falls in a perfect swatch across her bare shoulder, and every time I wake to find her waiting for acknowledgment, I wonder whether I'm still dreaming.

"Welcome back," she says with a smile.

"To the land of the living?" I smile back at her as her fingers trace the arches of my brows and run lightly across my bottom lip. I have asked her repeatedly not to greet me with "Good evening," which she and the rest of her family use as a salutation at the start of each night, though I had difficulty articulating why it bothered me. Stela took the criticism in her stride, and like everything that concerns us, made the necessary adjustments. She's been testing alternatives ever since, my favorite of which so far is "Good morrow."

Stela tilts her chin, feigning consternation. "In a manner of speaking, I suppose." Her obsidian eyes shine jovially which delights and disappoints me at once. She's a much better sport on nights when it is her turn to feed, a necessity I resent only because it means an evening without her.

Her bare thigh presses between mine as she stretches above me, like a cat after a long nap. She is without doubt the greediest and most generous partner I've ever had, especially in the first few hours of wakening. Stela's palms slide beneath my shoulder blades as she pulls my body directly beneath hers, placing me as she would have me. Not that I'm complaining. This preference for evenings is one of the most predictable things about Stela and ranks among her most endearing traits.

Lips the color of turned strawberries ghost along my clavicle. They press lightly against the last scar I'll ever receive, nestled in the crook of my neck. The scalloped muscles of her back tighten under my hands, but her resolve falters and then her affectionate ministrations cease.

"You dreamed of me again," she says.

I find it more than a little bit irritating that she doesn't even ask anymore. Her body relaxes and she lays both hands against my sternum to rest her chin atop them. Stela arches an expectant eyebrow when I'm less forthcoming than she would like. She quakes her hands gently, as though shaking me out of my silence. "Were you there?"

"Elizabeth, you know that I was not."

"Then how do you know I dreamt of you?"

Stela plants her forearms on the bed, the convivial gleam exchanged for something more serious. I run my fingers through her faultless hair, scouring her unobstructed gaze for deceit. She made a promise not to pry into my mind, an agreement that now goes both ways, though I'm still fighting to control that ability. Stela shifts her weight to her right side, pulls my hands from her hair to plant a kiss upon each palm, and then she folds my hands pointedly over my heart.

"Your touch is desperate, my darling. Troubled."

"I'm not troubled."

An exasperated sigh threatens her otherwise tranquil expression. She leans forward and grazes my jaw with her teeth. I hadn't realized I held my body clenched until it unfurls from her playful nip. She kisses my cheek and pulls her thumb down the cleft of my chin. "Tell me about your dream."

I twist toward her and place my palm on the small of her back, urging her to resume her place above me. She smothers a victorious grin which sharpens the corners of her mouth into two satisfied points and reclaims her perch.

"It was the same dream," I say.

"Was it day or night?"

"Night this time."

The time is the only variation I've noticed in the dream. The rest follows an eerily simplistic and specific track.

I'm walking along a cliff and find Stela is standing at the edge. My heart soars with longing and my stomach clenches with dread at the sight of her motionless silhouette. I call her name, but she remains fixated on the moon's reflection in the ocean below. I scream at her and still she doesn't move, so I run. But I never reach her.

"Does it frighten you when I leave to hunt?" she asks. "Are you afraid that I will not return?"

I hook my calf around the back of her legs and pull her body against mine. "What worries me isn't the thought of you leaving to hunt. It's the way the dream feels."

"How does it feel?" she asks quietly.

"Like a memory."

Stela says nothing. My arms lock around her neck and I tug her down into a kiss that is equal parts punishment she doesn't deserve and the adoration she quietly craves. Her mouth remains open afterward, an unspoken invitation, our faces only an inch apart. I hesitantly pull the swell of her bottom lip between my teeth, appraising her reaction. A second set of incisors slide down over my human teeth. When I feel Stela's lip pull taut in a taunting smile, I seize upon the offering in earnest and gouge the resilient flesh. The blood that mingles in our mouths causes my body to convulse as Stela cradles my face in her hands, a delighted hum crawling up her throat. I clench my fists so ferociously that every knuckle and both my wrists crack from the strain.

When she pulls away Stela is the portrait of a sage tutor and I crane my neck to chase her mouth.

"Very good, dear one."

She guides me back down against the bed, her palm pressed to my pounding heart. She closes her eyes, no doubt remembering the way my human heartbeat once raced against her fingertips at the slightest provocation. "Soon you will be fit for a hunt of your own."

Her eyes remain closed, fingers drumming against my sternum as the thirst takes hold. The few meager drops of blood I wrenched from Stela's lip are just drops of gasoline to the flame of my persistent hunger. Every fleck of dust sharpens into a pinpoint of light, casting a shimmering cloak across the room. My pulse—normally twenty beats per minute—thunders behind my eyes, my fingers curl into talons gripping the edge of the mattress. My vertebrae shiver and then snap into alignment. My legs twitch and I expend my last vestige of control to wrench the first syllable of her name from between my clenched teeth.

Stela needs no warning. Neither worried nor surprised, she blocks my involuntary attacks before pinning my wrists above my head in the tender fingers of one firm hand. The other hand she uses to muzzle my mouth, pressing gently down until my head rests once more on the pillow. Her bright laugh roils in my belly as every muscle rails against confinement. She whispers my name between breathy laughter, the pale curtain of her hair tickling my cheeks. My pulse slows, restoring me to myself.

We can't cry, but my body hasn't forgotten the need. Stela stills, releasing my face and limbs as she rears back on her knees. She pulls me with her, holds my cheek to her chest.

"No, my dearest," she gently admonishes, "you are making remarkable strides." She rocks us slowly back and forth.

"Stela—"

"I know."

I swallow another impotent whimper and scrub my face with my palm, which comes away clean and dry. The lack of tears only underscores the many unwelcome changes to my physiology. Frightened to face the monster I sense inside, I clasp her face despairingly. "I would never hurt you."

"Elizabeth." She pulls my hands from her face and wraps my arms around her waist. She kisses me lightly and presses her forehead against mine.

"You need to feed," she says.

"I'm fine for now."

Stela purses her lips, frowning. We've had this argument many times before. She leaves the safety of our bed in a rush, gathering her black silk robe from its haphazardly flung heap on the floor and my blood roars for her the moment she secures the belt around her waist.

No amount of intimacy or proximity is ever enough to satiate this terrible magnetism. Sometimes she can feel it too, the gut-deep pull, though I doubt her affections are as eclipsing as mine.

Stela descends the three generous steps into the sitting area and selects an emerald-green forestscape for the window panels. I leave my own robe where it lies on the floor as I stand behind her.

"I'll eat soon. I promise." I drag my nose along the side of her neck and she reclines into my waiting embrace. Her fingers dance across my knuckles, but her back is tense.

"I wish you would stop this self-inflicted hunger strike. It changes nothing, Elizabeth. Over time the need for daily feedings will abate, but first you must indulge your body. Give yourself time to grow stronger."

I press my face between her shoulder blades. "I don't like feeling this way."

Stela turns in my arms. "You do not have to be in control of everything all the time, dearest." She splays her hand against my lower back, brushing her lips over mine. "Let go. Permit yourself to revel in the hunger when it possesses you."

"Stela, I literally just attacked you."

"If you wish to achieve restraint enough to enjoy me without the fear of harming me, you must accept what you are. You have to embrace these cravings to conquer them. I promise, my darling, if you do not, they will drive you mad. And I know you absolutely abhor the thought of being slave to anything."

She's right. She knows she's right and she knows she's won but has the good sense not to gloat.

"Come." She takes my hand and pulls me back up the steps toward the bathroom. "A shower first. Then you must feed."

* * *

I sit on the lip of the tub, wrapped in Stela's robe, with a blood collection bag on my knees. At first, I was wary of them, unlabeled and possibly riddled with contagion. Stela laughed it off, assuring me that my constitution was such that any virus would find my body an inhospitable host.

They won't tell me where the bags come from. Only that the family keeps a steady supply for my sake. Neither will they tell me where they store them, which is wise. Stela brings me three a day, unless she's hunting or otherwise occupied. In which case Bård usually procures my lunch.

If the act of ingesting human blood of unknown origin once sickened me, I can't remember. Not with the first bag or any that followed. My apprehension lasts only until the first taste. However, I do have trouble feeding in front of an audience and given my reluctance—in general—to assimilate, Stela rebuffs any attempt on my part to feed in private.

The blood bag sloshes around on my knees. Transfixed, I poke the carmine liquid.

"Having met the woman only once, I am certain that Claire told you not to play with your food."

My head darts up, the bag forgotten in my lap. Stela regards me scrupulously from the corner of her eye in the mirror as she pins her hair back. She drops her hands to her sides and kneels in front of me.

"I apologize. That was thoughtless of me."

I straighten my spine and clasp my hands in my lap. "I don't want to talk about her, Stela. Not even in passing. Not yet." The mention of my mother's name still carries an echo of her accident on the stairs, the sounds her body made as it shattered. Just one missed step. I had nightmares of killing her for months before she slipped. In the most recurrent, I stood over her sleeping body and smothered her with a pillow. That was the first nightmare I shared with Stela.

Stela kisses my cheek. I close my eyes but remain unresponsive as she stands and moves back to the sink. "I will not repeat the misstep," she promises. "It was careless."

She runs over her reflection with an appraising eye, one hand reaching deftly for the small hook beside the mirror. She selects a long, delicate white gold chain adorned with a nondescript medallion. She loops the chain over her head and buttons the front of her gray silk blouse so that the medallion is only partially visible. Enough to lure the eye if her physique somehow failed to do the trick. I feel fiercely possessive as I flop the bag between anxious hands.

"Elizabeth, eat. Please. Would you have me distracted on a hunt? Wondering whether or not you have fed?"

There's something vaguely juvenile about the moment. Waiting on the tub while she readies herself, my breakfast on my knees. I used to sit on the closed lid of the toilet in my mother's enormous bathroom, watching her do the very same thing. I chase the comparison away as a familiar pressure builds behind my eyes. I can't cry for her anymore. For weeks I wished the tears would stop and now that they have, I realize how important they were. I thought the grief would leave me but it lies dormant, coiled in my chest and immovable. Stela seems so in control of her limited emotions. I was expecting a similar alexithymia to afflict me, but nothing so far. Perhaps, like the urge to feed and the inescapability of sleep, compartmentalization is just another muscle that slowly strengthens through the passage of time.

I turn toward the shower wall for what privacy I can manage in the small en suite. The plastic of the blood bag is tepid against my lips as it punctures between my teeth. I'm only distantly aware of the sounds I make when the first few drops trickle past my lips. My senses flood with life, my tongue alight with elements. Notes of sodium, chloride, potassium, phosphate mixed together. I brace myself against the shale-covered wall as a starved and painful shudder wrenches through me.

When I open my eyes, Stela is towering above me, her hand extended and a haughty expression on her face. I take her hand and she pulls me flush against her. "Good girl." She wraps a fist in my hair as she closes her mouth over my parted lips. Her tongue chases the taste of blood as I gather her blouse in my hands and shove her against the wall. The sharp splintering of tiles halts my affection, shards of chipped black slate clattering to the floor. Her extrinsically girlish laugh rings in my ears as she rests her forearms on my shoulders.

"Sorry." I release her blouse, smoothing the silk, but Stela's brilliant smile tells me that this was precisely the reaction she was after. She sucks on her bottom lip and a rebellious lock of pale gold hair slips against her cheek.

"How do I look?" she asks, stepping away from the wall. She tucks the front of her shirt back into the waist of her black slacks. I retrieve a damp cloth from the edge of the sink and drag the frayed edges around her mouth, smeared with blood. I take a step back, her eyes locked on mine.

"Perfect."

Stela glows. The medallion nestled between her breasts shimmers, catching the light, and I know with sickening certainty that someone else will admire it tonight. Someone will feel her deliberate breath in their ear. Someone will put their hands on her body. Someone will thank whatever deity they worship for placing this creature in their arms, and they will adore her right up until the moment she rips out their throat. I wish their imminent death consoled me but seeing her dressed in an outfit that calls to mind our first encounter makes the knowledge unbearable. If she knows what I'm thinking, she chooses to ignore it, her expression one of good-natured indifference as she takes my hand and tugs me toward the bathroom door.

"You are unforgivably late for your sparring lesson. Bård will never let me hear the end of it if we make tardiness a habit."

My fingers close around her wrist and I drag her back to me with a strength that surprises us both. It only lasts a second, but the fingers of her free hand curl and I know she was startled enough to retaliate. "Take a man this evening."

She isn't pleased. "I take a man most evenings," she says in a diplomatic tone. "You were an exception."

The thin bones in her wrist flex experimentally against my fingers, like she's testing my hold. I drop her hand, disgusted that I caused her alarm. "Just—promise me. Just for tonight. Promise you won't make another exception."

She broods mutely, the air between us dangerously silent. I sense that I've crossed a line. I just don't regret it. Stela has never once apologized for what she is, has never lied to me about her nature. Her steps are soundless as she crosses the bedroom and stands beneath the hatch in the ceiling.

"Do not keep Bård waiting, Irina," she calls over her shoulder in a completely neutral tone. One I haven't heard since the night she told me that the choice to live or die was mine. The hatch settles shut behind her. The name Fane gave me echoes lamely through the room.

* * *

"You are quiet this evening."

Bård pitches a blood bag over his shoulder and I catch it with a reflexive ease that would have made my father proud. I clutch the bag to my chest with my left hand, my right arm hanging lifelessly at my side. Despite the commonality of guns in this country, he insists upon training with longswords, rapiers, and quarterstaffs. His preferred hand-to-hand combat is Krav Maga, but that is easily the most modern thing about him. To call the man an old soul would be as glaring an understatement as calling him a man at all. But combat, he says, is all about form.

He perches nimbly on his toes as he hovers over my shoulder to inspect his handiwork. I chanced one look at the wound as I collapsed. A scalene laceration penetrating to the sternocleidomastoid, shattering the clavicle. I've found it's better not to examine my injuries too closely. I discovered this on my first lesson with Bård. He shot me in the abdomen as I walked through the door. That's the only time I've ever seen a gun in his hands. He said I needed to know what a bullet felt like. Stela had responded by throwing him into a wall, but in his defense, how was he supposed to know I'd already lived through a shooting the night Stela chased me out of a nightclub and into the arms of my assailant. The scar on my left bicep still looks red and angry in a certain light.

As I tear into the blood bag the shards of bone slowly regroup with a series of disgusting snaps. I'm not immune to pain. I just experience it differently. But such a grave injury induces a hunger that is horrific. The more serious the injury, the more insatiable I become.

"You had an argument with Stela," he surmises.

I roll my eyes at Bård's knowing smirk. He drops cross-legged beside me to the floor with disregard for the impact, his spine straight, forearms on his knees. I test my right arm. My shoulder pops into place and the wound seals over with new flesh.

"There you are." Bård slaps my shoulder so hard that my legs skid across the marble floor. "No worse for wear."

I grit my teeth so ferociously the enamel cracks. I'm sure he hears it too, but Bård is entirely unflappable. I can see why Stela adores him. He's a warrior with a heart, a genteel murderer. He permits no weakness in his training room, has no time for social niceties, yet here he sits, trying to talk to me about girlfriend troubles.

"What makes you think we had an argument?"

Bård looks about the armory and picks up his discarded saber. His weathered face is that of a man in his early sixties, his hair salt-and-pepper gray. Yet the muscles of his chest are pronounced, his vast shoulders as defined as a rower's. He is unexpectedly kind, meditative in his patience.

"Do you know why you failed this evening, Irina?"

The light bounces off the blade as he spins the pommel. I'm grateful to have lost the ability to blush. Ever the clever student, I replay our lesson behind closed eyelids, my newly forged eidetic memory a welcome upgrade to my considerable attention to detail.

"Your lunge was a feint and my attack should have been a parry. My shoulder was vulnerable to your counter."

Bård guffaws. "You were not present. Your thoughts were of Stela and not your opponent. Technique is equal parts practice *and* focus."

I scoff and Bård smacks my forehead with the sword. "See? You could have blocked that easily had you been paying attention."

I stand up and snatch the weapon from his grip, gathering my own fallen sword as I make my way to the rack on the wall.

"Perhaps tomorrow we will practice with the quarterstaff, and tonight you can talk to Stela," he says.

His obvious fondness of Stela is the only thing we have in common.

"She won't listen." I shove the blades into their gilded scabbards and return them to their mounts. Bård remains silent, watching me closely. "Stela doesn't hear what she can't immediately solve."

Bård stands and strolls closer, his bushy brows drawn close together. I'm touched by how invested he seems.

"The two of you are more alike than either of you wish to believe," he says. "You remind me of Stela when she was young. Impetuous. Bullheaded."

"Thanks?"

Bård chuckles, nervously scratching the silver stubble along his jaw. He takes my hand. "The biggest lie we tell ourselves, Irina, is that we can no longer feel. It is an armor of sorts, because eternity is impossible for the faint of heart. In all the centuries I have known Stela, even during her mortal infancy, I have never seen her so happy as now."

I swallow nosily, my throat constricting.

"She fears disappointment as desperately as you do."

He drops my hand and retrieves his white shirt from the floor. He shakes his loose, wiry ponytail free from the collar and rolls up the sleeves. "You will be on time for tomorrow's lesson," he says over his shoulder, striding to the door.

He grips the doorframe on his way out, spins back inside the room. "And if you tell anyone of our conversation…"

"You'll kill me."

Bård bares his teeth in a roguish grin and nods contentedly. "You are a quick study. Almost as quick as your Maker."

"Thank you, Bård."

"Do not dawdle in the halls, Irina," he calls out. "Fane detests idle wandering."

* * *

The room is reverently silent. The sandstone walls slope up to arched ceilings covered with brilliant depictions of heaven and hell, the victors and the fallen of some long-forgotten war, a ghastly banquet of corpulent children—possibly cherubs—and an army of emerald-robed soldiers in a great valley. There are plush leather armchairs along the far wall, with coffee tables positioned between each. A long, sturdy lovingly polished table stretches the length of the room. Ornate sconces cast mandarin-colored ovals of light up to the rafters. Enormous carved-wood chandeliers dangle precariously from the ceiling on weathered ropes, anachronistically illuminated by LED bulbs.

I've never ventured into the library without Stela. The distant scribble of a fountain pen scurrying across parchment suggests that Darius is well-hidden somewhere in the stacks. He's the only member of Stela's small but formidable family who I don't find terrifying. I consider calling out to him, but not even the studious historian would miss my footsteps crossing into his lair.

The towering oak bookshelves stand thirty feet high, each one adorned with a polished brass plate that in elegant script offers only a date range. The rows are broken down by century, the shelves are regional. Every work of fiction is present and accounted for, from

Ivanhoe to *The Brothers Karamazov*, but not a single title following the birth of the twentieth century. As though no modern mind produced anything valuable enough to warrant inclusion in this staggering collection.

"Irina." Darius is stealthier than he looks, and I nearly drop the first edition *Anna Karenina*. "To what do I owe the honor of your visit?"

I slide the book gingerly back into place. "Good evening. I was hoping to occupy myself with some light reading while Stela's aboveground. I've been through most of her collection already."

"I see." Darius pulls the round wire frames from the bridge of his nose, hooks them on the front of his yellowed T-shirt. Stela has said that he's the strangest of her siblings, but I wasn't sure what she meant until now. There are no lenses in his glasses. "Well, I am certain we can find something here that strikes your fancy." He makes a dramatic sweep with his hand. "You were seeking fiction?"

I nod halfheartedly and wander down the length of the aisle, tipping book spines closer and immediately replacing them. Darius smooths his greasy black hair back around his ears, offering unsolicited critiques of every volume I touch. He licks his fingertip, drags it over the white strip of scalp that runs in a perfectly straight part down the middle of his head. I pretend not to notice his primping and drum my fingers against the shelf.

"Maybe something more substantial this evening," I say.

"Nonfiction is right this way."

My palm closes over his forearm before he has the chance to turn around and Darius freezes, his chinless jaw turned toward the floor. I reconsider my tactics. Stela has repeatedly warned me to not go poking around the compound with an agenda, and I don't want to scare Darius off by asking for too much too soon. "A biography, perhaps. Something unusual."

His somber black eyes run quizzically across my face. He politely extracts his arm. "Unusual?"

The look he gives me is the same I see every night from at least one of their lot. Distrust, a hint of fear, perhaps, though I can't imagine why. I shouldn't have touched him, but Stela is constantly mentioning my standoffishness.

"I beg your pardon." Darius shakes his head. "I so rarely have visitors apart from Fane. And seldom do I receive a request for historical documents." He takes a step back and gestures toward the belly of the library. "Right this way. I have much to show you."

Darius moves gracefully but quickly, speaking excitedly of ancient Sumerian scrolls which weren't so much lost as they were reallocated.

Occasionally he mumbles to himself, low and quick in a language I don't recognize. He takes me back to a clearing behind the stacks lined with glass cases, some that stretch floor to ceiling. Inside are yards of unfurled scrolls.

"What's all this?" I trace the cool edges of the cases I can reach, my head craned to scour the cases I can't. Despite their age and general wear, the glyphs are astoundingly clear, penned or painted in colors I've never seen before.

"Encounters, primarily." Darius clasps his hands behind his back, rocks proudly on the balls of his feet. "Works seized to protect our anonymity. The Vault contains over ten kilometers of papyrus and approximately three dozen confiscated stone tablets, many of which were chiseled from the walls of ruined empires." He deftly navigates the display tables littered around the daunting space, his eyes on the walls. "Each branch of the family has a similar compound, though Fane's is the most beautiful. The writings you see here were concealed by Fane and his ancestors from every civilization they confronted, or inhabited."

"Have you read all these?"

Darius pushes his spectacles up the bridge of his nose and chuckles. Everything about him seems worn out: his yellowed clothes, his antique glasses. Even his laugh is like an echo. "You see that one there?" he says, pointing well above our heads at a scroll in the west corner of the room. "That is one of the oldest in the archive. It tells the story of a young man who was lured from his bed by a beautiful woman. She sang through the walls of his domicile and beckoned him to join her outside. In the morning he awoke by the seaside, bleeding from his neck. His companion had vanished, but the young man recorded his story, which traveled by word of mouth before the boy was intercepted. The Greeks called us Vyrkolakas."

Darius flits from one scroll to the next, continuing without pause as I trail behind him in awe of this hidden history. Somewhere in all this disintegrating parchment there has to be mention of how Strigoi came to be, the origin of the Moroi—vampires from birth—and possibly a glimpse into Stela's past. He touches the glass cases with an intimacy that suggests he isn't reading anything so much as remembering.

"Here you have stories of the Dhampir from Albania. This one, from Belarus calls us Upyr." He waves a distracted hand at the rest of the collection. "The bulk of the collection was seized in Romania. They named those turned, as you and I are, Strigoi, and those born as Fane was, Moroi. I would estimate at least three quarters of what you see, and more that you cannot see, was taken from that region."

"Why that region?"

Darius twists a stringy lock of hair behind the hook of his glasses. "As I said, this archive consists of documents acquired by Fane and his forebears."

"So, Fane *is* Romanian…"

My tour guide freezes, those expressive hands still lingering in the air—stiff now, as though he's suddenly afraid to disturb the atmosphere. He tucks his hands into his pockets, glances anxiously about the room. He starts whispering to himself in a language I don't know.

"Shall we find you something to read?"

Darius marches toward a series of much shorter shelves.

A glint of light distracts me. Along the far back wall, in the center of the Vault, is an enormous glass case. This one set atop a regal and engraved podium, with steps leading up as though it were a throne upon a dais. The interior of the case is lined with emerald velvet, indented by some weighty artifact, but there is nothing inside. Above the case is a coat of arms gleaming in bright gold. The coat of arms, shaped like a shield, is cut into quarters. The first section holds two crossed swords. Beside it, a dark bird—a vulture, perhaps. Below is a coiled dragon with talons drawn, and in the last section, a scythe. All around the shield, spinning off at dizzying angles, are nine serpents all open-mouthed with tails twisted in elaborate knots. I climb the steps to appreciate the crest more closely. I set my hands on the empty glass case and a sigh moves from my palms through my entire body. I jerk away from the case, stumble backward down the steps. At the base of the podium is a placard inscribed with the words: "Praeteritum esse Futurum."

"Beautiful, is it not?"

Fane appears behind me, with a vein-riddled palm extended. His emerald silk robe is parted to reveal his ruddy chest. I touch his fingers and his whole hand encloses mine, swallowing my wrist. He pulls me beside him forcefully, covering with a blithe apology.

"Praeteritum esse Futurum. That's *past is future*, isn't it?"

Fane flashes a practiced smile as he steers us away from the podium, back toward Darius' work station. He drops a leather-bound ledger on the assorted texts open on Darius' desk. The family tracks expenses and favors in that ledger, but that's all I know.

"All that shall ever come to pass, has already happened. Already begun," he says. "Do you read Latin?"

"I took two years in high school. Four more in college."

Fane still hasn't released my hand. He holds it between our bodies, almost daring me to pull away.

"My Lord." With several astoundingly large volumes piled in his arms Darius stops behind Fane. "I beg your pardon. I did not hear your arrival." Darius hovers, his bespectacled gaze flicking back and forth between us. Fane doesn't acknowledge him and lingers on me. The pressure of his stare increases, building beneath my skin with a fierce electricity.

Darius recovers himself and drops his considerable armload on the table behind me, moving cautiously to Fane's side. Just out of his reach. "I took the liberty of gathering a few of my favorite volumes for Irina."

"Oh, thank you." I know enough to understand that Darius has given me an out, and I seize the opportunity to turn away from Fane and pretend to pore over the books. I sense more than see Fane's answering frustration.

"My Lord, have you finished your review of the ledger?" Darius asks.

"Yes," Fane hisses. He turns, focusing on Darius. "The numbers are without fault, as always my son. But I am more interested in learning the reason for Irina's visit. Some light reading, perhaps?"

I grab the first book from the stack and clutch it to my chest like a shield. Using my exact verbiage is as disconcerting as Fane intended, and I wonder how long he was with us in the Vault before he approached me. Then again, he didn't have to hear our conversation to know what brought me here. Fane has an intimate relationship with the truth, whether it's readily offered to him or not. Lie detection is not one of his preternatural gifts, but a side effect of having lived for thousands of years. He can hear the thoughts of Strigoi but only those he has named, and Strigoi get better at hiding their thoughts with age.

As near as I can tell from what little Stela will say on the matter, the only way a Moroi can bind a Strigoi to them is by naming—or claiming as it is sometimes called—because they cannot turn human beings. Stela has the distinction of being the only mortal Fane has ever turned and feeding from her very nearly killed him. I was intended to Fane when Stela turned me, and by naming me Irina he was claiming me as a member of his tribe, building a bridge between our minds. The bond Stela shared with me was supposed to transfer to him, as it has with all Fane's *children*, but the name didn't stick and my bond with Stela remains. Whether Fane knows this for certain is anyone's guess, but he suspects and that is dangerous.

He's glowering when I turn back around.

"Stela removed her laptop from our suite after I was turned, and I've been through most of her collection already."

Fane crosses over to me again. He runs his index finger down the spine of the volume I hold. "The directive was mine," he says. "It will be easier for you to acclimate to our way of life if you are completely immersed. No distractions."

I'm not sure if that makes it better or worse, knowing that Stela was acting at Fane's behest. I remember our argument over the laptop quite vividly.

"Well," I wave the absently selected volume in my hand and offer him a tight smile, "I'll just go about my acclimation then."

Fane's boisterous laugh halts my eager retreat. "Come now, Irina." He smiles. "We both know that the complete history of the House of Báthory was hardly the subject you had in mind. Although, it is an invigorating read."

Fane steps alongside me and whisks the book from the crook of my arm. He glances at the cover with marked distaste and pitches it over his shoulder. Darius is so quick to rescue the book from the fall, that he appears to be in two places at once.

With a firm hand on the small of my back Fane steers my course down a darkened aisle. He moves soundlessly—not even his silk robe rustles. The cracks in the towering bookshelves permit slivers of dusty light, which dance against his shoulders and stroke his white-gold hair.

The aisle opens to a hidden room. Inside, aged armchairs reek of decay beneath the roaring heat of two great torches on the far wall. The back wall is lined with unmarked leather volumes in unremarkable shelves, a dormant fireplace and above it, another coat of arms, this one depicting a serpent curled around the talons of a falcon in flight.

"This is our family's coat of arms," he explains. "It served us well through countless forays. You should have seen the pride with which Stela carried this emblem. Though we have little use for it these days." Nostalgia softens his voice, and his eyes—though clearly analyzing my reactions—no longer intrude.

"The crest above the podium out there?"

"That is *my* family's coat of arms. A single emblem to represent the sacred unity of all the great houses. A serpent for the Moroi of each household."

I scan the bookshelves, while maintaining a healthy distance from Fane. He continues to watch me closely, mouth twisting in a menacing smirk when he realizes I am as close as I intend to get.

"What are these?" I ask, gesturing to the leather volumes.

"The case upon the podium holds the collected history of all nine families. It travels between the houses, resting in their respective vaults for a century, before it is passed on to the next clan. I believe it is currently in Spain, and it will not find its way back inside our walls for another two hundred years." He steps back, sweeps his hand about the room. "This is our private archive."

I have to take a step back to appreciate the breadth of the shelves, and when I do, I see that behind Fane there are indeed plaques on the shelves. A name for each member of his tribe, excluding Fane, and of course, me.

"These two rows belong to Stela." He steps uncomfortably nearer. "The uppermost three belong to Bård. Over the years, the earliest drafts have been recorded anew onto more sustainable materials by Darius. The tradition of recording one's deeds and conquests has waned over the last few centuries, as you can see. But I trust there is more than enough here to occupy you for the moment."

A catalog of Stela's long life. So many eras that had nothing at all to do with me, and here they are mere feet away. Fane is pleased, lips slightly parted and crystalline eyes shining with feline iridescence.

"I should ask her first."

Fane laughs thunderously. His giant palm clasps my shoulder playfully. "You have my permission to read them, if it pleases you. Mine is all the permission you require, Irina." There's no way to backpedal, to feign disinterest. He knows I came to the Vault looking for this. He's shown me more than I hoped to find. Being bound to Stela offers me a measure of protection from his powers yet makes me very much a target in his home. She warned me that whether he could hear my thoughts or not, he is gifted at reading motive. Stela was right. I should have listened to her and kept to our quarters. I keep my hands at my sides, take a step back.

"Thank you for showing me these."

"You are quite welcome," he says.

I stroll casually back toward the Vault.

"Would you leave so unfulfilled?" Fane asks in a booming voice. Fane loathes refusal, this much I know, and he has offered me a gift he knows I want.

I step through the archway, turn back toward him. "It's a private archive, as you said. I wouldn't feel right reading Stela's words without asking her first."

Fane nods sagely and crosses his trunk-like arms over his wide chest. "Stela will appreciate your consideration." It wasn't the response I anticipated. "Get back to your quarters, Irina. I will not keep your mate long from you, when she returns."

There's a knowing edge to his words, an unspoken challenge. This dance of ours is growing tiresome. Fane interjects a similar comment into every single conversation we have. A comment that indirectly emphasizes his importance in Stela's life. It never fails to infuriate me, which I suppose is precisely the passive-aggressive point. I incline my head toward him as I have repeatedly been instructed to do and make my departure before he can find an excuse to keep me longer.

* * *

Before the wheezing of the hatch, or the feather-light strut of familiar boots striding through the tunnels, there's a gravitational shift in my blood.

She's close.

I feel like a small child, or an abandoned puppy eager to be reunited with her owner after what seemed an intolerably long separation, which in all actuality was only a matter of hours. Is it possible that I can already smell her? To think I once equated her scent only to flowers. Stela is a constellation of incense and earth, deep rich wood, aged linens, lily, lilac and lavender. The last things her victim smelled.

I wait beneath the hatch for her, bracing myself against the bubbling Victorian wallpaper. I hold the air in my lungs. I would absorb her completely if I could.

Love is the most degrading emotion.

There isn't a milliliter of blood in my body that's immune to her. Not a pint that's forgotten what it was to run through Stela's veins, and it's always seeking a way back to her. The blood tingles in my scalp, down my arms, prickling madly with her rapid approach and the promise of close proximity. It takes everything I have not to rush up through the hatch and tackle her to the ground. Which is a testament to my slowly budding self-control, aided, no doubt, by my wounded pride after the last time that happened. Lydia had cackled at our backs and advised Stela to invest in a leash.

The hatch opens and Stela lands mutely on the floor. Her practiced hands are as imploring as her insistent mouth. Her lips climb the column of my neck as my arms close around her shoulders, and her cheek is so deliciously warm she feels fevered against my skin. If this is what I felt like to her when I was still human, it's a wonder that I lasted as long as I did.

Stela abruptly disengages and thrusts a bag of blood into my reaching hands. I'm not in the mood to refuse her or rekindle any argument we've had about the dangers of hunger. I've already upset her once this evening and I suspect I will again when she asks how I've spent my night. I pierce the bag with my fangs. A smell I know all too well sobers my senses. She saw Fane first, which is to be expected, but the sharpness of him surrounds me in such brilliance that I know he fed from her tonight.

A feral growl escapes me as the bag relinquishes a final trickle. With keener sight and a clear mind, I note a heavy reluctance in Stela.

Stela welcomes the intrusion of my hands as I guide her chin level with mine. She stares directly into my eyes. I run my thumb along the cooling skin of her jaw and though I don't go looking I find the answer to my question all the same. There's a fight in her eyes. A brawny man in his late thirties. I can feel the pressure of his fingertips against her hips as clearly as though they were my own, and the delighted cadence of her laugh as she wrestled him to the ground. The relief is short-lived. Fane is also in her eyes. The breadth of his shoulders casting her face into shadow as he holds her neck in his hand.

"Elizabeth."

The sudden invocation of my name is both a chastisement and a weary plea. Stela pulls my hand away, holds my wrist between our bodies. Do I exhaust her? I take too much. I make demands when I should compromise. Stela shared what threads of her hunt I could grasp. I pried when I should have been satisfied, I spied for longer than I'd been invited. But no matter what Fane believes, or what passed between them before I was born—Stela is mine.

She brings my captive hand to her lips, places a kiss in the crease of my lifeline. "And you are mine," she says.

She doesn't reiterate that feeding Fane is "a sacred role" that every Strigoi in his home shares. That it is the duty of all Strigoi to give their life blood to feed the Moroi who rules them. She doesn't remind me that one day I too will be a meal for him. I will not argue with her. Not tonight.

Stela keeps hold of my hand, and her solemn expression tells me there's a pressing matter to be discussed.

She looks into my eyes. "I am not a subject to be studied," she says gravely.

Her displeasure quiets my visceral hunger for her. She relinquishes my hand.

This time I'm the one to divert my gaze. A part of me knew Fane would tell her before I'd even left his company.

"I trust you understand how serious an error you made visiting any corner of this house with an agenda."

I can only nod, barely recalling why I ever entertained the idea of violating her privacy. Stela sighs, and I know the storm has passed.

"I'm better at studying than discourse," I explain.

"That is hardly the point," she warns. "If you want to know something, you ask me. You do not steal into the library to scour my journals behind my back."

"Where would I even begin?" My voice breaks, and Stela laces our fingers together. "And I did want to discuss it with you first."

"Why do you obsess over the past?" she sighs.

I shake my head. "I'm not obsessing. I'm curious. Is that so strange? You've lived for centuries. You've seen old worlds crumble, and new worlds age. I want to know what that was for you, from you. I want to experience the minutiae of your life, Stela, but there are hundreds of years. How do I account for them all with questions?"

Stela relaxes and draws nearer to me. She presses her forehead to mine, her mouth set in a hard line.

"You may not like all that you find, my darling."

"You'll let me read the journals, then?"

She rolls her eyes and tugs me toward the bed. Stela lowers herself to the mattress and pulls me by the hips between her jean-clad legs. The soft light from the bedside lamp glows across her face.

"If it will bring you peace to read them, you have my blessing."

I mouth a silent "thank you" as I climb atop her legs, threading my fingers through her hair.

"Promise me this," she says, "should you read something that hurts or angers you in any way, you will bring your concerns to me. That I might explain."

I push her back against the bed and place a kiss to the middle of her throat—an action she has repeated many times over on me. Her answering smile is resplendent.

"I promise."

* * *

Stela's heartbeat resumes its glacial pace beneath my ear as I trail the tips of my fingers along her obliques. She pulls a white sheet up around my shoulders—an old habit—to warm me, though I'm never truly cold anymore. Through the fog of impending slumber, I recall a single unresolved point. Something I'd forgotten in the excitement of her homecoming.

"You called me Irina."

Stela's arms tighten around me, pulling my body firmly against her own. Whether to smother the conversation or reassure me, I'm not sure.

"I often call you Irina," she says carefully.

"Not like that. Never when we're alone."

She presses her cheek to my forehead and glides her hand up the length of my spine to hold the back of my head. It's one of the few actions that betray her steely demeanor, and I wonder how anxious my name actually makes her.

"No. Not when we are alone," she admits. "I should not have used that name in anger."

I tuck my hand beneath her shoulder as she rubs soothing circles against the base of my skull. My vision darkens as oblivion rises up to engulf me.

"It's not my name, Stela."

"I know. Elizabeth."

Her reverent whisper is the last sound I hear. She brushes her lips across my scalp, and just before the blackness carries me away, I taste the dread she so artfully disguises.

II

Latibule

For two months, Elizabeth has barely made it to our quarters before collapsing. Her studies have consumed her so thoroughly that on one particularly disconcerting morning, I was forced to retrieve her limp body from the library. So late was the hour that lifting her slight frame was a challenge even for me, and though her slumber was resolute her body immediately coiled around my torso the instant I heaved her from the armchair she has claimed in Darius' library.

Sleep pulled insistently as I labored to return her to our bed. I knelt against the smooth floor of the tunnel to collect myself before I reached the hatch. That was the first time my beautiful cargo had ever resembled a burden. Anything could happen to her. What if Fane found her and decided to slake his thirst on his newborn, perhaps one morning when I am late coming home? What truths would he discover in her blood?

I laid Elizabeth out along the bed and her hands reached absently for me as I undressed. That morning I lay awake for many hours, skirting the edge of sleep, and allowed myself to wallow in the relentless foreboding I take such pains to hide from my beloved. I have often wondered whether her persistent nightmares are influenced by my own morbid fixations.

When she woke, I suggested that she conclude her research or confine her studies to the safety of our dormitory. Elizabeth was predictably, adamantly opposed. Darius was a great help to her, she said, especially with regard to the translation of contemporary colloquialisms. I reminded her that the journals are mine and the Latin I used to record them—though I have not written in that language for many years—is as clear to me as it is to him.

Naturally, this spurred a heated argument in which I was wrongly accused of trying to control her, and then I was cornered into admitting that I fear for her safety when we are apart. I could see the fear in her eyes, but she has never been one to accept defeat. Elizabeth, when angered, is dauntless. It is one of my favorite things about her, and it causes me the most concern.

We reached a compromise shortly thereafter. Elizabeth reluctantly agreed to bring several volumes back from the library, that I might keep a watchful eye to ensure she is properly laid to rest before dawn. Her sole stipulation was that I make myself as available for translation as Darius has, and that she be permitted to study in the Vault on the evenings I hunt aboveground. I acquiesced, but with a condition of my own: she must promise not to lose track of the hour again.

Two nights of relative silence followed this tense détente. Elizabeth remained supine on our sofa, jotting notes on a legal pad, pausing only when meals or sparring lessons were forced upon her. Not once did she seek my counsel regarding the journals.

On the third night, when Elizabeth attempted to extricate herself from our bed, I conceded. I could not stand another evening of pointed silence. I could not tolerate having her so near, and yet unreachable. In this regard, Elizabeth is stronger than I am. She fights for the sake of winning, no matter the argument or outcome. She is the single most determined, focused, frustratingly stubborn person I have ever known, and as soon as I reached for her forearm to keep her in bed, she smiled at me.

Elizabeth laughed breathlessly against my neck as I pinned her wrists above her head. Her hair mussed, falling over her eyes. She stretched her body languidly beneath me.

"I have ended countless lives for considerably smaller slights."

"I know," she said, "you wrote about it."

Elizabeth returned my affections so readily I could see clearly that our silent standoff was a contest. A battle of wills which I had lost and trust I will lose again. The realization took me by surprise, and with my cheek pressed against her hip, a mirthful chuckle escaped me before I could smother it.

"What?" She lifted up on her elbows.

"You were trying to teach me a lesson." I smiled. "What was it?"

She shrugged her shoulders. "I was angry with you."

I pulled her by the arms until her legs curled about my waist and gazed adoringly upon her marvelously disheveled head. "Elizabeth, if you wish to continue your reading in the library, I will respect your decision."

"I wasn't angry about the library."

I am so frequently out of my depth with her.

"You were scared," she said. "You've been scared, and not just about the library. But you kept that from me, and then you blew up about it like it's something I should know."

"My darling." I trailed the tip of my nose along her collarbone and she tightened her arms around my neck, tracing patterns across my shoulders. "There will come a time when I will be able to share all my hopes and fears with you. That night approaches faster than you think. You are stronger than many of the newborns I have encountered over the years, but you wear your emotions on your face. Fane has and will continue to read them."

"He can't hear me, Stela," she promised. "I can't hear him."

I molded my lips against the old scar that marred her neck and she twisted her fingers in my hair, pressing me closer. We lingered contentedly for a few quiet moments. I regarded her gravely. "He does not have to peer inside your mind to read your emotions," I explained. "That is precisely what frightens me."

She ran her fingers against the jut of my jaw with the same reverence she showed my journals. Those countless, empty years she has spent weeks worshipping like a holy relic. And so, the argument and her devotion were one in the same. A boundless desire to know me as no other has known me.

"You're not going to explain it to me, are you? How he reads me."

I shook my head. "I could no sooner explain the ability within myself. One day, a measure of that will be yours. You will see the desires of others as clearly as though their truth was written on their face. Maybe you will be the one to explain the mystery to me."

The birth of a smile threatened her stony expression. "I love you, Stela."

She had lived ten months in the dark, in her new life as a Strigoi and she had never said precisely those words. I could not venture a guess as to how long it has been since I received those words, if ever I had received them honestly, without coercion on my part or the intent on someone else's. Elizabeth intuited this immediately.

"You didn't know?"

I am not particularly communicative, and actions are my preferred method. But Elizabeth's words carried a swift and irrevocable consequence. My heart hammered, and she placed her palm above my breast. I could not bear to look at her, though she sought my eyes. Every time I think I have found the depths of my affection for her, there is more.

"Stela..." she whispered sadly. "I know I'm difficult. But how could you not know that?"

I think it might have benefited us both greatly had she never spoken the sentiment aloud, and the only thought I had in response was the certainty that I would not be able to share her when the time came, or release her when she grew tired of me. How long have I sat with the knowledge that Elizabeth cannot belong to me forever? I knew before she was born into this life. From the moment I laid eyes on her, she was not mine to have, but all of this meant nothing with the cradle of her hips in my hands.

There, in the midst of what might have been a truly beautiful moment between us, I called upon an ability I had previously reserved for Fane. My pulse slowed, and my mind cleared as I raised a wall between us. When I met her perpetually intrusive eyes, I witnessed a curious expression flutter across her face, quick as a shadow. Her spine straightened, and it was evident that she knew something had changed.

"Of course," I replied. "You would not be here otherwise."

Gradually, Elizabeth brightened, yet her new eyes—still years beyond her complete control—continued their gentle assault. Her stare was persistent and she surmounted my defenses unconsciously. I was alarmed as well as proud of her, but our situation is precarious enough without feeding the fire of our inextricable bond. So, I improvised.

The images I needed to create that wall were simple enough to select. A memory of our first evening, followed closely by the night she first asked me what I was. All the while, Elizabeth kept perfect conversation with me, unaware of the force she was exerting back at me.

She managed to flounce her way beyond my barrier, drawing deeper, pressing forward until my mind grew so exhausted that I reached in desperation for a dream I had no business touching. The first of her nightmares Elizabeth pulled me into. Elizabeth in a black dress, smothering her mother's motionless body with a pillow. Just a nightmare, but it had tapped into Elizabeth's subconscious desire to hasten her mother's inevitable death.

In an instant the weight of her tunneling gaze vanished behind scrunched eyelids, her nose wrinkled, and Elizabeth shook herself violently as though she had nodded off mid-conversation.

"Elizabeth?" I did not mean to do it. I swear. I only intended to distract her with a vivid image and afford myself a measure of privacy.

"I love you." I whispered the words softly into her ear and traced her cheek with my thumb. It was not the first time I had told her, but it was different knowing that the love I gave her she returned to me in full. Why should redamancy change anything?

We spent the better part of the evening entwined on the mattress, Elizabeth's breakfast long forgotten and my own responsibilities considerably delayed. She chased my touch in earnest, no doubt afraid that if we parted, she would find her mother standing at the foot of the bed, waiting for her.

* * *

"Again."

Elizabeth scuffs the ground with her heel. "You know this is ridiculous, right?"

I turn to find her standing three paces back, hand on her hip, scowling. Beside me, Erebus rocks on his haunches, anxious to give chase. I pull my finger down his snout and he tilts his head pleadingly, begging for the command to hunt.

"Humor me, my darling," I say. Erebus deduces that Elizabeth is the cause for delay and whips his neck around to growl a pointed warning in her direction. I snap my fingers and he resumes his about-face.

"Your dog hates me," she broods.

"He is not my dog."

"This is essentially hide-and-go-seek," she says.

"The children's game?" I ask. Elizabeth nods. "Then I expect you to win this round."

"And how am I supposed to win when you cheat?"

My laugh trills against the weeping stone walls. Elizabeth—even harboring undisguised fury—glows with pale radiance. I run my hand down her arm before taking the bait. My impossible girl, far too lovely for this dungeon of tunnels.

"How do I cheat?" I ask.

"Well, for starters, you have help."

Erebus growls at her.

"Quiet, old man."

He drops on his matted belly and rolls on his side with an exhausted huff. Amazing that an evening with Elizabeth can tire him more quickly than a day's prowl in the tunnels. A smile crawls across my lips.

"There is no such thing as a fair fight, Elizabeth. Not up there, and never down here. When the time comes that you must hunt for yourself, or conduct affairs on Fane's behalf aboveground, we must be assured that you can do so without being tracked. Your safety, and that of the entire family, depends upon secrecy. If you want permission to leave the lair, you have to prove yourself."

"You're right," she sighs. "I know." She turns abruptly to face the cavernous dark, nodding silently to herself.

I press my myself against her spine and place my hands upon her hips. "I will never tire of hearing you say that," I tease. "Primarily because it happens so infrequently."

She reclines into my embrace, reaches back to cup my neck in her hand. "Don't push it," she warns. She spares me a brief kiss and straightens.

"I'm ready," she says. Elizabeth steps forward, crouches into a run. She vanishes from sight before the first and only echo of her footfall rings through the tunnel.

Erebus jumps up when the sound of her departure reaches his twitching ears. He scrambles up and comes to heel. I give Elizabeth a full thirty-second head start.

"Erebus."

He peels from his spot in a blur of black fur, tail stiff, his tall ears sloping forward scouring the tunnel walls for a clumsy footfall. He keeps his nose an inch from the ground as he darts from wall to wall searching out her scent. He cranes his neck over his shoulder to ensure he has not lost me and yips like a pup as he doubles his pace in search of Elizabeth.

There was a time when I could not have hoped to outrun him, but his prime has long since passed. The tell-tale signs of age are pronounced in his rocky gait, in the silvery hairs that line his snout and tail. Erebus has outlived the oldest of his bloodline and he remains a capable and eager protector, but he will not live forever.

I slow my stride and let Erebus take the lead. He darts down the tunnel, running headlong at full speed with a delighted howl, scrambling up the sloped edges. I will miss him terribly.

Alone at last, I plant my feet and brace myself against the sweating wall. Elizabeth is easy to find in my mind's eye, speeding through the darkened freight tunnels, kicking up debris. Gently, I slip inside her mind. The aim is never to alarm or to pry. Instead I focus on what she sees, the stretch of darkened tunnel ahead of her, the barely audible sound her nimble feet make as they smack the packed earth. I take these sensory images—nothing so personal as to upset her when she inevitably finds out what I have been doing—and I offer them up to the ether, hurling the image outward as hard as I can.

I have no idea whether these stolen offerings appease Fane's growing curiosity about the "shockingly quiet" Irina. But Elizabeth cannot linger in his encampment without a footprint. The silence of her mind infuriates Fane more than he lets on.

I slide down the tunnel wall, dizzy and disoriented. I place my palms to the damp stone in an attempt to wrangle my swirling thoughts. Dipping into Elizabeth's mind however lightly tends to distort my perception. The tunnel is darker than I remember when I open my eyes. I push off the wall and start down the path after her.

I miss her timid footfall as I round yet another nondescript opening in the wall. When she jumps triumphantly in front of me, I nearly seize her by the throat. Elizabeth brings her forearm against mine in a perfectly executed block.

"I did it!" she cries. "I snuck up on you!" She gathers a fistful of my shirt and playfully dots my face with kisses. I have to halt her celebration prematurely to throw her body behind mine.

"Stop." I command. Erebus heels mid-stride, his great paws skidding across the wet floor as he barrels into view, and despite his best efforts his chest collides with my thighs. He barks his arrival.

"We lost this round, old man."

Elizabeth sidesteps my looming shadow with a hand to her ear. "I'm sorry, what was that?"

"I said we lost. I lost. Erebus lost, and you are the victor, my darling."

She steps beyond my reaching embrace and furrows her brow. A ridiculous expression only ever intended to mock me, though it bears not even the slightest resemblance. "I will never tire of hearing you say that, Stela," she says in a deliberately grave tone. "Primarily because it happens so infrequently." She can only just keep the smile from her lips.

"You do a terrible impression of me." I smile and kiss her temple.

When Erebus butts his head against her hip Elizabeth nearly jumps back into my arms. "What does he want?" she whispers. Erebus repeats the action, this time with a high-pitched whimper, and he sits at her feet.

"He is waiting very patiently to congratulate you."

Elizabeth reaches out tentatively and Erebus butts his head against her hand. She laughs prettily and scratches behind his ears in earnest.

On three separate occasions I have had to chase him from our dormitory. He liked to corner Elizabeth when I was out hunting. I must admit I was touched that he took her safety so seriously, as he only ever cornered her when she was alone. Elizabeth was not touched, nor did she understand when I attempted to explain that he only intended to keep her out of trouble. I smile against the top of Elizabeth's head, pleased to watch her finally warm to Erebus.

* * *

We brace ourselves spine to spine as our injuries mend. Bård heals quicker than I do, his shoulder snapping back into socket with a pop as he turns around to help me. He pulls my bowed leg straight and snaps my hip back into place.

The armory is now dreadfully quiet and the silence I normally find so soothing in his presence is oppressive.

"May I ask you something?"

Bård does not reply. He bends down to retrieve his ridiculously ill-fitting navy shirt. One of Lydia's petty torments. She knows the measurements of every person in this house, but there is rarely a day when Bård is dressed in any garment befitting a man of his stature. The cuff of his pants grazes his ankles. His shirt buttons pucker and strain to cover his chest. Sometimes the sleeves barely brush his wrists or strangle his biceps.

"Is this a question regarding your ward?" he asks carefully.

"Both our wards, actually."

Bård bristles, but gestures for me to join him on the sparring mat. "When it comes to the raising of a newborn, I have no wisdom to impart," he cautions.

We sit knee to knee on the floor, where only moments ago he managed to twist out of my grip by dislocating his own shoulder and throw me head first into the ground by my thigh. Speed is the only advantage I have against him, but he manages to outmaneuver me all the same. He fights close, he feigns defeat, and he is wholly without fear.

"How long was Lydia in our company before she devoted herself to Fane?"

Bård rakes his knotted knuckles along his jaw. The uncomfortable silence lingers for so long I expect him to rise any moment without answer.

"She was always his, Stela," he says brusquely.

Was she? Bård claimed her life centuries ago, and it is true that I remember no tenderness between Lydia and her Maker. All these long years later, she still dresses him poorly, she argues with him openly. She dotes upon Fane, especially if Bård or I are near enough to watch. Bård meets every taunt with a smile, he wears the clothing she selects whether it fits or not. I suppose her hate is something. Anything is better than indifference.

"I know she was. As are we all. But—"

Bård raises a forbidding hand. "There is no other way to end that sentence, and you know it. Perhaps, you wish to believe otherwise." He shifts his weight uneasily, and I brace for his departure. This line of questioning is blasphemous. But Bård does not leave, he takes my hand in his and squeezes, as though imploring me to continue.

"Was there ever a time when you felt a connection with Lydia?" I whispered, suddenly very conscious of being caught.

"In what way?"

I shrug, but I feel anything but casual. "A tether, of some kind? A shared memory, perhaps? Some vague impression of her mind or wellbeing?"

Bård's gentle stare grows sharp and intrusive. There is a warning in his eyes, a clouded sense of fear. Though each of us walk on eggshells around Fane, his powers are limited at a distance. He can read our blood with astounding clarity but only when he feeds from us. His eyes can open doors into our minds, but this is most effective when our gazes are locked. Otherwise, Fane can only hear what thoughts and emotions we wish to share. This apprehension rolling off my brother in waves is entirely directed at me.

"Have you asked this of anyone else, Stela?"

"Of course not."

"Good." Bård stands abruptly and drags me off the mat by my wrist. He smacks me between the shoulders. "Bury this," he says. "Never speak of it again."

With a sideways glance that instructs me to keep stride Bård strolls toward the main hall. "Irina is proving herself a quick study," he announces quite unexpectedly. This change of topic is not meant for my ears alone.

"Yes." I match his pitch and follow his lead to the steps that separate the main hall from the sleeping quarters. "She succeeded in eluding my detection in the freight tunnels."

Bård swings into the narrow corridor above our heads without alighting on a single step. He crouches beside his hatch and offers his hand to help me—though I require no such assistance—as a gesture of goodwill.

But Bård does not pull me into that raised escarpment beside him. Instead, I am standing in the Vault. The air smells of aged fur, and the wall in front of me is littered with leather-bound volumes aglow in the torchlight. There is a book in my hands. No. Not my hands—Elizabeth's. She has breached my mind again. I have never been able to push my way into Fane's, but perhaps this is one of the many reasons naming is necessary. Moroi are better suited to manage their fledglings and keep these mental bonds from bleeding into incoherence. The landscape shifts and I am sprawled beside my open hatch.

Bård bends above me, his large hand gripping my shoulder but he is silent in his concern. I pull myself into a sitting position, my legs dangling down into my open hatch. The rug far below my feet swims in my vision. "Perhaps your thoughts were otherwise occupied," Bård says loudly. I stare at him in confusion as he barrels on. "She is young to be so skilled in evasion."

His voice is removed, a scream underwater. Slowly, I realize he has resumed our earlier conversation, the farce about Irina's training. None of the worry I see on his face is reflected in his tone. This is all the privacy he can afford me

"It is possible that my thoughts were elsewhere," I say for prying ears. "I could have given her the advantage of distraction."

"Test her again after a proper hunt," he instructs. "If she can elude your detection a second time, I will step up my lessons accordingly."

"Thank you, brother."

He hovers in the crawlspace, watching protectively as I drop down into my dormitory. He forces the hatch closed quickly, his eyes betraying his mute concern.

I run the tap and stand over the bathroom sink splashing cool water on my face to steady my frayed nerves. The impression of Elizabeth still lingers behind my eyes, but the dizziness is nearly gone.

"Stela?" Two gentle hands slide down my shoulders, slipping over my biceps. I find her face in the mirror, looking famished and confused. "Are you all right?" she asks, unsteadily.

I straighten and wave her away. "Never better," I assure her. Elizabeth sighs, leans against the doorframe.

"Would you like something to eat?" I dry my hands. "You must be ravenous." I chance a look at her to find that her patience is exhausted.

"What's going on?" she asks in a small voice.

I try to step around her, but she spins into the bedroom completely in step with me.

"A miscalculation of your strength, I suspect. You just intruded upon my mind, quite forcefully I might add."

Elizabeth does not share my amusement. "Intruded? How?"

"Did you read something of interest this evening?"

The realization dawns on her. She turns sheepishly, descends the three steps into the lounge. "I reread something," she admits. Elizabeth sits perfectly straight on the arm of the sofa. "I didn't mean to pry, Stela. I swear. I just—"

"Which expedition of mine was so enthralling as to merit a second reading?" I ask, sensing the answer.

"Your journey through the Carpathian Mountains, right after Fane turned you."

If I close my eyes, I can still see the purple brilliance of the setting sun dancing across the River Danube as I ventured onward toward Miskolc on my way to Budapest. I lift her chin with my index finger. I run my thumb along the swell of her bottom lip and her eyes close briefly at the contact. "I was searching for a cure. Fane turned me, as you said. But the Moroi cannot tolerate human blood. I will never fully understand what possessed him to take such a risk. My mortal blood poisoned him, nearly killed him. He was raving mad from the pain. Confined to his bed."

"You needed the blood of another Moroi."

"The source had to be pure for my Lord. I meant to take the cure with force if necessary."

Elizabeth pulls my hand from her jaw and shakes the hair back from her face determinedly. She is on a journey of her own in the Vault. She seeks answers to questions I have never asked. "But the story ends before you reach Hungary and resumes after you return to Brașov."

"Does it?"

"I know you found her," she says in a noticeably firmer voice. "You returned with a vial of her blood for Fane. He was cured."

"You seem so certain it was a woman."

"There are vague references to someone called The Lady in later entries, but there's no name," she says. "In fact, she isn't directly mentioned again until your family relocated to Rome, and you run into a woman named Antonia, who you seem to know very well."

A private smile curls across my lips as I feel a familiar ache. There are so many miles between us now, an ocean, but her Ladyship finds me at the most unexpected moments. Elizabeth is suddenly much closer and my face falls into something more neutral, but not before she catches the distant look in my eyes.

"Are we approaching a question, Elizabeth?"

She wears her mouth in a tight-lipped line. "There were pages missing. What happened to them, Stela?"

I wave her concerns aside. "It was a long journey. There were all manner of beasts and foul weather in the Western Carpathians. Perhaps the elements rendered my writings illegible."

"You're lying." The steely assuredness of her accusation catches me off guard. She sees this and inches closer. "Fane has already told me that over the years Darius has copied the journals onto more sustainable materials."

My apprehension gets the better of me, and in a panic, I seize her forearm before I can think better of it. "Who else have you asked about this? Did you question Darius?"

Elizabeth twists her arm free and my apology is as wasted as the breath that leaves me when she thrusts her shoulder into my sternum. The force of the blow sends me back a step, but what concerns me most is the look on her face. Lips curled back from teeth, fangs bared. Her rage charges the stagnant air and the ends of her hair seem to crackle around her face. Her breath is labored, nostrils flared, every inch of her body poised for a hunt. Whether through the sharp snap of her cracking knuckles or the startled look on my face, she grows aware of herself. Her muscles relax and then her fangs recede. When she pulls her anger back inside, all that is left is a sickening shudder and an unspent sob.

"I should not have touched you in anger," I say, reaching out tentatively. "This was my fault, Elizabeth."

"Why am I panting?" She cringes away from my hands and rests her forehead on the hearth.

"Your senses sharpen with the promise of a hunt, scent in particular. Fear and pheromones are a powerful aphrodisiac."

"That's disgusting."

I shrug. "That is the way of it."

Elizabeth slumps to the floor with her head in her hands, trying to remind her body that breath is unnecessary.

"You should feed. You push yourself too far." I leave her side to procure her dinner, but I make it only as far as the bed.

"No. This first," she says.

I lean against the bedpost and shake my head. "Why is everything an argument, Elizabeth?"

"We're not arguing. You're deflecting."

I laugh because there is little else I can do. She is impossible to placate or distract. "Please, my darling, leave this be."

Elizabeth crosses her legs, leans her head back against the hearth and stares distractedly at the ceiling. "Who is The Lady?" she asks in a whisper that might not have been meant for me.

"Does it matter?"

Elizabeth considers this quietly for a moment. "Something happened," she whispers. "I felt something in the library. Twice, actually. Once when I touched the pedestal in the Vault. Again, when I was reading about your journey to Budapest."

Her insatiable curiosity will be the end of us both. "What did you feel?"

"A presence. Like I was staring at something that was staring back at me."

"A female presence?"

She nods. "As near as I can tell."

I take a seat on the opposite side of the hearth. "Her Ladyship has many names," I tell her, "none of which you will hear spoken within these walls."

Elizabeth turns to face me. She wraps her arms around her knees. "Who is she to you?"

"The serpent has nine heads. The Lady is one of them. Another Lord for a different family."

"Then why was your encounter with her removed?" Elizabeth asks.

The question carries with it a swell of melancholy, but speaking so openly about Her Grace is strangely liberating. A gift Elizabeth never intended to give me. "The siblings are often at odds. There is a reason the clans keep to themselves. Too many masters in one house is a recipe for war. And wars we had, many times, over the years."

"So, she and Fane are related?"

"They are kin in the same sense you and I are kin, I suppose."

Elizabeth scrunches her nose and makes a grunt to show her disapproval. "Please don't say that. We're not related."

Her distaste is just the levity we needed. I reach across and offer my open hand, palm up. Elizabeth briefly lays her hand in mine. She sits beside me and tugs my arm around her shoulders.

"Were you close to The Lady?" she asks in the peaceful quiet.

"Is this jealousy?"

She runs the tip of her finger along my jaw, presses a kiss beneath my ear. "Curiosity."

I sigh wearily and hold her closer. "She was a mentor. A friend. When I arrived in Budapest her guards seized me, brought me to her. She had been expecting me, though I know not how. She embraced me like a lost child."

"Ah," Elizabeth says knowingly. "Fane must have hated that. Even more so, because you thought well of her."

"The Lady and Fane have had their share of disputes. If I had to guess, I would say that any portrait that painted her in a benevolent light was distasteful to him. Whether he owes her his life or not."

Elizabeth closes her eyes and her lashes flutter against my cheek. Deep inside my mind I sense her, like a visitor on the other side of a door.

"Elizabeth…" She straightens, brushes the hair back from her eyes. "Were you trying to picture her Ladyship? In the library?"

Elizabeth shrugs—ah the fickleness of youth—and I see plainly that she has lost interest. She has the answers she wanted. "There was something familiar about the presence in the library," she explains. "At first, I thought it was you. Then I thought it was Fane. But when I read about her—what little there was—The Lady was…familiar to me." She sits up, eyes casting about, trying to make her thoughts plain. "Familiar but still completely strange. I felt…I don't know, cheated? It was like I'd been doing a jigsaw puzzle only to find that someone walked off with a fistful of pieces."

Centuries have passed and I can still picture The Lady's face before me as plainly as I see Elizabeth's, but her likeness has no home under Fane's roof. If Elizabeth had unwittingly pushed much further, she would have found the image she sought buried in my mind, perhaps even her Ladyship's true name.

"Some stories have no end," I tell her, pulling Elizabeth up with me as I stand.

"What's that supposed to mean?"

"Maybe you will meet The Lady yourself one day." I smile peacefully at her, and retrieve a bundle of kindling from the cupboard beneath the bookshelves. I busy myself with the beginnings of a meager fire.

"Yeah, maybe."

The eagerness I expected to see in Elizabeth is eclipsed by her fretful tension. I doubt very much that curiosity alone drove her to the depths of the Vault—the depths of my mind, for that matter—and back again. I am a fool for not having realized it sooner. This fleeting encounter with The Lady has rattled her.

I take Elizabeth by the hands and lead her back to the sofa. When I kiss her, she curls her free hand around the back of my neck, holding me in place for several moments longer. I withdraw to see an emboldened smile on her face.

"You will never know how beautiful you are to me," I say. Her smile grows impossibly wider. "I will return before long." Elizabeth feigns a pout as I stand up. "You must eat."

"Stela," she calls as I reach the hatch.

"Yes, my darling?"

When I turn to look at her the apprehension has returned. Elizabeth's stare burrows straight through me. She shakes her head gently, focuses her eyes on mine, offering a rictus grin.

"Nothing," she says.

III

The Vault

The overwhelming issue with Stela's journals is that they were written with complete disregard for the reader. In fact, they assume that anyone reading is as familiar with the events of her life as she is, which makes it all too clear that I am not reading the epic of her life, but an account of how she spent her time. And why should the great and powerful Fane require such an account?

Clearly, he is not as omnipresent as he would like his household to believe.

Stela uses seasons to mark the passage of time, but rarely records the date. The only reference to passing years is her own age and even this is inconsistent. Many entries are simply marked: winter, summer, occasionally timestamped with her approximate age. Summer, One-hundred-third.

As near as I can tell, Stela and her family stayed in Rome for less than a year, and this is where she encounters Antonia whom Fane wishes to kill. This is the only recorded reference of The Lady, and she is mentioned only as warning from Stela to Fane. Stela tells Fane that any harm to The Lady's favorite daughter—Antonia, I believe—would cause a civil war between the houses. These Roman entries appear to span from spring until the early fall of Stela's two hundred and twelfth year of life, and there is reference to Pope Clement XI which corroborates my hypothesis that Fane reached Rome around 1717, assuming Stela's birth year was in fact 1505.

Before Rome, and from what I've read about the decades after, the family moved constantly. But the most disconcerting passages—those I've read four times now—take place during the sixteenth century when civil war ensnared Fane's house. It began just after Stela returned from Hungary with Fane's cure, and there was dissension in the ranks.

The mysterious illness that crippled Fane after he turned Stela was the cause. Fane's second-in-command at the time, a Strigoi named Asim—whom Stela intimates had been beside Fane nearly all his life—had taken charge of Fane's fiefdom in Brașov including the considerable Strigoi army Fane had amassed. Asim was reluctant to resume his place in the background once Fane was restored to health by her Ladyship's blood, and he staged a coup. Asim succeeded in persuading several captains within Fane's militia that the time for Moroi rule was over. That sparked the first Strigoi uprising in the long history of our kind.

What happened next is really anyone's guess, but if Stela's account is accurate a staggering portion of the rebel army—Fane's own children—was incinerated before a single sword was crossed. A handful of fledglings dropped their weapons and fled into the Southern Carpathians. The rest fell beneath Fane's insurmountable opposition—his forces must have been supplemented by humans loyal to him, or Strigoi warriors sent from other houses—two flanks fronted by Stela and Bård.

Bård is credited with besting Asim in combat. He brought the eviscerated torso of Fane's former lieutenant to his master's feet. Stela does not mince words in her recount of the fire that consumed what remained of Asim.

The whole story is written with such uncharacteristic effulgence and pride, that I found myself cheering Fane on, hundreds of years later, alone in the library. A testament to young Stela's infectious patriotism.

After this scrimmage, the mutinous fledglings who narrowly escaped the massacre carried this story with them. They spread the tale of Fane's cruelty, his infanticide, and most importantly they told any who would listen of his frailty. When these deserters were apprehended by another Moroi—whom Stela does not appear to know—they had amassed a small force of their own. Newly made Strigoi who belonged to none but their Makers—as I belong only to Stela—having never been named by a Moroi. Asim's rebels were canonized in the hearts and minds of Strigoi the world over. Soon, all nine families were embroiled in a power struggle between Lord and subject, Sire and fledgling, Moroi and Strigoi.

The Transylvanian populace, who had been unwaveringly loyal to Fane—and apparently remain loyal to him to this day—urged him to abdicate and take his war elsewhere. They were peasants clothed and fed by Fane, protected by him until this point, and terrified by the carnage. Fane needed these people, his human subjects. He needed the camouflage they provided, the commerce, their silence, and of course their blood which was the fuel that kept his immortal army alive. And yet Fane had left their lands and his palace. He parted amicably with the town elders and bestowed upon them what riches he couldn't sell or carry.

But is this fable or fact?

Fane was also said to have razed his own palace to the ground with dozens of his family trapped inside. Only two members of his once enormous household were spared, his right and left hand respectively: Bård and Stela. In exchange for their lives, his two remaining children would aide him in the disposal of the unworthy. That's when Fane took his campaign on the road and declared war on all unnamed Strigoi with the blessing of at least six of the nine great houses, many of which thinned their own ranks and cleansed their lands of the unclaimed undead.

And of the three houses to dissent in the vote for war, only one reserved the right to offer amnesty and forbade the hunting of Strigoi in her land. The Lady.

Fear, pageantry, and propaganda. Fane is a master of all. The War of Insolence, as he so aptly named Asim's rebellion, sparked mortal fear into the hearts of Moroi whose right to rule had never before been questioned. Fane fed off that fright and transformed a battle into a global crusade.

He capitalized on Stela's and Bård's fealty to mount a campaign that would carry them across Europe and eventually to the Americas. During this centuries-long sojourn they wiped the countryside clean of every turned Strigoi without a Moroi, and furthermore—as evidenced by his hostility toward Antonia—any Strigoi viewed more favorably than his or her master. Of course, Fane's little trio was not without help. Moroi sympathetic to his cause joined in, and when there was no nearby Lord to help, Fane encouraged Stela and Bård to spread rumors among humans and instigate hunting parties.

The irony, of course, is that the longer they traveled, the larger Fane's band of assassins grew. Darius was discovered and spared in Rome. He was near starving, having been driven underground by fearful humans. He lived beneath the city in the catacombs with several of his kind, surviving—if you can call it that—on animal blood and the occasional vagrant. Darius' companions had stories similar to Bård's. They went to bed as men with families and trades and awoke one evening with a lacerated neck and no memory of where they were or how they'd gotten there. Darius was spared because he was literate and well-spoken. He was recording the stories of his companions in an effort to find a pattern, possibly, a cure that would render them mortal again.

Darius taps my yellow legal pad against the table once he's finished reading and reclines back in his seat. His face is inscrutable.

"So, what do you think of it so far?"

"What do I think of what?" he asks softly.

I arch my back against the splitting seams of the warped leather armchair but as usual nothing pops or realigns, and I realize that despite spending hours hunched over this paper-cluttered desk I'm not the least bit tense. "What do you think of the timeline?"

Darius frowns deeply, flings the stringy black hair from his eyes. "What year was it when you believe the family recruited me?" Darius asks, as though he was not present when it happened. "Sometime between 1700 and 1721, yes? But that's quite a large margin for error."

I snatch up the legal pad and scour the contents of my newest page. He knows the year down to the day, but he will not answer questions I have not expressly asked. Darius settles beside the bookshelves, dragging his finger through the velvet dust that has made its home there. I toss the legal pad aside.

"It's the best guess I can make with what I have. The least you could do was date the entries when you recopied them. What is it with you people and your blatant disregard for dates?"

Darius shoves his ink-stained hands into the pockets of his trousers. He chews on his lower lip thoughtfully, stares at me from under a mess of dark bangs. Stela would kill me if she knew what easy intimacy he and I share, and it would have nothing to do with jealousy. I can't quite explain why I trust Darius with all my prying.

"What, exactly, is this reconstituted family history all about, Irina? Is it a timeline you're after, or are you trying to paint Stela's past in a favorable light?" He watches me closely, never blinking. "Do you think..." he begins gently, "if you can validate her choices, understand them, you can learn to live with your own?"

"I'm not trying to paint Stela's deeds in any light. I'm trying to make sense of them to better understand her. I want a firm timeline, a clear progression of character. Answers."

Darius nods gravely as if he understands. He couldn't possibly.

I shove the legal pad into the leather satchel he gave me along with two yet unread volumes and stare back at him. He doesn't flinch but looks uncomfortable with my attention.

I need to understand what makes Stela so special. Different from the others. Her mechanics, not her character. I haven't come across a single account in her journals, or any others', of a fledgling named and claimed by the Strigoi who turned them, and I won't.

If my answers exist, I won't find them here. Fane wanted me to read these journals. He wanted me occupied, distracted, and it's working. I know something about secrets. They're only powerful while they're kept. Whether or not I'm still down here in two hundred years when that collected family history finds its way back to the podium, I'll never lay hands on it. Fane will see to that.

I stand and stack the volumes I've scattered in my arms, trying to arrange my mess for Darius' sake, but my twitchy companion quickly joins in. He's anxious to be rid of me. Ours is a strange, reluctant bond. I'm the only company he receives, apart from Fane. He looks forward to the distraction, while remaining wholly untrusting of my motives.

"Until tomorrow, Darius." I hand him the last of Stela's vellum-covered journals as he finishes rearranging the shelves.

"Yes." He nods sullenly. "Yes, tomorrow then."

* * *

Down a narrow hall smashed between the lounge and the armory are the stables. Not stables in the classical sense, with horses and lofts, but a drab basement. The hounds are kept there in cages that must have been stolen from a zoo. The area also houses enormous black iron boxes, stacked with antiques that no longer suit Fane's aesthetic, and broken weapons the family will never mend but keep because waste disposal is trickier than one might think down here.

Normally, Stela comes with me to get Erebus for my stealth exercises, but not tonight. Crogher twists his thick neck in my direction. I find that no matter where I end up within these walls, somehow, I'm always expected.

"Irina." He nods and turns back to his work.

Crogher isn't as tall as Bård, nor as broad as Fane, but there's nothing slight about him. He wears his hair in long, thin dreads, tied back most days. Lydia dresses him far better than Bård, and he always looks expertly tailored. His button-up shirt is pressed, a subtle lavender color that contrasts beautifully with his rich brown skin and makes this drab chamber seem a bit warmer.

Crogher was the slave of a cruel Irish dignitary who made a fortune investing in the Royal African Company. Fane's small family included Darius, Stela, Bård and Erebus' great-grandfather, Cronus, by that time and they were camped on the slave trader's land when Crogher set four wolfhounds on their trail.

The hounds put up an admirable fight, but in the end Crogher was crouched behind a rock and forced to witness the slaughter of all but one of his beloved animals at the jaws of Cronus.

The lone survivor of Crogher's pack was a female named Macha who Cronus took an instant shine toward. Though Macha's head was very nearly severed Cronus lay beside her and let Macha lick the weeping scratches on his face until she healed.

Crogher saw Cronus approach and thought the beast meant to finish his beloved Macha off. Enraged, he grabbed the largest rock he could wield and proceeded to best Stela and Bård for a round or two. He knocked the sword from Stela's grip, crushing her hand in the process. He nearly crushed Bård's skull before Cronus pinned him to the ground, snarling, prepared to devour him completely.

Fane called Cronus to heel and discussed the matter briefly with Bård. Crogher—near death—witnessed Macha's resurrection before he fainted, and when he awoke it was to Fane's soothing voice. Bård was still wiping Crogher's blood from his chin as he explained the transformation to their stalwart adversary turned newest addition to the family.

And then there were five, seven counting the hounds. The family left for Portugal the following evening, and from there to Morocco. What year would that have been? After 1700, surely, because Darius was one of them.

"What brings you?" Crogher's voice rumbles from deep within his chest, intimidating even when he's being cordial. I inch into the dusty room as he kneels down beside Erebus' little sister Macha. Stela told me that Crogher names all the females Macha, after Erebus' great-grandmother. He took it pretty hard when she died.

"I was wondering if I could take Erebus for a walk?" Crogher doesn't turn. The fluorescent lights buzz above his head. He pokes and prods Macha's exposed belly gently. I crane my head over his shoulder, but Macha has not been attacked by another transient in the tunnels. Veterinary medicine is hardly my area of expertise but she seems perfectly fine. "What happened to her?"

He stops prodding Macha's belly. His hand remains buried in her spiky coat for a moment. When Crogher snaps his fingers, Macha immediately slinks back into her cage. She flops down heavily on a mess of fur-covered blankets. I realize she's tired. I've never seen one of the dogs tired.

"She will birth a new guard soon," he says sadly.

"Puppies?"

The look Crogher gives me is enough to make me rethink the entire trip down here. He walks toward the large industrial sink in the corner to wash his hands, carefully cuffing his long sleeves up around his massive forearms.

"I studied medical science," I explain, "and I was a nurse. A good one. I can help when the time comes. Not that you need my help, I just…"

Crogher plants his hands on the basin. He stares directly at me, and I don't need to share blood with this man to know he's sizing me up. It's his thoughtful silence that pressures me to fill every moment in his company with useless chatter. His quiet reserve unnerves me. Stela has repeatedly warned me against being overly social with others until I can perfect my poker face. I haven't come to Crogher with an ulterior motive that needs to be hidden, but neither would I invite him to learn my tells. Although he can't read my thoughts the way Stela can, I keep my eyes averted and watch my feet.

"Forget I said anything." I wave my hand dismissively as I turn to go. "Good evening, Crogher."

I feel his hand on my shoulder and every muscle in my body tenses. He releases me just as quickly and when I turn around Crogher is twisting a towel in his hands.

"The mother never survives," he says thoughtfully. Crogher has said more to me in five minutes than I've heard him speak in all my months among them.

"Maybe I can help." I take a step closer. "I'd like to help, if you'll let me."

He focuses on my face, his brow furrowed. "The mother has to die," he says with a shrug. "Without her blood, they are only dogs. Dogs are no use to Fane."

My interest is piqued. I lean forward on my toes to catch a glimpse of Macha. She's sprawled on her back, breathing quickly in her dreams. "The puppies eat their mother?"

"They eat the mother first, and then they eat each other. We never keep more than two from a litter. One male, one female."

"Fascinating."

Crogher straightens and narrows his eyes.

"Not—I mean, it's awful, of course. I just—I had no idea how they…Never mind. I'm sorry to have disturbed you."

"Do you always talk so much?" he asks with the faintest hint of a smile.

A nervous laugh rattles through me. "Yes, actually. Every day of my life."

Crogher shakes his head and casts his beautiful umber dreadlocks back over his shoulder. He walks to Erebus' cage and opens the door. Erebus promptly heels without being told. "Tell him to come," he says, gesturing toward the statuesque hound.

I hadn't given a single thought as to whether Erebus would actually mind me without Stela at my side. I needed a reason, any reason for a walk. And during the observation period, I'm not permitted in the tunnels without a chaperone.

"Erebus," I call, slapping my knees excitedly.

Erebus looks to Crogher for approval, but Crogher merely crosses his arms. He pays no attention to the hound.

"C'mere big guy." My voice goes up an octave like he's some stray at a dog park and not an alarmingly sentient animal. Crogher grins. Erebus tilts his head, not in confusion, but disbelief.

"Erebus! Come."

The hound risks a step forward, looking back to Crogher for confirmation. He inches forward until he's standing in front of me.

"Tell him to heel," Crogher instructs.

At the sound of his master's voice, Erebus takes a step backward.

"Heel!"

The hound sits at my side, staring up at me expectantly and I'm more surprised than Crogher appears to be. Crogher nods in approval and jerks his thumb over his shoulder.

"Use the back exit. If Fane sees you taking him for a stroll at this hour he will not be pleased."

"Thank you."

I have to put my shoulder to the exit and the rusted hinges protest with a scream. Erebus trots out into the tunnel ahead of me, and Crogher lingers beside the open door.

"Did you tell Stela you planned a walk this evening?" he asks rhetorically. I open my mouth, but he couldn't be made to believe a lie. Crogher drums his fingers on the steel door as though deliberating. "Return him to me promptly."

"I will."

And with that, the loud steel door slams shut between us.

At the mouth of the tunnel, Erebus bellows a shepherding bark. He sits with his head craned forward, like he means to collect me if I don't catch up. His wide black eyes shine with silver at the edges.

When I join him at the fork of three possible paths, he nudges my right hip with his snout, guiding me to my left. I realize, quite suddenly, that I'm the one being walked. At every turn, Erebus nudges my legs in the direction he would have me take. We come upon a stretch of tunnel that ambles for an age to a collapse that has been hollowed out only enough for a hound to pass. Erebus barks encouragingly and disappears into the rubble.

Begrudgingly, I crouch down on all fours and follow after him. I can see light ahead of me, glinting off Erebus' black coat. When I emerge, the ceiling is much lower and I sense myself on higher ground. Overhead are iron grates and manhole covers. They permit the light to beam in blue columns and water trickles down the cement walls. It's not the sewer, but some kind of service tunnel.

I'm not supposed to be here.

I linger under one of those iron grates and eye the rusted rungs stuck into the wall. From above, I hear the distant sounds of the city. We must be further removed from the main roads than I realized but mixed in a fog of exhaust is the unmistakable musk of human beings.

Erebus growls and snaps his jaws. His hackles stand on end and he knows exactly why I've stopped walking.

"Sorry."

I edge out from under the grate and he stamps his paw to say I'm still not moving fast enough for him. He waits for me to pass him and then he presses his muzzle against the small of my back, forcing me ahead.

The tunnel narrows the further we walk, and the subtle incline continues until the ceiling is nearly within reach. There is light seeping through the dark from somewhere in front of us, and the roar of the city has been replaced by a gentler sound.

Our midnight journey dead ends at a circular grate. Erebus trots ahead and lies on the steep slope of the wall, his nose poked between the iron bars. I perch beside him with my boots planted against the damp concrete. Outside the cobalt night sky rests heavily atop the white-capped coastline of Lake Michigan.

I hook my fingers around the bars and press my nose through the opening, inhaling the heady breeze, the wide-open night the wide-open night.

"I'm gonna make a break for it."

Erebus shuffles and snorts, rubbing his head against the side of my crooked leg. I scratch behind his ears.

"Have you brought Stela here?"

Erebus paws at the iron grate and whines at the sound of her name. His eyes dart across the water and every few seconds back to my face, as though he's making sure I'm paying close attention. There are tufts of fur matted in thick black rows along the bottom of the grate that tell me he visits this spot often. But dark fur, not bright and silver like Macha's or ghostly pale like his brother Raghnall's.

"Thank you for showing me this."

Erebus plants his wide paw against the bars, and I find myself humming a song my father used to sing when I was small, watching the steady waves roll against the wall below us. Stela is out there, dressed in her finest, wearing her most enticing smile. She's feeding, or covering her tracks, or already on her way back to me. It's a wonder she manages. A miracle she doesn't run away. Not for the first time, I wonder what keeps her down here. What keeps any of them?

"I could never run away from her," I say softly. Not to return to life aboveground. Not to live in a world without Fane. Erebus swipes his paw down the bars and whines. It took every ounce of my resolve to banish Stela from my mother's sick room and out of my life. A decision I was able to make only to protect an invalid, and one I regretted immediately. Stela and I argue, often, and over the most trivial misunderstandings, but I am raw without her. Like every nerve in my body has been exposed to the elements. I wish I could chalk this up to our bond, but my affinity for Stela began before I knew her name. In those first few minutes when she was just a beautiful stranger sharing an empty waiting room with me, I could have sworn I'd known her all my life. That my blood recognized her, even then.

She unsettled me. She excited me. She still does.

It's easier to gauge the hour with the help of the fresh night air. I can sense the approach of the sun. We don't linger for very long.

He takes an easier route home—faster, too—twisting his head over his shoulder occasionally to ensure I haven't strayed. When the overhead grates appear again, Erebus soldiers on, and I repay his trust in me by keeping my eyes on him. I wouldn't want to jeopardize my chances of a future excursion with him.

As we near the compound my thoughts return to Stela. When I was alive, she had to leave my bed to return to this bleak prison. I remember the way the streetlights spilled through my bedroom window and swam across the pale expanse of her back. I remember how the whole of my mother's brownstone felt when Stela was waiting inside. I remember my mother's perfume, and the musk of my father's wardrobe, and freshly brewed coffee before the sun was in the sky. Could I still drink coffee? Would it make me sick? I should ask.

As I cling to these memories, I fail to notice that Erebus has stopped walking. The footsteps of another are nearly upon us. An anticipatory thrill runs down my spine and I turn around to embrace her only to find myself pinned to the wall. Eyes I was not expecting lock with mine, and a thin arm that might as well be marble presses against my throat.

"Sorry," I choke, "thought you were Stela."

Lydia's mouth is only an inch from mine and she keeps her arm on my throat, not to deprive me of air, but to ensure I can't look away. "You wound me."

"I wasn't paying attention," I rasp.

She pats my cheek with her free hand and I am so enraged that the whole tunnel seems to brighten. I know she senses this because she smiles. A taunting smile, as though I'm the most pathetic thing she's ever seen. "Lost in thoughts of your lover?" she asks. "How adorable."

I grab her wrist, but barely manage to jostle her. She is grounded, feet shoulder-width apart, and I've lost my footing. What would Bård think? The harder I pull at her, the closer she leans. Her straight black hair tickles my cheeks. Her wide almond-shaped eyes bore hungrily into mine.

"Ah-ha," she says, "thoughts of your lover, indeed, and something else. Homesickness, is it?"

I slam my eyes shut and shove my palm against her sternum. Her vise-like grip vanishes and she stumbles backward with a raucous laugh, her head thrown back in delight. Lydia all but doubles over in her glee as I storm off, tugging my clothes into place.

"Erebus, come!"

I hear his nails clips against the ground.

"Heel!" Lydia cries, and Erebus sits beside her, still as stone. She kneels in front of him, running her fingers over his chest, whispering praise. She stands up, knowing I can't return without him. She's won.

"How did you know what I was thinking?" I ask.

She tilts her head and spares me a bemused smile that flashes in the dark like a blade.

"Please," she huffs. "You are a child, Irina. You were either thinking of blood or home, and I did not see lust in your eyes." She scratches Erebus' muzzle. "Well, at least not once you realized it was me."

My jaw clenches and I stare at Erebus, pleading with him silently to follow. But he remains perched beside her.

"He will not follow you," she sing-songs. "You are outranked."

I lean against the tunnel wall and cross my arms. "What'd you want, Lydia?"

She snaps her fingers at Erebus who falls into step with her, closing the distance between us. Lydia turns me toward home and slips her arm in mine. "If it were left up to your guard dog, we would never get acquainted," she says teasingly. She slows our pace to a leisurely stroll and for some reason I play along, despite sensing a setup.

"He isn't my dog." From the corner of my eye Lydia's lips curl and her face brightens. Out of all of us, she looks the most human. Her skin is a soft golden tone, whereas Stela, Bård, and Darius are all ghostly pale. She's petite, about three inches shorter than I am which makes her the smallest member of the family. But it's her playfulness more than anything else that gives her the bloom of life.

"I was not referring to Erebus," she says. She runs her hand down my arm and pulls me closer, cackling proudly. She shakes her black hair out of her eyes. That hair alone would be reason enough to hate her, if her sense of humor failed to do the trick.

It stands to reason that Lydia's attire should stand out. She's flashy, with several thin gold necklaces, and tasteful rings stacked in threes up and down her fingers. Where the others wear nondescript blacks and grays, Lydia is fit for a photo shoot. Tonight, she's wearing black leather pants and a sheer cream-colored silk blouse that flatters her warm complexion. An extravagant indulgence considering this is her second look this evening. Everyone burns the clothing they hunt in before returning home to ensure that trace evidence of their kills never follows them back to the compound.

She notices my appraisal without comment. She tugs me past the main entrance toward the stables. I would have thought she'd be keen to get me caught with Erebus at this hour, and the fact that she doesn't push me into the main hall is no small courtesy.

"What is it with you and Stela, anyway?" I ask. "Sibling rivalry? Or have you always hated each other?"

Lydia's smile never falters, even as she drops my arm in favor of a guiding hand on my shoulder blade. Erebus tries in vain to wedge his head between us but she nudges him out of the way with her knee.

"What has Stela told you about me?" she asks, more diplomatic than Stela led me to believe.

"Very little."

Lydia makes a small, noncommittal sound. Erebus comes to heel at the exit door, but neither Lydia nor I move to enter. Even in the dreary light Lydia gleams, as if her zest for life emanates from some secret place inside her. She wears death better than anyone I know.

"How far have you read in Stela's journals?" she asks. "Has the family reached Constantinople?"

"What makes you think I'm reading Stela's journals?"

"Fane told me."

"Of course." I smile. "What else has he told you about me?"

"Fane tells me everything," she says seriously.

I doubt that. I don't even think she believes it. "The family has just set sail for Morocco."

She smiles again and runs her eyes up and down me. "Hard to make sense of it all without a computer. I would imagine that has slowed you down considerably, having to cross-reference everything for dates."

I shrug. "Goes against everything my generation stands for."

"And what is that?" she asks, amused.

"Wikipedia."

Lydia chuckles and swats my arm. Were it not that I distrust her because Stela must have some reason for hating her, I think we might actually get along. I like her. She's playful and witty in a way that reminds me of a few good friends I had in college. She dresses like they did, makes me feel like they did—her opinion of me matters more than I'd care to admit.

"Well, the sooner you settle into our ways, the quicker you can return to your modern conveniences. I shall procure your smartphone myself, as soon as Fane permits," she says.

It's reassuring, coming from her, though Stela has assured me of the same. Lydia is the closest to me in age, and she knows what it means to be in my position. Low man on the totem pole, the awkward new kid, the youngest member. She raises her hand to knock on the door.

"You're nothing like I thought you'd be."

Lydia freezes. She regards me seriously, still faintly amused. "You are exactly as I imagined you would be, Irina."

I don't get the chance to ask what she means. Crogher yanks the door open before Lydia's first rap. He stiffens at the sight of her.

"Good evening, brother," she says. "I found something of yours wandering the tunnels."

Erebus slinks inside with his head down and marches straight for his open kennel. Lydia follows him. Crogher slams the door shut behind me and his look says that I won't be taking Erebus for a stroll again any time soon.

Crogher clears his throat and clasps his hands behind his back. "Macha is carrying heirs."

Lydia claps gleefully. "A spot of good news for our Lord!" she exclaims. She pats Crogher's broad chest. "You should tell him. He will be pleased."

Crogher shuffles but doesn't move away from Lydia. I keep my distance, inching widely past them toward the hall. There's an uncomfortable familiarity between them that embarrasses me.

"He will be just as pleased to hear the news from you," Crogher says, taking a step back. "I have no *other* reason to call upon him at this hour."

The implication is clear, even to me. Lydia's eyes burn in her skull, but that beguiling smile remains plastered on her face. Her gaze snaps in my direction before I can slip away.

"I should get back. Stela will be home soon."

Lydia catches my wrist. "I would not mention tonight's outing to Stela," she whispers. Her face is so close to mine, I can't tell if it is a threat or a warning. Her eyes are serious, but there remains a hint of suppressed smile on her lips. "The thought of you wandering the tunnels by yourself would only worry her."

I give a quick nod and take another step.

"Your secret is safe with me, Irina." She winks and turns back to Crogher. He glares at her, and I know without seeing her face, she's staring just as savagely at him.

* * *

I managed the fire on my own this evening. The logs hold their position and don't collapse in a smoldering pile. The fireplaces had initially seemed an odd inclusion. It's not as if the tunnels lack climate control, and as Stela once told me, we don't suffer the temperature the way humans do. Our bodies adjust to our surroundings. Then I realized that the rush of warmth one gets from standing in front of a fire is not unlike the blush of a feed.

I'm not surprised when two smooth arms encircle my waist. I counted her every step the second she dropped into the tunnel, and I hated every single one that wasn't meant for me. Fane had kept her longer than expected.

"Your body is warm from the fire," she purrs. Her lips pressed to my ear as I lean readily into her embrace.

"You're warm too." Warmer than she would be if Fane had fed from her, so Lydia must have satiated him this evening. This does not explain what kept her so long from me, and I doubt she'll offer a reason. Judging by the dance of her fingers along my waist she's in too good a mood to talk business. Stela buries her face in my neck and inhales greedily.

"Macha is carrying a litter," she says. "Erebus' sister."

"Crogher told me."

Stela withdraws her right arm and pulls a collection bag from her back pocket. When I take it from her the plastic is still warm from her skin. Warm blood is enticing and I don't waste a moment, tearing into the bag with my teeth.

Stela smothers a chuckle against my shoulder, her thumbs rubbing circles in the dimples of my hips. I barely register her presence. Once, every few days, she offers me a bag of blood heated by her flushed and fed body. Bag or no bag, embarrassed or enthralled, disgusted or starved—it makes no difference to me when the blood is closer to the temperature my body knows it should be. The last few drops are wretchedly cool, and I crumple the empty bag in my fist and toss it into the fire.

"When did you see Crogher?" she asks, conversationally, pulling her black long-sleeved T-shirt over her head.

"I dropped by the stables after the library."

Stela drops her shirt on the floor, her mouth frozen in a tight-lipped smile. She steps down into the living area and perches on the arm of the sofa to remove her boots. Beautiful, buttery leather ringed at the soles from snow or rain. Is it winter?

"What drove you to the stables, dearest?" she asks carefully, sensing her own impending displeasure.

If Stela already knows, she's putting on an incredible show. Is it possible Lydia didn't mention running into me? I was so sure she would. Still, a secret is leverage.

I stand between Stela's legs. Guarded in her expression she raises her eyes to mine. I bend down and kiss her cheeks, holding her head back in my hands.

"I wanted to go for a walk. I asked Crogher if I could take Erebus with me."

Stela's lips twitch. She closes her eyes, inhales deeply and pulls me close, her body still as stone. "Was Crogher angry with you?"

"Not at all. He wasn't exactly enthusiastic, but I doubt he's prone to whimsy. He told me about Macha, and I offered to help him with the birth. He told me the mother always dies, which, while gruesome, is also intriguing. And that was the end of it. He let me take Erebus out through the back."

Stela tilts her head, acutely aware that there's more to the story. "Just like that. He let you leave with Erebus in the middle of the night?"

I shrug and Stela laughs. She holds me by the neck and kisses my exposed throat. She hikes up my blouse, stops as though remembering something important. "Elizabeth, the hounds need their rest, as we do, and this was not a training exercise," she gently admonishes. "If someone else had seen you taking him for a stroll—"

"About that," I interject. "I ran into Lydia on my way back."

Stela's body tenses and I can practically hear her internal monologue: do not get angry. She keeps her eyes from me, flitting them about.

"What did she say?" Stela asks quietly, willing herself to remain calm.

"She told me not to tell you."

"So, why tell me?"

"Because she said I shouldn't."

Stela's sardonic grin grows into a genuine warm smile. She tugs at the edge of my shirt. I shirk it off and toss it behind me. Stela slips her fingers into the waistband of my jeans and places a kiss above my heart. "You might just survive this house," she laughs, but there is genuine relief in her face. "You are sharper than I credit you for."

"I really am."

Stela giggles into the crook of my neck and shakes me by the hips. She kisses my neck, my cheek, my lips. My mind wanders and Stela pulls back concerned.

"Sorry. I was thinking about something Crogher said. About Macha."

"It is the way of things."

"I gathered as much. He said…actually he said exactly that."

Stela sits up straighter on the arm of the sofa and tugs me closer, hooking her calves around the back of my legs. "And this troubles you?"

"Not exactly. He said the mother *has* to die. Without her blood the puppies are just dogs."

She tilts her head and waits for me to continue or arrive at some sort of punchline. "Yes…" she says. "What use do we have for mere dogs? Everyone has a purpose here, Elizabeth. Even the hounds."

"That's what's bothering me. Does the mother bite her offspring?"

Stela's fingers falter, she looks taken aback by the suggestion. "Of course not. Why would she? Macha's instinct will be to guard her litter. Their survival will be her only concern."

"Right, but I didn't turn when you injected me with your blood to save my life. You had to drain my blood and then I yours. So how is it that the puppies are changed just by drinking their mother's blood. Shouldn't Macha have to feed from them and then they from her? Why would the rules be different?"

Stela rears back with a hearty laugh.

"Why is this funny?"

"I misunderstood," she explains, waving my exasperation away. "I mistook your questions for concern. I should have known it was the science that bothered you most."

"Christ, Stela. It's not like I don't care. I offered to help Crogher." I step out of her embrace. "Couldn't we just inject the puppies with some of Macha's blood? She doesn't have to die."

The humor is still high in her cheeks, but she stands sighing. Stela cups my chin gently, encouraging me to look at her. "What would we do if Macha had—shall we say—a litter of six, all of which survived? And Macha herself survived?" she asks earnestly. "Where would we keep them? How would we feed, and care for and train them all?"

I narrow my eyes. This reasoning bothers me almost as much as the sloppy science. Stela senses this, and a look of resignation settles over her.

"So, you just let the herd thin itself out? Remove the weak links."

"Survival of the fittest." She shrugs. "Surely you can appreciate that." She reaches for my hand and tugs me toward the bed.

"Is that what Fane's crusade was all about? Weeding out the undesirables?"

The moment the accusation leaves my mouth, I regret it. Not because it's untrue, but because Stela will never agree with me. This is her life's work, and she is proud of her service. She stares at me as though she's never seen me before. She drops my hand. I watch her walk the short distance to the mattress. She shoves her pants down around her ankles and keeps her back to me. She flings her bra to the floor and slips between the turned-down covers still wearing her underwear, which is never a good sign.

I finish the job Stela started, undressing myself without expectation. Sometimes we're on the same page, usually when we're on each other. Other times we might as well exist on different planets for all the trouble we have understanding each other. I crawl into the vacant side of the bed. Stela doesn't look at me, just stares blankly at the ceiling.

We lie motionless in the dark, the silence between us a physical entity, a third body in our bed. Stela doesn't reach for the lamp on the nightstand. The fire casts eerie shadows, and when I turn over on my side her face is blank. Her stony expression wills me away. I reach across the bed to make sure I can still reach her.

"I'm sorry." I rest my hand beside her arm. Close but not touching. "I was out of line."

Stela's eyes, unblinking, don't shift from the ceiling. My hand is vehemently ignored. She gives no indication that she even heard my apology, and for a second, I wonder if she sleeps with her eyes open. I wouldn't know. She always falls asleep after me, and she's the first to wake.

I flip back over, pulling the covers up around my chest.

"The pups are born of the mother," she whispers. Her voice is small, distant. "Macha's blood will be the catalyst to the beast already inside them. If they did not feed from her they would stay as they are, but the hound would remain, dormant for all their considerably shorter lives."

If I understand Stela correctly, the pups carry the gene. It must be a gene. Does this mean both parents have to be carriers to produce viable offspring?

"Is it the same principle with the Moroi?" I ask, so quickly I don't think to consider my timing.

"Go to sleep, Elizabeth."

I can't will myself to sleep—Stela knows as much—and for once, I wish the incapacitating blackness would arrive ahead of schedule, if only to be done with this night. I take to counting the books on the shelves instead.

"Is that really what you think of me?"

I lift my head and turn to look at her over my shoulder, uncertain as to whether she said the words aloud, or I wished them into existence, or perhaps gleaned the thought from her somehow. "What do you mean?"

Stela's eyes fall miserably along my face. It could be the fire, the obscuring shadows, the space between us, but she looks small and impossibly young. Stela curls on her side to face me fully, and I flip hurriedly around though neither of us move any closer.

"Do you think, all those years, that I played the happy executioner?"

I don't. Honestly. And what choice did she have? She was following orders. Looking at her now, she's as vulnerable as I've ever seen her, and I hate seeing her this way.

"No," I answer truthfully. "I swear, that's not what I meant."

A familiar darkness steals over her face. She doesn't turn away, but she has walled something off. "But you do think it of Fane."

"Stela...a lot of people died."

"They were not *my* people," she says.

"They were someone's—"

"You did not live it!" Her fist tightens around the sheets and it's obvious that she's one clumsy word away from losing her composure. She can be frightening, but this is different. I'm frightened for her. She knows I'm right. I can see her fear that she was wrong, or god forbid, that Fane was wrong. All that blood spilled for sport, and nothing more. She's a killer, she knows that. But she's also a solider. And to Stela, that makes all the difference.

"You're right," I nod. "I wasn't there."

Stela remains propped up on one arm, and I stare back at her with all the understanding I can muster. This isn't an argument that can be won. She lingers on my eyes for a breath, a second, and finally she turns away from me again. As she settles back into bed, she slides toward the center. I move slowly, giving her every opportunity to pull away, or tell me to leave her alone. Instead, she presses her spine against my front as I wrap my arm around her waist. She doesn't relax into my embrace, and despite this closeness, Stela is miles away as my vision clouds over with sleep.

IV

Trust

I waste entire evenings in pursuit of the precise moment I lost control over the course of my life. It would be so easy to blame Elizabeth. But I do not hold her responsible for my actions. My footsteps strayed from the path long before we met in that dreary little waiting room, with the blood of her patient William Moore still sliding down the back of my throat.

One particularly bleak night, I actually searched his name. I spent hours immersed in his various social media profiles and read through every record the Chicago PD had on the poor man. Larceny, armed robbery, possession, intent to distribute, arson when he was a juvenile. William Moore was a bully and a petty thief, and everything I found out about the man, I had already learned from his blood.

It would be poetic to find that young Mr. Moore was a hero embroiled in a torrid love affair. That his blood poisoned my reason with romantic whims as he slept in that drug-induced haze. That a piece of his heart splintered free and lodged itself in my cold chest, creating a hole just large enough for Elizabeth to wind her way inside.

The noble thing to do is to admit fault. There was a time when I would have fallen on my saber if it meant protecting the honor of my position, my family. I was proud of that person. But this person now who scurries around the rules, who dotes on and falls at the feet of a woman she has only just begun to know and truly understand? I do not know this person.

So, why do I bend Fane's laws? Why do I conceal my deception? Why am I constantly seeking to subvert his knowledge of Elizabeth's true allegiance? I see my trespasses for what they are, and still I persist. Is love more important than loyalty?

Elizabeth is part of me now. She is inextricable in a way I once considered Fane to be, but clearly, I overestimated my attachment to him. Elizabeth is vital as a limb. The only comfort I find in this new self is the certainty that without her, I could not continue. I am as sure of that fact as I am that I will feed this evening, that the sun will blister the sky tomorrow.

Outside, the evening unfurls peacefully. The crystalline lights of Tinley Park twinkle in the distance. In every building, behind each window is a life. Which world will stop spinning this evening, I wonder? Who will wait on a loved one who never returns?

"Kathryn. So sorry to have kept you waiting."

Andrew has extended his hours to accommodate our unsanctioned meetings. I truly hope tonight will mark the last time we have to discuss the matter. My secrecy makes him noticeably uncomfortable.

"Think nothing of it." I wave my hand toward the window. "I was just admiring your view."

My good Mr. Opes shuffles behind his desk and stands beside me, his hands clasped behind his back and I slide my sunglasses back into place before I turn to him. Andrew releases a breath that loosens his whole body.

"It has been a number of years since I was able to loiter beside this window. You keep impossibly early hours."

"A reasonable woman would hardly call six p.m. an early hour, Kathryn."

He uses the alias so playfully. Strange to think that even as my co-conspirator, he has no right to know my name. Our true names have the ability to bind mortals to us for life, such was the case when I gave mine to Elizabeth. Like the sunglasses I wear which keep him safe from my thrall, the alias is for his protection.

I sweep my black wool blazer off my shoulders and walk around his wide desk to drape it over the back of my seat. Andrew, buttoning down his suit coat, takes his rightful place behind the desk and rolls the crisp cuffs of his pressed sleeves up to his elbows.

We have come to an understanding, he and I. I am the devil he knows, and after meeting Lydia—Dilay or Ms. Sadik, as he calls her—he is less than enthusiastic to pursue a change of representative. He is the steward my Lord selected, and with a bit of intimidation, a capable one at that. To look at him now, so polite and accommodating, one would never guess that this same pencil pusher had the gall to steal tens of thousands from our mutual benefactor.

Andrew sorts the documents that Rachel has compiled for this meeting, everything that requires Elizabeth's signature.

"Tell me Andrew. How is your darling Christine?"

His sole heir is still a sore subject. His face clouds predictably. But avoiding it will not impede Christine's birthright. A part of him has already begun to accept her fate, and so he leans back in his chair.

"She's well. Thank you," he says cordially. "Top of her class."

"I would expect nothing less. Her major is business, is it not?"

He curls a plump finger in the knot of his tie and pulls the fabric slack around his ruby throat. We have miles to go, Andrew and I. Christine's major, her dorm room number, her preferred study nook, the friends she keeps, the friends she should not keep, her favorite professor (with whom she had a brief and heartbreaking affair), her best and worst subjects. I already know it all. If I meant to cause the child harm she would have been drained and incinerated ages ago.

"Yes, business," he says. "Her focus is finance and corporate management. She's off to a strong start, laying the foundation she needs for her MBA."

I nod appreciatively. He has come such a long way in such a short time. He has nearly repaid Fane—Mr. Radu to our dear investment banker—in full for the money he skimmed from Fane's largest account, and the other accounts he manages for us have profited greatly from his reinvigoration. Which is precisely the reason I remind him, on occasion, where his loyalties lie.

"I was pleased to hear of her acceptance to Harvard. We wish her all the best, Andrew."

Hard to say what causes him the most discomfort: name-dropping Christine's current location or my use of the word "we" and all that it implies. His eyes drift to her portrait on his desk and they mist over.

"Shall we get to it, then?"

"Of course."

Andrew arranges several documents and with a closed pen, traces down the edge of each sheet listing the inventory that has been liquidated, the value of each item, Claire Dumas' hospital bills, her life insurance, checking and savings accounts, the money left to Claire by her husband, the endowment she received when her father passed and finally the sale of the brownstone.

"You are certain we have secured a buyer?"

"As certain as anyone can be, yes. They're waiting on the appraisal, but I can assure you, Kathryn, the value is there."

"What do you require from me?"

Andrew flicks open a large manila envelope and drops several documents inside before extending it to me.

"Ms. Dumas will need to sign all the forms I reviewed with you." I cringe at Elizabeth's last name, her powerful first name splashed all over these pages. There was no other way to make good on my promise to Elizabeth that her inheritance would be secured and secreted away for the time being. Andrew has spoken that name aloud only once. I swore to him that if I ever heard it pass from his lips, in this office or anywhere else for that matter, it would mean the death of everything he holds dear. "We'll need a copy of her driver's license, or some form of government-issued photo ID for our own records. When we close on the house I'll call you with the final number and present a net dollar amount to be deposited into your…client's…existing trust. Then we can talk about her portfolio."

"Something modest, I think. More conservative than the accounts you currently manage for Mr. Radu."

I retrieve my blazer and Andrew rises from his seat.

"The returns will be much smaller than your benefactor's accounts, if we go that route. But the fluctuations will be less volatile. It's a give-and-take," he says, making scales of his hands.

I lean over the desk and extend my hand to him. Andrew shakes it firmly without recoiling from my tepid skin. In moments like this, when Andrew is all business, he reminds me of his dearly departed father. The Opes family has been good to us.

"I can assure you, Andrew, I will discuss the matter at length with my client. The decision is hers, but she is a practical woman. I think something more conservative will suit her needs."

"Quite right." He nods. "May I show you out?" I wave him off.

"You have done all that I require and more this evening, Mr. Opes. I know the way. Good night Andrew." I slip into the darkened hallway, dimly illuminated by the building's harsh auxiliary lighting, but the office door does not close behind me. I turn to see Andrew braced against the threshold.

"Kathryn, should El—Ms. Dumas…"

I remove my sunglasses and tuck them into my breast pocket. The near slip drains the color from Andrew's face.

"Will your client require the same series of protocols we use for your family?"

My eyes stretch wide in the dark, swallowing the thin streams of light left in the hall. Andrew retreats a step, pulling the door tight around his squat body.

"Ms. Dumas *is* family, Andrew."

Small beads of perspiration dot his temples. He nods emphatically. "Of course. I'll see to it personally."

"I have faith in you, Andrew," I call out. "The documents will be returned to you by a courier the day after next."

The office door closes with a thud and the sound of the lock clicking into place is music to my ears. He finally knows his place.

* * *

The air is sweet with perspiration. Dense as a bog. Bodies ripe from exertion drape themselves on strangers, brace against unfinished cement columns, collapse against the bar. Some have expired completely, heads slumped to their chests as they drift in and out of consciousness on rectangular sofas. But the true warriors dance on, crushed together on the dance floor.

This is not my preferred hunting ground. Those who frequent such decadent establishments usually arrive in groups. Men are easy enough to isolate, but not without a few lingering jealous glares from their dateless brethren. Still, the club has a certain charm. A revelry, a carelessness that I admire. Bodies against bodies, sharing the same air, yet, isolated in pursuit of their own amusement. They move like an ocean, waves upon waves, rising and falling in time with the music.

Though I have refused her offer of a drink, turned my body toward the churning crowd, and rebuffed her every attempt to make conversation, this evening's mark has sealed her own fate. Elizabeth will not be pleased, but what can be done? Her angled and possessive posture coupled with a few gratuitous touches to my shoulder have deterred several young men who would have gladly taken her place. Resigned and considerably more irritated than the situation warrants, I spin on my stool and give her the invitation she desires. My shin brushes her bare calf and her hand falls upon my knee.

Her name is Natalie. Not a day over twenty-three. She studies Theoretical and Applied Mechanics at Northwestern. She has a dog named Julian, a rescue who really rescued her. She is the only child of two successful restaurateurs in Philadelphia and could not stand to waste another long weekend in her parents' presence—much to her misfortune. She arrived here with friends from school, but an argument broke out and drove the party their separate ways.

It never ceases to amaze me how much you can learn about a person with a simple sympathetic nod.

Natalie has indulged in more than alcohol this evening. Her pupils are nearly as wide as mine, swallowing her hazel irises. She speaks rapidly and jumps from one topic to the next. Occasionally, she runs a finger or the back of her hand across her cheek to sweep away a thin layer of sweat. Cocaine, most likely.

"What about you? Are you from here?" she asks abruptly.

The question catches me off guard and I chuckle. "No. My family moved around often."

Natalie flicks her heavy bangs back from her face and leans in conspiratorially with a hand to her mouth. "Let me guess. Military brat?"

"Something of the sort."

"Thought so," she says around a messy slurp of drink. "You've got the kind of intensity that comes from a strict upbringing and you don't look like a preacher's daughter."

I lean forward on my stool, run the tips of my fingers along her sweat-dampened jaw. "How perceptive of you." Natalie presses her torso against my forearm. She beams at me, and for an instant her overstimulated body grows still. She traces the lapels of my jacket and presses her glossed lips against my ear.

"You wanna get out of here?" she asks, emboldened.

I run my fingers through her brass-colored hair and drop a few bills for the barkeep. "You read my mind."

My car is not parked as remotely as it should be. In my haste for a hunt after the meeting with Andrew, I hadn't the time to conceal it properly. The oversight works in my favor. Natalie would not have followed me willingly down the usual alleyways. The streets are teeming with college students, some snug in the crooks of the buildings we pass, others sitting with their heads between their knees along the gutters. Christine Opes comes to mind. But if the Opes heir was home for the weekend, we would know.

Natalie and I round the back of the club where the foot traffic is as heavy as the sidewalk. Though each pair of eyes is occupied by a mobile in their hands or the object of their desire, it is too populated to take her here. I open the passenger side door and Natalie drops inside with a giggle. A few faces dart up from the icy blue glow of their enrapturing cell phones as I slam the door, but at this distance, in a faintly lit parking lot in the middle of the night, no one can see

Natalie's face. I do not envy the detective who will have to explain this to her family.

"So, your place, or your place?" she asks, her head flopped back against the headrest, leaving the taut skin of her neck perilously exposed.

"Very well," I say and inch my way into oncoming traffic.

I have a mind to take her through the industrial park where I typically hide my vehicle, but there is a naivety about Natalie that I wish to preserve as long as possible. Besides, there are several sparsely lit service roads between the city and the funeral parlor, any one of which will suffice. She might even find it charming to pull off the main road before we reach our destination, before any sense of danger pervades her excitement. We need not fight or thrash or scream. This child is being reckless—her age demands it of her. And were I just another woman, this could have been a memorable night for Natalie.

Was Elizabeth rebellious at this age? She entered this vehicle more than once of her own volition. She gambled her life away in that very seat…

Natalie rambles beside me as we make our way beyond the city limits, and I am far more silent than I should be. Thoughts of Elizabeth still bursting with life at the forefront of my mind.

As we roll to a stop with the city skyline glinting in my rearview mirror, Natalie opens the clutch strapped to her wrist and procures a small silver vial from its depths. There are times when I yearn to be wrong. Natalie presses one nostril closed and snuffs the fine white powder from the lid of the small canister, throwing her head back ferociously. She sniffles, dabs at her nose and thrusts the vial toward me.

"No thank you." I brush her offering away.

"You sure?" She wiggles the smooth cylinder in her fingers playfully.

The light turns green and Natalie drops the vial back in her clutch. She sits a bit straighter, unnerved for reasons she cannot quite place. She ruffles her hair—dishwater-blond in the moonless night—and smiles sheepishly. Sensing that the night has taken a turn, I pull off on an unlit service road before the atmosphere can grow any more uncomfortable for her and cut the engine.

I turn in my seat and toss the keys on the dashboard. "I prefer to keep a clear mind."

"I get it. Sorry. That wasn't cool. I should've asked you first."

She fidgets with the snug hem of her skirt, which is three inches too high for the weather. Autumn approaches quickly, but Natalie wanted to make an impression tonight. Her eyes dart anxiously along the empty road ahead. When she meets my waiting stare, I know the question before she does.

"Wow. I never even got your name."

"Kathryn."

Natalie repeats the alias, nods to herself. A little tension leaves her body. "What do you do for a living?"

She is trying very hard to keep her voice even and polite, despite the effects of the drug. Her hands grip her knees, feet planted firmly on the floorboard to keep them from pumping. My mind is occupied almost entirely by the late hour, and the envelope sitting in my glove compartment. I wanted something brief and brutal tonight to celebrate the fulfillment of my promise to Elizabeth—her finances secured. Natalie was never supposed to happen. What she needs now is reassurance, encouragement, before she grips the door handle and runs for the highway. I push my seat back and extend a hand toward her.

She stares at my palm, swallows roughly. "Not much of a talker, are you?"

"Not particularly," I say with a smile.

Natalie smirks briefly and takes my hand, helping herself over the center console and into my lap. She tucks the hair back behind her ears and peers unsteadily down at me. Her lips hover above mine for a precarious breath and before she can close the distance between our mouths, I turn her chin and brush my lips from her shoulder to her ear. Natalie shivers, her hands grip my shoulders. She dips her chin, chasing my lips again. I pull away slowly, tracing patterns on the soft warm skin of her thighs and focus my attention on her throat. When her palm finds the back of my head, I open my mouth and pierce the skin as gently as I can.

Natalie's scream is immediate, guttural, but I lock one arm around her waist and curl my fist in the sweat-dampened hair at the base of her skull. She ruins her fresh pink manicure by tearing at my blouse, my neck, and when her hands fall limply at her sides her nails are edged in blood. I do not fight her, but cradle her close, drinking deep and languorous mouthfuls. Her ugly scratches heal almost faster than they were carved. I slide her gently into the void without a bruise or a broken bone.

She dies in a heavy swoon—the fear evaporated from her face—ushering out a final breathy sigh that carries with it every care she has ever had.

The body crumples down on top of me. When the last trickle passes between my lips, I lift her under the arms and place her back in the passenger seat. Her head thumps dully against the window. I prick my thumb and seal the wound with the balm of my blood.

As I turn the key in the ignition, I take a second glance, considering if it would be safer to throw her in the trunk before getting back on the highway. She looks nothing like Elizabeth, but with her eyes peacefully shut, her features placidly composed and ashen, I am reminded of the night my love took a bullet in the arm and compelled me to break every rule Fane has ever enforced.

Natalie doubles over as I grind the throttle underfoot, eager to conclude the brief remainder of my journey and rid myself of her company for good.

* * *

To my dismay, the parking lot is far from vacant when I arrive at Carrington and Sons. Lydia's silver Mercedes G-Class is pulled beneath the lamppost at the rear of the building. Bård's black Land Rover is parked right alongside her, still running. Both my siblings are posted against the doors of their respective vehicles, standing under the harsh white gleam while a cloud of jewel-bodied insects swirls dizzily overhead. Derek Carrington is with them, gesturing helplessly. All three collectively turn their heads at the intrusion of my headlights.

"Kathryn, there you are," Bård says.

"Good evening, Birger." I nod to him. "Dilay."

"Kathryn," Lydia responds with an undercurrent of amusement that unsettles me. Nothing pleases her more than delivering bad news, and her mood is too high—Bård's too low—for the cause of her joy to be anything else.

My siblings are still wearing their sunglasses, as a courtesy to Mr. Carrington. With a weary sigh I reach for my Ray Bans and slide them up the bridge of my nose. Lydia smiles ruefully and reclines against her car—like a cat in the sun—and Bård scratches the back of his neck. Derek opens his mouth, closes it, uncertain as to whether or not he should speak with so many of us present at once. It is a rarity.

"Is there a problem?"

"The cremator is broken." Lydia cocks her head, smiling bemusedly.

I sneer back at her and glance over my shoulder. Natalie is not visible from the windshield, still doubled over in her seat.

"It's been losing heat for months," Derek says. "I've made my concerns clear. I thought with Mr. Collins' help we could get a few more years out of it, but when he disappeared…"

I sigh wearily. Collins, of course. Bård's former associate. Mr. Collins was selling our kills, or pieces of them, to medical harvesting companies as part of a new business endeavor brokered by Bård. I terminated Collins' contract and his life when he began stalking Elizabeth at Fane's behest. How many times must I be made to regret killing that glorified corpse-butcher?

Bård bristles at the mention of his ex-associate. "Yes, you made your concerns quite clear. Thank you, Derek."

I don't know how much Fane has told Bård of my involvement in Mr. Collins' *disappearance*. This is the problem with compartmentalizing information. How was I to know the cremator was all but spent and that Mr. Collins was our sole contingency plan? The illegal trade of human remains was lucrative to be sure, but also—apparently—necessary to rid our family of the corpses we accumulate.

"Can you keep the bodies in storage until the unit is replaced?" I ask.

"I can't," Derek replies, pitifully. "The freezer is beyond capacity, Kathryn. What's left of the body Birger brought in is stacked on top of Dilay's in the only open drawer. I couldn't even finish the cremation."

Bård steps up behind him and places a grounding hand on his shoulder, spinning the wiry young fellow around to face him. Bård stares deeply into Derek's anxious eyes, holding him by the biceps. His sunglasses slide down his nose.

"Derek," Bård says soothingly, "we understand your position. No one is angry with you. You will have the means to purchase a new cremator tomorrow." He glares over at me. "Kathryn will see to that."

"This will be the third unit we've installed in twenty years," Derek says. "I'm worried. What if the city or the state steps in to make sure everything is up to code? I can't have undocumented bodies in my basement when that happens!"

Lydia's laughter is harsh. She twirls off her car to stand beside Bård, his aggravation showing. She places a hand on Bård's back and he steps away, giving her a turn with Derek. She wraps her arm around Derek's sweaty neck, brushes his cheek with the tips of her fingers and stares over her glasses deep into his eyes.

"If that happens, I can assure you nothing will come of it," she says. Derek swallows roughly. "Your family has been generous to us. Have we not repaid that generosity tenfold?" Derek is too far in the warm embrace of her black eyes to respond, he simply nods. "Be a dear and fetch the change of clothes I brought for Kathryn, would you?"

Lydia watches Derek stumble indoors, then turns to Bård. "You really should leave the convincing to me, Dede. You only ever manage to intimidate young men."

Bård ruffles his brow just for her and a grin flits across his face. Grandfather. He hates that nickname. She has called him that for as long as any of us can remember, but only when she is truly pleased with herself or particularly unhappy with him.

"What of your feed this evening, Stela?" Bård asks. The three of us make a formidable triangle in the parking lot.

Lydia pivots to face me, a sinister gleam in her eye. There is so rarely an interruption to our routine, and the opportunity to improvise disposal of a kill is as exciting as the hunt itself. I do not offer a solution for the body slowly spoiling in my car. Bård and Lydia take to brainstorming among themselves.

"Do we know a butcher, Dede? Fane would love that. Feeding the chattel back to the herd."

Bård shakes his head. "We had a butcher on Maxwell Street, but they closed shop in 1958 and he would not handle the bodies if they were whole. We had to bring them to him skinned and quartered, first."

"She could weight the body, drop it in the harbor."

"Not this time of year. The water is too low," Bård says. "Stela would need to secure a vessel first."

"What about a hospital? She could stow the corpse in the morgue."

Bård considers this, click his tongue. "Too many eyewitnesses, too many loose ends. Stela would have to strip the body and rub it down first. Clean beneath the nail beds. Trace evidence."

Derek's uneven footfall halts their ruminations as he rushes to my side with a brown paper parcel tucked under his arm. The three of us reach up in unison to secure our sunglasses.

"Thank you, Derek." The name Kathryn is printed on the brown paper in Lydia's elegant handwriting. "I will personally ensure that your account is credited with the funds to replace the cremator. Send me a quote tomorrow."

"Thank you, Kathryn." Derek dips subserviently. "Well. I'll say good night to you all then. Sorry again for the disruption."

"So, what will become of the body, Stela?" Bård asks once our company returns to three.

I tilt my head, considering the problem that is Natalie's lifeless husk. "We have not had a fire in quite some time, brother."

Bård claps his enormous hands and the sound echoes across the pavement. Without delay, he turns back toward his Land Rover to accompany me in the disposal.

"May I join you?" Lydia asks.

I open my driver's side door and stop short of the seat. "I would not dream of keeping you any longer from our Lord's side."

Lydia's face ices over, all amusement drained from her features. That old familiar indifference. She storms back to her Mercedes and is the first to roar onto the main road, pointed toward home.

Bård peels out onto the highway behind me, and I lead him to a condemned steel mill on the outskirts of the city. Natalie's limp body jostles with every pothole. In truth, I would not have minded Lydia tagging along for this spectacle, but news of the furnace will anger Fane. Lydia casually mentioning—in her deliberate way—that the body I burned was riding in the front seat, instead of the trunk, would be all the excuse Fane needs to strip me of my feeding privileges for as long as he deemed fit.

* * *

The drive back to the compound is anxious but exhilarating. Fane might disagree with my disposal solution. He may chide Bård for my behavior, blame him for not having talked me into a more cost-effective solution. But for now, we are both elated by the distraction—however fleeting—that this evening's romp has provided.

When my brother thrust the gas can into my hands, his irritation was as obvious as his anticipation. I knew he would not approve of a corpse in the front seat, but the only acknowledgment occurred in the few seconds before the inferno devoured my Mercedes and Natalie with it. Bård shook his head solemnly and called it a pity. I agreed. I loved that car.

Bård pulls his Land Rover into his usual spot, the empty space beside mine at the back of the parking garage that conceals the entrance to our family home.

"What will you choose for your replacement?" he asks.

I shrug and exit the passenger side, flinging the door shut behind me. "The Quattroporte will be an upgrade."

"The Maserati?" Bård laughs, falling in step with me. "What makes you think Fane will *reward* you for incinerating your transportation?"

"I do not intend to mention my preference unless he asks, and I doubt he will. Besides, Fane has always appreciated my good taste."

Bård smiles affectionately at me, opening the hatch and waving me into the tunnels ahead of him. He stops above the door to his suite. Fane will have all the company he requires between Lydia and myself. The safest course of action for Bård is to stow away quietly until tomorrow and let the storm pass.

"Stela…" Bård takes hold of my wrist as I maneuver around him toward the main hall. An early evening in the quiet of my quarters is not a luxury afforded to me tonight. Fane will have words for me, and I have to find Elizabeth first. "You took something from the glove compartment," he says, "before you burned the Mercedes."

I stare impassively back him. He would hear the lie if I told one, and I cannot venture the truth.

Bård releases my wrist, shakes his head. "Take your jacket off, throw it over your arm," he says. "The fabric bulges around the envelope. Fane will notice."

Bård is right, of course. I remove my jacket and drape it over my arm. Bård makes no effort to hide his concern, and his disapproval.

"Thank you, Brother."

He nods stiffly, no longer looking in my direction but staring down into his own darkened living quarters. "You would do well to thank me less and behave yourself." He drops soundlessly through the opening and his door settles shut.

I slink off the landing like a thief and follow the sluggish pounding of Elizabeth's heart. For her, another late evening stretched into early morning and all but wasted in the library. Where she has no doubt spent the last few hours rearranging the narrative of my life as she sees fit. I rest my forehead against the cool facade of one of the smooth marble columns at the entrance.

She is so young. Idealistic. Passionate, too. Was that not what first captured my interest? Did I not encourage her to ask any questions in her quest to understand me better? I handled it poorly. She was curious, possibly frightened by my journals—our crusade must have made a gruesome read.

I swallow my lingering resentment and stroll into the Vault as casually as I can.

Darius sits at his desk, strewn with ledgers. He jumps to his feet as he always does when he has been caught mumbling to himself and folds his empty wire spectacles in his hand.

"Good evening, Stela."

"Good evening."

"Have you come to collect your fledgling? Has the hour escaped me again?"

"Nothing of the sort, Brother. I only intend to steal a glimpse of her before meeting with Fane."

Darius has always been a romantic. He waves me on with an eager hand and ushers me behind the stacks toward the private archive, as though I have not found her there dozens of times. Elizabeth's pulse beats in my veins. If I were blind I could find her. If Elizabeth stood on the opposite side of the world, I could picture her as clearly as I see Darius now.

"Just through there," he says and steps aside. "At her usual table."

"Thank you." I pat him firmly on the back "Will you keep an eye on the hour for her? Send her back to me soon?"

"Of course," Darius says gravely. Undoubtedly the brightest of us all—at least until Elizabeth catches up to him—and yet, simple in his distracted and unassuming way. His easy enthusiasm. Always so proud to be tasked, no matter the size of the request.

"Good man."

Elizabeth's eyes are trained on the entryway, and from her sharp focus I suspect she has been waiting in just this position since I first stepped foot in the tunnels. The journal she was reading is collapsed against her chest, one leg flung over the arm of her chair, the other firmly planted on the floor. She is braced for a lunge but remains deathly still as I cross the room.

We have had unfortunate difficulty navigating each other since the night she accused me of genocide. She tried several times to apologize and I could see that she was sincere. Whether it was my duty to defend Fane in all matters, or my own wounded pride that kept me from accepting her penance I cannot say. But seeing her here, ready to rush into my arms at the hint of permission makes all my defensive posturing seem foolish. She loves me. Her obsidian eyes glow like two silver moons, deep and ensnaring. Impossible that one so young, so new to this life could hold such inexhaustible sway over me.

I stand beside the open journals spread across the table. Her eyes remain fixed upon my face, even when I turn away to read a few passages she has copied down on her legal pad.

"Viktor and Rolf," she whispers.

"Pardon?" I take a seat on the edge of the table, my ankles crossed just inches from her sock-clad foot.

"The perfume you're wearing. Flowerbomb by Viktor and Rolf." She tosses the volume she was reading on the table.

"The perfume is not mine." I sit up, clutch the table in both hands and brace for another fight.

"I know it's not." Elizabeth emits a humorless chuckle, nearly a growl, and raises her hands toward me—palms up. "I don't care."

I toss my coat aside and shove her back by the shoulders as she pulls me down into her lap. We are two famished creatures when our lips meet, our embrace greedy and rushed. She plants one hand on the small of my back and the other scurries up the front of my blouse. She pulls her mouth away to run her lips along my neck, and through the haze of her affection my concern gets the better of me.

"Have you eaten?" I whisper into hair. Elizabeth grabs me by the hips.

"Not now, Stela. Please." Her frustration is a balm to my heart and I lose myself a moment longer to her attention.

"I have something for you." I keep as quiet as I can—exposed as we are—letting my lips shape the words.

Elizabeth stills but keeps her hands on my body, nails biting into my hips. She leans back only enough to brush against my mouth. "What?"

"My coat. Stow it in your bag. Meet me in our quarters."

"What is it?" She arches her brow, lingers suspiciously on my discarded jacket.

"Not here. Take it with you. I have to meet with Fane."

Curiosity overpowers attraction and Elizabeth stands up before I have managed to step away. She snatches the coat up to fish around in the pockets and finds the manila envelope folded in two. She pries open the unsealed edge to glimpse inside but I catch her arm and shake my head sternly. She reaches for her satchel and slips the packet inside.

"I may be longer than you prefer this evening," I say. "There is an urgent matter I must discuss with Fane."

Elizabeth tilts her head and grabs my hand before I can turn away. She pulls me back with surprising strength. It might be time to start limiting her meals and test her tolerance.

"You came to me first," she says and her smile is blinding.

"Yes. I did."

She cups my face in her hands and kisses me slowly. "I won't open it without you."

"I promise not to linger any longer than I must."

Elizabeth pushes me back playfully, staring at me with adoration and intrigue. Whether I am punished anew for my mishandling of Collins and this unanticipated consequence, or berated again for my carelessness, I will cherish this memory of her scandalous excitement. Of all the punishments I can imagine, there is not a single one that outweighs the reward of her exuberance.

* * *

Loitering outside Fane's suite, I close my eyes and concentrate on Elizabeth. I steal quietly into her mind, settle behind her eyes. An insignificant tableau stretches out in front of her. A stack of journals, a paper strewn table, Darius' hands as he helps her tidy. I send this inconsequential glimpse of Elizabeth's perspective out to Fane, beyond the barrier of the bond she shares with me, the bond that seals her thoughts from him. Hopefully these stolen moments satisfy Fane's growing curiosity about Elizabeth long enough for her to ingratiate herself. Presently I return to myself, to the foyer in front of Fane's door. The dizziness that has always accompanied this voyeurism evaporates as quickly as it arrives. Perhaps the trick is a full stomach.

I shoulder open the brilliantly polished mahogany door. Fane's suite is oddly silent. Lydia lies tangled in his sheets, her shoulders bare, one golden leg thrown across the length of his mattress. She has a pillow crumpled in her hand, clutched beneath her chin. The evening proved too much for her to handle, so exhausted from his appetite that sleep came for her a few hours early this morning. A pang of pity pierces my heart.

"Would you keep me waiting when I have been so patient with you?" he asks.

Fane is stretched along the length of his sofa, a hand propped behind his flaxen head. His chamber is dotted now with Lydia's preferences, small touches, like the couch which is pushed in front of the blazing hearth. Two new paintings hang above the fireplace, dreadfully upbeat images, too modern for his taste. Here and there, an object of hers, evidence of the physical space a lover takes up in your life.

"Never, my Lord." I kneel beside him and kiss his troubled brow, smoothing the angry ridges away with my fingertips. He catches my hand and brings my fingers to his lips.

"Come. Sit with me." The fire has burned to flickering coals. Fane's legs are clad in fine garnet-colored silk, a strange color on him, another example of Lydia's influence. I sit next to him and the heat from his body is overwhelming.

"Lydia told you about the cremator?"

His iridescent blue eyes shine an inviting shade of violet when they catch the light from the coals. "She did. You can trouble Andrew with the figures."

The fury I was so prepared to soothe is absent in the uncomfortable quiet that follows. If I ignore Lydia's sleeping form in his bed, the evening has the tint of a great many nights and mornings I have spent in his company, talking of nothing, thinking of little else but him, content to remain in his presence for as long as he wished. It is enough to remind me fondly that we once shared peace and clarity.

"What did you cost me this evening, Stela?" There is no irritation in his voice, rather an undercurrent of exhaustion I do not hear often.

"Between the impromptu disposal of my kill tonight, the new cremator and installation, I would estimate north of a hundred and fifty thousand."

Fane sneers, runs his hand along his thigh. He drums his thick fingers impatiently, turns toward me. I follow suit, bringing my leg up on the sofa.

"That figure does not take into account the profits you robbed from me by murdering Mr. Collins." Fane reaches behind my head and reverently strokes the soft hair at the back of my neck. He does not seek another apology and he knows that if it meant saving Elizabeth's life, I would do it again.

"No," I say simply. "The summation of his service would be closer to five times that amount by now."

He wraps a tendril of hair around one finger, twisting it tightly and releases me. The silence stretches on, seconds mounting into painful minutes. Me, left to my shame, and he with his eyes on the dying fire. There was a time when I would have been content to drape myself across his legs and bid the minutes to build into hours. Now it is all I can do to keep my body language open and inviting, smothering images of Elizabeth before they can blossom into thoughts. His jealousy is not something I intend to provoke. Not now. Not ever if it can be helped.

"What have you given me as recompense?" he asks. "Another mouth to feed. Another to clothe. Another to shelter."

"You have my unwavering loyalty, my eternal gratitude for the charity you have extended to Irina, and the mercy you have shown me." I place my palm over his heart.

Fane traces the fingers on his chest and takes my hand in his. He turns it over, studying it closely, kisses my palm but does not let go.

When his tongue darts between his teeth to taste my skin, I push every thought of my darling girl as far from my mind as I can manage. The force of Fane's bite and his grip shatters every bone in my wrist and hand. I remain stoic even as he twists my arm, locking his prying eyes on mine. He is cruel with his feed, angling for an outburst, possibly a plea. When I give him neither he throws my limp arm aside. It hangs bloodless and ruined in my lap.

He pushes off the sofa, repeating my name over and over. Fane perches beside the hearth, his arms outstretched along the mantel, which shudders from his added weight. "You cannot solve problems with platitudes, my dove. And you have brought me nothing else since the day you met our lovely Irina." He dives behind my eyes, searching for fear, hoping for a lie. His presence knocks around in my skull without his usual finesse. He wants me to sense him.

"I will bring you a solution. A tangible financial endeavor to repay my debt."

"You have already been given ample time," he says. "Far more leniency was shown you than our dear Mr. Opes when he thought to rob me."

I stand up and my left arm dangles lifelessly at my side. I force a smile I do not mean. He arches his brow incredulously and howls with laughter.

"Get out of my sight, Stela." The amusement softens his bitterness, camouflaging his disgust. Striding across the floor toward his bed, he stands above Lydia's motionless body, and for a second I fear for her safety. But there is an affection in his gaze that was once reserved only for me.

"When next I call upon you, I expect a profitable solution for my financial pain."

"It will be done, my Lord."

He settles on the edge of the bed and the springs pop and creak to cradle him. Fane runs an adoring hand up Lydia's bare calf, watching me closely as I cross to his door.

"How does my fledgling progress?" he asks before I can take my leave.

I school my features before I turn to face him. He has never claimed her as his own in front of me. "Strong. Ready to be weaned."

Fane trails his fingers up Lydia's hip and her body opens to his touch. Even in sleep she mewls a contented little hum.

"Nearly time to take her aboveground," he says, allowing Lydia to curl around his massive torso as he lies down beside her.

"So it seems."

Fane brightens with an infectious smile I almost mistake for pride. "I should like to call on her before long. Taste her progress for myself." His eyes darken with the portent of a rebuke, and through this I know that I have failed to mask my hostility.

I dip my head to him. "She is yours to evaluate, my Lord."

"Yes, my dove." He kisses the knuckles of Lydia's small fist. Holds her hand against his ruddy chest. "She is."

* * *

I slip down past the stables to the scullery to procure a bag of B Positive from the ice chest for Elizabeth and tuck it in my waistband. My intentions to wean her all but forgotten. There is comfort in routine, and the longer she takes, the longer I can keep her to myself.

I mistakenly hoist myself inside the tunnel on my injured arm. The pain makes me recoil back into the hall, and a small gasp reaches my finely attuned ears, though I never heard her footsteps. Elizabeth clearly occupied herself with her reading longer than either of us anticipated. She tosses her satchel into the tunnel and gently inspects my crushed arm.

"What did he do to you?" she whispers against my cheek. There is possessiveness in her voice I have tried to curb. She helps me ease myself into the mouth of the tunnel. My sluggishly mending muscles cry out—surely she has strength enough to share her own resilient blood with me tonight. I shuffle deeper into the corridor on my knees, and glance back at Elizabeth. She casts a curious glance back at the hatch above our living quarters, but asks no questions and follows me. When we reach the main entrance, she nods for me to lead as I clumsily mount the ladder to the parking garage above.

Elizabeth emerges a moment after, the soles of her sock-clad feet blackened by wet earth, her chestnut hair glowing with streaks of auburn under the white lights of the car park, black eyes shining with concern. I have not seen her under this light since the night she was made, and the woman before me is not the human she was all those months ago. That version of Elizabeth was alive and terribly afraid that all her careful life choices had led her to die beneath a garage. Was she right to fear? And what has she gained but an eternity in the dark? I did not want this life for her. Neither did I want to damn myself to a life without her.

Now, my injury is what troubles her, and more than that, she does not know what she will do once I confirm that Fane caused it. She trembles violently and I drag her by the hand toward the Maserati. The key is kept under the carriage in a magnetic box. As I hit the lock release Elizabeth stands at the passenger side door with her eyes shut to gather the night air. The city—so perilously close—swims around her head, filling her ears with the hushed sounds of mortal breath, the hasty steps of people rushing through the end of their night and into the embrace of a new dawn.

Elizabeth opens her eyes and stares straight through me, her eyes on the closed garage door. She pitches her weight from one foot to the other like a great cat, preparing to sprint. I smile sympathetically. I did not consider how taxing this field trip would be for her. She straightens haughtily and dips down into the passenger seat.

When I was made—when Lydia was made, for that matter—the world was ours, and fledglings were not corralled. They were free to hunt as soon as they pleased, so long as an elder was with them. And an elder was merely any family member familiar with the area. Someone to guide the young ones away from tribes and towns where they might be recognized by humans from their past, or worse, a loved one they had left behind. Such reunions never end well.

Mine was not a time of traffic cameras on street corners, CCTV, DNA profiles or missing-persons registers. I never feared that a young urchin would snap a photo of me on their mobile, that my image would spread across the Internet like wildfire. Enclosed in this luxurious vehicle beside Elizabeth, my heart aches as she hits the lock on her own door to trap herself inside.

"You should give yourself more credit." She stares daggers at me but says nothing. "If you cannot believe that you are in control of your impulses, believe that I would not allow you aboveground if I had any reservations."

Her fingers tremble in her lap, and she crosses her legs, leans back against the buff leather seat. "Lock your door," she says. She gnaws absently at her bottom lip, blinking her sensitive, powerful black eyes under the glare of the fluorescent lights. I do as she asks and wait.

"Why are we here?" she asks. "And what happened to your arm?"

I pull the collection bag from my waistband and offer it to her. She snatches it from my wounded palm and tosses it into her leather satchel, which she promptly discards on the floor. I hear the blood slosh, and grip the steering wheel. Elizabeth twists in her seat to face me, furious.

"Fane saw fit to remind me that I owe him a debt," I say. "I have for some time now."

"Because of me?" Elizabeth's voice suddenly soft and childlike.

"No." I trace her cheekbone with my thumb and pull her forward into a soft kiss. "This has nothing to do with you, my angel. I took something from him."

"This is about Mr. Collins." Her wide eyes are impossibly close, and her gaze digs deep. An artful lie is out of the question. She already knows the truth.

"Everything was set into motion by my own selfish actions. Mr. Collins was my failure, not your fault. This evening everything spiraled out of control because of the choice I made to end his life all those months ago."

"What happened tonight?"

"The cremator at Carrington and Sons was unable to cope with our family's demands. The unit will have to be replaced immediately and at great expense. Worse, I had to be creative in the disposal of my feed this evening."

Elizabeth brings her legs up in the seat. The satchel on the floor tips over and the collection bag tumbles out. My head roars watching the blood—black as ink against the dark carpeting—slip lazily around an air bubble.

"Where's your car?" she asks, surreptitiously inspecting our current hiding place.

"Burned. Along with the body."

Elizabeth stares dazedly out the windshield and repeats my words to herself, presumably until they make sense to her. Burned car. Burned body.

My compromised hand flexes in my lap and we both hear my splintered ulna snap back into place. Elizabeth's hand hovers, suspended in air above my wounded arm. I throw my head back against the seat and grit my teeth. Despite Natalie's contribution, my injury has left me ravenous.

"Would you please, just this once, make quick work of your food?"

She recoils and gropes along the floor. I have to turn away when the plastic punctures between her teeth. A starved shiver runs down my spine at the sound of her swallowing.

"Come here." She reaches for my chin, the bag still clutched in her hand with only two ounces missing. Her lips are stained crimson and intentionally smeared. I lean forward to capture them and she drags me closer by the front of my gray T-shirt. "Finish it. You need to heal."

Before I can protest, she taps the pierced plastic against my bottom lip. I drain what remains with a blissful groan. The blood is cool, unpleasantly so, and I can appreciate how it is possible for Elizabeth to resist a meal until urged to eat. The sweetness has long since faded and what remains reeks of death.

My right arm straightens of its own accord, twisting between us while Elizabeth stares with rapt attention as the skin blushes, and the bruises fade from blue to green. The carpal bones snap like trodden twigs and the damage is neatly mended.

The atmosphere is charged with humiliation on my part, and tactfully unspoken satisfaction on hers. She leans back in her seat as the tendons knit muscle neatly to reformed bone. Elizabeth runs a scrupulous eye at the car's interior, dragging her fingertips along the stitched leather seat, across the wooden inlays in the dashboard.

"This is your new car?"

"No one else has claimed it."

"Quite the upgrade." She leans over the center console to trace the silver pitchfork embellished on the wheel. I suppress a laugh, and she chuckles delightedly. I drop her satchel into her lap and procure the envelope I entrusted to her earlier.

"Care to do the honors?" I offer her the package and Elizabeth snatches it from my hand with obvious excitement.

For several minutes, the only sound is the shuffling of papers. Elizabeth reads silently.

"This is everything?" she asks distractedly.

"Nearly. We have secured a buyer for the brownstone, pending the results of an appraisal. Andrew assures me the value is there, and a background check on the prospective buyers convinces him that they can pay. He needs your signature."

Elizabeth arranges the paperwork into a neat stack and slides the forms back into the envelope. She whispers her thanks with a remorseful sigh. Her reaction is never what I anticipate.

"I thought you would be pleased." My jaw tightens, her apparent sorrow is a far cry from the happiness I envisioned.

"I am," she says with a forced smile.

"I have done exactly as you asked." Surely, she must find some peace in knowing that her personal finances have been secured.

Elizabeth takes my hand. "Stela, I appreciate the trouble you've gone through to safeguard my inheritance. I'm sad about the brownstone. I grew up in that house."

"Homesickness?"

She answers me with a weary shrug. The memory of my human home has largely disappeared beneath the sands of time, but one image remains clear. It seems so very little to offer her.

"I remember Fane's palace in the old country perfectly. The towering columns, the freshly swept stone floors. Pastures to south were dotted with wildflowers, and the mountains were always capped with snow."

Elizabeth leans over the console, rests her head upon my shoulder. "What about your home before that? Your mother's home?"

"I have one memory of my mother's home—the smell of fire in the hearth, sitting on the floor with a blanket of deer hide wrapped around my shoulders. My sisters were huddled around me. I was cold. It may have been winter."

Elizabeth stiffens. "You had sisters?" Her incredulity indicates I should have mentioned them sooner.

"I had four sisters. All had black hair, like our mother."

"What were their names?" she asks.

"They were older than me. There are times when I can almost see their faces. Their names were swallowed with the rest of my first life."

She grows silent and introspective again. "Will I forget?"

Her life, she means. The mother she feared and the father she worshipped. "Eventually. Not everything, and not all at once. It happens so slowly, one barely notices."

Elizabeth opens her mouth to speak, closes it again. She places her head once more on my shoulder. I expected a protest, a defiant refusal or vehement rebuke. Instead the silence spreads out between us, and she gazes blankly at the steering wheel. Claire's memory plagues her more terribly than she admits, but she is not yet ready to forget.

"Elizabeth," I squeeze her hand, still resting on my chest, "I have news."

"Bad news?"

"Not entirely.

"Fane agrees that we need to start limiting your meals. The time approaches when you will have to hunt." The decree unsettles her as I feared it might. "He will want to inspect your progress for himself before he releases you upon the world."

Elizabeth's expressive eyes go intentionally blank. Her expression neither shocked or saddened, simply neutral. "What does that mean?"

"He intends to feed from you before he will permit you aboveground. You can avoid his eyes and keep to our quarters but blood never lies. He is very curious about you, my darling. Dangerously so."

She nods solemnly. "Well," she says decisively, "we knew that was coming." Her face is twists into a snarl. "I'm not going to bed with him, Stela."

I am certain that now is not the time to touch her, yet painfully aware of my need to do so. "Elizabeth, that is not—"

"That's *exactly* what he wants," she says. "Don't undermine my understanding of the politics in this place. Lydia gets whatever she wants because she gives him what he wants. You were his unrivaled favorite for centuries because you..." She hesitates. I watch her awareness blossom.

It is not a baseless accusation. I have never hidden my involvement with Fane. Elizabeth has read about it for herself in my journals, in my own words. Perhaps that is why it is so painful to hear my relationship with him summed up so succinctly. Purely transactional. I have never considered our relations in such simple terms—as a bartering system.

"Stela, I didn't mean to imply—"

"Yes, you did."

"I'm not judging you," she says. "I just don't want that. I don't want him."

I nod absently. Her refusal brings me undeniable peace of mind. I want all of Elizabeth entirely to myself, precisely as we are now. He will feed from her. But perhaps that is all. She does not want him... Incredible.

"We will need to prepare for that meeting," I say.

"How?"

"Your truth is in your blood. The trick is to teach your brain to tell your blood the truth you wish to share, and nothing more. He cannot know that you belong to me, my darling. That he suspects as much is dangerous for us."

Elizabeth unfurls her long limbs, smiling faintly, comfortably preoccupied by the prospect of a goal, a new talent to master. Would that it were so easy. For her, it may be. Who knows? But like my resilience to the sun, my ability to shape my truths in a more digestible, safer narrative might prove uniquely mine. Unfortunately, there is only one way to know for sure.

The sun moves quickly now, embracing the city with lavender arms. The temperature inside the garage has risen a few degrees. Soon sleep will overtake my love. Her movements are languid. She leans forwardly slowly, tugs once at my shirt collar.

"Not here." I kiss her long fingers. "Climb in back."

Elizabeth smiles slyly. We exit together and seal ourselves in the rear. Time is running short. I pull Elizabeth against me.

She climbs onto my lap and ghosts her lips along my cheeks, my eyelids. "What was her name?" she asks as she closes both hands over my jaw.

"Whose?" I ask, deliciously distracted.

Elizabeth noses at my ear, hunting for scents that do not belong. "The reason you didn't want to do this in the front seat."

"Natalie..."

Elizabeth leans back, she whispers the name against my parted lips. She regards me with a curious intensity. "I've always liked that name," she says.

V

Inertia Alone

A blistering breeze scatters tattered scraps of paper that drift through the pre-dawn air like a dress rehearsal for snow. The rooftop of the parking garage is desolate, and though the wind is vicious up here there is a remote stillness like that of a long-forgotten attic. Following my first successful hunt, my privileges were extended immediately to encompass the whole of Fane's facility—his bedroom notwithstanding. Supine on the cement, I can see the stars piercing through a milky film of smog.

Nearly October again. Almost a year in the dark, and I am none the wiser. The nights stretch on, but the weeks have blurred together. It seems it was only yesterday that Stela found me beside my mother's grave on that brisk fall night. One year of my life…

It shouldn't matter, and why I should measure time when I have more than I will ever need?

Stela assured me that there is nothing after this life. No choir of angels or chariots of gold to usher us into the beyond. That we are, each of us, alone. I made my decision to join her in the dark, to tie my life to hers. After my mother passed away, after my budding relationship with James imploded, I couldn't lose anyone else. Stela promised forever, and she has delivered. She's given me a family, whether I like them or not. She has freed me from death.

I've faced one death already. I tried to explain to Stela not long after I was turned—what I remembered of the darkness that enveloped me that night after I died. That I was alone but surrounded. There were bodies rushing past me in that ether, dragging me along in their slipstream as though the power grid went down on Michigan Avenue but the pedestrians kept moving, fighting to make their way home. There was a crowded nothing dragging me onward, but in the middle of that chaotic march, she had appeared.

Stela's voice had reached me in the dark. Stela told me to *rise*. She brought light with her to that dreadful place, and the light was gold, brilliant and pale. The foreign bodies all around me noticed her light even if they took no notice of me. My hands were one pair in thousands, clawing and pushing to grab hold of that light. Stela knew my hands, she found me, she pulled me free.

When I returned to this plane Fane was at my side, but I could still hear Stela's voice ringing in my ears.

This evening, I took the train to UI Health and stalked the parking lot outside the emergency wing. When I was still a student, I had a summer internship there. The parking lot was full of worried family and nurses in blue scrubs savoring their smoke breaks. I recognized the weariness in their faces as they bemoaned this cantankerous patient or that arrogant attending. How many times had I voiced those same complaints?

I entered between a carousel of ambulances, and just as Stela had the night we met, I avoided the cameras as best I could and found the long-term care ward. It was immediately clear to me why the family avoided this method of feeding unless absolutely necessary. Not only is it risky, the pungent odor was repugnant. Beneath the disinfectant swirled a sharp fetid rot.

Hospitals were once my sanctuary, with their buffed floors and antiseptic decor, horrible wallpaper and uncomfortable chairs. Between the stench of the sick and the endless chirp of monitors in unattended rooms it was a challenge to find my mark.

Stela considers herself a one-woman jury. When I've lived alongside human beings for more than five centuries, perhaps I'll be as good a judge of character as she professes herself to be. But with only two decades and change under my belt, I picked my victim the only way I knew how. I skimmed the charts of slumbering patients until I found someone I was certain would never recover.

He was a weathered old man, slight in his bed, but his frame suggested he'd once been broad-shouldered. His close-cropped hair had a dewy silver sparkle that danced in a horseshoe around his skull. A veteran, if I had to guess. No family photos in the room, no balloons, no flowers, no cards for a man who was admitted ten days prior. Stage IV glioblastoma. It doesn't get much worse than that.

The feed was nearly as intoxicating as my first hunt with Stela. He didn't struggle. It was almost like a kiss goodbye. His memories were wearing at the edges, blurred. He shared boxing matches and the jungles of Vietnam with me. A vintage Ford pickup with the windows rolled down blaring "Lover Man" from the speakers. An airplane where everyone was wearing their Sunday best—men in three-piece suits, women in pillbox hats—standing in the aisles as they smoked.

I was careful not to spill this time. Gentle with the body. Isn't that a better way to die? In the arms of a woman young enough to be your granddaughter, while you give the last gift you have to offer anyone in the world? I hope a part of him was aware of our intimate exchange and unafraid. I thumbed the silver crucifix nestled in his wiry chest hair and imagined that he was happy just to have a push, a little help along his journey.

After I sealed the wound, I tucked him in and slipped out into the hall before his heart stopped beating. I took the exit stairs two at a time, the screaming monitors at his bedside echoing in my ears. A handsome young doctor passed me on my way down, checking his smart watch. He never even looked at me.

The ride home was harder than the ride out. The pounding in my head had subsided after my feed, but my stomach sat like a rock. Not painful, but certainly not pleasant. Strange, Stela is always so content and sated after she hunts. I ignored the mild discomfort and tried to enjoy the soft crush of human bodies all around me, the chorus of their heartbeats, now without the overwhelming urge to rip into their throats.

The whole ride home, I thought about my first hunt.

Stela and I had prepared as extensively as we could for Fane's evaluation. She assured me that the moment he tasted my blood he would be privy to all my secrets, unless I found a way to clear my mind and focus only on what I wished to share. Every night for nearly two weeks she drank from me before my feeding. My job was to avoid thinking of anything contentious and I managed to ruin the exercise every time by thinking of a shared conversation—wherein, at some point, she called me by my true name—or by remembering my parents, inexcusably human and therefore weak. I thought about that night in the Maserati, when she told me about her sisters, which was dangerous because Fane had not given her permission to take me beyond the tunnels. I thought about studying in the library, which was risky because Fane might ask about my findings and I had already made my feelings about Fane's crusade abundantly clear to Stela. And throughout it all, the truth of my allegiance to Stela remained crystal clear, written plainly in my blood. Night after night this continued, and as the days became weeks Stela grew frightened to the point of fury. All the while I was either starved or was too heavy in the swoon of a feed to be reasoned with.

Stela feeding from me was unlike anything I've ever felt before, and a far cry from the tiny mouthfuls she's taken in the past. Better than sex, with her or anyone else. The blood that sings in my veins every time she's near cried out at the opportunity to return home. Every cell in my body surged with excitement. The sensation of being devoured by her, without dying, was like falling without end. When I could no longer raise my head on my own, I begged her to continue, so weakened that Stela had to hold the blood collection bag to my lips. Several times she tore her own wrist to give me the added fortitude. I was able to accept her offer without attacking her for more afterward.

Nothing on earth tastes the way she does. Intensely familiar and yet painfully exciting. Smooth and without a single acrid note. Human blood has a certain tartness, a gamy aftertaste that satisfies but pales in comparison to her. Feeding from Stela is like coming home. Feeding from Fane was…

Despite all Stela's meticulous testing and training, I let her down more often than I made her proud. I tried to explain what I saw behind my eyes when my blood was rushing into her. A jumble of images and half-realized memories. How was I supposed to control images I could barely recognize? She delicately suggested that I wasn't focusing hard enough, and insisted we keep practicing.

My success ratio was abysmal. Until one evening when we found that feeding prior to Stela's tests actually improved my focus, however marginal. We could only repeat that success twice more before Fane summoned me. Despite my protests that I wasn't ready to face him, Stela stated calmly that to postpone would only make him suspicious.

I couldn't possibly have been less prepared when the time finally came.

Stela had been too gentle with me. She savored the experience, intentionally disregarding memories which might cause me discomfort, artfully whisking away the painful moments of my past life in favor of something lighter, happier. In Stela's blood I relived memories we both shared. Never a scrap from her day-to-day life before I was made, nothing private or depressing. I didn't consider at the time that my first human feed should be any different.

Fane, dressed in his usual emerald silk robe, stood just beyond the door when we arrived. He dipped his head cordially and waved me toward the living room. I took a seat on the sofa and kept my eyes on Stela who stood motionless at the door. I'm still not sure why he invited her. Was it an act of respect, or the simple torment of forcing her to watch? But Stela did not watch, she stood ramrod straight like a sentinel and kept her eyes on the floor, looking to Fane only when spoken to.

The sheer size of the man. Nothing human about the way he moves, his gliding walk, thunderous when he wants to be. The energy he exudes can only be explained as an undiminished vitality, coupled with the certainty that it never will. He thanked me for taking the time to come and meet with him—as if I'd been given the option to decline—and sat uncomfortably close. I know Stela heard my heart calling to her, not that she flinched or met my stare. She remained by the door as Fane took my neck and shoulder in his hands.

When Fane stared into my eyes, any objection I had fell silent. The fire crackling in the hearth died, the hum of the air purifier, the squeak of our leather seats. That was only the second time he had peered into my mind that way, and it was as though all he had to do was reach out and he would have held my soul in his giant palm. Most unsettling of all, a part of me wished he would.

Fane was not gentle, neither was he a brute. I was dimly aware of his hands on my body, his lips on my neck. He had pulled me into his lap so that I could not see Stela anymore. When his teeth sank into my jugular, I watched my own hand—as though it no longer belonged to me—cradle the back of his head. My last concrete thought was that Fane had no fangs. But his teeth—at first glance the same as any omnivorous mammal—were scalpel-sharp.

There was no pain. In fact, I'm sure I made a sound to the contrary because I heard Stela shift on her feet. I could sense more than see Fane watching, daring her to move. The memories came faster with Fane, as though he was able to filter more from me in a fraction of the time. I smelled my mother's brownstone. I heard both my parents calling me down to dinner. I remembered guest lectures at school and cafeteria gossip and Helen. Sweet Helen, my mother's secret favorite night nurse, waking me from a nightmare. My mother's body, encumbered with wires and electrodes. Stela, my beautiful girl. Her hair in her eyes as she leaned above me in bed, as she drew close, her lips parted and pressed to my ear to whisper… I opened my eyes and planted both hands firmly against Fane's chest.

He didn't release me right away and I was too afraid to push him back. He touched my cheek with disconcerting gentleness. There passed a moment of quiet confusion between us. Then, two things happened simultaneously: Stela stepped forward and I heard the telltale sound of a blood collection bag sloshing in her hands, and Fane bit his wrist.

"My Lord," she said, but I couldn't hear anything else. Fane's wide, red chest rumbled against my cheek and my vision narrowed to a pinprick. It was as though all that existed in this world was the blood running down his wrist.

I fed from him.

For how long, or how much I took, I can't say. He tasted of Stela and so much more.

Fane twisted his wrist from my mouth and laid me down on the sofa. I watched him rise with open arms and walk toward Stela. He kissed the top of her head, but Stela did not return the embrace. She stared at me, horrified, color completely drained from her face. After that, the room went black.

When I regained consciousness, I was lying in the center of our bed with Stela curled around me. There was a bag of B Positive on the nightstand. On instinct we first stumbled over each other's attempted apology. Stela had no idea Fane would spare his precious blood for the sake of a lightheaded newborn, and so, it never occurred to her to prepare me for that. She was as puzzled by my apology as I was of hers. What did I have to be sorry for, she wondered? For my part, how should I have explained all that Fane's blood showed me? The ecstasy he felt when he crushed Stela to him, when he bore her into a new life, is as much a part of me now as it is of Fane. What right did I have to speak that aloud? In the end I apologized for what I could put into words: I never meant to betray her by feeding from him.

Stela wouldn't hear it. She was flush with excuses before I finished speaking. She did not blame me, but she was afraid. What was Fane's angle? Did he know something of his powerful blood that Stela did not? Would he be able to hear my thoughts now, was that his game? In over five centuries of life, Stela could count on two hands the number of times he had let her take her fill of him that way. There had to be a reason for his *generosity*, but Stela was at a loss.

When we had exhausted ourselves with worry, Stela handed me the blood collection bag from the nightstand but I was not hungry. I was completely and entirely without thirst. It was as though I would never be hungry again, as though I'd never known hunger. For all my fear of Fane, I felt powerful, strong. I didn't want a tepid bag of B Positive. I wanted to drain the life from him. The craving was so intense—*is* so intense—sometimes I can think of nothing but that. I haven't told Stela. I'm not sure I ever will. This desire isn't sexual, if desire is even the right word.

We lost something that night, Stela and I—an innocence, a degree of intimacy. All the memories of mine that Fane tasted and all the memories of his that linger in my mind still. How close will Stela keep her secrets now that I am someone she's expected to share?

Two days later, Stela accompanied me on my first hunt and the family was positively brimming with excitement. Once cleared by Fane the sidelong glances and clipped conversations to which I was so accustomed stopped. I was embraced by Stela's siblings, more fully than I had been since the night I became of one of them.

Lydia went to great lengths to dress us for the occasion, preparing with more pomp than prom night and all the fervor of a Bat Mitzvah. She went so far as to double-check my measurements—despite having dressed me for months—and delivered my painstakingly selected wardrobe in person. Her deep-seated aversion to my lover was temporarily forgotten. She chose a crimson cashmere Donna Karan sweater for Stela, with a billowy cowl neck that dipped drastically in front, and toffee-colored satin-lined wool trousers cut in a skinny leg. Certain that Stela would protest any heel, Lydia commissioned calf-high boots just a shade darker than the pants and crafted in the softest Italian leather I've ever touched.

My own ensemble was Lydia's artistic rendering of a blood-drenched christening gown. A burgundy Dolce & Gabbana dress, three-quarter sleeved and covered in floral-patterned lace, with a sheer bodice and arms. She paired this with heels that were mercifully only three inches high and that matched Stela's pants exactly. The trench coat was undoubtedly from the same tailor who crafted Stela's pants. I mourned the senseless tragedy of having to burn the coat before morning the moment I slipped my arms into the sleeves.

To my eternal shock, Stela actually invited Lydia to sit with us while we readied ourselves, so that she could see her handiwork before we left for the night. As we changed in the en suite I teased Stela playfully for the kindness she showed her least favorite sibling. Stela smiled but said nothing and averted her eyes with all the bashfulness of a bride until I was covered. We cut an intimidating sight in the mirror, and if there'd been any doubt of our appeal it vanished at the sound of Lydia's exaggerated inhalation. Lydia clapped like an excited child and twirled me around, bonding with Stela over the fit of the dress, which hit me two inches above the knee and held my body as though it were bespoke.

The feeding schedules had to be rearranged for the week so that Stela could chaperone me, which meant Lydia was forgoing her meal for my benefit. There was no hint of animosity toward me or Stela, and Lydia asked to accompany us as far as the garage. When we reached the car, Lydia fussed over my coat and hair, she offered words of encouragement and brushed off my thanks. Before we parted, she held me by the shoulders and kissed my cheek. Stela smiled graciously, she thanked Lydia for her trouble.

I must have offered half a dozen alternatives to hunting in a public space. To transition from hand-delivered blood bags to seducing and murdering someone is a considerable leap. Why not allow me to hunt transients in the tunnels first, alongside the hounds? But the hounds had to eat too. Why not lure someone to me, say in a park or an alley, and let me finish them off on my own? But then, what would I learn? I even suggested conducting my first feed at a hospital, despite the lingering sense of responsibility I felt toward the infirm. But Stela and Bård only laughed. Now I know why. A hospital is a gruesome place to hunt.

Stela chose the hunting ground and drove. Simply being in the car on the highway was a sensory overload. The blur of lights, the noise, even with the windows rolled up I could smell the people we passed. Stela took my hand at the first red light, and didn't release it. I shook in my seat, a curious mixture of fear and hunger knotting my gut as we drove through Old Town.

When Stela pulled the car around behind the chosen club, I recognized the building immediately. I'd been there before. I renewed my misgivings as she searched for a place, both secluded and accessible, to conceal the car. At the time, I wondered if this was her way of reliving what might be considered our first date.

"What if someone recognizes me?" I asked as she pulled the keys from the ignition.

"One look from you will be enough to confound anyone," she said. "Just remember your lessons."

"Stela, it's too crowded." I shook my head. "I can smell them from here."

"That is precisely the point, my darling."

Stela came around to my door and offered her hand. Hesitatingly, I accepted her chivalry. The night breeze whipped the gentle folds of her billowing collar. She wore her hair pinned back, as she usually does to hunt, and the wind loosened a few strands around her face and neck. She was a vision in red.

"Your drive to feed will overpower any moral quandary that troubles you now. Trust me." She tugged me along after her, headed for the nightclub.

"Is that supposed to be comforting?"

Stela turned on her heel, stalking me backward until I hit the old brick of the building. I knew what she was doing, and I let her quiet my mind. Stela's eyes, black and obliterating, bore into mine. She pushed past all the worry and noise, parted the belt cinched around my waist and pushed the coat apart to run her hands up my abdomen.

"Take a deep breath, Elizabeth." I did as I was told. "Good girl." She smiled. "Hold that breath."

The air in my lungs saturated my senses. I could taste perfume, cologne, hair products, car exhaust, rain that had fallen hours before but remained trapped in the concrete, acrid sweat and human pheromones. Everything intermingled but still each scent distinct.

"You can release it now," she said.

To exhale was to experience each scent all over again in a rush that threatened my footing.

"Better?" she asked. She knew the answer.

My eyes widened with thirst, and Stela's outline, even in the darkened alley, grew sharp and clear. The protests, the moral issues that congested my thoughts were replaced by a level of entitlement that I've never felt in my life. I was more connected to my body than I'd ever been, and completely present in the moment. No one was deserving of mercy, and no one was innocent. I was neither evil nor righteous. To kill was neither right nor wrong.

There was only one thing I wanted then, and I knew with unshakable conviction that I would have it.

"Lead the way," I said.

Stela grabbed the lapels of my fine coat and pulled me into a kiss that radiated throughout my entire being. The thought of watching me hunt excited her and I understood why. I'd watched her feed many times, though I'd never been present. The blood makes a voyeur of us all.

Stela wrapped her arm around my waist and drew me close as we made for the entrance. The music was wretchedly loud, and the bass thumped like a pulse point obscuring the pulse of the humans. Without one heartbeat to draw my attention, the crowds waiting outside were easier to view as a collective organism. I wasn't hunting a person, I was taking an appendage. Nothing that would be missed.

Stela shoved her way to the front of the line with me in tow and shouldered past a group of rosy-cheeked young women arguing with the bouncer. He was a large man with a pierced lip, and the name Veronica tattooed on his throat in elegant script. His neck was thick and meaty, and the veins in his neck and arms suggested prolonged use of steroids. I wondered if I would taste them in his blood.

"Names?" he asked roughly, focused on his clipboard.

"Anything you like," Stela purred. She stroked my hip as I watched the veins in bouncer's neck pulse and engorge with blood. He glared at Stela, met her dark eyes, and I knew he was lost to her. She laughed, that frightening peal of bells, and he laughed too as though Stela was terribly clever, as though they were old friends. None of this was true, but what did it matter? We strode inside and the line waiting to gain entrance became an angry mob.

Across the threshold the smell overcame me so quickly, I thought I would fall to my knees in tears. Stela shoved me into a corner and over her shoulder I could see streams of light cutting across a mass of bodies, slick with sweat. With every intention of murdering as many of them as I could I surged against the barricade of Stela's torso. They belonged to me.

"Elizabeth!" Stela grabbed me by the chin and forced my attention on her. "Push-it-out." She meant my breath, I hadn't realized I was holding it again. I nodded dreamily and exhaled. There was one scent I couldn't rid myself of completely, familiar and begging to be known.

Gradually, my head cleared and Stela stroked my jaw where she'd manhandled me. She reviewed the plan. We would part ways so as not to draw unwanted attention or lessen our chances of being approached. She wouldn't be far, keeping watch while she hunted her prey.

Breathing is not obligatory for Strigoi. We're vulnerable to fire or beheading and catastrophic blood loss will weaken us considerably, but we can't be drowned or suffocated. We do retain the ability to breathe, be that to soothe ourselves or to assess the air. Scent, after all, is vital to the hunt. However, I was not to take another breath until I was safely outside with my chosen victim as the added stimuli was clearly too much for me. If she caught me breaking this rule, if I gave her the slightest inkling that I was losing control the hunt was over.

It would be easier to isolate a man, though ultimately it was my decision and she would respect my wishes. I glanced over her shoulder again and could see her point. Not a single woman moved anywhere alone.

With that, Stela squeezed my hand and walked away. I followed her down the stairs but paused at the dance floor to give her time to make her distance. Stela stopped unexpectedly and turned to meet my eyes across the crowded room. A pleased grin spread across her lips as she caught me watching her. A moment later, when two impeccably dressed young men drifted between us, she was gone.

I opened my coat and headed for the bar. A dapper gentleman, prematurely gray at the temples, passed me a vodka cranberry. I took it just to have something to do with my hands, and because there was malice in his eyes and the drink was safer with me. He leaned in to shout something into my ear, but I wasn't listening. Part of me wanted to wipe this man from the face of the earth, but a human part of me, the woman I used to be was afraid of him.

My skin seemed to taste the air, even if my tongue could not. Every step I took the scent at the back of my throat grew stronger. I was sure I knew it. Fingers trailed from my shoulder to my elbow, with such easy familiarity that I smiled through my ravenous appetite and turned, expecting to find Stela behind me urging me toward a particular mark.

"Hey there, stranger! When'd you get back in town?"

My smile was not meant for him, but he answered it with his own boyish grin. He patted the vacant stool beside him and opened his arm for a hug, of all things.

"James…" My former coworker turned lover and almost-friend.

Of course. Was this not the bar he'd chosen for our first date? A date which had ended with a gunshot wound and a gallon of Stela's blood to keep me alive? Overjoyed, he wrapped me in his arms and lifted me off my heels. I didn't need to press my nose to his neck to place the scent now. He was always in trouble for wearing too much aftershave at the hospital. The warm rush of his giddy laugh tickled my cheek as he eased me to the floor.

"You look incredible," he said. "Seriously." He leaned awkwardly against the bar, shy and unsure.

"What are you doing here?" I asked. James, whose smile never faltered, simply sat back on his stool.

"Good to see you too," he said, and nudged me with his elbow when I took the seat next to his. I thanked the seductive design of this pretentious pit that he could not get a good look at my eyes in the spartan lighting that edged the top of the bar. "So, how was your trip?" He propped his chin on his fist, clearly already a few drinks into the evening. He set his drink down clumsily.

I didn't know where Stela was, but I sensed she was close. It was dangerous talking to him with her near. She wouldn't be happy to find me catching up with him.

"My trip was good." I had completely forgotten my cover story, but I couldn't bear the thought of leaving him unattended when Stela was hunting nearby. James gave a disapproving snort and flicked the sandy hair back from his eyes. Only his hair wasn't long and shaggy anymore, it was clipped close to his head and the top was longer than the sides. Styled with enough product to render it immobile.

"So..." he leaned forward conspiratorially. "Where'd you go? What'd you see?"

His drink had been replenished and it sat undisturbed beside my own abandoned glass. He was brimming with the same teasing exasperation which had always met my reticence, and the normalcy endeared me to him all the more.

"I spent some time in Italy, then Morocco." Not a complete lie. I had studied Stela's journals so closely there were times when I could picture the places she described as though I'd been with her. And James didn't really care where I'd been or what I'd seen. He was doing what he'd always done, asking open-ended questions to keep me talking.

"Alone?" he asked. I was wondering when we'd get to that. He took another drink and wiped his perfectly pink lips dry. Had his lips always been that shade?

"No. I was with family." I smiled privately to myself and toyed with the damp edge of a cocktail napkin.

"Oh," he said, tilting his head. "I thought it was just you and your mom." He didn't mean it unkindly, and he was certainly paying closer attention than I thought. We'd spent many evenings eating horrible takeout in my kitchen, talking into the night while my mother wasted away in a care facility, and I was trying desperately to think of anything but Stela. I didn't want to be alone in that brownstone—which was so much lonelier without my mother's shadow—and James was only too happy to distract me.

"Distant cousins," I covered.

"It's good to have you back," he said, and patted my shoulder. He was different, I realized. "Been, what? About a year?"

Gripped with panic, I stared blankly at him. A year? How was that possible? After far too long a silence, I nodded dumbly. James went back to his drink, content to share the bar with me but that was the extent of it. He welcomed me as a friend, not an ex, though I'm not sure we were ever really an item. Once the initial awkwardness had gone, he was positively chummy.

"Hey check this out." James leaned back on one hip and fished his wallet from his back pocket. He flipped his billfold open and brandished a sonogram.

My pulse pounded in my temple, like the distant tick of a detonator. The first warning. If my chest started heaving, that was the end of the evening for me and anyone within arm's reach. My only hope was that Stela would subdue me before my misplaced rage devoured half the bar. I cleared my throat. "Yours?"

"A son," he said proudly, flipping the wallet closed and shoving it back in his pocket. "You know Nicole, in radiology?"

"Of course. The blonde."

"Yeah, we had a thing…that was after you and I…you know." He waved his hand, as though brushing the not-so-distant past aside. Perhaps I was right, and we'd never really been a couple. I certainly pushed him away after my mother passed, and I kept him at better than arm's length before that. What right did I have to be jealous, or hurt? I had chosen Stela.

"Congratulations." I tipped my glass toward him. He finished his drink, I set mine back down untouched.

I stood up. I needed to get away from him, get some air. Where the hell was Stela? But James wasn't going to let me disappear on him again. He caught my arm, offered to buy the next round. He hated drinking alone. I wondered why he wasn't at home with Nicole.

Stela appeared as though she'd always been perched in front of us. She was just on the other side of the bar, with her victim fawning all over her. It was the gray-templed man who'd handed me a drink. Stela was admiring the cut of his suit coat. Her hand stroked the satin lining. He wasn't her usual type. Stela likes her prey brawny, physically imposing, rugged. This man was tall but lanky and beautifully dressed. I wondered what she saw in him. I must have been right about him slipping something in my drink.

Stela chatted with him distractedly, but her eyes were set on mine. With her forearms draped lazily against the bar, the dip of her collar was dramatic, and the exposed expanse of her chest was as white as porcelain. She didn't seem angry with me, but she slid her eyes to James.

"Let's get out of here." I pulled James roughly by the arm. He chuckled and wavered on his feet.

James, his confusion exaggerated by his drunkenness, put his hands out. "Whoa Liz," he laughed. "I gotta settle up first." He stared at my hand, still wrapped around his bicep.

"No need." I slipped my arm through his. "I came with a friend. She'll cover it."

James wasn't a fool, and my generosity and sudden proximity made him skeptical. "Where's your friend?" he asked shrewdly, searching the faces at the bar.

"Over there. Red top," I said, pointing out Stela.

I wasn't sure what to expect. I was fairly certain that Stela had at least casually stalked him when she and I first met. Neither Stela nor James ever mentioned it, but he did get awfully skittish around me after our first failed date. He only met her unwavering glare for a second before grabbing my hand protectively. He took a staggering step backward. "Yeah…we need to go," he whispered. "Now."

James wasted no time in reaching the exit stairs. He hurried me along, pausing occasionally to whip his head over his shoulder, certain that my mysterious *friend* was close behind. I didn't need to sneak a glance at Stela—her eyes never left me.

On his feet, James was noticeably more intoxicated than he'd been at the bar. He leaned heavily on my shoulder and took wide, unsteady steps. He laughed loudly in my ear—a wracking, nervous sound—and apologized profusely for his state. The faint stroke of his warm breath caused the hair on my arms to rise.

We made it to the exit without incident, but neither of us had a car. My first impulse was to get him out of sight, and I firmly believed—at the time—that this was out of fear for his safety.

James had taken the El into the city from Cicero. There was a platform two blocks north and he insisted he knew the way. He tugged me down the same alley Stela and I had used, speaking in a slurred but passionate voice about his son-to-be. Apparently, Nicole had wanted very little to do with James after discovering a series of incriminating texts not long after that first sonogram.

"She threatened to leave me off the birth certificate," he lamented, leaning heavily against a Dumpster. We were running out of alley, and James had run out of steam. "Who does that?"

I peeked my head around the corner. The El platform was only half a block away, lit like a beacon of safety. It felt like another round of hide-and-go-seek in the freight tunnels. I turned back down the alley and expected to see Stela close at my heels. But we were alone, apart from the occasional pedestrian and the usual traffic.

James slumped against the brick wall of an old pizza parlor I used to frequent with my parents when I was small. "Your friend," he mumbled and glared at me accusingly. He shook his head emphatically. "She's not good."

"You're drunk," I said, and grabbed him by his coat. I thought I'd have to drag him the rest of the way to the train. "Everything will be better tomorrow."

James didn't help me, and he seemed to have no interest in walking any further, Stela or no. He fell back against the wall and hit the back of his head hard enough to make me wince. "You never liked me," he said.

What shocked me was how sober he sounded, how collected. James was not having a drunken epiphany beside that pizza parlor. This was something he'd thought about for a while, maybe something he'd practiced saying. It wasn't true, no matter how hard he'd convinced himself. I'd had only two friends after I returned home to care for Mother: James and Helen. Three, if Stela was to be counted, but our relationship had always been too complicated for me to consider her simply a friend.

There were fat tears in James' eyes that threatened to stream down his cheeks. God he was drunk. His severe frown made him appear years younger. I didn't know if his sudden shift in mood was the alcohol, or thoughts of never knowing his son, or Nicole, or the fact that I never wanted him the way he wanted me. Maybe a combination of all four. His pink lips trembled.

I put my hand on his flushed cheek and traced his bottom lip with my thumb. His pulse began to climb and I didn't hide my smile. James had been good to me once, when I desperately needed a shoulder and a willing ear. He had needed someone too, and while we didn't have time for a drunken therapy session, I realized that it was possible to give him some peace.

I neared to him and he straightened, his back to the wall. I took his face in my hands and guided his downcast eyes to mine. James steadied on his feet. The booze had made him sluggish, and my eyes made him drowsy. Gradually he collected himself, his frown melted away in placid contemplation and he placed his hands on my waist. He pulled at my hips and I stiffened, certain that a pass was inevitable at this point. Instead, I found myself encircled in his arms, his forehead pressed to my shoulder.

I think he said "I can't lose him," but James was still slurring and the crying didn't help. The baby, I suppose. He couldn't lose his son. In the moment, I could only focus on his warm breath rustling through my hair. His body was so warm he felt fevered and I leaned into him, pressing every inch of myself against the furnace of his skin. He was speaking through his sobs, but I wasn't listening. Our slight height difference meant that his shoulder was level with my mouth. I could see his collarbone through the top two buttons of his shirt.

And then I made the single most ignorant mistake of my unimpressive life.

I inhaled.

When his hands slid down my back, I ran my palm up the back of his head, pressed my face to his neck and breathed him in. His scent was overpowering. James held me tighter and pulled our bodies back into the shadowed nook where the Dumpster sat beside the wall.

I was transfixed by the hard lines of his body. Every nuance from his fabric softener, to his liberally applied cologne and the salt of his blood—singing in his veins—urged me on. So, when James' tongue darted between his too-pink lips to taste the skin just below my ear, it seemed the greatest thought that anyone had ever had.

There was no world beyond his carotid artery. The second I tasted his skin his blood was all that I could hear and the only song I ever wanted to listen to again. But it wasn't enough to feel his life force pulse against my lips. It will never be enough, I know that now. The hand that cradled James' head became a claw, and when he struggled to right himself, I gripped his shoulder and exposed his throat.

James cried out, he pushed at my chest and face, pulled at my hair. He screamed my name until the volume of his voice threatened to drown out the hypnotizing melody I longed so desperately to hear. I couldn't have that. I muffled his screams and he began kicking and kneeing me as I opened my lips along his carotid. My mouth became an amphitheater for his chorus and his thundering blood resounded like applause. When my fangs broke through the fragile barrier of blushed skin I collapsed to the pavement in ecstasy, and I took James with me.

The blood was sedative and stimulant all rolled into one. My heart spasmed to life as though I'd just self-administered a milligram of epinephrine. The blood spread through the endless web of my arteries and capillaries—luridly warm and impossibly quick.

James moved inside me—not for the first time—deeper than he'd ever been, dragging memories of Christmas mornings and bicycles with red seats. He shared his conquests with me, his escorts, and most treasured was a homecoming queen in the bed of an El Camino. I saw his father's face in every expression, his birth mother who died so young he'd forgotten her features until that final volley for life. I saw Nicole—the mother-to-be—giggling underneath him, then clutching his hand fiercely during that first sonogram. And then I saw myself smiling sardonically from over my shoulder at him, sauntering away in the opposite direction. I was above myself in bed and felt the awkward rumble of an untimely chuckle against my lips, the chaste press of my own lips afterward in an effort to reestablish intimacy. I stumbled after these glimpses, I sought them out as though some key to the woman I'd been, the woman he loved, was buried in his memory. I stayed in his blood until the pictures grew dark and over-exposed. I brought them to my face, but I couldn't make them out.

I couldn't see anything anymore. Nothing but blackness in every direction, swallowing me from all sides. I braced my body and to my horror a hand reached out and clasped me by the wrist.

I don't know how long I'd been screaming her name, only that when Stela yanked me up by the arm, I did not recognize her. She threw me into the wall and pinned my arms to my sides, repeating my name over and over again until I calmed. When I came to, the only blackness I saw was in Stela's frightened eyes. I think I'd lost consciousness for about five minutes. My senses returned in a tunneling rush and I didn't know where I was at first, or how I'd gotten there. Once it was clear I wasn't going to take anymore swings at her, Stela leaned in and held me close. Her hold on me was odd, heavy-handed, she turned me toward the dark alley and away from the street.

"Go back to the car," she said. "I will join you shortly." She stroked my cheek with her thumb and kissed me hungrily. The blood of her feed was still on her tongue and I held the back of her head to make the kiss last. Normally, Stela melts against me when that happens, but she wrenched herself free almost immediately. That was when I noticed the taste at the back of my throat, and saw the arterial spray drying down the front of my gorgeous dress.

Barely visible behind Stela's legs was a pale hand curled on the pavement. Several nails had been ripped clean off, and the index finger had been ground so low that the bone was exposed. Stela called my name in warning, but I stepped around her anyway. James' exsanguinated eyes—clouded by death—gazed up at me from the blood-splattered cement. Stela tore my beautiful coat trying to keep me from the body. It slipped off my arms and I fell to my knees in front of him. My whole body seized with a sob, and I know I said a lot of things in that moment but I can only remember one: It was an accident.

I apologized profusely to his inert corpse, as though he would wake at any moment because his murder was an honest mistake and I was so very sorry. But James did nothing of the kind. His lifeless limbs flopped grotesquely in my arms as I shook him, as I hugged him tightly enough to snap a rib. I covered the gaping hole in his neck shut with my palm despite the fact that it wasn't even weeping anymore. I screamed for Stela to do something, but she was unflinching and cold.

She pried me away from the body dispassionately. Stela knelt and her exquisite wool pants sopped up a puddle of black blood. She bit her wrist and closed the wound on James' throat, dabbing at the torn flesh like a painter smudging shadows across a canvas. Then she hoisted the corpse over her shoulder and carried what remained of James Henry Atwood to her car. He was one more body to dispose of, a task to be handled. Beyond the fact that it obviously mattered to me, it made no difference to her that I knew him. She didn't care that a son was never going to know his father, or that Nicole would never receive a single support payment. She didn't care about James' elderly father now alone in a nursing home without his favorite visitor, or a hospital that would have to replace a talented and beloved nurse, or the friends whose lives would be forever changed. None of that was out of character for Stela, of course, regardless of how alone I felt at the time.

No, what eventually made me suspect that I'd been set up to kill James—from the club Stela had chosen, to his inexplicable presence on the night of my very first hunt—was that she had no discernible reaction at all. That's what worried me. She could have stopped me, she could have caught up to us at any moment, but she didn't.

I stood in the center of that damned alley and watched her disappear. I listened to the blood drying on the pavement, felt it cracking where it had smeared my neck and chin. When Stela returned she walked out in front of me twenty yards off and stared. She didn't call out to me, or even wave her hand. There was no whisper from her heart to mine, and no pull from her eyes. With the clock ticking against us and two bodies to incinerate, we squared off in that alley and I realized that Stela wasn't the least bit jarred by this horrific *coincidence*.

I had no proof. I walked back to that car because there was no other choice. My clothes were ruined with blood and a strange vertigo was making it difficult to be objective.

The recycled air in Stela's beautiful car was undisturbed for the length of our drive to Carrington and Sons. Stela left me to my silent reflection. I considered all I knew about the woman next to me—the details of her first kill, a story she told me that predates her journals. She had fallen in love with her sparring coach and when Fane found them together, he turned her that very same night. The next night she was reunited with her lover who had been imprisoned in Fane's dungeon. She killed him, of course. She was a fledgling and he was the first human she'd seen.

On the one hand, I don't believe in coincidence. On the other, I don't believe that Stela would ever knowingly cause me pain. So where did that leave us?

When we arrived, Stela placed her hand on my thigh, and I knew she wanted me to wait in the car. For once I didn't argue. I couldn't. I still felt unsteady. Vaguely dizzy. If drinking from Stela and Fane invigorated and satiated me, why should feeding from James be any different? Was it grief? Was it all in my head? Did the last blood-collection bag Stela gave me have an adverse effect?

Derek Carrington jogged around to the front of the Maserati and I rolled down my window. He thrust his trembling hand in my face. He wore the black scrubs of a morgue attendant. An older man, mid- to late forties, handsome in a clean-cut and unassuming way, but noticeably exhausted. I regret the impression I must have made. Stela called him to the trunk to help her unload our cargo.

When she came to collect me from the car my head had cleared and the bodies had already been moved into storage. There was still an odd sensation in the pit of my stomach, like an air bubble roiling around inside me. Stela led me across a poorly paved parking lot. She knew I was trapped in my own mind.

I recognized the embalming room, even if I didn't remember Mr. Carrington. The steel table was cold beneath my palms. Stela disappeared behind a blue cotton partition with a brown paper package tucked under her arm. The furnace had changed, larger and sleeker than I recalled.

Stela returned in a fresh change of clothes—a simple black Henley shirt and jeans, standard issue for the family post-hunt. She set a parcel beside me with "Irina" written in Lydia's elegant script. Stela leaned forward to unzip my dress. I felt foolish, but I couldn't move and she wasn't asking me to help. To move, to speak, to do anything at all was to admit that once the vertigo receded and my stomach settled, I'd never felt more alive. A truth I wasn't prepared to embrace.

A decent man was dead, and I had killed him.

She drew the dress down my chest and arms, and I could tell by the way she stared at the scar on my left bicep that she was thinking of the last time I was on that table. Her right hand drifted briefly over my puckered skin—the gnarled bullet wound I received during a robbery gone bad. I can still hear the sick crack of my would-be assailant's spine shattering in Stela's crushing embrace.

After she'd stripped me of the evening's attire, she folded the dress around my blood-smeared pumps and laid the heap gently beside her own clothing. She handled the dress carefully, as if she didn't want it to wrinkle before it was burned. Clearly, she loved it as much as I did.

The rag was warm as Stela brought it to my neck and scrubbed my skin clean. She kept her eyes on her hands and away from my body. She cleaned my fingers and chest reverently. Our eyes met when she traced the rag around my lips and chin, and in her anesthetizing black gaze, I saw exactly what I needed to see the moment she found me in the alley with James—concern. She was showing it the only way she knew how.

I covered my face and leaned forward against her with a muffled scream. I didn't deserve her concern, and it was the closest to pity I'd ever seen from her. I was a murderer, and if I were honest, I enjoyed every second of his death. I will remember it always.

Toward morning, as the sun ascended and Stela and I were safe in our comfortable bed, she explained that what I encountered as I fed from James was a common occurrence for inexperienced Strigoi. I had fed from him for too long, followed the memories too far and witnessed the instant of his death as though it were happening to me. In other words, I'd made a rookie mistake.

Stela was curled around me in bed, her cheek pillowed on my shoulder as she traced the angle of my ribcage. I nodded thoughtfully to acknowledge that I'd heard her. I meant to ask her about the vertigo, but the soft swish of the sheets falling to the floor stopped me. We had no need for a fire that night—our bodies were warm from the flush of a feed and the friction of each other.

Afterward, Stela filled the void left by my discomfort with chatter. My home had been sold, and it was time to discuss the final steps needed to secure my finances. She would speak with Andrew Opes. The dress Lydia chose looked beautiful on me, did I like it? The trunk of the Maserati was not suitable for two bodies. I would require my own vehicle. She would see to that.

All the while, James' ghost sat at the foot of our bed, his shoulders slumped against the bedpost. Blood the color of pomegranate juice caked the back of his pale blue shirt, wept from the claw marks that ran down the back of his head.

* * *

Sitting on this empty rooftop is the longest I've been without Stela's company since I was turned and the difference is only a matter of hours. I can't stretch the time for much longer. My eyes ache. The pain grows more pronounced with every lifting shadow that peels away from the horizon. It's nearly morning and even if it weren't, if the world decided to stop spinning and plunge humanity into endless night, I still wouldn't last much longer without Stela. My blood begs for a reunion.

How does it work? This seemingly biological addiction to Stela? She's in my marrow, but how much deeper does she reach? Why was I not successfully named by Fane? What does it mean that I'm still Elizabeth? Why can't I find a single example of this ever having happened between a turned Strigoi and their fledgling? And why has no one mentioned discomfort or dizziness after a feed? Stela is unique, that's the consensus among her family, but I am not.

My little experiment here on the rooftop is a resounding failure. The sun has barely wrinkled the shade of night and already my skull is on fire. Shouldn't her inexplicable resilience to daylight have transferred to me when I was turned?

"It is nearly late enough to wish you a good morning."

Either I'm fatigued to the point of deafness, or Lydia's prowess as a hunter has been undersold. There wasn't a single footfall to give her away. I didn't even hear the ancient steel door at the top of the stairs close behind her. "Good morning to you too," I say over my shoulder. But Lydia has already settled to my right on crossed legs. She blinks back the sleep threatening to drown her and places her palms on her knees as if meditating.

"Testing your strength?" she asks, her head cocked to the side with a conspiring smirk. My mood lightens considerably.

"Stela stays up well into the morning and she rises early," I concede with a shrug.

"Is your mistress' hearty constitution catching?"

I rub my weary eyes. "Decidedly not, I'm afraid."

Lydia's long black hair, perfectly straight, whips in the shrill wind and brushes my face. "Are you quarreling?" she asks conversationally, shifting her legs toward me for a better look at my face. I nearly turn away from her, more out of habit than anything else.

"Not exactly." I mirror her posture. The front of her intentionally large sweater dips down from her shoulder. A lovely thing, cream-colored, cable-knit and cozy. There's something about her eyes, the shape of them, their impossible width that gives her face a perpetual adolescent youthfulness. Stela's journals say nothing of Lydia's age when she was made. Younger than both Stela and me, I can tell. "Why do you ask?"

It's Lydia's turn to shrug absently. "Stela was talking to Fane in the den. I asked after you. She said I could find you here." She squeezes the bridge of her nose as she speaks, and I know she's as encumbered by the approaching daylight as I am.

"Stela telling you where I am translates to the two of us arguing?" I ask, amused.

"No," she corrects with a finger. "Stela telling me where to find you and leaving me to do so without accompanying me hints at discord." I say nothing, and Lydia stares back at me intently.

She's right about Stela, but she's wrong about the fight. There hasn't been one, and I don't know which is worse: one of our petty arguments that flare to life in a blaze and extinguish just as quickly, or one of our silent bouts of suspicion and distrust. I'm not sure we're embroiled in either at present, only that navigating conversation has been tricky as of late.

"Things have been difficult since the first hunt," I confess.

Lydia nods solemnly. "The regret you feel is perfectly normal, Irina." Lydia places a hand on my exposed ankle.

"The whole night felt wrong," I say, my jaw clenched. I don't know that I should share any of this with her.

"I did not seek you out to judge or ridicule you," Lydia says softly. "You can unburden yourself, should you need to. It was not so long ago that I was turned." Lydia laughs dryly. "A few hundred years may sound like an eternity to you now but trust me when I say it passes in the blink of eye."

I would like an outside opinion of that night, of James, but Lydia is biased against Stela and unquestionably loyal to Fane. Beyond that, I don't think you're supposed to kill people you know. People you're connected to, or people that could be traced back to you. It's conceivable that Stela would be the one punished if a rule had been broken. After all that Stela has been through with Fane for the sake of loving me, I don't want to be something she has to defend yet again.

"You know what I think?" Lydia interjects in light of my continued silence. "I think that blame is a balm we use to protect ourselves from grief."

I rest my chin on my knee and turn toward her. Lydia's eyes are faintly rimmed with red, and I know my own can't be faring much better. "Did you blame Bård for your first kill?"

"I blamed everyone. Bård and Stela in particular."

I nod and stand up stiffly, smacking the dirt and dust from my pants. "I think you're right. Blame *is* a balm for guilt. And grief, like glory, demands an audience. I'm sorry to have kept you up so late to bear witness to mine." I offer a hand to help her to her feet.

Lydia laughs deeply, a warm and hearty sound. She loops her arm through mine, tugging me close. We trudge across the rooftop toward the stairwell and away from the bruised morning, arm in arm, with Lydia's head on my shoulder, quite like old friends.

VI

An Exciting New Venture

She had said she felt like a prisoner stripped of her most basic human rights, chiefly, her freedom. A sentiment in which no irony was intended, nor did she take kindly my reminder that she is no longer human. So, I guided her through dozens of exercises meant to prepare her body and mind for Fane's intrusive evaluation, which she passed, thus extending to her the exact same liberties the rest of our family enjoys. No more, no less.

I chaperoned her first hunt—as was my duty—disposed of her kill, cleaned her, dressed her. Elizabeth regarded me with silent suspicion for a fortnight. Fine.

She wanted her autonomy, her financial independence. I bartered a favor with Andrew to make her wish a reality, having little regard for my own precarious position in Fane's good graces if it meant her happiness. She grew morose at the news that her mother's brownstone had been sold, the final hurdle before consolidating her finances.

A written history was her desire. Unmitigated access to my personal records, a mirror into my past. I gave her my blessing and she met me with insult and accusation.

Now the lady wants a laptop, a vehicle of her own, a mobile phone, a private meeting with my good Mr. Opes, and unspoken though this desire may be, the time and space to decide whether I am the villain of her story. When I explained that these requests would take time, that a laptop and mobile are expenses which must be approved by Fane, she commandeered my personal laptop. Twice I caught her perusing articles online about Opes and Sons, their public holdings along with several articles written about the man who holds my family's fortune in his hands. A man who works with no one but me, and a man I promised would never be forced to meet another of the family after Lydia nearly murdered his daughter Christine. But what of it?

In an unscheduled meeting without my consent or a word of warning, she solicited a vehicle directly from Fane. Her wish was granted and she had her choice that very same night. Though Elizabeth did not gloat, it was abundantly clear that she was blithely unaware of the price he might have attached had he been less taken with her brash approach. And who is to say that Fane does not intend to collect on that request? He has always held courage in high regard, but that is not to say that he is unwary of it. He has lived long enough to know the difference between bravery and ignorance. He asked Lydia to secure a mobile for Elizabeth too. Two gifts in one night...

My company is desired when it suits her, or if she has come to an impasse in her "research" as she calls it. During those evenings, my praise and reassurance are required first.

Each evening she falls asleep upright in our bed with the ghastly glow of the laptop bathing her face in pale blue, and I tell myself that tomorrow I will speak with her. But come dusk, before Elizabeth has stirred, when her face remains troubled in repose my resolve crumbles. For even in sleep she appears braced for calamity. Her dreams prey upon her. Some evenings she mewls into her pillow, others she thrashes in bed or clings to me desperately. I catch flashes of James' exsanguinated face where once there was only Claire's ghost.

She wakes more beleaguered than ever and flashes a smile that does not reach her eyes. She pulls the laptop onto her thighs and resumes her work, scouring news outlets and medical journals. For what purpose? She is no longer a practicing nurse, and she abandoned her dream of working in medical research when Claire became ill.

Elizabeth has taken to hunting on hospital wards almost exclusively. Whether this is a moral dilemma or a matter of convenience remains to be seen. Questioning her hunting patterns would mean confessing that I have been following her and that would doubtlessly result in a confrontation.

She stalks her childhood home every time she leaves the compound to hunt, much the way I did when Elizabeth ended our relations. A young couple resides there now, prominent attorneys in their mid-thirties with two cherub-faced children aged six and nine. She loiters in the alley, in the shadow of the privacy fence, and watches them. On more than one occasion I thought I would have to collect her as she let herself in through the back gate—with its troublesome lock—and stood on the patio to hear the sounds of the unsuspecting slumbering family.

Had I failed to follow her, I would have had no way of knowing that the monotony of life after death is already proving a bit much for my beloved. This is the very reason Fane decreed that Lydia would be our last newborn. Lydia suffered a similar malaise that culminated in a blind rage for two decades. We moved often in those days, and more often than not Lydia's penchant for reckless slaughter was the precursor. Elizabeth's problem is that she cannot take an active role in the world, where social justice and the importance of the individual had been her religion.

What else could be expected? I waded into this monotony inch by inch over the years. When I found Elizabeth, I clung to her as though she were a life raft. I gambled with my life, my family's safety, I killed for her. I would have done anything to keep her with me, because the banality of life without her was so unbearable. What did I think would happen when I plucked her from the world? My brilliant, beautiful girl…

My laptop lives on her nightstand now. Her Bentley Continental is parked in the garage beside my vehicle, and I no longer presume an invitation to accompany her when she is outside our suite. A meeting with Andrew is not something I can arrange in good conscience until I know more about Elizabeth's limitations. Lydia was frightening enough for him, and she is no newborn.

However, I did arrange a video conference so that she could speak to him face-to-face, on her own behalf. I pretend not to notice that she keeps James Atwood's social media profile open in a tab on her mobile, that she has read every condolence posted to his page, every photograph he shared, every photograph shared of him. I hearken to her rants. I answer any inquiry about my journals—rare as of late—and my hunting experiences as fully as I can. I listen at the top step of the roof above the parking garage to her chatting cordially with Lydia about night-sky constellations—about which Lydia is exceedingly knowledgeable—and slink away without interrupting.

When she returns to me at the tail end of the evening, I return her affections as well as she allows and I ask her what she needs. "Work," she says. "I need to work." So, I retire early and Elizabeth opens the laptop and mumbles to herself about platelet structure, the hippocampus and so forth.

This much is within my power to give, and I would give her all that I have and more if it meant that she could know some modicum of peace. If she could taste for even one moment the tranquility and sense of purpose her existence has given me.

* * *

I spent the first three hours of my evening parked one street down from the parking garage, waiting for Elizabeth to leave for her hunt. Through fragmented impressions that made less sense to me than usual I was dimly aware of her distraction. She has not strayed one foot from the sofa on which she was reclined when I left.

When last I saw her, she was scribbling notes on the legal pad, scrolling through a medical article and rambling excitedly to herself—perhaps, to me also—about rodents. This began shortly after sunset. Dressed for a hunt when I emerged from the washroom, Elizabeth was exactly as I left her.

"Dearest, do you intend to feed in those clothes?"

A distracted mumble and an arched brow were my answer. Slowly, she turned away from her reading and there followed an exaggerated silence before she registered my question. Elizabeth glanced down at her robe as though completely unaware of her attire.

"What time is it?" she asked and looked lamely at her naked wrist.

"Half past eight," I said and took a seat on the arm of the sofa. Autumn is a welcomed reprieve from the brevity of summer nights, and during this time we make as much use of the extra hours as we can.

Elizabeth briskly scrubbed her face with her hands. I toyed with a lock of her beautiful chestnut hair. "Sorry," she said. "Stanford University has published this article about blood transfusions and spatial memory in mice." She pushed the laptop away and let her head fall back upon the cushions. "I completely lost track of time."

I have no interest in medicine—why should I?—but Elizabeth remains passionate about it. She is better with a distraction to occupy her mind. We are better when the focus of her attention is not on my past. Freed from her research, she ran an appreciative eye over my apparel.

"C'mere," she said with a jerk of her chin and a sly smile.

"Absolutely not." I narrowly escaped her grasp and stood again, straightening my sweater. Elizabeth pouted and leaned over the arm of the couch. "The hour grows late. You need to get dressed."

She sighed but remained as she was until I could deny her no longer. I cradled her jaw in my hands and kissed her parted lips. When she encircled my wrists and tried to drag me down after her, I pulled back and there she hung, suspended over the arm of the sofa like a marionette.

"Dress." I kissed the corner of her mouth. "Hunt."

Elizabeth was happier this evening than I had seen her in weeks. The playfulness that so endears me to her had returned and it threatened my resolve by the minute. She made no move to release my wrists, brushing my knuckles with her lips.

"You're right. I know. I'll get dressed."

"What was that?" I asked and craned an ear toward her. Elizabeth chuckled that droll laugh of hers, breathy and sparse as a breeze.

"You're right, Stela," she said gravely, good humor evident in her eyes. "I'll make myself presentable if not enticing. You go. I won't be far behind."

There was no mischief in her voice. I was without reason to demand we leave together. She believed I was respecting her space and allowing her to hunt in private. Still, I was concerned that James lay behind this request. That Elizabeth's reluctance to invite me along was rooted in the suspicion that I facilitated his death by her hand.

"Very well," I said, and stroked her cheek. "I hope when you return to me your mood is likewise prurient."

Elizabeth laughed and shoved me. "Go on, Romeo. I'll be right behind you."

But she did not follow, and now I am left to confess that I failed to leave without her.

* * *

The suite is in an alarming state of disarray. Elizabeth managed to move from the sofa only to sit cross-legged in the center of the coffee table with a moat of torn notebook paper sprinkled all around. Several volumes of my journals are stacked along the floor and the sofa is covered with open medical textbooks.

Elizabeth is so withdrawn into her own mind she took no notice of my arrival, which was admirably silent, but still…I could be anyone, with any intention. I take a step in her direction and thankfully, I notice an instinctual stiffening of the spine.

"You're home!" she exclaims, shoving the laptop aside. She wraps me in a crushing embrace and adorns my face and neck with exuberant kisses. "I have so much tell you—my god, Stela. Where to even being?"

Her laughter follows maniacally as she drags me down the three steps into the living area and deposits me in the armchair.

"Remember the mice?" she asks. "The Stanford article about blood transfusions in mice? Absolutely fascinating. I must have read it four times, and that got me thinking..."

What follows is a one-sided diatribe. Elizabeth is giddy, gesturing wildly with her hands, referencing her medical-journal articles to illustrate a point I cannot hope to follow. She doesn't notice my stunned silence.

"So, the brain is the organ the blood is protecting when we feed. The body rushes blood to the brain to maintain brain function. But as the brain dies the prefrontal cortex, the hippocampus, the cerebellum and the basal ganglia are firing on all cylinders, right?" she asks, pausing for input.

I nod my head uncertainly.

"These regions of the brain are looking for a skill set, a lesson that will serve the injured body. Some way to prevent death. That's the torrent of images we see. Sights, sounds, faces, places. It's the brain trying to categorize what it knows and what is happening to it, as it's happening. The brain just starts replaying everything in the hope that something will save the body."

She snatches up the laptop and brings it to me, shoving the screen in my face. She doesn't seem to notice when I flinch. "And this study might actually hold the key to understanding how our bodies regenerate. Well, Strigoi brains, at least. What they've discovered is that spatial memory in older mice improves if they receive a blood transfusion from younger mice. In these older mice new synapses formed in the hippocampus, where memory is thought to live."

"Dearest, come with me." I offer a hand over the armchair. "My mind is beleaguered with hunger, and so is yours." Elizabeth drops her arms, frustrated, and stares down at the crumpled pages under her feet. "Perhaps when we have both fed, I will be better able to follow your train of thought."

Elizabeth stills. She locks eyes with me unflinching for at least thirty seconds. Her soft, full lips purse into an unforgiving line.

"You haven't eaten," she says calmly.

"Of course not."

She stares down at her feet, her face hidden behind a curtain of hair.

"Elizabeth, you have several lifetimes to be angry with me." She snaps to attention, frowning. Her outrage smolders like coals behind her eyes, however, her disappointment is greater than I feared. "Let us hunt first, and when we return you can explain…" I take a long lingering glance around the room, "all this once more. You will have my full attention. I promise you."

I expected shouting. Instead, Elizabeth gnaws nervously at her bottom lip, her shoulders slumped and the evening's excitement forgotten. "Yeah," she says with a sigh. "I should eat." She sounds so much like a child.

She places her hand in mine and permits me to lead her to the washroom where her attire hangs untouched in the garment bag behind the door. I slide the robe from her shoulders and it pools around her ankles.

"How long have you been following me?" she asks with eerie assurance. I unzip the garment bag and slide the pine-colored cashmere sweater from its wooden hanger.

"You know the answer to that."

Elizabeth nods and faces the mirror, shrugging on the sweater. I face the door and unclasp the wool trousers Lydia has selected for her.

"You know where I've been?" she asks in a juvenile tone, finding my eyes in the mirror. She takes the trousers from me without turning around. Elizabeth's palpable fear has nothing to do with being caught hunting in hospitals, and everything to do with stalking her childhood home. Frequenting a neighborhood where she is likely to be recognized. She knows that I am aware of her thoughts, as though the murder of tenants would mean anything to me beyond the inconvenience of a cover-up. No, the shame in her face is because her contempt did not exclude the children…

"Yes." I take hold of her shoulder. "I know."

Elizabeth pulls on the trousers. She runs her palms over her beautiful sweater, then stares intently at her own reflection.

"Why did you seek to conceal your sorrow from me?" I rest my hand on the small of her back. Elizabeth finds my eyes in the mirror.

"Would you have understood if I'd told you?" There is no judgment in her voice, just weary exasperation.

"No," I admit. Elizabeth's eyes fall, fix on the drain at the base of the sink. I press my front to her back and Elizabeth straightens, she pulls my arms tightly around her. "But I would have tried."

* * *

Shards of shattered glass still cling to the half-moon windows, shining brightly in my headlights. The decrepit wooden doors are barred with rusty padlocked chains. I remember when this factory was a paper mill that employed north of five hundred union workers. It's now derelict.

Flames flicker deep inside. I cut the headlights off and circle the building at a crawl, certain that someone calls this abandoned kingdom home. If we are fortunate, we will find more than one vagabond inside.

"What are we doing?" Elizabeth asks, and in so doing, breaks the strained silence that ensued when I refused to allow her to drive herself.

"Searching for the point of entry."

The building is U-shaped and in the west corner of the interior wall lies a basement access door, strapped shut with untarnished steel chains. I nod toward that door.

A bowed awning sags above the west arm of the building, overgrown with ivy. I pull the car beneath the covering and cut the engine. Elizabeth stares out the passenger side window, breathing swiftly in anticipation of a kill. She shakes her head.

"I don't want to go in there, Stela."

"We are short on time. This is not up for debate."

Elizabeth turns slowly, her eyebrows pitched, and folds her hands primly in her lap. "You know, I do a lot better with sound logic than I do with blanket commands. So, let's try that again. Why this place? Why not a hospital?"

Strange that one who was so dedicated to the healing of the infirm would be so quick to prey upon them. Then again, human beings do so crave familiarity. I take a fortifying breath and detect an easily identifiable scent in the night air. Someone is hiding here. I give Elizabeth a satisfied smile and lean upon the center console. "We cannot use a hospital because you have made an unfortunate preference of them as of late."

"I've been careful," she counters with a flourish of her hands, "I haven't visited any location more than once."

"That much is true. How long do you think it will take before an administrator or the police begin to suspect a connection between the sudden rash of critical patients terminated due to unexplained blood loss?" Elizabeth stares at me coldly. "Two more weeks? Three, perhaps?"

She opens her mouth, but a snappy rebuttal eludes her. She clenches her jaw and closes her eyes, taking a deep breath. "They're in there," she says, acquiescing. "I can smell them."

I exit the vehicle and open her door. "Shall we?" I ask, offering a hand. Elizabeth balks, but accepts my hand.

"The sweet illusion of choice," she says. "See? That wasn't so hard, was it?" she teases with an infuriating wink.

I laugh dryly and steer her toward the chained door. "Have I called you impossible lately?"

"Not since last night," she says with shrug.

The chains are wrapped between two rusted iron handles. There is no padlock to break, thankfully, so we maintain the element of surprise. I usher Elizabeth inside.

Elizabeth whispers concerns about leaving my vehicle unattended in such a notorious neighborhood. I assure her that the car is safer here than in our own garage. A fine automotive in a poverty-ridden area indicates a very specific form of employment.

"Drugs?" she asks, slinking in the dark.

"Drugs, prostitution, arms dealing, human trafficking." I lead her toward an eroding staircase at the end of a damp hallway. "The flamboyance implies the confidence of the owner, which suggests a fearless and possibly violent temperament."

Elizabeth walks soundlessly on the balls of her feet up the steps—her back pressed against the ice-frosted wall. "Your family chooses their hunting grounds based on crime rates, don't they?"

"*Our* family," I say, stepping around her into a wide entryway with a peeling linoleum floor. "Yes and no. We choose heavily populated cities, because crime is a given when humans are kept in close quarters."

"Bleak."

"Factual."

An unintelligible mumble catches both our ears, and I bring a finger to my lips. We move along the darkened wall and wait. Quickly, our care is rewarded with the sound of shuffling steps. Elizabeth's heart pounds, her pulse racing. I squeeze her hand.

There are at least five men in this building, and the end of the corridor is noticeably lighter. A scent of smoke from damp kindling laces the air. Visibility on the second floor is greater than I hoped. Decades of rain and snow have eaten through the roof, making way for the moon to shine a light on our position.

"Find them," I whisper. Elizabeth turns toward me, her black eyes large and starved. "We need take only two." She nods and slips away, letting the scant shadows dictate her approach.

Elizabeth straightens up before she rounds the corner. She listens to her blood. Three men on this floor, one of them asleep. Two more somewhere on the wing. She darts her head around the corner. She holds her position and waves for me to follow.

This will be an excellent learning opportunity for her.

The peacefully slumbering gentleman is upright in the corner, covered with all his clothing to guard against chill. His face is a mask of wrinkles, trimmed with a wiry gray beard. He rests with three black trash bags clutched in his fists. Elizabeth takes a step toward him, and I pull her back by the wrist. She stares at me, confused, and I point to the adjacent room at her back.

Our marks are close, talking lively to one another about war and government. Elizabeth falls behind me, following step for step until we part to occupy opposite sides of the generous opening. No doors conceal our approach.

The men have a fire burning in an oil bin, and the room is regretfully well lit. Their conversation continues, both of them pacing in tight circuits, alert from the unforgiving breeze which means we must wait. The pulse of their blood calls to her, compromising reason and exhausting our patience. I whisper to her mind and she hears. She pries her gaze from the two inviting forms and finds mine. I urge her to wait until their backs are turned. Cover the mouth first.

Elizabeth is trembling with hunger, but she silently insists I take the larger of the two. I smile and dip my head. She knows me so well.

When my mark turns the back of his tattered wool coat to the door, I retrieve the knife from my boot and warn her not to drain the body as she did before. Elizabeth's bloodlust wanes for a moment and she nods curtly. She does not appreciate reminders of James. The lay of the room is better from her side, and I move when she does. Her mark bends down to get something from his duffel bag, and mine stands warming his fingers over the fire. We move in without a sound.

The hunt is not much of one, but the fight is fierce in my prey. He bites my hand as soon as it closes over his mouth. Elizabeth scoops the younger man up off the floor and into her arms. They thrash wildly, kicking their feet in the empty air.

Though I am loath to rush a feed, Elizabeth falls to her knees with her victim tight in her grasp and I know she has no intention of heeding my earlier warning. Consciousness fades from my mark and I drop his body to the floor.

"Enough, my darling." I take Elizabeth's throat in my hand and push the young man's body away from her. She whimpers, and then growls. "We need him alive."

Elizabeth releases her hold and slumps back against the wall, her hand to her stomach. I drag the blade of my knife across my palm and smear it over the wound.

"Why are we leaving them alive?" she asks, grimacing.

"You need spilled blood to stage a crime scene."

When the wound on his neck has healed, I slit her mark's throat and what blood is left soaks the front of his dirty clothes. Elizabeth recoils and looks as though she might faint. Perhaps the sight is ghastlier from a few feet away. She stands up, leaning heavily against the wall, still clutching her stomach as though ill. I drag this corpse beside my own unconscious fellow. An abdominal wound for my mark, variation is key. I arrange the body and step back, checking their oozing injuries. I wrap the handle of my knife in the fist of Elizabeth's kill.

"Murder suicide," she says, standing on noticeably firmer feet.

"Only to be used sparingly, too risky otherwise." I appraise my work from a new angle. "I doubt anyone will call the police for these two. More likely, the remaining tenants bury them somewhere on the grounds. They can keep their lodging only as long as it remains a secret."

Elizabeth looks on forlornly, hugging her arms around her chest. She shivers—sickened or chilled? Neither seems possible—and walks out.

I follow Elizabeth out onto a walkway connecting the two wings of the building. The tile is intact, though the windows have all been shattered inward. She lingers, standing tall and breathing the night air. Her hands are tucked in the pockets of her overcoat. Gone is the sickened grimace, and the distant glow of the streetlights on the service road illuminates her silhouette. I stand beside her and appreciate the contrast her beauty provides to our ramshackle surroundings.

"Are you all right?" I ask.

"Killing in hospitals is easier."

"Because you can choose victims you know are destined to die?"

Again, she does not answer my question. She holds herself by the elbows, rubs her hands over her biceps as though cold. "Is this the part where you tell me that we're all destined to die?" Elizabeth stares at me, pained and depressed.

"No. This is the part where I remind you that you are destined to live and designed to kill. You are not one of them Elizabeth, though I know you feel closer to human than Strigoi. That will not last forever. A murder in a hospital is still murder. If you can consider that a mercy, why should tonight be any different? You spared that man a life of hardship and squalor."

"I am become death," she muses. "Destroyer of worlds."

"Vishnu, one of my favorite false idols. But human beings do a fine job of destroying the world on their own."

Elizabeth turns toward me, wraps her arms around my neck. "I was thinking of Oppenheimer, but you're right."

"A fine illustration of my meaning. I remember when the bomb was dropped on Hiroshima. Not one among us could understand the reason for such excess…"

"What did you feel when that happened?" she asks. Her favorite question. What was it like? What were you feeling? What are you thinking, Stela? My answer rarely satisfies her, but my memory of the bombing is sharper than many I carry concerning human affairs.

"Disgust. No honor in a death like that."

"Is it so strange that I feel disgusted with what we've just done?"

"The mass murder of countless innocents, some feeble, the elderly, even infants are not equal to the execution of two squatters able to fight for their lives."

She pushes the coat off my shoulders and down to the floor. She unbuttons the front of my black silk shirt. "The tally of murders doesn't stop at two, Stela." She leans forward and presses her lips to the hollow of my throat, running her fingers along my exposed torso. "When you take our strength and speed into account, our victims are as mismatched against us as any atomic bomb."

I lift the edges of her sweater and trace my thumbs along the dip of her waist. "Life is rarely fair, dearest."

She rocks against me, still wrestling with the conflict of her conscience, but relishing the distraction my hands provide.

The night is very nearly spent and I do not have to remind her of the time. Elizabeth forgoes foreplay and her touch carries conviction. She hooks her leg around my waist but resists when I try to pull her to the glass-littered tile. The silver radiance of the moon dances in her hair as she leans back against the window frame. Has she counted the days since we were last intimate? I am a slave to this woman in the worst way, and to some extent she must know. Her lips curl up in a smirk when she touches me, and a helpless sound falls from my mouth against my will. "I missed you too," she whispers in my ear.

We find our way to the floor amongst the glass and years of dirt. The glass and the force of our affections shreds the back of my shirt and smears her palm and forearm with blood. Our wounds heal only to be reopened whenever we move. Everything about her is overwhelming—her intelligence, her emotions, her touch—and we arrive at the edge together.

"Did you want me like this when you found me with James?" she asks, breathless.

"Always." I grab a fistful of her hair and pull her body back so that I can sit up beneath her weight and look into her eyes. "I always want you like this."

She finishes soundlessly with open eyes and I follow the next instant, keeping my cry contained. I do not manage to hold her stare, and her pleased expression when I blink my eyes open is spiced with friendly competition.

Elizabeth pokes her fingers through the shredded back of my shirt, tracing the newly healed cuts before they vanish completely. She remains perched on my lap as she buttons my blouse, in no rush to stand. She picks up my discarded coat, carefully straightening the collar. "It must have been enticing for you," she says, "watching me kill him. Knowing that James and I had a history."

I snatch the coat from her and shrug it on. When it becomes obvious that I do not intend to reply, Elizabeth, watches my expression closely. It is as distasteful to me to think of James as her lover as it is for Elizabeth to acknowledge that he died in her arms. But jealousy has no place among my people. Our lives are long and I myself have enjoyed many bedfellows. Elizabeth will have many more lovers to come, whether she believes that now or not. Eternity is a tundra, the monotony disrupted only occasionally by a new conquest or acquisition—intimate or otherwise—and I will not be new to her forever.

I tug at her freshly secured waistband. "Tell me more about this discovery of yours."

Elizabeth tilts her head and stares impassively back at me. She does not appreciate my changing the subject. She wants an answer to a question she has not asked, and if I am to be accused of something, I prefer a direct approach. We can converse or we can sit in silence, but I will not play this game with her.

"I want to understand where we fit in the world," she says. "How our bodies work on a molecular level. What are our limits."

"You were quite animated this evening. Did you have a breakthrough in your studies?"

Elizabeth watches me from the corner of her eye, as though she fears I intend to tease her. "The blood transfusion study in mice, for one thing. Increased brain function when transfused with the blood from younger mice."

With the clear head granted me by a successful hunt, her implications are much more obvious the second time. "I can see how that would be true for me. Every human I feed from is hundreds of years younger than I am. But would that regeneration be applicable to one as youthful as you?"

Elizabeth is encouraged by my willingness to postulate. "It would explain why I haven't experienced the euphoria you've described to me when you feed. My own experience has been a mixed bag. Feeding from a human does not produce the same effects as feeding from you, or Fane for that matter."

A mixed bag?

"Elizabeth…you should not compare the two. And what do you mean by—"

"You also assume that my blood is still mine. I am not convinced that is true. For instance, when you feed from me, when you're nearby my blood races as though desperate to reach you." She takes my hand and places it over her heart. "Do you feel it?"

"Yes." I stroke her cheek. "But you remain distinct when I drink from you. Tinged, perhaps, but still uniquely yourself."

She smiles radiantly, pleased to hear that she remains—in some small way—the Elizabeth she has always been.

"So, it's possible that my makeup was drastically altered when you turned me. What I want to know is how severe that transformation was."

"And what of the memory flashes when we feed?" I ask, hoping to steer her toward a less invasive study. Something we could extrapolate from our victims without analyzing ourselves. The road she is headed down is one I doubt our Lord would condone. Our people have been the subject of countless investigations and speculation throughout history. To call our very biology into question—whether by a Strigoi or the town priest—is not a pursuit he welcomes.

"An overzealous theory on my part," she admits. "There's no concrete evidence to suggest that blood carries memories. Only that blood flow has an effect on their formation. Still, if Fane can control a flood of fragmented thoughts and arrange that information into a cohesive narrative, I see no reason why you or I wouldn't be able to do the same. Excluding the superiority of his genetic makeup."

"You believe then, that Strigoi might have the power to withdraw information that benefits us while we feed?"

"Why not? Even if the reason Fane is able to probe our minds is some kind of evolutionary tier, the Strigoi are still genetically superior to human beings."

I have tried to teach her how to guard her thoughts and control the memories in her blood and failed. Could my ability to control the tide of my own memories be just another of my inherent gifts? Or is that ability a result of my advanced age? Surely Bård must know the trick of it. How else would he last so long in Fane's service? Unfortunately, this is not a question I can ask him.

Elizabeth's thoughts rush haphazardly along any time I feed from her. The truth of her allegiance to me and to herself, the fact that she is not my Lord's Irina at all. Blind luck that the memories Fane tasted when he fed from her did not find us both out. How strange a happenstance, indeed. How improbable that we have won so many rounds of roulette. Either he knows and has a punishment in store for us, or he will learn the truth very soon.

"If we could control the images our victims share with us, the benefits could be boundless," I say.

Elizabeth brightens. "Could you imagine the knowledge? Say you fed from Stephen Hawking or Einstein. Well, assuming you understood their memories, of course."

I stand up and start pacing beside her. "Social security numbers, account pins, banking and routing information…"

Elizabeth ices over and stands up slowly. "Stela, this isn't some money-making scheme."

Now is not the time to argue. The future is too full of opportunity. "Of course not, my love. But as with all great discoveries, one must start somewhere."

She smiles sardonically. "And you think petty larceny would be prudent?"

"If you want permission to pursue this research there must be some recompense for Fane. That is the way of it."

"You know I hate it when you say that. Besides, I don't have enough evidence to support my theory. I mean, we could try to herd our victim's thoughts, but without a substantial understanding of our own bodies we'd be groping in the dark."

My body is buzzing with excitement. I know, better than she, that such a thing is possible. The night she was shot I saw into Derek Carrington's mind and removed the memories he had of her. His compliance was mostly thrall. He was mesmerized by my obsidian eyes. However, the near surgical removal of his memories was a different muscle entirely. I have thought very little of that exchange for fear that it was one more oddity which set me apart from my lot. Worse, that it was a strength only Fane should wield. I am not entirely convinced that Fane would believe otherwise, but I have lain awake in our bed scouring my brain for profitable opportunities. Some means by which I could redress my debt to him. To think that all this time the answer lay in the mind of the one slumbering peacefully beside me.

"What would you need to do the study yourself?" I ask, slipping an arm around her waist. She wades into my embrace, presses her temple against my shoulder.

"A lab of my own. Somewhere private, secure, where the materials wouldn't run the risk of falling into the wrong hands. Samples from as many of us as I can get."

I tap my fingers up her spine and turn toward the dimly lit sky. The stars have all retired and the pale horizon has begun to warm. We are nearly out of time and I have so many questions for her. Elizabeth twists in my arms and reads the approaching light herself. She has been weaned and fully fledged, but I cannot grant her access to any blood beneath Fane's roof. All blood belongs to him. Hers and mine and most of all Fane's which is most certainly high on her list.

"Do you trust me?" I ask. She nods firmly. Heaven knows I have not always made it easy for her. "We must hurry home. The sun will pain you and you need to rest."

I climb through the jagged window and drop to the ground below. Elizabeth follows close behind, sure on her feet. She walks around to the passenger side door and waits for me to open it. Not because she cherishes my chivalry—she thinks it arcane most days—but as an unspoken truce.

"I will bring your proposal to Fane and present it as enticingly as I can," I say, backing out onto the service road. Elizabeth is wise enough to know that there is only one way to reach what she desires. We must approach Fane first. The decision is his alone. "I expect he will call upon you to address the concerns he will undoubtedly have."

"Understood," she says gravely. As we turn toward the highway her hand crosses the console and rests on my thigh. "You still owe him, don't you? The cremator. Mr. Collins. Me."

"Yes."

Elizabeth withdraws her hand and retrieves a pair of sunglasses from the visor. She slides them on as we merge onto the highway, glittering faintly as night wanes into morning. Her tolerance for sunlight is abysmally low, but she is young.

"Then I'm glad I can help." She drops her head back against the headrest and shuts her eyes behind the dark lenses.

* * *

Beside the hearth Elizabeth undresses clumsily while I arrange the fire. She kicks her bloodstained clothes into a haphazard pile as the kindling catches. Both our outfits will need to be burned when I return.

She stands just behind me with my black silk robe draped over her arm, watching me undress. Her eyes are sharp, shrewd in their appraisal, and her steely silence fills me with foreboding. The fire snaps sending a thick curl of smoke up the flue.

"I have to discuss this evening with Fane."

Elizabeth says nothing. She steps closer and reaches behind me to unclasp my bra. She does not look away from my eyes as she drags her nails down my hips, taking my underwear with them. With a flick, she holds the robe open for me.

"Do you discuss everything with him?" she asks, securing the belt around my waist with a little more force than necessary.

"You of all people know how much I hide from him."

"Did you tell him about James?"

There is a storm inside her. I would have to be a fool not to sense it, but her eyes reveal little else. Black as an ocean, and curiously empty. She is growing stronger, and so quickly… The question about James appears, on the surface, only a query. A curiosity on her part. Her seeming indifference troubles me more than her frequent outrage.

"Elizabeth, if you mean to indict me, have it out." But she only smiles back at me, taking my hand in hers and placing it above her heart. "I will not dance around this subject with you any longer. Accuse me now of facilitating James' death so that I can deny having any hand in the matter."

She rises up on the balls of her feet and holds my face gently in her hands, our lips only inches apart. "Would you?" she asks, incredulous. Still staring deeply into my eyes—not prying or digging past my defenses—she shakes her head. Even my righteous indignation palls in the light of her unsettling certainty. I back away from her, unable to meet her stare any longer.

Elizabeth grabs me in a fierce embrace. When I fail to return her affection she laughs dryly, just once, and presses a kiss to my cheek. "Good night, Stela." I watch her drift silently away from me and turn down her side of the bed. "I do love you," she says. But she will not look at me.

* * *

Fane is awake at every hour. I slip silently inside his sizable quarters and find him upright in bed. He has a large vellum-covered book open on his bare legs and one arm curled protectively around Lydia, who slumbers. Fane does not look up from his reading, but waves me over, and I stand at his bedside while he finishes the page.

"My dove." He smiles, closing the book quietly. "To what do I owe the pleasure of your visit?" He is not one to whisper, and I must admit the sound of his softened voice warms my heart. There is no disturbing Lydia at this point, but still he considers her. My own child sleeps now, safe in her dreams until they turn upon her—they always do—and the sun crests over the tops of buildings aboveground.

"Irina brings me to you, Lord."

He cranes his head back gently, but the eyes hint of calculating appraisal. Elizabeth has driven me to his mercy several times, and always to ask for more than I deserve.

"Come," he says, patting the vacant edge of mattress, "sit with me."

I find myself taking care not to jostle Lydia, of all people. Perhaps his fancy and Elizabeth's fondness for her are finally rubbing off on me.

Fane delicately pries his arm from Lydia's grasp, and she promptly wraps her arms around his waist.

"All my children are so lovely when they sleep," he whispers, doubling over to kiss her shoulder. "You are the only other in this house who knows that to be true." The only one with the ability to stomach the daylight hours. He slides so gracefully into our once-easy camaraderie. Maybe all that was good between us will be again. We might yet salvage some kind of friendship. I miss him. Just a moment in his presence restores my peace.

"Do you watch Irina sleep?" he asks.

"As often as I can for as long as I am able."

"What have you come to ask of me, Stela?"

Ask *of* me, not ask. I can hardly blame him. When was the last time I visited him with good news? Or visited him at all, without a summons?

"Irina studied medical science, as you know." He nods. "An article about blood transfusion caught her eye early this evening. She was so excited by the implications of what she read, I had difficulty convincing her to leave the lair." A half-truth though it may be, Fane accepts it for now. "She believes that this particular study may hold the key to understanding our own regenerative abilities."

Fane laughs loudly, showing no consideration at all for the soundly asleep Lydia wrapped around him. I recognize this laugh—he thinks such an understanding is an absurd pursuit. I thought the same, until Elizabeth expanded upon her hunch.

"Stela, we are as we are, and that is enough," he says, chuckling quietly. "That is everything there is and all there will ever be."

"Irina's interest is not limited to our miraculous constitution, my Lord."

Fane sobers, clearly intrigued. "Explain."

"She believes that the memories and thoughts writ in the blood of lesser beings can be herded and controlled via their blood."

Fane sniffs and smooths the sheet down around his thighs. "What do the thoughts of mortals matter to me?"

"Think of it. If we could control those flashes in their blood, we could hunt for thoughts that interest us. Nothing would be private as long as we were feeding. We would hold all their most sensitive information in our hands."

He brings a finger to his mouth and taps his lips as he mulls over the possibilities. Fane never rushes to a decision. Why should he? He has all the time in the world. His diplomacy is the reason we are kept safe. I have long desired to be as deliberate as he is in everything he does or does not do. For many years I tried to model this behavior. But loving Elizabeth as fiercely as I do has made me glaringly aware of my own shortcomings, my quick temper and my tendency to be reactive.

Finally, he says, "You were thinking of personal information?"

"Banking information, specifically. Blackmail is always an option."

Fane leans back against the headboard. He stares at his palms open on his lap, and the skin is ruby red with bright blue capillaries pulsing from Lydia's blood. He flexes his fingers and clenches his fist. "What would convince you that such a feat is even possible for a Strigoi?"

The thick bones in the back of his hand ripple like tightening cables. I watch those hands as his gaze pierces my right temple, my whole face flushes with heat but I do not flinch. "Irina is not entirely convinced herself. She wishes to study our own blood to better understand how the memories are translated in the first place."

"I never suggested she was," he says calmly. "After all, Irina is not the one who came to call on me this morning, is she?" He places two fingers under my chin and raises my eyes to his. "You brought this to my attention. Therefore, you must believe her hypothesis is possible."

Around his black pupils there is a neon yellow ring that keeps his pale blue irises at bay. I have always thought that the heat of his stare originates from that band, radiating outward. Perhaps Elizabeth will one day explain that phenomenon too. The heat builds in the base of my skull and Fane is there, waltzing through my thoughts in search of some memory that will damn me.

"I merely consider it an interesting avenue to pursue," I say with a shrug that shakes his hand from my face. Nothing so direct as a flinch.

Fane folds his hands in his lap and with a roguish grin flashes his white teeth. "Who was it then, Stela?" He raises a finger in warning. "If you lie to me, I will be deeply disappointed."

The fire in my skull subsides and his presence in my mind withdraws. He will not pry the truth from me. He wants me to present it as an offering. I grip the tangled bedsheets and sit up straight, braced for the back of his hand or worse. "Mr. Carrington," I admit and keep my eyes on his. Fane despises cowardice.

"You controlled his thoughts?"

"Once." I nod. "Elizabeth was wounded. She needed medical attention. I took her to him. Afterward, I removed the memory from his mind."

Fane, clearly intrigued, straightens in bed. "How was she wounded?"

I never imagined the circumstances surrounding my treachery would matter much to him. But Fane can be surprising. "Bullet wound. She was shot." I swallow compulsively, the thought of all that wasted blood seeping into her black dress. "A man followed her into an alley. He was…he wanted to hurt her. The gun went off in his hand when I overpowered him."

"I know the wound. Her left arm." He taps the same spot on his own bicep. "I recognized the scar for what it was the night you turned her. A girl born in the city walks unaccompanied down a dark alley. Why would she do that?" he asks himself and smiles suddenly. "She was running from something."

I nod.

"She was running from you." Fane needs no response from me and takes my hand. "I will not pretend to understand the guilt you harbor over this woman, Stela. Being as I am, such emotion has never been a driving force in my life."

For one fleeting second, I want to rebuke his implication. I want to align myself with him, be as he is, beyond the petty torments of conscience. Such indulgence is weak, mortal, unbecoming of a warrior especially of my age.

"What does Irina need from me?" he asks, patting my hand gently. And I am once again my truest self—a loyal subject.

"Medical equipment. A laboratory in which to work."

"And?" he presses.

"Your blessing to study our own biology while pursuing this theory."

"That is a lofty request," he says, shutting his eyes briefly. "Well… I do not intend to decide this morning. It concerns the whole household. Bring Irina to the monthly meeting. We shall discuss the matter as a family."

I thank him profusely for his time and graciousness. Fane smiles warmly. He takes my hand again, cupped in his, and kisses my knuckles sweetly. Is Lydia the reason for this new tenderness in him? I stare down at her sleeping face. The kinship I felt for her earlier wanes, and I consider the joy it would bring me to drag her from this room by her perfect hair.

"Get thee to bed, my dove," he says, slipping down beside Lydia. He cradles her head on his chest. "If you hurry, I trust you can manage a few precious minutes of watching Irina sleep."

I leave them to each other. What good is it to wish to emulate him in all matters, if I am unable to quash something as trivial as envy? Envious of James and the way he comforted Elizabeth when I was forbidden from her life. Envious of Lydia and the space she now occupies in Fane's heart.

The scent of the fire rushes up to greet me as I drop into our quarters. Elizabeth mewls in her sleep, reaching across my side of the bed, aware that I am near enough to touch even in her heavy slumber. I gather our discarded garments and toss them into the fire.

I slip into bed and before I can settle myself, Elizabeth throws her head on my chest. She grips my waist and pulls me close, thrusting a leg between mine. Fane is right, of course, I can manage a few moments to appreciate her beauty. Her wild chestnut hair obscures the right side of her face, but I can still make out the quick darting movements of her closed eyes, the pout of her lower lip. I cannot savor her for long before the darkness calls to me.

VII

Written In The Body

The first notable difference is the smell: disinfectant, rat poison, fumigation fog, and fresh paint. The linoleum in the hallway has been replaced by Bård's henchmen, and the Pathology door at the end of the hall omits a sterile white gleam through its wire-threaded window which casts diamond patterns across the floor. The building is much quieter than I remember. No vermin scurrying inside the wall, no buzzing electrical wires swaying from the ceiling.

It's hard to believe this is the same empty clinic Stela showed me a month earlier. Less than that. Equipment was cataloged and tested. What could be salvaged was marked accordingly, and what I had no use for was piled up in one of the vacant offices. She then forbade me to step within fifty feet of this building. She turned complete control of the renovation over to Crogher, who staffed his team with ex-cons—fall guys for the family's more conspicuous kills—that Bård owed a favor.

"Are you ready?" Stela asks as she places the keys in my upturned palm.

"As I'll ever be."

Stela drapes her arm over my shoulders, holding me close. She smiles against my temple. "Would you like a moment alone?"

Her perceptiveness often surprises me, because she will demonstrate sensitivity toward things I know she considers trivial, even though she denies possessing empathy.

"Would that be all right?" I ask.

"Of course." Stela squeezes my shoulder, takes a step back from the door. "I left something in the car," she says. "Take your time."

As Stela's boots retreat leisurely down the hall I take a deep, grounding breath and slip the key into the lock. The door swings open and blinding light radiates down from the fluorescents and glints across the polished steel bench tops.

I trail my fingertips along the island in the center, leaving a smudge of prints against the pristine workstation. The microscope I ordered sits beneath the new shelves on the left, the centrifuge we salvaged glistening like new beside it. Each cabinet is neatly labeled as are the drawers. There's a new sharps container beside the door, and a lightbox beside the fridge. I smile to myself, wondering if it was Bård's idea or Crogher's, and imagine my brothers standing in the center of the room, wondering what detail was missing.

"Hmm," I remark to myself, somewhat amazed. "*My* brothers…"

I suppose they are.

I test the faucet in the polished steel sink and nod approvingly as I turn in a slow circle. They really thought of everything and it endears me to the family more than I thought possible. I lean back against the sink and consider the decisions leading up to this moment, the culmination of my dreams.

The monthly meeting was astoundingly pedestrian, held in an offshoot of the common area, a door I'd never passed through before. There was a long table—American Cherry, I believe—and six black leather office chairs, evenly spaced. A seventh chair had been relocated from the library, positioned awkwardly between the head of the table and the chair to the left.

There were two whiteboards scribbled with dates and figures, a dozen or so oversized Post-Its stuck to the dark walls and covered with names penned in either black or red marker. I only recognized one: Andrew Opes. I wiped the recognition from my mind immediately, thankful that Stela and I were the first to arrive.

Gradually, the family filed inside, each with a legal pad and pen in hand. They sat according to their rank. Bård to the right of what could only be Fane's chair, so ridiculous was the size. Stela to Fane's left, though my armchair had been wedged between her and Fane.

Lydia arrived on her Lord's arm and he stopped to hold a chair out for her, the chair to Bård's right. Crogher was directly across from her, and most surprising Darius took the seat at the far end of the table, directly opposite Fane. He arrived with two giant ledgers in hand, and the meeting did not start until he found his page. Darius bowed his head graciously toward Fane.

With three resounding knocks of his fist, Fane called the meeting to order and all eyes fell upon him. He welcomed me and placed a hand atop the back of my chair, which irritated Lydia. I doubted I would be sitting so near to him for long. I felt very much like a guest speaker.

Fane turned our attention to Bård who proceeded to present a rundown of the family's standing with various allies. I couldn't believe how far their influence reached. Andrew Opes—The Money—and Derek Carrington—Disposal—were the only players familiar to me. Then came the police chiefs, detectives, and beat cops. There were allies within every influential gang in the city of Chicago, but the list didn't stop there. Bård's "associates" had met with hospital administrators—three of whom I knew by reputation—the Mayor, and a contact in the Governor's office.

Stela must have sensed my nerves because she reached out to hold my hand just before I began drumming my fingers. I felt foolish sitting among them, thinking of the liberties I'd taken without knowing the cost. Namely, my frequent hospital hunts which Bård's men must have covered up. No wonder Stela was always so frightfully on edge. The line we walk is so much more precarious and political than I'd ever imagined.

Crogher updated everyone on Macha and the fast-approaching birth of the new guard she was carrying. He shifted then to talk of the tunnels, their infrastructure and integrity in astounding detail. Repairs he had made himself, and private contractors he'd consulted. There was a particularly worrisome crack in the foundation of the weathered parking garage above us. New concrete would have to be poured, though not by the man Crogher hired to examine it. He had not escaped Erebus. Far too slowly, and far too late, I realized that Crogher is not merely compound security. He's Fane's chief architect. Every hallway, every tunnel, every room is his design.

Lydia presented a tally of our living expenses, charged as she is with all the creature comforts: vehicles, cell phones, our bespoke wardrobes and our astronomical electric bill. How did no one suspect a parking garage that drained so much of the city's power? I suppose Bård has people in utilities, as well.

The sheer cost of our keep left me speechless. And during every report, all the way around the table, Darius never stopped jotting down the minutes of the meeting in his comically large ledger. He looked like a younger, sadder Ebenezer Scrooge.

Stela was the last to speak, and when she did even Fane sat forward. It became quite clear how deception of this magnitude was possible in the modern age: shell corporations. Stela was the Vice President of Finance, or the Chief Financial Officer of at least a dozen completely fabricated companies, and Andrew Opes was her right-hand man. She was eloquent as always and intimidatingly knowledgeable about market trends. Stela wasn't parroting what Andrew told her. We were spending at a rate three times higher than we were taking in.

The room grew tense, silent. Fane pinched his bottom lip, thanked Stela for her efforts and asked that she extend his gratitude to "her Mr. Opes." Bård, ever the gentle giant, broke the icy chill by ribbing Stela, saying she'd lost her touch and that Andrew clearly lacked *motivation*. Stela responded with a grim smirk. Lydia followed Bård's example, offering to accompany Stela on her next trip to Opes and Sons. Crogher offered to station the hounds outside Andrew's office. But it was the sharp clang of Darius' round wire frames that put a stop to all their friendly teasing.

Darius stood wearily with an eraser in his long hand. Like Stela, he was a different person in this room. It wasn't that I'd underestimated the family's intelligence, more that I had not yet been exposed to the sheer breadth of their collective wisdom. Together, they are a powerfully practical force. Darius didn't twitch nervously or talk to himself. He didn't obsessively wipe the stringy black hair from his eyes or laugh suddenly without reason. Darius walked to the nearest whiteboard and updated the figures, his weighty ledger discarded on the table.

The family was trending in the red. With their current spending we would have to tap into our emergency reserves in less than a year. A reserve which, as I understand, had not been touched since the family first relocated to America. We were not without ways to cut cost.

I became uncomfortably aware of just how large a gamble Stela was taking with my research. I caught a fleeting whisper exchanged between Stela and Fane and backed myself out of her thoughts as quickly as I could. Her wary side-eye told me that I hadn't acted soon enough, but when I'm nervous Stela is where I go. When Stela is nervous, her defenses fall and sometimes I just get dragged into the maelstrom of her mind. It had happened in the worst possible place, sandwiched between Stela and Fane.

I missed my cue to address the group. I hadn't been listening for the name Irina. It was Stela's thunderous "Elizabeth!" echoing in my mind that made me bolt upright in my chair. Fane threw his head back with a hearty laugh, Lydia snorted at me and Bård merely shook his head.

"Give your attention to the infant of the family, would you? Irina believes she can offset our financial woes," Fane said, leaning back in his enormous chair. He gestured broadly with an open hand to say the floor was mine.

My hypothesis was not well received. Crogher chucked his pen clear across the room where it wedged in the wood paneling. Lydia regarded me cautiously. Darius' marker sank slowly down the dry erase board in a bright red line. Bård, Fane and Stela sat perfectly still, arms crossed, and waited patiently me for me finish. My proposal was this:

"The blood tells a story. One memory after the next, in chaos until the brain dies. Why? How? What do we carry in our blood that bonds us to our victim's thoughts? How vastly altered is our brain chemistry to allow us to partake in this final assault of the mind? Everything in our lives begins with our blood. Our strength, our prey drive, the blood is the reason we can hear and sense one another.

"If we could understand the intricacies of our own biology, the scope of our uniqueness, then we may also be able to unlock hidden potential. What if we could learn to hone traits we only ever use on instinct?"

And finally, when all else failed to excite them: "Controlling the blood memories would mean carte blanche access to anything and everything our victims knew."

The room regarded me with the same hostile suspicion of my first few weeks among them. Absently, I thanked them for their time and sat. Both Stela and Fane placed a consoling hand on my forearm and shoulder. Fane opened the floor.

Lydia and Crogher were both adamantly against participating in any study. I wasn't surprised. From what I'd read in Stela's journals and gleaned from Darius' history lessons, I was not the first medical zealot who sought to put them under a microscope. Everyone, excluding myself, had been driven from their native lands by prying eyes and simple human curiosity.

Lydia went so far as to name drop Fredrik, the Strigoi captured by the Nazis in 1942. Darius had shown me the documents of his live dissection. Fredrik was unnamed—he belonged to none of the nine Moroi, but word travels quickly in small circles. Four members of the nearby Russian clan—under the direction of Fane's brother, Pytor—came for Fredrik in the night. They massacred any soldiers they encountered, seized the official records and burned the laboratory to the ground with Fredrik inside. I was offended by Lydia's comparison.

Crogher nodded alongside Lydia. He kept his muscled arms tightly crossed, shook a perfect dreadlock away from his face, and watched me closely for the faintest hint of animosity. I didn't argue with Lydia.

Bård, who had remained silent, spoke once Lydia had exhausted herself. He only had one question. "What do you need?"

Stela smiled warmly at him and picked up the reins of our debate. She turned in her seat to speak only to Bård, Fane and myself; effectively barring any interruption as no one would speak over someone addressing Fane. She said that to start I would require a fully equipped laboratory with as many samples of Strigoi blood as I could acquire.

Bård chuckled uneasily and leaned back in his chair. He stared grimly at Fane. "Establishing an area within the compound would be preferable, my Lord. But space is at a premium."

"The installation of instrumentation would be an obstacle, even if we had the space," Crogher said. He was not warming to the prospect but he is prized for his practicality in all matters.

"Crogher's right," I said. "Not only would cost play a factor, we would then have to buy the equipment and have it installed. I couldn't calibrate the instruments on my own." I shrugged and looked to Stela. "That would mean paying contractors to rough out a laboratory down here, then we would have to purchase the equipment and invite technicians down here for installation and programing."

"The hounds would have food enough for a fortnight," Crogher said. A droll laugh rippled through the tense atmosphere.

Stela shook her head. "The paper trail alone would incriminate us."

"My son," Fane said and snapped his fingers at a pouting Darius. "What have you to say against, or in defense of Irina's proposal?"

Darius tented his fingers beneath his weak chin. The family waited in suspense for his take.

Darius cleared his throat. "In my humble opinion, my Lord, I believe Irina may be onto something." He retrieved his wire spectacles from the margin of his book and pushed them up his aquiline nose.

"Why say you, Darius?" Lydia asked with respect. We had all inched to the edge of our seats. He shut the ledger in front of him, stacking his assorted books one at a time into neat columns.

"We have all tasted the memories for ourselves," he said. "They are not something Irina has imagined. To her point, there is no reason

I can fathom as to why blood should carry memory. It is a subject worthy of study, evidenced in our daily lives, and to begin we would first need to understand our own bodies."

Not one dissented. The room waited breathlessly for Fane's final judgment. He stood with hands the size of dinner plates splayed atop the table and his gaze took the temperature of each of us before he spoke.

"Bård, reach out to your associates. Have them scour the city for closed properties. A foreclosed medical laboratory or testing facility would be ideal. We may be able to find something at auction."

Bård nodded and offered me a sly wink.

"Stela, work with Bård and Andrew to facilitate all purchases. If we cannot find a location fully stocked and up for sale, work with Irina to itemize her needs. Again, an auction lot would be my preference. I want individual purchases kept to a bare minimum, and all purchases subject to my approval."

Stela bowed her head. "We will be discreet, my Lord."

Fane straightened to his towering height and his voice left no room for protest. "You will all contribute to Irina's study. Unless an individual can provide a more lucrative endeavor, contestation will not be tolerated." Fane stared solemnly at the room, his focus moving from one face to the next. "This meeting is adjourned."

Fane requested that Stela and Bård hang back to discuss "the finer details." In dismissal, Fane patronizingly congratulated me on a job well done. He assured me of his optimism and his confidence that my research would produce. Never has a vote of support sounded more like a threat.

Lydia and Darius were loitering in the common room, lost to each other in a hushed debate which stopped the moment I approached. Lydia smiled sheepishly at me.

"I do hope you can respect my apprehension," she said as she linked her arm in mine. "It was not personal." Together we walked toward the hall, Darius a step behind us. I bumped against her shoulder and admitted that I did. "You realize the risk should your little project hit a wall?" She turned and squeezed my hand.

I hadn't really considered it a personal risk until Fane's parting remarks. I was seduced by the possibility of discovery and I desperately wanted to help Stela. How was I supposed to know our finances were in dire straits? I flashed Lydia my cockiest grin and she kissed my cheek before disappearing down the hall toward Fane's quarters.

"She worries for you," Darius said, stepping out from behind me. "I worry for you too." The sconces cut thick shadows across his face, lending menace to his mien. He juggled the towering stack of books in his arms and whipped the black hair from his eyes. Everyone seemed intent upon impressing the severity of my situation upon me, as though the stakes were unclear. Perhaps I should have taken more caution not to overpromise.

"Spotlight is a dangerous thing," he warned. "Stela could tell you all about it. So could Lydia, for that matter."

"You mean being in Fane's line of sight is dangerous."

"I mean nothing of the sort. In fact, I have not said a word."

Darius turned away with a grave expression and made his way back to the safety of his library.

My request for a laptop had been fulfilled in the nick of time. Gone were the evenings of Stela's loaded silence while I busied myself reading medical texts, as she and I were both plugging away every free hour to scour the city for suitable real estate listings. Our new normal was a night spent at opposite ends of the sofa, our feet touching, laptops on our thighs. Stela fielded nightly calls from Mr. Opes about the condition of various abandoned properties around town. Her tone had changed with him, which made me painfully curious about the man she once reviled and with whom she had grown increasingly informal. I wanted to meet the money-laundering mastermind for myself. After all, I had a personal stake in his prowess.

Bård became a frequent visitor during those hectic weeks. Those nameless associates of his were also coming up empty, and it seemed we would be forced to renovate a vacant office space. Bård was becoming such a fixture in our suite that Stela changed the window projector to a portrait of an ice-capped lake. I asked her about that once, and she said it was her brother's favorite. Something that reminded him of home. I couldn't pronounce the name of the lake as beautifully as she did.

On occasion, Stela would converse with Bård in his mother tongue. They didn't intend to leave me out and were quick to apologize and explain. One evening they had an animated discussion entirely in French. The family had spent time in Paris at the turn of the 19th century. I only caught the gist of what they said—I hadn't spoken French since eighth grade—and I didn't dare interrupt them. No one makes Stela laugh the way Bård can.

When he finally bid us farewell, I laid my head in Stela's lap. She ran her fingers through my hair and leaned down to kiss my forehead.

"You speak French."

"*C'est vrai*," she said, playfully tracing the shell of my ear.

"Can I ask you something?" I held her hand and brought it my heart. Stela nodded. "You and Bård…"

"Never."

"Never?" I sat up on my knees. "I wouldn't be angry, Stela. You two are so close, and he brings something out in you."

She smiled and shook her head, the humor slowly slipping away. "I would not conceal something as trivial as a romantic entanglement from you, my darling." She pulled me closer by the wrist until I was nearly in her lap. "Bård and I have always been close." She fiddled with my fingers, lost to her thoughts for a moment. "Actually," she said with detached amazement, "he is the only member of my family that I have not—"

"The only?" I gaped dumbly. "As in, everyone else?"

Stela tossed her head back and laughed heartily. "Forever is far longer than you realize, Elizabeth. One bores easily."

"But…even Lydia?"

Stela tilted her head and leaned closer. "Are you jealous of her or me?" I shoved her shoulder lightly and she wrapped her arms around my waist.

"You don't even like each other!" I said as she brushed her lips against my neck.

Stela nipped at my jaw playfully. "It was always in Fane's company. Lydia and I were never alone." I stilled, and Stela drew back sensing a cold shift in my mood. She huffed and sat up straight. "Must you be so puritanical?"

"I didn't say anything."

"No," she said, leaning back against the arm of the sofa. "Nor do you need to."

"Can you stop acting like I don't have a right to feel…" I had plenty of words for it, and they all sounded painfully insecure.

"Feel what?" she asked softly.

"Insufficient."

Stela cupped my chin and raised my eyes to hers. "That is the most ridiculous thing you have ever said to me." She pulled me into a drowning kiss that ebbed and flowed until all my doubts became irrelevant. Our foreheads rested against one another lazily, and I laughed at myself.

"Come to bed with me," she demanded, her hands on my hips. "I will speak French to you, if you like." Her knowing smile was enough to make me remember the need to blush.

"Maybe…"

It was all the encouragement Stela needed. With her usual grace she lifted us both off the couch and crawled up the bed while I clung to her. She was more tender with me that night than any since before I was turned. Her touches lingered, and though I barely understood a single lilting word I felt her meaning throughout my whole body.

In the last few minutes of intimate silence, before the sun blossomed across the sky and took me away from her, I mused on Stela's seemingly perfect French. She could assimilate anywhere, to anything, and she had been forced to do so countless times. She was brilliant, cultured, she had a warrior's knack for survival and a certain ruthlessness that I was fortunate to be barricaded behind, instead of standing in its destructive path.

"Let's go away together," I whispered.

Stela smiled against the top of my head. "Where should we go?" She ran her hand down my back, urging me closer.

"Anywhere."

"Paris, perhaps?" she asked playfully. I tilted my head up to look at her, and she read my sincerity. Her smile faltered, and I hated to watch the light leave her bright eyes. I didn't expect her to sound so weary. "Beloved, we are home now, but this will not always be home. We will all be forced to move on, eventually."

"No," I said, leaning up on my arm. "Just the two of us, Stela. Let's cut our losses and go."

"What losses?" She laughed and nudged me gently. "Why should we run?" I shrugged and lay back down, my head pushed under her chin. "This is about your experiment," she surmised, running her fingers through my hair.

"Yes and no," I said. "Does it have to be about any one thing? Or anyone else? Can't it be about us? I want a life with you, Stela. Just you and me."

I didn't expect her to understand, or to throw off the covers and whisk me away right that instant. It wasn't about making her choose between her family and our relationship. I needed her to know what I wanted more than anything, even if it was something we couldn't have, or something she would never give me. Words have the power to shape our reality, and I hoped that on some level just speaking my desire aloud was enough.

"Our world does not work that way," she said cautiously, her voice soft. She took my face in her hands and examined me closely, as though she was seeing me for the first time, committing my eyes and mouth to her memory. "Thank you," she whispered, and placed a delicate kiss on my parted lips.

"For what?" I asked.

"Wanting me all to yourself."

It was a quarter to nine the next evening when Stela's phone vibrated on the coffee table. She'd kept it on silent since I changed her ring tone from an innocuous chirp to Bonnie Tyler's "Total Eclipse of The Heart," which for the record was hilarious—even Bård thought so. But I had since been banned from touching any of her electronics—and being better able to respect boundaries than she believes—I made no attempt to answer the call, certain that she could hear it rattle against the table.

Stela emerged from the bathroom in a cloud of steam, rubbing the wet tendrils of her blond hair briskly with a white towel.

"Yes," she answered. Her warmest greeting. She fixed me with an unreadable expression. "Then we will have to move quickly," she said and settled between my legs. My fingers traced up the razor edge of her obliques, and she swatted my hand away with a crooked smile.

"Andrew, I will not be alone this evening. The space is not intended for my use." I sat up and stopped trying to distract her. Now that I was certain the call was meant more for me than Mr. Opes could possibly know, I focused my hearing just in time to catch his vehement refusal. Stela snapped her fingers at me and pointed toward the bathroom. I stood up to ready myself.

"My ward," she said. "You met her on video conference. This is not a negotiation, Andrew. She has the final word on the matter." Perhaps reading the understandable hesitation in his voice, she moved beyond her own annoyance and into reassurance. "She will be on her best behavior," she promised and glared at me with an arched brow. "I will not leave your side for a moment," she said, hanging up.

"He's found a space," I said.

"Wash up. We have a long night ahead of us."

Stela extended a towel toward me as I stepped out of the shower. "We need to discuss the ground rules before our meeting, dearest,"

"*Rules*?" I said, wrapping myself up. "Something new and different for us."

Stela winked at me in the mirror. "Yes, rules. Your favorite. Repeat after me," she said. "I will not attack, threaten or otherwise unsettle

Mr. Opes." I humored her through stiff lips as she swiped at my mouth with a wand of gloss. We were pressed for time and she was nervous.

"Elizabeth," she sighed. "This is of the utmost importance. Andrew plays a crucial role in the safety and comfort of our family."

"Jesus, Stela. I said I wouldn't hurt him." I shirked away from her and appraised myself in the mirror.

"You know, for an agnostic, you use that name quiet liberally when riled," Stela replied, head tilted.

The drive was tense, but not because of me. I hadn't demanded that we drive separately. I didn't protest when she told me she would be driving. I hadn't even asked her where we were going, and she did not offer that information.

"What is it about Mr. Opes that makes him special to you?" I asked, not really expecting an answer.

"The Opes family is a legacy we created. Fane and I," she said. "A bargain was struck between Fane and Harold Opes, Andrew's forebear, generations ago. The Opes' fortune is entwined with our own. Their successes, their failures are ours, and vice versa.

"Harold Opes entered into a pact with Fane. In exchange for his service as a financier, and the service of at least one heir in each generation, an immense wealth would follow the Opes family through the ages."

"So, Andrew Opes is in bed with Fane because of a deal his great-great-grandfather made?"

"Precisely." She nodded.

"That doesn't bother him? Or you?" I asked.

"Andrew is the first Opes to object to our arrangement. I never considered the morality of what we asked before he inherited the company, and he is generously compensated for his pains," she said. The more she talked about the Opes family, the more her mood improved, but I didn't believe that Andrew was the cause. There was a jewel in this arrangement, but it wasn't him.

"So, Mr. Opes does resent Fane."

"Andrew resents me, because I am the face he knows," she said wearily. "Just not enough to terminate our arrangement."

"And how would he do that?" I asked. Stela turned briefly in my direction, and the answer was written in her grave silence. "Death really is the only out with you people, isn't it?"

Stela huffed a dry menacing laugh. "I do so wish that you would stop referring to your own kind as *you people*."

"And I wish you'd give me the whole story for once, but here we are."

She pulled the car beneath a graffitied viaduct on the outskirts of an industrial park. The crumbling buildings sagged heavily, squat little structures.

"Andrew was a taciturn little boy who grew into an entitled man," she said quietly. She closed her eyes briefly, took a centering breath and exhaled the worst of her temper. "When his daughter was born it was clear to us all that she would be twice the steward her father is."

"What does his daughter have to do with it?" I asked.

"We could sense the potential in Christine Opes, much like we can smell cruelty on others. She is fated to us."

"You know, for a nihilist, you talk about fate an awful lot."

Stela fought the tug of her approaching smile and tossed a pair of sunglasses in my lap as she slid her own up the bridge of her nose. "I resent that description."

I leaned over the center console and kissed her cheek.

A black Mercedes SUV cut its lights and pulled alongside us. Stela tapped the frame of her sunglasses and pointed at me. "Put those on," she said. "Under no circumstances should you remove them in his presence."

I did as instructed and not a moment too soon. The elusive Mr. Opes appeared at the hood of our car. Stela and I exited in unison and kept close to our respective doors while he steeled himself.

He was clearly the man I first met on video conference. I hadn't been able to get a sense of him through a screen. Without so much as shaking his hand I could see it, the weakness Stela reviled in him. The egoism. His proclivity for scotch which anyone could have smelled on him.

"Kathryn." He nodded. "And you must be—"

"Andrew!" Stela's sudden outburst made both Andrew and me jump. She took a step forward and slid her sunglasses down and her wide eyes devoured all the light within a city block. "She will be Natalie to you."

Natalie? I did mention that I liked the name. And then I realized that Andrew Opes knew my name, my real name. Elizabeth Dumas was scrawled across several hundred pages of paperwork he had signed off on to ensure that my mother's brownstone was sold, that my trust was intact. I didn't know what would happen should he use that name, only that when Stela told me her name upon our first encounter it forever bound me to her. I desperately did not want this angry little man bound to me for the rest of his natural life.

"Natalie. Yes," he said, visibly shaken and staring blankly into Stela's black eyes.

"Good evening Mr. Opes," I said, careful not to rattle him further.

"So, Andrew," Stela said, flicking her glasses back into place, "shall we survey the space?"

Andrew gestured for Stela to take the lead toward a short, flat building with no windows. She walked behind the car to my side and took my hand. Mr. Opes stayed behind a few paces, holding a manila envelope against his chest like a shield. He hobbled over the rough pavement. I couldn't blame him for his wariness—apart from the threat Stela and I posed to his physical safety, we were not in the best area. In fact, the boarded windows, the crumbling brick facades riddled with tags from local gangs were all enough to unsettle me until I remembered the only threat to me comes from my own kind.

The door was padlocked and Mr. Opes struggled to open it. The air inside was stale, rife with mildew and rats. I could hear their sharp nails clicking in corners, soft bodies thudding within the walls. In all my time in the tunnels I'd never seen a trace of a single rodent, thanks to the insatiable appetite of the hounds. Stela entered first with an arm around my waist, more to protect Mr. Opes from me than anything else.

"Can you see, Andrew?" she asked.

"Well enough," he replied. "There should be power to the building, but I think it would be wise to keep things dim in this neighborhood."

He was right. The building had been a clinic that closed at the end of the Gulf War because of poor management. After that the property had been sliced up and several small medical practices moved in and then out. There were still names printed across the glass windows of reception areas, everything from physical therapy to orthodontics, which boded well for the possibility of salvaged equipment.

The hall ended at a door. Stela took the key from Mr. Opes' outstretched hand and unlocked it. Andrew entered last and groped for the interior walls for a light switch and the fluorescents flickered to life.

"This room is completely contained," he said, markedly more comfortable now that he wasn't fumbling in the dark. "Only one door in or out, no windows. Pathology was here in the first clinic, a private practice later on, drug testing after that. It's all in the file."

It had been a dumping ground for at least ten years. Crumpled specimen bags littered the floor. Three centrifuges were stacked on the cabinet in the corner. Two exam tables bent back toward the ground, a stretcher tucked between them like an ironing board. Busted slides in the only sink, and sharps containers ripped from the walls and spilled on the ground. Two lightboxes sat propped against the island in the center. A phlebotomy cart sagged against the far wall on broken wheels, but a small refrigerator with a glass front gleamed like new nearby.

Stela stalked the edges of the room, keeping conversation with Mr. Opes. I had withdrawn from their back and forth, drifting my hands over each discarded instrument. I knew enough of Stela's temperament to tell that she was less than pleased. She had begun speaking more rapidly, and by the time I turned around she'd stopped walking to pull a dirty needle from the heel of her shoe. She held it like a knife, asked Andrew if he considered himself a funny man. Did he believe this rancid hovel was befitting of her patronage? I reached her the second Andrew's spine slammed into the door. Her face inches from his, the needle a hair's breadth from his chin.

"It's perfect."

Stela blinked. Mr. Opes let his head thud back against the doorframe and loosened his tie. Stela turned toward me slowly, incredulous. She tilted her head menacingly and glared at Andrew's sweat-soaked face.

"Is this a joke?" she asked, more to Mr. Opes than to me. "Have the two of you been in contact without my knowledge?" Andrew stumbled over himself to assure her we had not. "Absolutely not…Natalie, I will not have you working in squalor." She clasped her hands together firmly as though the matter was decided.

"Dearest," I said, prying her hands apart so I could hold them. "Look at this space." I took her around the room again, helping her to see the potential. It was self-contained, full of equipment that could be salvaged or sold, largely removed from pedestrian traffic but still readily accessible if we needed anything delivered. Should anyone think to ask about the new business moving in, we were just opening another clinic and not even Stela could put a price on a cover like that.

She softened and forgot all about our audience as she leaned in for a kiss, which was cut too short by Mr. Opes' foolish and revelatory intake of breath.

Andrew floundered, peeled his gaze away with some difficulty and searched for any distraction that would conceal his considerable shock. In the heat of the moment I failed to realize that poor Mr. Opes simply couldn't believe that "Kathryn Radu," the woman of his nightmares, my Stela, was capable of such tender affection. Instead, his reaction seemed like garden-variety homophobia to me. I didn't decide to approach him. I don't even remember crossing the room. One minute I was kissing Stela and the next I was towering over Mr. Opes, wondering what kind of effort was required to split someone in two.

Stela never gave me the chance to find out. She gripped me by the shoulder with enough force to promise pain if I tried to shake her loose. "I want to thank you for your pains, Andrew," she said from behind me. She didn't position herself between us. The color had drained from his face completely. "I know this was a strange request." She placed her free hand possessively on my hip. Andrew looked down quickly, then back up to me. I was a weakness he did not know she had. There wasn't much to be done to minimize exposure, but Stela could make it clear the lengths she would go to protect us.

"I can't tell you how pleased I am," I told him, and stuck my hand out. He stared down in disbelief at my offered hand. I tilted my head down and peered into Andrew's face from above my sunglasses. "As I'm sure Stela has told you, I'm difficult on my best days." His hand closed around mine, but he did not shake it. He was lost the moment he looked into my eyes. Despite my raging hunger, I don't have Stela's bloodlust. So, what Andrew saw in my eyes was not the image of himself dismembered. Instead, I focused my thoughts on the terrible pressure I was under to perform, the ferocity with which I loved the woman behind me.

Andrew yanked his slick hand away, the blood pounding in his temples, and with a smile I slid my sunglasses back into place. He blinked away the lingering effects of the invasion and groped blindly for the door handle. He ripped open the door and spouted hasty assurances that he would email the documents first thing in the morning, promising us discretion. His footfall down the hall was frantic. Twice he stumbled in the dark. He prayed out loud until I heard his car door close and the engine turn over.

Once we were alone, Stela spun around. She raked the back of my head with her nails, her eyes afire. "That was quite the gamble," she whispered. Her lips traced my jaw, kissed the soft patch of skin below my ear.

"You loved it." I leaned into her embrace, my body opening to her mouth, her hands. "Besides, it worked. He's terrified of me." I tugged her lower lip between my teeth and licked the blood that bloomed. My mind raced, though Stela's intentions were clear I couldn't help but consider all the work ahead to prepare the lab. Stela, who had moved to my neck, sensed my distraction and groaned. She pulled back and held my cheeks.

"There will be time later," she said, stroking my cheeks with her thumbs. "For now, let us celebrate."

"You want to hunt," I said, smiling.

"Can you think of a better way?" She took my hand and flicked off the lights.

All the other vacant offices would need to be inventoried, as it was possible there was equipment of use. I tallied the mental checklist of tasks ahead as we walked back to the car.

"What should we have this evening?" she asked, her eyes wide and starved. She took my hand and held it against her thigh. Her flippant attitude about death still bothered me, though not nearly as much as I claimed. My hunger was constant, and the more I considered what I wanted the more upset I became. Feeding from Stela or from Fane was the only time my thirst was satiated. She would let me, if I asked her. But it was getting much harder to stop myself once I started.

"Someone violent for you," I said. "Someone beautiful for me."

Stela was quiet, but her smile said that she approved. She turned the key in the ignition. "Let us find a lovely couple to share on the Riverwalk."

It would be wonderful to say that I found her proposal distasteful. It would not, however, be true.

* * *

The starched white cotton tickles my wrists, the fabric a durable but abrasive material, heavily bleached. Everything I've ever wanted and nothing I earned. I run my thumb across the bright blue thread stitched into the breast pocket: M.D. and a blank space where my name should be. Probably best to leave it this way. To see Irina stitched here would have broken my heart, and Elizabeth Dumas would have given us away.

"I thought..." Stela begins. "Where are you?" she asks, and I smirk at her choice of words.

"I was just thinking about how we got here."

Stela runs her hand down the lapel of my new lab coat, the one thing I hadn't included on any supply list. Couldn't bring myself to request. "I can return it," she says, tugging on the coat. I shake my head. "Let me have a look at you," she says.

"I'm not a doctor."

Stela laughs, cocks her eyebrow. "According to whom?"

"The medical board, Stela."

"I was unaware there was a license required to study our kind." She doesn't want to laugh, but she finds my ambivalence absurd. "You would think that Fane would inform me of the criteria before authorizing a purchase as exorbitant as this facility."

"Stela…"

"Take it off. You are not required to wear the coat simply because I gave it to you."

"It's not the coat," I say, and Stela crosses her arms protectively. Stela who is usually steadfast and so confident in her decisions. We don't really do gifts, or material gestures of any kind and I am ruining a lovely thought by failing to explain what the coat means. "I wanted to earn this."

Stela knots her fists in the front of the coat and shakes me back and forth in a lazy, exhausted way. "My darling," she says, "your life will be so much easier when you stop measuring your success against the masses. You may have taken an unconventional route, but here you are, in a lab of your own, with the white coat you worked for and your very first subject."

She drops onto a stool and pushes up the sleeve of her ivory sweater. She splays her arm across the polished steel table and stares up at me expectantly. Her alabaster skin glows eerily under the harsh lights. I open the drawer and retrieve a tourniquet and syringe.

"She dresses like a doctor," Stela says, "has the instruments of one."

"You're a little turned on by this, aren't you?" I pull up a stool and secure the tourniquet around her bicep. The skin is completely opaque, not even the hint of a vein. She must be starving.

"Would you think less of me if I admitted that I am?" she asks.

I purse my lips, pull her arm straight. "You wouldn't be the first patient or subject to crush on their doctor."

Stela grins. The median cubital is barely visible in her arm, a hint of a shadow.

"Will I bruise?" she asks, still smiling brightly. Incredibly pleased with herself.

I release the tourniquet and retrieve a tube from the counter. "You're in rare form this evening."

Stela shrugs. "Must be the uniform."

Stela collects the single drop of blood that blooms in the crook of her arm on the pad of her finger, pops her finger in her mouth. She stands behind me as I hold the vial toward the light and a carmine shadow cuts across the steel table. "Is it everything you hoped and more?" she asks, staring expectantly at the tube in my hand.

I invert the blood tube and place the vial onto the rotating wheel. "If I knew what a willing participant you'd be, I would have taken more than one."

Stela takes a step back, her hands raised in mock surrender. "That was quite enough for one night," she says. "Besides, one of us should hunt."

The mere mention of the word causes the walls of my stomach to clench, and suddenly that vial of Stela's blood is the only thought in my mind. Who would know if I failed to study it and drank it instead? Stela's blood…probably still warm…

Stela kisses the side of my throat, chuckles as the unexpected contact makes me jump. She scoops her jacket off the counter. "Focus on your work," she says. "I will handle the rest. Hunting for two is hardly a task I begrudge."

"Should I meet you somewhere?" I ask, distracted, my eyes never leaving the enticing sample.

Stela slips her arms into her buff leather jacket. "I will bring your mark when I collect you. The logistics will handle themselves," she says, brushing my concerns away. She makes it to the door, stops, turns back toward me. "Have you any ether?"

Ether? The request is just odd enough to distract me from my hunger. "What? No. Why?"

She bites the corner of her mouth, drums her fingers on the door. "Pity."

* * *

After collecting a sample from Bård and wishing him a fruitful evening, I pull my stool alongside the island, eyeing the vials. Every cell in my body aches with hunger. The pain is so sharp, so clear I swear it almost has its own distinct voice.

Focus on the science.

Focus.

I slide Stela's sample from the wheel, turn it over in my shaking hands, as the cautioning of all her siblings rings in my ears: Do not compare yourself against Stela.

How many times have I been warned? I know firsthand that her sleep schedule is unique. Her ability to focus her memories. Her tolerance for sunlight. I was in the lab for less than an hour when the fluorescent lights began to test my eyes, a persistent ache that built until I was forced to wear my sunglasses indoors. My fingers tremble as I place Stela's vial back on the wheel.

When in doubt, know thyself. I retrieve a fresh slide, print my initials along with the date on the white edge and prick my finger. My blood spreads in a perfect circle between two pressed pieces of glass and I pull my open laptop toward me as I note the obvious. The color is as I suspected, a shade I'm intimately familiar with at this point. The smell, however, is rich in copper, like a handful of tarnished pennies. I spin my stool around toward the microscope.

My sample is thrilling. The shape is distinct. My erythrocytes are larger than they should be and perfectly spherical. Not small biconcaved discs like usual. I glance at the blood tube sitting on the bench and observe that the blood is moving independently. It seems to be throbbing in the vial, almost trying to escape. I have to remember to take a sample from my victim when Stela brings my meal, to see for myself the way these cells react when human blood is introduced.

As I record my observations an unwelcome sound reaches my ears. I close my laptop and turn toward the door. The footfall is light—not intentionally so, but graceful—the faint indication that one of my kind approaches and wants to make themselves known. Not Stela, my blood would have warned me. Would the sample in the tube show that? Would blood removed from my body crawl across the counter and reach for her? I get up from my stool and unlock the door.

"Good evening, *better half*," Lydia says with a smile, pushing the door wide. "I heard you were accepting donations."

"Lydia, what are you doing here?" I step aside as she prances into the lab, sliding her dark Ray Bans over her sensitive eyes. She turns on a four-inch heel, ruby-colored and satin to match her slip of a dress. She slides off her black leather jacket and tosses it carelessly on the center island.

"I came to make a deposit, of course," she says with a shrug, clicking around the lab in her Manolos. "Unless my currency is no good here."

"You know that's not what I meant." Lydia takes a seat. I stand in front of her, my hip braced against the metal edge. "What are you doing here tonight? I wasn't expecting you for another two."

Crogher, Darius, and Lydia are on the same feed cycle and no one goes aboveground without permission from Fane for any reason other than hunting. When Stela would sneak off to visit me for a few hours before I'd been turned she was perpetually terrified that Fane would find out.

Lydia's lips curl into a sly smile. "I must say, I am impressed by the leniency Fane shows one as young as yourself," she says idly. "This little project of yours has secured you at least one extra outing a week.

True?" She swivels back and forth on her stool while I open a new syringe.

"Apparently I'm not the only one. How'd you manage to sneak out this evening?" I ask. I pull up another stool and sit in front of her.

Lydia chuckles and leans forward as though sharing a secret. "Fane appreciates my enthusiasm."

"I'll bet he does," I say. "So, you what? Told him you just couldn't wait to volunteer for the study you very nearly crushed with your protests during the monthly meeting?"

"You seem surprised," she says, shaking the hair out of her eyes. "Am I incapable of changing my mind?"

"Incapable is not a word I'd use to describe you. Dogged, perhaps."

"That is my favorite thing about you, Irina," she says. "You are honest to a fault, as am I."

"Straighten your arm out for me, please." I tap her elbow and she extends her hand into my lap, resting her palm on my thigh.

"What are the gloves for?" she asks, snapping the latex against my wrist.

"I'm just super method about this whole thing," I reply dryly. Lydia glowers at me.

Though her skin is darker than mine, much richer than Stela's, it's just as smooth and unobstructed. Not a vein in sight. I hold her arm, rub the skin between my thumbs. "A doctor and a masseuse," she says. "No wonder your Maker is so taken with you."

"Just hold still."

The muscles in her forearm tense and the needle splinters into half a dozen pieces, the tourniquet busted and hanging off her bicep. Lydia throws her head back uproariously. "Oh Irina," she cries, "you should have seen the look on your face!"

I toss the busted syringe onto the table and retrieve a fresh needle and tourniquet. Lydia makes a show of calming herself in between delighted giggles. She mocks my seriousness with an exaggerated frown. "You know, it's moments like these that help me understand why Stela finds you so irritating," I say, tying her arm off a second time.

"Well, there is no reason to be insulting," she says. "I was only trying to get a rise out of you."

Lydia has fed more recently than Stela has and the blood flows more easily. I'll need to make a note of that. She watches me closely from behind her dark sunglasses. She pushes the hair back out of my eyes and her knuckles brush my furrowed brow. "I am glad to have fouled your first attempt," she decides. "You take yourself far too seriously."

"All finished," I say and pat her arm.

"What now?" she asks.

"Now I record my observations."

Lydia leaps up from her stool to sit on the island instead, her legs crossed at the ankle. "That sounds dreadfully dull."

"Tedious."

Lydia watches me closely as I label her sample and place it with the others. "I thought this science of yours would be a bit more..." she waves a whimsical hand, "glamorous."

I laugh in spite of myself, though I'm still anxious to get rid of her. Not because I don't enjoy her company. I just can't shake the feeling that Fane sent her here to observe and report back. "We can't all be as glamorous as you are, my friend," I say. Flattery goes a long way with Lydia.

"How kind of you to say that of a poor merchant's daughter." She loves a misleading statement. Perhaps she does it intentionally to see how far I've read in Stela's journals. Whether I know the truth of how she came to be. And like any Type A personality, I can't resist correcting her.

"Hardly. Your father was a very wealthy man. He owned a fleet of trade ships."

Lydia's smile wilts. "He was to be the wealthiest merchant in the Empire upon my marriage."

"To Selim III," I say. "Sultan of the Ottoman Empire." Lydia nods distractedly. "Well, for what it's worth I can't picture you as anyone's eighth wife."

Lydia stiffens, and it's clear that flattery was not enough this time. "I was betrothed but not delivered." She clenches her fists. "My father was executed. My family was ruined."

"I'm sorry." I place my hand over hers, expecting to be shaken off. "I didn't know."

"Imagine that," she says with sneer. "Stela neglected to mention all the facts."

I withdraw my hand and Lydia hops off the counter.

"Do you still think of them?" I ask. "Your family?"

Lydia frets over my lapel. "You want to know if I can still see their faces," she says with unsettling certainty. "The answer is no, dear sister. I lost their faces long ago. All I have now is a silhouette."

I don't know if the answer is comforting or terrifying. I suppose it depends on the relationship one has with their family. My mother is persistent as a plague, and I think even if her image is destined to fade, her voice in my ear will remain a constant. Lydia presses against me, reaches around my back for the vial labeled with her name.

"You still think of her," she says. "Your mother. Claire, was it?" Lydia doesn't need my answer, so I don't offer. She raises the vial of blood to the light. "You loved her very well. I would venture to say that the only thing you love better in this world is Stela."

This is not the first time that Lydia has known more than I've shared. I'm starting to wonder if Stela has exaggerated my muteness to Fane. What if he can hear my thoughts? Lydia certainly seems to have a beat on me. "You told me once that I was exactly how you pictured me."

Lydia giggles, leans forward to drop the blood sample into my breast pocket. "And you want to know how I had any impression of you at all," she surmises, delighted at the prospect of a new game. "Stela showed you to me," she says. "It was an accident. I was in a bad way and I fed from her. She did not betray you."

"You knew about me before I was turned?"

"I knew of you before Fane was certain of you," she says. "You were written all over Stela. Your compassion, your fire, your sorrow."

From this angle she has unmitigated access to my face, and I'm careful to conceal my emotions before she can read them, her black irises just visible above the top of her frames. "You told Fane about me." I focus on the wheel, the spinning blood samples, anything to keep my eyes off her. But Lydia is patient and still as stone. She follows my gaze.

"All this fuss and equipment for something that should be tasted, not examined." She stands up abruptly, leans around me to throw away a piece of the needle she shattered. When she straightens—directly in my face—her sunglasses are gone.

I've been intruded upon by Lydia before, but at a greater distance. She's intentionally caught me off guard, and I'm certain that was the motivation behind all this polite conversation. The sound of her blood thunders in my ears. "Drinking the samples won't answer my questions," I say.

Lydia cups the side of my face. "Perhaps you ask the wrong questions." The full weight of her stare feels like sinking into a warm dark pit. Not as soothing as Stela's gaze, or as sedate as Fane's, but compelling none the less. She smiles at me with fangs extended and pierces her bottom lip. I can't look away. She brushes her blood-smeared lip against my mouth and I catch it between my teeth. Lydia makes a delighted sound and wraps her arms around my neck. *Don't.*

Don't do this. But it's too late. My mouth is open to her blood-tinged tongue.

I shove against her sternum with one hand, but my other arm is locked around her waist. Her blood shows me what she would have me know. A distant laugh, sharp as a scream. An image of a bustling port, Lydia's mortal home, rosy at dusk. Swept streets beneath her sandaled feet. Stela standing at the mouth of a dark and deserted cul-de-sac, waving her down and begging for help. Bård lying in wait behind a kiosk, scooping Lydia up in his giant arms while Stela watches without interest.

"Stop." I grab her by the hair as the puncture on her lip heals. My palm spreads across her chest, pushing her back, but she still has me by the waist.

Lydia laughs dryly but doesn't let go. "Would you rather wait for your Maker to join us?" she whispers, running her hands up my back. "It would not be the first time that Stela and I shared a mate." She drags the tip of her tongue against the needle point of her incisor.

I grab her by the throat, force her back at arm's length, my body trembling, my eyes glued to the smear of blood at the corner of her lips.

"Stop!" I scream into her bewildered face.

"What is the meaning of this?" A voice booms in the windowless room.

Lydia's hands leave me in a rush, she raises them beside her head. Stela steps through the door lugging a young man behind her, his wrists and ankles bound with zip ties. Stela drags him by his black hair, so dark it shines with blue hues. She tosses him in the corner beside the fridge and plants her hands on her hips. "Irina…" she says calmly, strolling toward me. "Release her. Now."

My arm trembles from the force of my grip, and I grit my teeth so hard the blood I taste at the back of my throat is my own. Deep inside, that hungry, child-like voice urges me on. Lydia gapes at me, her eyes darting frantically to Stela. Stela presses against my right side, her fingers loosening my grasp as she lifts my hand away. "Enough," she whispers. "Let her go."

Lydia bolts upright, holding her neck protectively. The hunt has hold of both of us now, Lydia's snarl a mirror of my own twisted face. She screams at me, but the words are lost. All I can hear is the pounding of her heart.

Stela turns toward the young man she carted in with her. "One more word and I will rip out your tongue." She places herself deliberately between Lydia and me.

"Fane will know of this," Lydia says with a venomous glare.

Stela laughs—a sound too coarse to be genuine—and seizes Lydia by the wrist. She straightens her least favorite sibling's dress, her hair. "You intend to tell our Lord that a fledgling bested you?" she asks incredulously. "By all means Lydia, tell him. In fact, allow me."

Lydia rips her wrist free and takes a clumsy step back. She opens her mouth but closes it again without a witty rejoinder. The look she gives me from over Stela's shoulder brooks no misunderstanding. Our easy camaraderie is a thing of the past. She storms out of the lab, the door thrown open, her footsteps shaking the foundations. Beside the door, the young man Stela brought with her weeps silently, his jeans soaked with urine. Still, he is beautiful. A soft, patrician face, tall even curled up on himself. My taste to the letter.

Stela turns around slowly, her eyebrow arched imperiously at me, her mouth tight. "Dearest, have you completely lost your mind?"

"What?" I ask, pulling my attention away with some difficulty from the meal on the floor. "Me? She forced herself on me!"

"Did she now?" Stela crosses her arms.

"She enthralled me in my own lab…" My chest is heaving.

"And you thought," Stela says, pointing absently at me, "that the appropriate response to an unwanted advance was to strangle Fane's favorite?"

I clench my fists and my nails split my palms, anything to keep from lashing out at Stela. "You weren't here."

"Did you try talking to her?"

"Of course, I did," I whisper through clenched teeth. "I told her to stop. She didn't. So, I stopped her."

"With force."

"Are you seriously lecturing me on gratuitous violence?"

"No." She's as unaffected by my rage as she was by Lydia's panic. "I am cautioning you against impetuousness."

"How dare you."

Stela's lackadaisical air shatters. She towers over me, dwarfing the entire lab and gestures wildly with furious hands. "You were out of line!" she shouts. "Lydia is fond of you. That is no secret. Fane is partial to Lydia. That is no secret." My pulse pounds in my throat, but I'm too disgusted with her to speak. "Do you have any idea the kind of power Lydia has in our house? The unholy hell she could visit on both our lives?"

"She kissed me Stela," I say, bewildered. "How is that irrelevant to you?" I'm not sure what is worse: Lydia playing me to steal a kiss or that Stela doesn't have the decency to be sympathetic or jealous.

"It was a compliment, Elizabeth. And you rebuffed her by shaking hands with her neck."

"A compliment?" The fire in my belly threatens to engulf me. Every muscle tenses for a fight and part of me wishes Stela was just a little bit closer. "What would you have had me do?" I ask, my voice deadly calm.

Stela closes the space between us, clenching her fists, her face an inch from mine. "Politely decline," she says, completely serious. The fury in her eyes is meant for no one but me.

"Oh god…" I shake my head, repulsed. "What *am* I to you?" Stela blinks but says nothing. "Some kind of party favor? Is that how this works? You have your fun with me, then pass me around to your family?"

Stela's right arm twitches. I flinch and hate myself for it. She takes a step back to collect herself, slowly flexing her hands. "Must you be so childish?" she asks wearily. "You are not my property, Elizabeth. You are my heart's joy, but you are not my possession." She shakes her head sadly. "Lydia fancies you, and she is Fane's. I adore you, and I am Fane's. We belong to him, dear one. Not to each other." She looks toward the open door. "Not even to ourselves."

There it is. The truth I've been waiting for and fearing all along. The fury is transcendent. I press myself against her, even as she inches back. "Well, aren't you a *good* little soldier."

I wish the pain in Stela's eyes was enough. I wish it was enough to know that my point was made, that somewhere inside she understands. It just isn't. Stela is the first to look away and when she does, I know beyond the shadow of a doubt that I will never forget this moment.

I take off my lab coat and hang it up beside the door. The dinner she brought me curls his legs close to his chest, mumbling ardent pleas against the tape across his mouth. Abstractly, I consider Stela's earlier request for ether, and the memory of our playful banter is the final twist of the knife.

"Where are you going?" she asks as I step out into the hall.

I turn only halfway. I can't face her again. "To our palace in the fucking sewer."

She takes a small, uncertain step. "Feed first." Her voice betrays nothing.

"You eat him. I've lost my appetite."

VIII

The Inviolable Truths of Immovable Objects

I believed it in the moment. I had recited that speech to myself many times: We do not belong to each other. We are not our own. A mantra that served to remind me that no matter the depth of my connection with my reticent fledgling, she was not mine to keep. The look she gave me...crestfallen, then bleeding into contemptuous. I had not seen that side of Elizabeth since the evening I showed up uninvited to Claire's sickroom.

Naturally Elizabeth shut mc out, as she had before, as she will certainly do again. I trailed her at a respectful distance to ensure that her anger did not cause her to act rashly. I watched her storm out of her laboratory and walk down empty streets, courting traffic, disappointed when none came. She knew I was there but kept her face forward, her arms crossed.

A block before she reached the subway platform her right arm shot out to seize the lapel of a sharply dressed gentleman in his early forties. From the cut of his suit and the slicked back hair a banker of some kind. Elizabeth wheeled him around the corner of a theater without even bothering to cover his mouth. She feasted until the screaming stopped.

The body was left in a crumpled pile and I could follow her no further, which I suspect was the point behind abandoning a kill. She knew I would be forced to cover up her mess. What was strange was the blood spatter, if you can call it that. There was a black pool beside the body, as though she had spat several mouthfuls upon the ground. She was furious with me, that much was obvious, but furious enough to waste her only decent meal in three days? For one so young, it hardly seemed possible.

It took me far longer than it should have that evening to dispose of three kills instead of two. I had to return to the lab after Elizabeth gave me the slip and finish off the young man I had brought back for her. He wept unprotestingly through the shoulder of my sweater until the blood stopped. A pitiful kill that left me sluggish and gorged.

Mr. Carrington certainly had his work cut out for him, and to his credit he did not bat an eye when I told him that the third corpse had been for research. Not the truth, but a lie disconcerting enough to squash dissension.

When I descended into the tunnels around dawn I did so with a sigh of relief. The atmosphere changes when Elizabeth is close—the air grows heavy like the heat of summer, subtle and electric. I could sense her immediately.

I sat in the corridor above our chamber door, listening for sounds of life from below. The candles over each hatch had long since been extinguished for the night and the tunnel smelled of warm wax. Elizabeth was safe in our bed with no movement to give her away. Her mind was intentionally a brick wall, as the time for her expiration was still a quarter of an hour off. She was only fifty feet from me at most, but I would not be welcome.

I hunched in the narrow enclosure and tried to find my earlier anger, but it kept slipping through my fingers. Yes, she had behaved foolishly. She had no idea the sway a woman in Lydia's position holds. The longer I sat there the more I considered Elizabeth's words. In all honesty, I would have sworn that she reciprocated Lydia's desires. And how could I begrudge her? Lydia is enticing in her own way, convincing when she wants to be.

When I found them together in the lab my first thought was to back away unnoticed, to let them have their moment, which I assumed had been building for at least a few weeks. But quick on the heels of that acceptance came a fury that blinded me to all else, a red haze across my vision. I recognized that Elizabeth meant to strangle the life from Lydia, and still I could not find peace. The jealousy rose thick and hot in my throat like so much blood. My only clear thought was of Fane and what he might do to Elizabeth when he found out.

Elizabeth became the threat. I attacked her character. I dismissed her, a failure I will carry with me for a long while. How I wish that my only worry was of Fane, and not the fear of being replaced in Elizabeth's heart—as I have been replaced in Fane's.

Elizabeth deserved an explanation, a sincere apology at least. The truth is that I felt I deserved one myself, for the dig she made at my fealty to Fane, for getting too close to Lydia when I warned her away, and for some reason my pride demanded that this be the argument in which Elizabeth admitted fault first.

I must have lingered too long, because just as I was about to slip out of the corridor and sleep in the library, a hatch opened cautiously behind me. We did not need to exchange words. My state of mind was written on my face. Bård motioned me to drop down into his generous suite.

The bedchamber was filled with soft chanting from the speakers in every corner. Bård had already resumed his place in front of the fire, his legs crossed atop a threadbare Persian rug, hands laid gently over his kneecaps. The windowscape was a winter scene. A lone Norwegian pine leaning in a crisp bed of snow. No mountains, just a barren pewter sky that stretched on for an eternity.

I reclined stiffly against the hearth with my knees pulled up to my chin and tried in vain to keep my eyes from Bård's peaceful face. He told me once that meditation had been Fane's suggestion, and that over time he had learned to master his volatile temper that way. After several quiet minutes Bård released an audible breath and his high chest fell, shoulders slouched forward.

"Out with it then," he said.

"Out with what?"

Bård smiled before he opened his eyes. "Tell me what happened to the lovebirds. Your silence is so deafening Stela, I can focus on nothing else."

Life seemed so hopeless in that quiet moment, utterly devoid of all its promise. Was it possible that Elizabeth had asked to run away with me? Was that real? I was so far removed from her thoughts that despite the pricking of my blood—another sign that Elizabeth is near—I could almost convince myself that I invented her.

"I found Lydia with Irina tonight."

Bård nodded. "They have been rather close as of late," he said. "I must say, I did not think it would happen so soon." He stood gracefully and walked down into his sitting area. "Irina is obviously enamored of you," he added as an afterthought. He flopped down on the sofa.

I followed him down the three short steps and watched him stretch his wiry limbs along the deerskin sofa. I kicked off my boots and paced. "She attacked her," I said, avoiding Bård's piercing stare.

He lifted on his elbows. "Lydia attacked Irina?"

"Not quite."

Bård narrowed his eyes. "But there *was* a brawl?"

"Oh yes," I said, slowing my steps. "Irina says that Lydia enthralled her while they were alone in the new laboratory."

That got his attention. "What was Lydia doing in the laboratory?" he asked. "She is not due a hunt for another two days."

"I never asked." That simple question suddenly seemed to me incredibly important. "Irina grabbed Lydia by the throat before I could announce myself."

"I believe it of Lydia," he said with a shrug. "Do you doubt Irina's account?"

I had not doubted it for a moment. That was the worst part.

"What I do not understand," he continued, "is why Irina would react with violence. Lydia is very attractive." He clucked his tongue, rubbed his hands together briskly. Bård had a strategic mind. A quality that Fane has always lauded. "What did Irina say when you asked her?"

I looked up and stared back at him. "When I asked her what?"

Bård laughed, incredulous. "When you asked her why she attacked Lydia?"

"Only what I told you. That Lydia forced herself on Irina. Irina said she asked her stop."

Bård furrowed his brow. "Thrall is not what I would call force, but I suppose everyone is entitled to their own interpretation." Was that not what Elizabeth had tried to impress upon me? That she felt forced, even threatened.

"You had words," Bård deduced.

"We had several," I said. I took a seat on the opposite end of the sofa. "I cannot for the life of me understand how she could be so careless as to attack Lydia, of all people."

"Irina's impulsiveness is one of your favorite things about her, Stela. And a trait the two of you share."

"I was afraid of what Fane might do if he found out."

Bård huffed and raised his bushy eyebrows. "This from the child who repeatedly lied to him. Who disobeyed direct orders to get what she desired most?"

The unwelcome truth came barreling out. "I want her all to myself, Bård. Constantly." I bent forward and held my face in my hands. "When I first found them, I could have killed her."

My brother said nothing, and I was emboldened by his strained silence. "Fane would tear Irina apart in front of me as penance, if he knew."

Bård placed his large hand between my shoulder blades.

"Somehow, everything became her fault. The things I said—"

"Enough," he warned, though not unkindly. "Stela, I understand why you find Irina so beguiling, I do. She has a bit of you inside her. Something deeper than blood." He patted my thigh and stood. Bård walked to the windowscape, his silver hair tied in a loose bun at the back of his neck.

"I will not warn you again to be cautious, as we both know that has never been your strong suit," he said with a pained smile. "You run headlong into any challenge." He took my hands in his, bent his head to kiss my knuckles.

"I have a challenge for you," he said. "Think of your life, Stela. Before you met this woman, your life with and without her. Ask yourself: are you stronger now? Or is Irina a weakness. Does having Irina in your life make you better or worse?"

I opened my mouth, but gave no answer. The longer we sat there the more anxious I grew that no protest on my part arrived.

"Irina asked me," I said, "if you and I had ever been intimate." I expected him to balk, as I had, but his features darkened. He clasped his hands together tightly, unamused.

"What did you tell her?" he asked calmly.

"Simply that we have always enjoyed a certain closeness," I replied and laughed uncomfortably. Bård turned his body away from me, staring at the windows. "We had just never been lovers." I finished softly as an unaccustomed uneasiness grew between us.

"It will be morning soon," he said and gestured to the sofa. "You are welcome to sleep here for as long as you need."

"One day will suffice," I said, not wanting to impose more than I already had. Bård pitched his bony shoulders as if to say that decision was entirely mine and walked silently up the steps toward his bed. I sat perfectly still until he returned with a blanket. He hovered for a moment, one foot behind him in retreat.

"The world will be less bleak by nightfall," he said.

I smiled. Bård turned his back without smiling in return.

"Thank you, Brother."

* * *

There are a great many creature comforts one can do without, however, forfeiting one's bed in favor of a wrestling mat is among the least desirable. Thankfully, I have never needed my surroundings to be amenable in order to sleep.

Elizabeth and I have not exchanged a word, even in passing, for nearly six days. The armory seemed as good a place as any to ponder Bård's question, and I was reluctant to keep his company after I had exhausted my self-imposed allowance of a single day's lodging.

The weapons' cupboard has become my retreat. Tucked in the corner of the armory, it consists of a swept dirt floor and dusty blades hanging on mounted racks. Out of the way and largely hidden from sight, though not private as it lacks a door. On the third evening Bård found me folding the sparring mat and he reiterated my welcome in his suite. He was kind enough not to laugh when I stubbornly declined.

A high-pitched whine, and the scuffle of the evening begins with more urgency than usual. Crogher's clomping boots pound down the tunnel. He seems to reconsider his rush, turns and knocks on another hatch.

The whisper of conversation piques my interest when I realize that half the dialogue belongs to Elizabeth. I catch only the shape of her voice in the air, not the words themselves. Elizabeth climbs out into the tunnel and closes the hatch behind her as she scurries after Crogher. It is a small mercy not having to wait for her to leave our chamber so that I can dress myself for the night. I mean to do just that and stand up to fold my mat away when, much to my unease, I find that my garment bag is hanging from a rack of quarterstaffs just outside the armory.

So, Lydia knows where I have been sleeping. But I have not seen or spoken to her since that evening in the laboratory. Did Bård tell her? Elizabeth? The thought that she has confided in anyone about our argument is one blow too many first thing in the evening. I rip the bag off its post and send the quarterstaffs trembling. As I change the whole household awakens, and a palpable excitement radiates throughout.

When I emerge stretching my arms through the sleeves of my black sweater Lydia stands at the end of the hall. She closes Fane's bedroom door quietly behind her. Gone are the days of bonding over my fledgling's charms, and Lydia crosses her arms at the sight of me, as though the mere thought of moving in my general direction is more than she can bear.

Thankfully, Darius peeks his head out from the library and traipses down the hall with a volume we know well tucked under his arm: the record of births. Curious, Lydia and I fall in line behind him, the three of us headed for the stables.

Tonight is an auspicious one, though not for the hounds. Crogher has Macha's head in his lap as he speaks to her softly. As always, one Macha dies so that the next might live and Crogher is despondent. The beautiful gray hound nuzzles his thigh and rakes her large ashen paws through her nest of quilts, desperate to rid her body of this precious cargo.

Elizabeth's shoulders tense when I stand behind her. Clad in a somber navy shirt that rides just above her waist, she stoops to gently prod Macha's swollen belly. She senses my eyes move across that patch of exposed skin as clearly as an unsolicited touch and tugs her shirttail into the waist of her jeans. Her obstinacy would be enough to garner a smile had I not been forced to spend the last week sleeping on the ground.

Macha's jealous brother Raghnall throws himself against his cage, frothing at the mouth and howling in protest of offspring that do not belong to him. Erebus stalks the short length of his cage, growling low at Raghnall. I rap my knuckles against the bars and Erebus, the new father, sits obediently though his hackles remain on end. I stroke the top of his large paw through the bars and hum a tune I have carried all my life, despite having misplaced the words centuries ago.

Lydia has one foot on the dirt floor and the other propped against the wall, her thigh exposed through the folds of her robe.

Darius has already begun sketching in the open volume, his hip pressed against the large oak worktable.

I sense Elizabeth staring. The half-remembered lullaby catches in my throat, chased from my mind by the welcome heat of her familiar onyx gaze. She collects herself when my song stops, as though startled from sleep, and drops down on the swept dirt floor next to Crogher.

"How much longer?" she asks. Her thin fingers disappear into the dense white fur of Macha's belly.

Crogher brushes her hand aside, traces the protruding shapes of the litter. He shakes his head solemnly. "Not long," he says as he cradles Macha's gray snout in his hands.

Bård arrives with a thud, having skipped the last two steps. His hands still working the buttons of his shirt. "Have I missed it?"

Lydia spares him the same smile one would grant a disruptive child and rubs his arm. "Take a seat, Dede," she says, straightening the collar of his shirt. A shirt that is a surprisingly accurate fit, as are the trousers. Either Lydia has tired of humiliating him, or she has taken up a new torment. I check Elizabeth once more, but her jeans are an ideal length, her shirt a perfect fit. The outfit is lackluster, true. My own is a bit drab. But neither ensemble is an obvious mockery.

"Oh quiet, you!" Bård pounds his fist against the top of Raghnall's cage. The hound whimpers and flops theatrically on his belly as Bård lifts himself to sit on top of the cage. Erebus relaxes.

"Move," Crogher says, and Elizabeth moves behind Crogher to sit at Macha's head. That earns her a pointed growl, but Elizabeth is undeterred. She lifts Macha's head into her lap and begins to hum the same tune I used on Erebus. Macha nuzzles into Elizabeth's embrace and the whole family falls silent. Crogher, who had been busy pulling Macha's tucked legs into position, takes Elizabeth's hand in thanks.

The smile that splits my dear one's face is a sight so precious I forget that we are entrenched in a standoff. Elizabeth is regularly at odds with every member of the family, sometimes through no fault of her own. She chooses the wrong words at the wrong time. She pushes when she should be patient.

I think it shocks us both how long we permit ourselves to smile amiably at one another. Macha's ear-splitting howl puts an end to that. Elizabeth, who had fallen silent, beings to hum anew. How does Elizabeth know the song so well?

"Here they come," Crogher says bleakly. He scoots forward into position as Macha omits an eerily human scream. The whole of our company leans in.

Macha struggles with the first pup. Elizabeth whispers to her, stroking her snout. A breath of new life enters the world and drops into Crogher's hand with a feeble yip and the sound of tearing flesh. Blind and black, the first of Macha's daughters has arrived.

One pup becomes three, becomes seven. All of them slick from the womb and black-furred like their father. The weary new mother curls forward, running her pink tongue across the flesh she has created.

"Seven…" Bård says dumbly. He stands behind Elizabeth. "No wonder Macha was so lethargic."

"Eight." Crogher lifts a lifeless pink mass in his giant hand. "Nearly eight," he says. The pups nestle closer to the teats, groping for something they sense in their blood but have never tasted.

Elizabeth stands with Crogher. "May I?" she asks, gesturing to the stillborn pup Crogher is protecting. In an odd moment of uncertainty, he looks to me for reassurance. Elizabeth wraps the pup in one of

Macha's unused rags and sets the corpse on Crogher's wooden work bench.

Elizabeth turns to inspect Macha who has fallen silent and very still. Three of her offspring have begun to feed and beneath their slick bodies faint specks of blood dot the dusty floor. Elizabeth moves closer, but Crogher shoots her a warning glare to keep back.

"How are they feeding already?" She shakes her head grimly.

I lift the small sticky body from the table and pull back the towel. I slide the slack jowls back to reveal a row of razor-sharp iridescent fangs, no longer than the point of a pen. Elizabeth spares me a tight smile and nod. She takes the dead pup from my hands and wraps it carefully, setting the body beside her.

Macha's bright eyes have begun to dull, a cloudy halo threatening to extinguish her vision completely. Five out of seven babes bleeding her dry by the miniscule mouthful. The two forgotten pups mewl helplessly, twisted in the quilts. Their superiors grow more ruthless with each swallow, tugging at their mother's skin with newfound strength, planting their paws on her belly for support.

"My god..." Elizabeth places a steadying hand on my bicep. "Look at their eyes." They have indeed opened, ten new black irises to match their present company. The bitch, Macha's firstborn, has already grown. I exchange an appreciative glance with Bård and Crogher, the new Macha crowned prematurely in our minds.

A weakened whine slips from the mother, and Elizabeth turns her head in pity. She gathers the motionless bundle to make a hasty exit, presumably having had her fill of death for one evening. The moment her hands lift the corpse from the table Crogher is on his feet, and Lydia appears behind him.

"What are you doing?" Crogher asks.

Elizabeth stiffens and turns cautiously on her heel. "I'm taking it to the lab."

Lydia all but claps with glee as Crogher presses forward, towering over Elizabeth. "He." Crogher sneers. "The pup is male." Arms crossed, Bård rocks on his feet and casts me a look of concern to say that he intends to intervene if I do not. "He is not your experiment Irina."

"Comparative study," she says, which does not help. She holds the cargo closer to her chest, as defiant as the day we met. Crogher reaches out, and I seize his forearm before he can claim his fallen pup by force.

"No more." I step between them, and Crogher drops his arm. His chest rises, and from behind Lydia strokes his shoulders, her eyes trained on Elizabeth.

"Let Irina take him," Lydia says, trailing her fingers down his arms. "She digs her own grave not asking Fane's permission first."

Macha releases a sigh, and with it she leaves the world more peacefully than she entered. Crogher whips around with two outstretched hands, but for all his imposing strength he is powerless to stop nature from taking its well-worn course. He does not move toward the body—the pups have already begun to nip and growl at one another. Macha belongs to her litter now. Instead he moves to Erebus and Raghnall, releasing the latches on the door.

Elizabeth is gone when I turn around, and Lydia is slinking up the staircase, perhaps after her. I shoulder past Darius, who barely looks up from his sketches. In the yawning hall I find only Elizabeth, standing at the top of the stairs with her souvenir cupped protectively to her chest.

"I didn't need your help," she says.

A weary chuckle rattles in my throat as I brush around her. "You should try thanking people, dearest." I make my way toward our suite, aware that she is keeping in step with me.

"I'm not in the habit of expressing gratitude out of obligation," she says.

"Politeness should never be an obligation."

"You sound so much like my mother when you talk down to me." She slips beside me in the passage.

"Well, whatever you need to fuel that inexhaustible ire of yours."

Elizabeth radiates a dozen retaliations she does not voice, flips her hair over her shoulder and scampers up into the corridor. To keep my distance, I linger in the passage. The urge to argue with her is overwhelming, because at least she speaks when provoked.

I catch the hatch before it closes and drop down into our suite. Though I have lain my head here for more than a hundred years the whole room smells of her. The strength of her presence strangles me. Such a wonderful yet painful taunt.

Elizabeth emerges from the bathroom with her leather satchel slung over her shoulder. She clears her throat, shifting from foot to foot. "Why are you here?" she asks.

"Collecting my keys." I snatch them off the desk in the corner. "Or did you fear that I was moving back into my *own* room?"

"Our room," she corrects. She shakes her head and sits on the edge of the bed. "Where have you been sleeping?"

"Does it matter?"

"Stela…" she sighs, dropping her head back dramatically. "Would I ask if it didn't?" She turns toward me, bringing her knee up on the bed.

"In the weapons cupboard."

Elizabeth laughs unconsciously. "Sorry." She smacks the vacant stretch of bed beside her and we sit together like two strangers on a park bench. "Better to hone your brooding around all those instruments of destruction?" she asks. Too playful, too familiar.

"We absolutely must do this again soon," I say and make to stand.

Elizabeth grabs my wrist before I can take my leave. "Don't go," she says wearily. As if I could with her hand on my skin, and that forlorn look.

"I'm angry with you," she says, her eyes on the floor.

"How about that?" I nudge her with my shoulder. "We agree on something." I need not examine her face to sense her answering smile, and it is safer to keep my eyes forward.

"That doesn't mean I hate you," she says.

"Nor I you." Nor will I. Should she turn her back on me as Lydia turned on Bård and make an enemy of me time and time again, I fear it matters not. She is mine, and in a way she always has been.

"You should get going. Science waits for no woman."

Elizabeth stands and clutches her satchel closed, which no doubt contains the pup she spirited away from Crogher. He will get over it. He likes Elizabeth, her forthrightness if nothing else. He likes so few…

In the freight tunnel she asks me why Crogher opened Erebus' and Raghnall's cages. Was he not afraid for the safety of the pups? She accepts my offered hand but not my explanation. The fallen member of the pack is the business of the pack. They honor her by finishing what remains.

"They eat their dead?"

"Yes," I say, climbing up the ladder to the parking garage. "But it sounds much less poetic when you put it that way."

Elizabeth stifles a laugh.

"What's on your agenda tonight?" she asks, lingering beside my vehicle. I humor her small talk because I know it pains her to make it. Her reluctance to part ways is at least something. We lean against our respective cars, and the dreary atmosphere of the garage does nothing to lessen her charms.

"I have a meeting with Andrew."

"You're finalizing the lab?"

A creak catches our attention. We both stand upright, listening for intruders. No one emerges and all is quiet. I press the lock release and open the driver's side door. "Andrew and I have another matter to close."

She does not press the Andrew question, a first for her. She stands awkwardly, debating inwardly.

"We should talk," she says quickly. I pause with half my body inside the car. "Sometime soon. About everything. Us."

After nearly a week in the armory I am no closer to answering Bård's question. Am I stronger with her, than without? Perhaps it is not something I can answer alone. She and I are, after all, inexplicably entwined.

"Yes. We should talk."

Elizabeth nods enthusiastically, less to affirm and more to clear her head. Sorted, settled, onward. Only this action gives me insight to her state of mind as she is keeping her thoughts very much to herself. I could press for more, but that would be a betrayal. Whatever she thinks or intends to say should be offered freely, and on her own time. Elizabeth takes a hands-on approach to everything but her anger and her pain—of those she is afraid.

"Dearest," I call out before she unlocks her door. "How did you know that song? I never finished serenading Erebus."

Elizabeth smiles privately, her eyes alight, and shrugs. "Must have heard it from you."

I seal myself in my vehicle and watch Elizabeth slide behind her steering wheel. A shadow passes across my rearview mirror, a black flash and then nothing. I turn around in my seat and peer out the back window. The garage is utterly still, only the red glow of my taillights.

* * *

"I see you've made yourself at home." Andrew drops his coat on an empty chair and I push my black-framed sunglasses up into place. Andrew's mangy Lhasa Apsos paw at my pants. The smaller of the two can barely see through his milky cataracts and nestles behind my boot. No dignity in aging, whether human or animal.

"You said the documents would be ready this evening."

"Indeed, they are," Andrew says, dropping heavily into a leather chair. "I waited around the office for you. You never showed."

"Is that concern I detect, Andrew?" I lean forward as he loosens his tie. He very nearly smiles.

"You're never late, Kathryn. I didn't know what to make of it." He sits up and reaches for a bottle of scotch on the coffee table.

"A private matter kept me longer than I hoped," I say. Andrew raises his brows, but his greedy mouth is occupied by the glass at his lips. He moans and settles back in his chair. "No cause for concern, Andrew. We are stuck with each other."

Andrew gives me a lazy grin that does not reach his eyes. As he rummages through his paperwork, I examine the carpet. Different from the last time I invited myself into his home office, ripped a hole in his neck and left him in a pool of his own blood. Such was the punishment Fane demanded for his thievery. I wonder, did he try to have that mess professionally cleaned, first? Or did he rip everything up at once and replace it? What must he have told his wife?

"Everything is sorted, Kathryn." My name draws back my attention. He clicks a pen and slides it over with the paperwork. "The estate of Claire Dumas has cleared probate. The trust of…"Andrew swallows, shakes his head, "your *client's* trust remains intact, all assets have been liquidated and deposited into that account. I just need your signature."

"You require *her* signature, Andrew, and you have it."

Andrew blushes and flips through the signed documents as though he has forgotten something. As though this was our first liquidation. He helps himself to a second glass of scotch. "So, you don't intend to be trustee?"

My laughter is so abrupt that the mutts at my feet jump to life and scurry behind Andrew for protection. He pats their trembling heads absently. "She would never allow it," I say, waving the question aside.

Andrew sits taller in his seat, blinking heavily. "Kathryn," he says, folding his hands on his belly. "I owed you a debt. I did my part. But I never agreed to deal with anyone else." He finishes his second scotch. "Mr. Radu is my client, and you are our liaison. That's all."

"Andrew, your obvious favoritism is heartwarming."

"If Mr. Radu finds out about this—"

"You disappoint me, Mr. Opes." I rise from my seat and stalk around the edge of his desk, letting my fingers trail the scattered documents—knocking them about. I sit on the arm of the chair next to him. "I am still Mr. Radu's liaison, and I will act in the same capacity for my client, your newest client. You will not meet with her directly unless you wish it. But my name is not to appear on any account belonging to her. Is that clear?" I place a hand on his shoulder, and he releases a held breath.

"Wouldn't it be easier if—"

"Indeed! Far easier if I could make decisions on her behalf." I drop my head back, shaking my head at the indifferent ceiling. "But Natalie desires control."

Andrew stares at me intently, almost as if he wants to see my eyes. I arch a brow and face him straight on, but he does not flinch. An expression passes over his face that might be pity.

"This is important to you too," he says carefully. "I see why you're so taken with her."

Andrew Opes has taunted me, reproached me, questioned me. Once, just to insult me, he even gambled with his life in this very room. But never in all our years of business has he successfully disarmed me. It occurs to me that I have never once sought his services for myself. I have always worked on behalf of someone else. Elizabeth said as much. *Well aren't you a good little soldier?*

I stand abruptly and gather my things, while Andrew swirls scotch number two in his hand, still watching me with that same curious intensity.

"I trust you have everything you need?" I ask, shirking on my coat. Andrew nods solemnly.

"If Mr. Radu *were* to find out about this, nothing could be done in heaven or on earth to save either of us."

Andrew, who has heard it all before, raises his glass with a wink. "To the grave, Kathryn." He seals the bargain with a drink.

"To *your* grave, Mr. Opes, and into Christine's capable hands."

His face hardens. After all, if a requirement has not been met, the duty of remedying the oversight may very well rest on the shoulders of his only child.

* * *

Fane called me home hours before I was expected. His urgency brought an icy chill to my blood. My mark was still nursing his drink at the bar when I heard my Lord's voice and I nearly left him to live. But Fane would also need to feed, and though Lydia has been carrying that burden almost exclusively for some time now, it would not do to tempt fate and arrive at his door half-starved.

I could not savor the hard-won mouthfuls of a victim so clean of influence. He was still clearheaded when I led him away, understated in his allure. The animated way in which he spoke reminded me of Elizabeth. Inherently wealthy, but with the confidence of someone self-made. Adam, he told me, though that was not his name. I suppose everyone is entitled to a bit of mystery, but the blood is beyond illusion and gave him away: Michael.

What compelled Michael to follow me out of a well-lit bar and down a dreary alley with an alias fast on his lips? And why should he call himself Adam, even to a stranger he trusted enough to want to take home? What need did the false name fulfill?

I sense Fane the moment I exit my vehicle and note that Elizabeth's car is not parked in the garage. Her absence is reassuring and my relief is short-lived as I realize why: one less life to worry about. Fane rarely calls to me anymore, not unless to review his accounts and that will not happen until the first week of the new month.

Wherever Elizabeth is, I hope she flirts with dawn before she returns home.

The door to his chamber is open, spilling soft yellow light across the stone foyer. An uncommon sight. For a Lord who abhors secrecy among his subjects, he makes no effort to hide his preference for privacy. As I cross the threshold the door slams shut behind me unaided.

Fane sits in his ebony chair—a throne at least in size—and from the edge of the room only the back of his head and the hem of his emerald robe are visible. We are alone, and I have never wished for Lydia's disruptive presence more.

"My dove," he says, brushing a wrinkle from the bunched silk gathered at his knee. "You know it pains me to wait." I force a sense of calm to penetrate my mind and stand in front of him, prepared to kneel. "Be seated."

Fane rests his head heavily on his clenched fist. He does not sigh although his pained expression suggests an irritation that borders on fatigue. The fine edges of his robe are drastically parted over the breadth of his veined and ruddy chest, and I see the blood rushing beneath skin, surging around his heart.

"If I asked you where you were this evening, would you tell me?" He does not look at me.

"My Lord?"

Fane lifts his head up toward the ceiling, a smile spreading across his lips. He rubs his lips softly, thoughtfully. "No," he says. "I suppose not." His arms drop limply against the armrests, and his eyes—always so piercingly curious—pass distractedly around the room on everything except my face.

"I know where you were, Stela." He nods solemnly to himself, patting the armrests with his restless hands. "I have known." He cranes his neck and every muscle in my body locks into place. "What I do not know, is why?" That piercing blue stare cuts to the core of me, and the only subterfuge I can manage is to keep my mind completely blank.

He laughs once, cups his chin in his hand as though caught in the most pleasant daydream.

"We could do this all night, could we not?" He stands violently and paces in front of the sofa. "You never had a mind for strategy, Stela." He says this so simply that I question my right to take offense and sit patiently with my hands clasped. "Not like your brother." He sits on the coffee table, his face inches from mine. "But you were always headstrong, fearless," he tilts his head incredulously, "faithful…"

"My Lord, if I may—"

He taps my lips with his finger. "You may not."

Fane strokes my jaw, and the fury he so adeptly conceals burns in the tips of his gentle fingers. The pressure of his stare increases dramatically, creating such heat that my cheeks and neck blush and the muscles in my face twitch. He releases me just as quickly, looking sadly at the rug beneath our feet.

"You may not be the lieutenant Bård is, but you are smart enough to let your opponent show their hand first," he says with a smile. I remain silent, painfully aware that the menace radiating off of him has not yet peaked. "You learned that from me." He shakes his head and stands up, still so close that I have to crane my head back to look at him.

Fane strolls toward his nightstand and fetches a notebook from the drawer. He smacks the worn cover against his palm and takes a seat on the bed. I know what the notebook contains. This confrontation has been building for weeks, in some ways he and I have been on this road for years.

"The first deviation was noted just days after Irina was turned, and on my honor Stela, I thought nothing of it then." He wags his finger at me, but there is nothing playful about him. "From that initial unsanctioned meeting a new ritual formed. Care to comment?" He glances up from the notebook gripped in his hands. "No?" He arches his pale brow, but I remain still and damningly silent. Confounded innocence is the only play I have left. "I thought not," he says bitterly. "The frequency of your meetings with the loathsome Mr. Opes tripled once Irina was turned, and as of late—due in part to the new lab, I have no doubt—I dare say, they have quadrupled."

Weakness will not serve and the meek inherit precisely nothing in Fane's kingdom. I stand up with conviction and cross the room. Fane waves his hand and I take a seat beside him. He smacks my knee and holds the book further from his face so that I can read the report for myself. I would recognize that whimsical scroll anywhere, and I knew it was her without the penmanship to ruin the surprise.

"Lydia is a surprisingly efficient shadow," I say, strangely calm and close to laughter. I knew there was someone with Elizabeth and me tonight in the parking garage, and I ignored it. "I have never given her due credit."

Fane turns me roughly by the chin. "I have warned you before not to blame your sister for your own misdeeds."

"Of what do I stand accused, my Lord?" Even I am shocked by my tone, and the steadiness of my voice. The righteous affability of the wrongfully accused, though we both know this is no baseless accusation. Fane snaps the notebook shut and whips it across the room with a flick of his wrist. The spine smacks the far wall, and the force of impact sends several pages flying. They flutter dreamily to the floor.

"Tell me why, Stela." He turns to reestablish eye contact. In that instant the hatch in the parking garage opens and my stomach drops like a stone tossed down a dark well. Elizabeth is home.

Fane tilts his head up and sniffs the air. "The bloom of my budding fledgling," he says dreamily. "Shall we bid her to join us?"

My vision darkens to two black tunnels focused solely on his eyes. His grip on my mind loosens in a rush. For as long as I live, he will not harm her.

"I was careless with your Mr. Collins, my Lord." I place my hand on his cheek. He turns toward me, eyes narrowed to skeptical slits. "It was selfish and thoughtless of me. I have a debt to repay, you made that perfectly clear." I speak as one split in two: the part of me that placates him knows how to handle Fane, but the other half screams in protest for what will be required to distract him. The trust fund that Andrew now manages on Elizabeth's behalf cannot be discovered. We are not permitted to have independent funds.

Fane tolerates my hand on his cheek but he does not reciprocate. "My debt has yet to be resolved, but have I not shown progress?" His outrage flares, I can see it in his eyes, but he says nothing. Progress is not resolution. "Your concerns are my concerns, my Lord." I reach up to brush a wisp of blond hair away from his eyes. "By your assessment I am heedless and self-obsessed. And by the intelligence Lydia gathered I am damned by my efforts to right the past." I take his hand in mine and the old affection is still there, chipping away at his ire. "I have been meeting with Mr. Opes to see what can be done to supplement our losses."

Fane cups my hand in his, palms as warm as smoldering coals, and brings my knuckles to his lips. "Why hide this from me, Stela?"

"I fear that nothing can be done, my Lord." His eyes dig deep into mine, but there is nothing for him to find. My indiscretions, my motives, my fears cannot be sifted through or reached. Those eyes that I have loved and feared for centuries, eyes that both laid me bare and elated me, that once seemed bluer than the sky in spring now are just two pale pools in his head. I listen to the sounds of Elizabeth shuffling around our suite as she readies for bed.

"I want to believe you," he says, closing his eyes briefly. "But your mind is as quiet as Irina's." He casts my hand off and smiles cruelly. "Let us summon the blithely silent youth, shall we?" He makes to stand up. "I have no doubt that the secrets you keep from me have been shared with your bedfellow."

"I have no bedfellow!"

One should never raise their voice to Fane. One should never stand against him defiance. I rarely see him shocked, but then I have surprised myself tonight. He knows Elizabeth and I have been at odds. If Lydia knows I have been sleeping in the armory, Fane knows it. For once the truth is on my side.

"Irina wants none of me."

Fane stares down at me with pity in his eyes. He places his huge hand on my waist, but I feel only the weight of it and a sensation like chills. "My dove," he says softly, sneaking his thumb under the edge of my shirt. I stare down at his intruding hand. When did his touch become so galling?

"Irina is a child of this era." He strokes the skin beside my navel. "Fickle and narcissistic. She knows nothing of honor, or duty. You cannot say you were without warning." Fane presses a kiss to the top of my head, my temple, his hand pressed to the small of my back ushering me closer. He leans forward to force me backward, his mouth in view and my body locks into place, then shudders.

A minuscule movement. I did not recoil. I did not push him away. But I have never met his affection with anything less than eagerness, not once in over five centuries. The two of us stare at each other, mouths agape, both stunned into complete silence. Time leaves us here, suspended, neither believing what has just occurred. The shock dissipates when Fane seizes the back of my neck. He looks at once furious and horribly sad. His grip so tight he raises me up on my toes.

"Get out of my sight, Stela."

* * *

I stand at the mouth of the tunnel for as long as I can. The blistering sun rises and warms the earth over our heads. I listen to Elizabeth sleeping until my strength gives out. It would be such a comfort to slip through the hatch, to nestle in bed beside her and without a single thought of who is right or wrong watch her body respond to my nearness. And in the evening when we wake entwined, would she have me then? Will this fight end like so many others, the needs of the body quieting the mind?

The empty sound of my fatigued steps is my sole companion as I trudge back to the armory. The rack beside the wall is adorned just as it was this morning, with a garment bag hung beside the quarterstaffs. Is it possible that my life was never in jeopardy? Clearly, Lydia expected that I should live to fight another day if she bothered to choose an outfit for me. The real question is will the bag still be there by evening? Or will Fane strike while I sleep for causing him offense?

Will he strike?

I hang the garment bag in the cupboard. To think Lydia followed me all the way to Andrew's home undetected. Elizabeth has commented on her stealth before, mentioned that Lydia caught her unaware. I should have listened. Vigilance is the mark of a warrior.

I kick the roll of blue mat underfoot and watch my makeshift bed unfurl like a tongue. The compound is quiet, not even a stirring in Fane's quarters. I cast my boots aside and stretch out on my back, my hands pillowed beneath my head.

A large part of my mind is still locked away, swept cleaner than this cupboard. Never in all my years have I succeeded in barricading my mind this way. And to resist Fane's eyes completely? To remain stalwart under his intense scrutiny, and bar his intrusion into my mind? That was no mere misdirection on my part.

Of course, Fane will know all soon enough. He will call Andrew and hear the lie in his voice, or Lydia will catch me in the midst of one deception or another and report back. I have no doubt she will redouble her efforts tonight. For the moment there is time to marvel at another evening lived.

As unlikely as it is to discover a strength so late in life, it is precious and to be savored. The mechanics of this new ability must be understood. I was terrified of Fane, until I was not. I was whole and then I was split in two. The good soldier remained, and she pacified Fane, defended her actions and position. Meanwhile, the traitor did not flee but raised a wall around my mind and stood guard. Two selves united in their troubles and bound against a shared threat, but this was not self-preservation at work. The common goal was clear: protect the girl at all cost.

Elizabeth was the cause.

From my chamber comes a whimper and then the rustling of a sheet. I can sense her disquiet growing. An arm knocked out beneath the pillow, a leg kicked out across the bed. A second sound, softer than the first reaches my ears, a pained moan from her sleep-parted lips. I will not leave her to unpleasant dreams when we were so close to losing each other this morning. I close my eyes to find her.

Rest now, dear one. Elizabeth's body relaxes with a sigh, and I sense the tension leave her body as though I held her in my arms.

There are differences to manage, more numerous than either of us could have known. Tempers on both sides, conviction, and stubborn pride. But there is also immense tenderness, kindness, selflessness, and bravery. I close my eyes and roll onto my side, thankful to finally have an answer.

I am undoubtedly stronger with her than I was without.

IX

Preconceptions

The platelet count is impossibly low. Using a human metric, every Strigoi in Fane's household suffers from severe thrombocytopenia, even immediately following a feed. Prior to feeding, counts drop even lower. When fresh blood is introduced to the sample the Strigoi red blood cells excite. They tremble in the vial and swell to three times their normal size, absorb the human cells. Somehow, the platelet numbers rebound too.

Oddly, Strigoi barely bleed when injured and clot fast. Which begs the question, why? The answer must lie in our erythrocyte's ability to assimilate if not digest human blood.

I had hoped that Macha's dead pup would offer some insight into how these unique cells begin but found nothing of note in the pup's red cell structure or platelet count. It leads me to believe that Strigoi blood is somehow parasitic in nature. If that dog had lived long enough to feed from Macha, his cells would have mutated to mirror his mother's. Just as my cells were manipulated by the introduction of Stela's blood. Still, I had to be drained completely of my blood first. The samples I took from his healthy sister, "The New Macha," are eerily similar to our own. Her platelet levels, however, are normal.

Which brings me to the Stela problem.

I've collected four samples at various intervals around her feeding cycle, and unlike the rest of us, her platelet count never dips below what would be considered normal for a healthy human being. This could explain her resilient composition where sleep and light sensitivity are concerned. Stranger still, Stela's erythrocytes are an opaque, blush-colored replica of the rest of the family's.

Stela's been accommodating. Once our resolve to stop speaking crumbled, she dropped by the lab three times in one week. She never asked me why I wanted so many samples, and I didn't explain. What would I say? She's heartier than the rest of us, and that is hardly cause for concern.

Besides, Stela is sensitive about these subtle differences. Her genetic superiority is a point of contention amongst her siblings. I can see why—she certainly has an enviable constitution. What I don't understand is, how? If the cause were attributable to feeding from Fane, then the benefits would be widespread throughout his progeny, myself included. No, if the mutation of cells were that simple, Stela and I would have similar lab results. And without a hypothesis as to why she's different, it doesn't make sense to tell her what I've found. The information would only be one more irregularity for her to downplay and conceal.

On an utterly unscientific note: I am fiercely protective of Stela. If it served no other purpose, my discovery of her dissimilarities helped to clarify a few of Stela's fears. I understood that it alarmed her that I was never properly bound to Fane and this is why she insists upon calling me Irina when we're not alone. Now, what I don't understand is why it matters to whom I'm bound, beyond the challenge it could mean to Fane's authority. But what I get is her instinct to compartmentalize and keep up appearances. In some form or another, she's been doing it all her life.

I slip the blood film from the microscope stage and hold it under the recessed lighting beneath the cabinets, as though my microscope is the problem. Stela's name labeled on the edge seems suddenly dangerous. Stela's vials—each one emblazoned with her name—sit with the rest of the samples. I pick hers out and place them in a container of their own.

I manage to miss my own vein twice. The blood gurgles into the vial, thick and reluctant. A false sample, a forged label, that'll hide Stela for a while longer. My paranoia catches up with me in the middle of my search for my discarded pen.

I print Stela's name on the sample I faked and place it with the others. I gather her vials and the slide and lock them in the cupboard under the microscope.

What's Stela doing now? Pressing herself against some unsuspecting stranger? Chasing a frightened giant of a man down the middle of Michigan Avenue with a song in her heart? Once, the thought would have made me green. Now, I just wish I could watch her work.

I snatch up my cell phone and tamp down my disappointment when a new text alert fails to arrive. Whether we're fighting or not, I had expected that she would sense my thoughts turning toward her. Is she actually angry enough to give me my privacy? Stela, my perpetual stalker?

I shoot off a quick text instead, asking her to meet me in our room. We've avoided each other long enough.

My phone buzzes. Stela's text says simply that she will be there. I frown at my phone. Was she right? Did I overreact with Lydia?

"Am I interrupting something?"

The air tingles, static charged, and the hair on my arms stands on end. My heart pounds and the persistent hunger—my constant companion—builds a scream in my skull. Never a footfall to give him away. Not the click of the door when he opened or closed it behind him, as though he just teleported in to say hello. It would be such a comfort to believe that teleportation was beyond his ability. But as his visit is no doubt intended to remind me, I know almost nothing about him.

"Fane..." my voice is little more than a whisper. "This is a surprise."

He dips his head cordially and helps himself to a tour of the new laboratory his money purchased. I can count the number of times I've seen him dressed in anything more than his favorite emerald robe. Lydia has chosen charcoal pants and a white oxford. The disheveled but expensive look of the shirt softens him.

He takes easy sweeping strides, pausing every other step to examine a cabinet or fondle a discarded instrument. He runs his finger around the rim of an empty beaker, and the glass sings under his touch. He adjusts the base of the microscope to center its position on the counter, looks at me and smiles. I've been in close quarters with him before and I recognize his manipulation. My pulse slows, despite my desperate hunger. Every cell in my body craves more of his blood.

The control he exerts over the emotions of others is a tactic employed to get to the heart of things, no different from the effect a Strigoi can have on a human. A calm mind is an exposed one.

"I was under the impression you never leave the compound."

Fane continues to pore over the lab, undeterred. He pauses to test the cabinet at his shin, rattles the lock once and stands to his full height. The ceiling is only half a foot from the top of his head. Foolish, locking Stela's samples away. He can smell her, as surely as I can smell him.

"A confidence I trust you will keep," he says. He folds his arms across his chest and leans against a cupboard that groans against his weight. I take a seat on the stool because standing in front of him does nothing to level the playing field and I have to crane my neck to see his face either way. His size is actually the least intimidating thing about him, though it was the first thing I noticed when we met.

"You are skilled at keeping confidences." Spoken like an afterthought—the way he insists upon the word "confidences" when the inflection is clearly *secrets*. I lace my fingers around my knee, try to maintain a neutral expression, and think of something my mother said: "Secrets are only powerful while kept." At the time, I thought she meant that the power resided with the keeper, but I see the implications differently now. To be entrusted with a secret is to share a burden. Fane tried to ensnare me with a secret when he granted me permission to read Stela's journals without her permission. He was wiser this time. He turned up announced in an unexpected place and forced the secret on me.

"What can I do for you this evening?" I ask with as much humility as I can manufacture.

Fane steps closer and runs his fingers up the side of my neck, pulling my chin forward. "You can start by addressing me properly." A fire gathers at the back of my eyes, warm but not yet burning. The yellow ring around his pupils expands, threatening to inflame his delicate blue irises. "I have been more than patient with your postmodern sensitivities, Irina."

That much is true, and I didn't expect to get away with my casual refusal for this long. The white lights overhead dull to a tolerable gray and my eyes—held hostage by his—seek them out as a reprieve. His stare reaches inside, as indelicate as a groping hand, and so engrossing that I can't remember a time without their smothering influence. He's digging deeper than he ever has, but I sense my memories slip right through his fingers. A drop of fear trickles into my heart. The budding disquiet that follows, the fading edges of that blissful calm he inspired is deliberate.

"What can I do for you…my Lord."

Fane's lips curl back over perfectly white teeth, pulling the cleft of his upper lip flat. The sight is both welcoming and threatening. He drags his finger down the bridge of my nose. Stela touches me the same way when she's particularly pleased with me. Fane looks toward the vials sitting on the island.

"The question is always what can *I* do for my family, Irina." His fingers dance atop the vials, making the blood inside slosh. I take a sobering breath and hold it captive in my chest as he removes the sample I just faked and examines Stela's name on the label. "I have demanded a metaphorical pound of flesh from each of my children to further your study." He waves the falsified sample around carelessly. "But I have recused myself from your study, and I do hate to play the hypocrite."

It takes every last shred of self-preservation I possess not to laugh in his face. The science helps, and he knows that. A sample of his blood would be everything. The answers I seek, and a temptation I'm not certain I could resist. It's hard enough to keep Stela's samples without drinking them. But as Stela has warned me many times before, Fane gives nothing for free.

"I thought this would please you," he says, and takes a seat on the empty stool. He tilts his head curiously and gone is the feral grin. He looks for all the world like a little boy, albeit a very large one.

"A vial of your blood would be…" wonderful, fascinating. Fane is clearly flattered, a triumphant smile spreads across his mouth. I've never seen him so pleased with me. Does he look at Lydia this way? Stela? His face etched with violence, but still somehow ethereal. How long was Stela enslaved to his gossamer hair and clear eyes, the promise of dimples that never arrive? "Thank you, my Lord."

Fane leans back and slides three fingers into the pocket of his pants. He retrieves one of my vials, already filled, and rolls it around in his outstretched palm. "Lydia commandeered a vial the last time she was here," he says. Though my fingers tremble in my lap and my blood sings, I don't reach for the vial. "You have been far more gracious with me than you were to her."

I lick my lip and the ghost of Lydia's kiss intrudes upon my senses. Fane raises a brow and slips the vial onto the wheel with the others, as though his sample was of no more importance than any other contribution. "I understand why you were so enraged by Lydia's advance."

"Well," I hesitate, crossing my arms, "you're the only one so far."

Fane stands up, shaking the cuff of one leg free from his ankle. How Lydia can find anything large enough to fit him is a wonder. I peer over at the wheel, inspecting his vial. Did Lydia steal a tourniquet for him as well? I slide his sample from the cradle and lift it toward the light. At first blush the blood appears perfectly ordinary if not dark. Fane barks a dry laugh and smacks me on the shoulder. I nearly drop the sample to the floor.

"Ever the skeptic," he says, shaking his head. "That blood is quite real, I assure you." Despite the seal, his scent is detectable. Sweeter than honey and darker than syrup. I set the sample back with the others. "Your needles would be no use, Irina." He taps a finger against his forearm, and I have a clear vision of him sitting on the velvet sofa in his lounge, opening a vein with his razor-sharp teeth.

"Do you know your greatest fault?" he asks, unprovoked.

"I can think of several," I say, laughing nervously as I clasp my hands tightly.

Fane does not laugh and begins to pace again. With his chest high, his hands behind his back, a tenured professor preparing for a lecture. "You see deception where there is none. You anticipate hidden motive and miss the larger picture."

"Is that what I do?"

Fane turns on the toe of his black leather loafer. Under the harsh white lights, his skin looks a bloated, beaten red. The veins in his forehead spin a web of blue that clusters around each eye. "You thought Lydia's interest was a threat to your *relationship* with Stela. Some effort to subvert what you have." He wags his finger at me and smiles when I scowl. "In contrast to the rising divorce rates, your lot values monogamy. You believe love requires a focal point."

He spreads his hands out wide, empty. "And you are the only one among us who views the bonds we share through such a provincial lens. As something to be coddled and strictly controlled. A gift to be given or taken away. Indeed, the only one who would bother to label such a bond as love in the first place."

I fix my sight on the microscope and an unamused smile slides across my mouth. Stela loves me in ways I can quantify and in ways I can't hope to understand. I've tasted her love on my tongue.

Fane bends down and takes my hand in his. The warmth of his skin is shocking, it leaches into my hand as he pets it. "Stela's affection for you is beyond question," he says, and gives my hand a reassuring squeeze. I consider it a personal victory that I don't flinch away from him. Instead, I think of every time Stela has said the words out loud to me. I think of my lab coat, the sale of the brownstone and my own swelling trust fund, the pillow she held over my dying mother's face, the centuries she's tacked onto my life. All the countless demonstrations of her love, no matter the method of expression. No matter the cost.

"I have felt Stela's affection for you myself. With my whole being." He strokes the side of my face, my hand still caught in his. Fane slowly runs his fingers through my hair.

There's intimacy in his touch that I haven't granted him, but what worries me most is that the touch is almost familiar.

"She was like a woman possessed last night. I cannot remember a time when Stela matched my affection with greater zeal, and for that, I thank you."

My hand goes slack in his palm and my body chills with icy dread as Fane's bright and terrible eyes bore into mine. Stela is everywhere at once. She surrounds us as though the invocation of her name was enough to pull her through space and time and place her between Fane and me. I know it's Fane's doing, but her breathy whimper licks the shell of my ear and my stomach drops. Fane releases my hand and breaks eye contact. This glimpse of his interaction with Stela the previous evening may not have come together quite as vividly as he intended, as my connection to Stela is no doubt blocking the way. But her pleased whimper still rings in my ears. He dips his head to the side and stares at me with pity.

"I can see that you are displeased," he says.

A pricking sensation builds at the back of my eyes, and my vision tunnels. Every ounce of self-control I can muster is required to keep me seated on that stool. He would kill me before I so much as scratched him. Fane waits for a reaction I will not give him.

"I trust there is no need for idle threats between us?"

I shake my head, half blind with rage, barely able to hear him.

"All creatures behave truer to form when they perceive weakness," he says, and slips his arms through the sleeves of a dark trench coat. "If you tell anyone of my visit this evening, Irina, if I hear so much as a whisper about my time aboveground…" he pauses until I look at him. "I will incinerate your beloved in front of you."

Fane doesn't wait for my acknowledgment. He picks up a hat I didn't even notice and flips the collar of his coat up around his cheeks. He leaves as quietly as he came.

I remain perfectly still on the edge of my stool, the toe of one foot braced against the floor. My pulse roars in my ears. I begin to doubt what I've been shown. She wouldn't do this to me. Not after everything she's risked and everything I've given up. She wouldn't sleep with him. She would tell me, warn me if it couldn't be avoided. My legs tremble when I stand, and my hand reaches out as if possessed, knocking samples aside to retrieve the one small vial of Fane's blood.

My hands shake but I get the cap off quickly and tip the vial into my mouth. Half the sample spoils on my tongue. My body quivers as I fight to secure the cap, but I can do no more than that and the sample slides from my grip. The tube clatters around the others, stopped from falling to the floor by Crogher's vial.

A rush of color explodes behind my eyes. Fane's blood slides down the back of my throat, boiling me alive. I hear my own gasp as though watching myself on film, I see myself drop to the floor on my knees, gripping the steel island for support. What comes is not a memory at all, but a fleeting glimpse. A wave of emotion, euphoric and sedate. Stela's face, her eyes closed, lips parted and then nothing. I focus my thoughts on what lingers on my tongue, but while the blood is alive the brain is removed and can offer no insight—another theory approaching confirmation.

My heart pounds, threatening to burst. I sit on the floor and fight to regain control of my thoughts, but Fane is everywhere and nowhere. It's not the first time I've tasted his blood. I've learned nothing to confirm or refute Fane's insinuation that he slept with Stela last night, yet the lack of proof does nothing to quell the nauseating certainty I heard in his voice.

Badly shaken, I can hear the approach of the sun, though dawn is still a few hours off. I slow my pulse, take a centering breath.

When I open my eyes all I can see are the samples glinting on their wheel. I can hear the cells moving, pulsing in the vials. That small voice inside, so childlike, so petulant, promises peace if I just drink a bit more. So many samples. Why do I have so many? Why wallow in human blood when I could have this?

A sound like a gunshot pierces my ear. A car backfiring. Three blocks north. Fane's formidable blood has sent my senses rioting.

I lift what remains of his sample with two fingers and slide it quickly back into the wheel, afraid to touch it for too long.

On the edge of the island is a perfect indentation of my right hand pressed into the steel. I ghost my fingers across the ridges, marveling that I could possess such strength and not know it. My awe is short-lived. What I need to know now is if what Fane alleged is true. There's one way to find out for certain.

I don't look back as I flick off the lights and close the door.

Outside, the moon casts a hollow silver sheen on every available surface. Heavy, wet snow melts in a puddle of oil, it weighs down my hair, and my new eyes can see prisms of color refracted in each flake. The wind is murderous, bitingly cold, and the sting of the breeze dances across my cheeks but the chill ventures no deeper. The howl of what will undoubtedly be a significant storm serenades me on the short walk back to my concealed car.

A hunt won't do this evening.
I have a particular craving to satisfy.

* * *

The meager warmth of a new fire glows in the hearth. Stela leans against the arm of the sofa. She has changed the windowscape to a stark winter scene. An odd choice, a photo we've never used: that of a single bent tree in a bed of undisturbed snow. The hatch settles quietly above my head, and I watch Stela stare at the projection from the edge of the room.

"What do you think of it?" she asks. Her attention remains on the windows. "The image, I mean. Does it move you?" She tilts her face toward me, a cheek, the point of her nose visible but the rest of her face is hidden by her hair—still damp from the snow. I flex my fingers at my sides and use everything I have to keep from approaching her.

"The scene reminds me of something." She gestures vaguely with a sweep of her hand. "A feeling more than anything, not a memory, exactly."

I drop my bag to the floor and Stela turns and appraises me quickly from toe to forehead. She crosses her arms and faces the windows once more.

"Like the dream I have of the day Fane claimed me," she continues. "It speaks to me," she says of the damned landscape in front of her. "I have no idea why."

She warms her body by the fire. She's wearing a standard black long-sleeved shirt and dark jeans, the usual attire for a journey home—post-feed. How long until she comments that I've arrived home in the same clothes I was wearing when I left? And is there any other way to begin this conversation?

"*Affinity*," she says triumphantly, one finger raised in the air. "Am I making sense?" Her black eyes soak up the smoldering flames and glint like two black opals. My lips part, the start of an accusation. Nothing comes. Stela smiles weakly, as though testing the waters. "I felt similarly the night we met."

I take one wavering step deeper into the room and her scent—warmed and freed by the fire—rushes up around me like a snare. The shy smiles, the flirtatious and romantic whimsy of her meditations are too late or too soon, I don't know which.

It's as though the storm outside followed me, chilling me to my core. The hair on my arms rises, charged and warning. Stela trembles as though touched by the same cold and her smile vanishes.

"You said we should talk." She narrows her eyes, ventures a step closer.

"I know what I said."

Stela raises her eyebrows, purses her lips. She nods to herself and clasps her hands. "I can leave if you prefer."

My pulse thunders in my temple. With the swoon heavy upon my senses, and the taste of her heavy in the air, catastrophe seems inevitable. Stela matches me step for trepidatious step, and we meet at opposite ends of the bed.

"You neglected to feed." Her concern is as palpable as her disappointment.

"Neglect is an interesting choice of word. It implies carelessness."

Stela, sufficiently ruffled, implores me with her eyes. Digs for some clue as to my frame of mind. I avoid her eyes and inch closer. Stela plants her feet, never one to shy away from confrontation.

"Why did you send for me?"

I trace the edges of her with my eyes, and then my fingertips. She doesn't flinch when I press against her. She doesn't embrace me either.

"I want you to tell me the truth." I stroke her cheek.

Stela, indignant, tries to shoulder past me and we collide. I grip her by the shoulder and shove her back against the bedpost. The wood splinters but Stela blinks slowly, mildly impressed. She relaxes into my hold and wraps a hand around my wrist. Her fingers rub soothing circles over my skin, like an unspoken encouragement. A veiled smile slithers across her mouth—she's asked me more than once not to be gentle with her.

"What truth, my darling?" She knots a fist in my sweater and pulls me flush against her. The bedpost behind her groans. Stela's eyes chase after mine, desperate for their familiar depths. She breathes my name, sotto voce.

My grip slackens and my hand falls to her beautiful neck. The intention is clear and Stela leans in to my hand, baring herself to me. She cups my face and forces me to look at her. Stela's eyes reveal her desperation. Desperate to reach me, desperate to touch me. But she does not find that same willingness to bend in mine. Instead she's sucked into the maelstrom that's been drowning me for the last two hours. No images to help her decipher my state of mind without a conduit of blood, but the emotions are there, streaked in messy arcs like a Pollock of grief.

Stela's hands fall limply at her sides, but the muscles in her throat spasm to test my hold. My fingers tighten, though she's made no effort to free herself. "You spoke to Fane," she deduces, standing to her full height. Her voice is utterly resigned and notably devoid of guilt. Even her soft, intentionally understanding eyes are remorseless.

"Stop talking." My arm trembles, and though Stela's mouth is closed her upper lip protrudes ever so slightly—the telltale sign that her fangs have emerged. "I don't want words, Stela. I need you to show me."

Stela's eyes narrow. She places a steadying hand on my shaking elbow, then presses her thumb deep into the joint to buckle my arm. I keep my hold only barely, and with white knuckles Stela clutches her hips. Every inch of her body urging her toward a bloody culmination, an impulse she arduously ignores. I twist her neck to the left with a shift of my hand and force her shoulder down. Her pale blond hair slips away and I watch the muscles of her throat jump beneath the skin.

Her temper gets the better of her and I get the fight I courted. She tears at my sweater, wraps a furious hand around my throat. My name bubbles up in Stela, beating beneath my fingers. The hand at my throat, keeping me at bay, disappears. Stela stands there, half slumped, her eyes bright with warning and her voice thick in my ear. She calls me a jealous fool and pulls me forward.

My fangs sink into her neck and she sighs beautifully, clutching the back of my head with an angry claw. She clings to me as the blood floods into my mouth, and the small voice of my bottomless hunger sings joyously. Stela's knees grow weak and I shove her back against the bedpost. I have only one thought, immune to her pleas and her unvoiced pleasure. The images I seek are right at the surface, as though Stela set them to the forefront of her mind.

Fane holds her close, his hand on the small of her back, his nose pressed to the top of her head. Stela stands rigidly in front of him, willing her body to soften. *Protect the girl.* Fane nuzzles closer, obviously seeking, his lips parted and eyes closed. His want is palpable, a beating pulse, as obvious to me as it was to Stela in that moment. *Protect the girl.* He cranes his head and she pulls back to stare him in the face, to see what's coming, certain of what is required.

She flinches.

Fane opens his eyes, mute with horror.

He sends her away.

I tear my mouth away from her with a gasp that sends a spray of blood across her pale chest. Stela slumps in my arms, her eyes vacant and wide, lips moving without sound. We collapse together to the floor and I hold Stela's face against my neck, braced for a bite that doesn't come. Her head lolls to the side, like a nightmare I've had before. One I had often when Stela was still training me to control my impulses.

I bite my wrist and press it against her absently moving lips. The letters take shape against my skin though Stela emits no sound: protect the girl. Her lips stop moving and her muscles coil in my arms. Her eyes alight with life, then shut completely as she grips my forearm with both hands and wrings my veins of all I've taken, everything I have to give.

The sensation of being drained is nothing like death. Stela is hunting for her own truth now, and every image I show her is devoured. Fane standing in my laboratory, the things he said about her, about them. She sees me open and taste his sample. Above and below all these moments we share is a swift undercurrent of emotion. Stela's was fear. Mine is the most heart-wrenching pain I've ever known. Stela braces a palm against my sternum and shoves me away. We drop to our sides both caught in the swoon of the other's emotions.

She was merciful, more reserved with her feed than I was. We lie silently on the floor, each with a cheek pressed to the scuffed wood, our eyes fixated on each other.

"Are you satisfied?" she asks in a broken voice. Her eyes are soft, wounded. She curls in on herself, limbs pulled in tight. She looks like an abandoned child. I suppose that's exactly what she is, no matter how old she gets. I reach out for her and she places her hand in mine.

"Are you?" I ask. With effort Stela pulls me closer. Her considerable strength has taken a hit.

"Not quite," she says. Stela pierces the pad of her index finger before I can ask what she means. She smears the blood against my bottom lip, pushes her finger past my teeth. The blood is scarce from such a small wound, but I don't have to hunt, only receive. I see Stela standing in the doorway of the lab, a young man dragged in behind her. I see myself curled around Lydia. It looked like an embrace. The inevitability of that moment to Stela, her certainty that I am something she is destined to lose. The overwhelming sadness came first but was not long for this world. It died on the heels of her blinding rage toward Lydia.

"Oh," I offer dumbly as she withdraws her healed finger. We both roll over on our backs. The fire in the hearth pops to break the silence. I can't think of a single thing to say to her. An apology is due to both parties. I never should have doubted her. She shouldn't have taken her fears and frustrations out on me. My reluctance to say this out loud has nothing to do with stubbornness. A spoken apology just seems so empty after such an intimate yet aggressive exchange.

"The picture," Stela points lazily at the windowscape, "does it resonate with you?"

I turn to regard the image she chose more carefully this time. "Lonely," I reply. My eyes drift back up to the sharp shadows overhead. "The picture makes me feel lonely."

Stela sighs, always an awful sound.

"Everything makes you feel lonely," she says. Her observation isn't an attack and even if it were, her sorrow and helplessness would soften the blow.

"You don't." I take her hand again and she squeezes back weakly.

"Sometimes I do."

Sometimes she does. Often, we aren't what the other needs, or think we need. We say the wrong thing and what we've built goes up in flames. We build it again, on the same ground, in the same way. Is that just life? Are the bitter disappointments unavoidable? Stela is the only person I've ever wanted, and I know the feeling is mutual.

In one swift movement Stela is poised above me, one thigh between mine and both hands in my hair. She stares beseechingly into my eyes and kisses me, just once, soft and chaste at the corner of my mouth. "I would never willingly cause you pain," she whispers. Her lips brush my cheek like a falling tear. I pull her down against me and hold her close and take a greedy breath of her hair. It seems like years have passed since we held each other this way, and for a while that's all we do. Our touches gentle, careful, shy.

Stela breaks our timid embrace and hoists herself up as though jolted awake by a terrible dream. "Fane actually came to you."

I nod solemnly. I had hoped she'd forget for a while in favor of the moment. Or that the revelation that Fane can and does travel aboveground would be buried. But it isn't every day you find out that your *embattled* overlord enjoys a frolicking night on the town whenever the mood strikes him.

"He knows you do not belong to him," she says.

"We don't know that."

Stela is not convinced. "He shared a secret with you. That was no accident, Elizabeth. It was a test. He came to the lab as he wanted you alone. Perhaps in an attempt to listen to your thoughts without distraction. To see if he could…"

I lift up on my elbows and Stela rocks back on her heels. "You're scaring yourself. And me." I hold my palm over the quickly mending flesh on her neck. The skin there is warm to the touch. I find myself oddly regretting the fact that I'll never mark her body the way she's marked mine. But she'll carry Fane's mark all her long life.

"You drank his blood," she says, horrified. "How much did you drink?"

I sit up as best I can with Stela perched on my thighs and take her wrists. She's looking right at me, through me, as though searching for some hint of him. "Not much. I didn't even drain the vial, Stela. Stay calm."

"Not much this time. How much have you had?"

"I don't know." Lie. "A couple encounters. Once when he tested me to see if I was prepared to go aboveground. And…"

Stela scrubs her face with her hand. "Just tell me."

"There were two or three times when he caught me in hall. Said Lydia was late coming home. He fed from me, just my wrist, he didn't take much. But…he gave it back to me. I… It was weird. I should have said. Why would he need to feed from someone and then let them feed from him immediately after?"

Stela shakes her head, laughing weakly. "Lydia is never late. She can barely stand to be apart from him. And it was not about your blood. It was about getting his blood in your veins."

"Why? You've said yourself Fane rarely—"

"To read you!" she shouts, grabbing my face desperately. She calms herself as quickly as she can. "Fane cannot hear you, and he knows why. He knows, Elizabeth. He knows you are not his. He might have been counting on you drinking the blood he brought to the lab…"

I grab her by the shoulders and force her look at me. "Stela, I'm still me. I'm still Elizabeth. I'm not now, nor have I ever been Irina. I don't belong to him. He can't hear me. Okay?"

She stops gripping my face and starts stroking my cheek. No one has ever looked at me the way she does—as if I'm something precious to her, a gift…

"He's not going to kill me," I tell her. I've never been more uncertain of anything, but that's what she needs to hear. I stand up and take her hand to help her to her feet. "At least not yet. He needs me. He needs the lab to produce results."

Stela wraps her hand around the back of my neck and kisses me. She's rushed in her affection, despondent. I can taste myself on her tongue, that bright copper tinge of spent blood. Her hands roam down my front, they probe and stroke as though she means to examine me for fresh injuries. I hold her hand over my heart and break our kiss reluctantly. "Stop. I'm all right. He's trying to drive us apart. That's why he came to the lab. That's why he told me he slept with you."

"We are not safe here, my angel."

"We don't have anywhere else to go, Stela. Your words, not mine."

"I did this," she says. "I brought this upon you."

"I made my choice. I chose you."

Stela laughs derisively. "A decision made considerably easier without knowing all the facts."

We've never addressed her pointed omissions so directly. Stela has never affirmed or denied that she downplayed how hard a transition this life would be for me. And I rarely speak about the particular challenges her world has created for me. What would be the point? Stela was Fane's ward for two decades before she was turned. She never had a life of her own. She never made a decision unless Fane sanctioned it. Sometimes I forget.

"Dearest," I say, though I rarely use terms of endearment with her or anyone else. "Knowing what I know now…I can honestly say that given the chance to take it all back, everything we've shared, I would make the exact same choice."

Stela smiles widely, her bright white teeth gleaming. She takes my hand, brings it to her lips. "I will fix this."

"It's not all on you, Stela." I rest my forehead against her temple and wrap my arms around her waist. It's not often that I get the opportunity to comfort or calm her. "So, what do you want to do?" I ask.

She shifts out of my embrace, deliberately tames her anxiety, and becomes in an instant the Stela I see every day. The brazen Stela I fell in love with.

"We will require travel documents," she says and starts to shift on her feet. "Passports, money, attire, incidentals." She plants her hands on her hips, drumming her fingers on her waist and looks blankly across the room. "Andrew can procure them. Afterward, he will need to make himself scarce."

"Fane will find us." I don't know why or how or what makes me so bitterly certain.

"We will be hunted," she affirms. "We will travel light. See the world, if you wish. But I suspect we will have to keep moving for quite some time."

For the first time I recognize the mistake I made by reading Stela's journals. She puts her own delicate spin on this grand adventure, but I know what it means to be without a clan. We'll be outliers, unclaimed

Strigoi without allies or protection. I would give just about anything to have maintained my ignorance of the politics that govern beings like us. Blind optimism comes readily to the naive.

What would The Lady say if Stela asked for sanctuary?

"Banish the thought," Stela says with a wave of her hand. But Stela wasn't looking at me when I had the idea, and I didn't project it to her. What the hell kind of power does this woman have if her moniker can be heard even in one's private thoughts? "I returned the favor of her grace centuries ago. We are not indebted to one another."

"You saved her daughter Antonia in Rome. You mentioned it in your journals."

"Yes, and she saved my Lord's life before that. Her Ladyship would start a war were she to claim us. Another war, when each of us remember all too keenly the cost of the last." I cup her chin and kiss her ruffled brow.

"You should sleep." Stela lets her head rest heavily in my hand. "I'll take the couch tonight."

Stela jerks her head up, and her wounded eyes are enough to crush my resolve. "Must you?" she asks. It's the closest she's ever come to begging. I don't resist when her hands slip around my waist, or when she pulls me down onto her lap. She presses her cheek to my collarbone.

"I don't want to keep repeating the same unhealthy pattern with you," I whisper, raking my fingers through the soft hair at the back of her head. "I think we need to be gentle with each other, listen more, exercise patience. Cultivate patience, since we're both sadly lacking in that department."

Stela raises her head and looks at me as though I've just asked her for a divorce. Which is ridiculous. We're not married. "Elizabeth, please." She keeps hold of my waist, tugs me imploringly. "Just to sleep," she says and stares up at me with her unnerving naked eyes. "I need you."

Not, I love you. And not an apology or an offer of forgiveness, which we're beyond now. What kind of monster could refuse her?

"You're on my side."

Stela smirks and heaves herself dramatically off the bed. We each move silently to our respective sides and disrobe more timidly than we did our first night together. Eyes averted as we slip beneath the sheets and keep close to the edges of the mattress.

I stare up at the unadorned posts of the canopy while she settles her limbs. "I need you too," I whisper in the fresh dark, seconds after Stela extinguishes the bedside lamp. The mattress is firm and unwelcoming, unfamiliar to me after having slept on her side these last couple weeks.

Stela's hand slides across my belly and I roll instinctively into her arms. We settle our heads on my pillow, her fingers stroking my ribs, my fingers caressing the smooth planes of her face. The fire in the hearth is only a bed of red coals, but I can see her as plainly in the dark. Despite the shadows beneath her eyes, she's as beautiful as she was the day we met.

"He's going to kill us," I say, accepting for the first time what Stela tried so desperately to impart to me.

She pulls the back of my knee and guides my leg over her hip. "He will undoubtedly try."

I hold her that much tighter and press myself as close as I can. Strange to get something you've always wanted. I thought I would do anything to have Stela all to myself, but the cost is steeper than I could have imagined. I would do anything to keep her safe, except risk losing her, and that is precisely the reason we're in danger.

"Will everyone come for us?"

Stela runs her finger down the bridge of my nose as she has dozens of times before. "Bård is unwavering in his loyalty to Fane," she says. She doesn't sound hurt or even frightened. Not anymore. She's resigned herself to this course, to whatever tomorrow brings. She kisses my eyelids and closes her own.

I stroke her forehead, her cheek, and make a point to commit her resting features to memory. Stela never expires before I do, and I hold my gaze steady until the encroaching blackness blurs the edges of my vision and pulls me down with her.

* * *

Perfectly round spheres…and all with the same pink tinge. His platelet count is high. Impossible to say whether he fed immediately before and I'm most certainly not going to ask.

Of all my samples, from every member of the family, only two fall within the normal human range. Only two have the same inexplicable iridescence and bashful hue. Is it because Fane turned her? Was this the result on a biological level? Does that begin to explain Stela's resilience to light?

I massage my eyes with the palm of my hands and lean heavily against the counter. The clock is running out. We could have days left in the lair, hours if Stela's meeting with Andrew goes well, and

I'm no closer to understanding the role blood plays in memory than I was when I started. That memories can be channeled seems highly probable. But how, if that matters at all, remains to be seen. In fact, the only success I've had has been to double my list of questions.

I heave my notebook from the depths of my bag and begin poring over my hastily jotted observations. My platelet count is consistent with the rest of the siblings, the color of the red cells doesn't vary in anyone but Stela. If this were the result of her being turned by Fane, why wouldn't that odd color have been passed along to me? I skim through most of my notes and read through the post mortem on Macha's stillborn pup once more. Perfectly normal platelets. A stark contrast to the pup's hearty sister's cells. The pups were by all outward appearance—aside from the presence of milk teeth at birth—perfectly normal dogs prior to feeding from their mother. There had to be something inside them. A dormant gene lying in wait.

Unbidden, a memory of Stela grinds my search to a screeching halt: "I had four sisters, all with raven hair like our mother."

"Black hair…" I snap the notebook shut. Blond hair is recessive. How the hell was Stela born fair-haired and fairer skinned than any member of her family in a tribe of no more than two hundred people? Every member of her mortal clan had to be related.

My stomach sinks. I can picture Stela's mother as clearly as my own thanks to Stela's persistent dream of the last time she saw her. Small-boned with a sun-leathered complexion and waves of black curls that spilled to her waist. Beyond the strange sentiment that passed between Fane and Stela's mother, the way she thanked him for taking her child away from her, I never paid much thought to the dream. Stela's screams, her mother's tears eclipsed the obvious. Of every member in attendance when Fane collected Stela, she physically resembled only one person…

I peer over my shoulder at the blood film sitting under the microscope. I reach for the slide and hold it gently, as though it could combust at any moment. Fane's neatly printed name sits heavily in my palm. A hypothesis is only an educated guess, but there are some things in this life that once spoken can never be unsaid. Stela would never forgive me for saying the words out loud.

Does she know? Could she already suspect? The question sends an involuntary shiver down my spine. I slip Fane's slide in the tray beside the others and lock them in the cabinet.

I keep hold of the counter as I stand up, shaken and faint with hunger. The task of gathering my things and righting the lab is a welcome distraction. I toss my notebook and laptop back in my satchel and retrieve a collection bag from the fridge. The delivery of donated blood had been an unexpected gift from Stela. Not quite as thoughtful as the lab coat, more a condition than a gift. Still, she knows me, and was sure I'd linger here until the last possible second. This was Stela's unobtrusive way of saying that if I mean to burn the midnight oil in a very literal sense, it won't do to miss anymore meals for the sake of discovery.

The blood bag is cool in my hands, lifeless. No more appealing than a raw slab of meat on a plate. I tuck it in the waistband of my pants—a trick I picked up from her—and pace aimlessly around my clinical refuge. This could be the last time I ever step foot inside this room.

I pull the blood bag from my waistband and drop down onto the edge of my stool, sending myself into a lazy spin. The skin of the bag bursts beneath my teeth and a mouthful rushes down my throat. There are no memories, or passion or heat. Just the tepid promise of another feeding cycle complete, another night sustained this side of the grave. Two draws from the bag and the blood comes right back up in my throat.

I barely make it to the sink in time. There is no strain or retching involved, but the reaction is faster and more thorough than my previous bouts of unexplained reflux. The blood pours out of my mouth, spatters into the sink and slides down the drain. That's when the shaking starts. I toss the rest of the collection bag into the sink and sit down on the floor until the dizziness passes.

Something is wrong.

I should have told Stela the first time it happened. When was the first time? James. I didn't feel right after James, but I kept his blood down. Up until that point I'd been taking blood collection bags as meals with no side effects. Feeding from Stela has never been a problem, nor has feeding from Fane. Sometimes I can manage a successful hunt and lose only a mouthful or two. I can offset that loss and correct my dizziness and disorientation by feeding off Stela later. But this? The blood had barely reached my stomach before I spat it back up. I need to tell Stela. She should know. Maybe this is just part of the transition from human to Strigoi, one more difference she forgot to mention because it had been so long. It's been over a year though…

I drop my head back against the cabinet and force myself to concentrate on something else until the shaking stops.

What will we do together, Stela and I? What will we do for ourselves beyond surviving for the sake of each other? Without Fane's far-reaching influence and considerable wealth, we'll be scavengers. A blight on humankind, draining the life from their veins and no doubt robbing their still-warm corpses. My own inheritance will only take us so far.

I check my phone. Though a whisper would be welcome to Stela I don't trust my ability to keep my emotions from bleeding through, and she has enough to worry about. How could I even begin to broach the similarities I've uncovered between her blood and Fane's tonight? Worse, what if I manage to cover the topic and she resists the bigger picture? Will I have to spell it out? I don't know if that's something I could forgive were our positions reversed. And what if I'm wrong?

She'll be out hunting now, no doubt having terrified Andrew even more. I send her a quick text to hurry home and decide against citing a reason. She won't ask for one. I envy that trait, I truly do. Stela doesn't need to know why—only when and where.

I stand up and scour the sink, hiding the blood bag near the bottom of the trash. I take off my lab coat and gently hang it on the hook beside the door. Satchel in hand, I take one more look around my pristine workspace, my sanctuary. I flick off the light and lock the door behind me.

* * *

The hearth is ablaze with a roaring fire and the room is almost uncomfortably warm, bathed in orange light that makes long shadows of the furniture. A smile plays at my mouth, Stela must have sensed something was wrong if she managed to beat me home.

"Stela?" I drop my bag on the desk in the corner. The bathroom door is open and dark. She isn't seated on the sofa or curled up in the armchair. A chill creeps into my blood and races down my spine.

Her car wasn't parked in the garage.

I tiptoe toward the darkened bathroom, searching for her reflection in the mirror.

"Still out and about, I fear."

I freeze. Fane is perched casually beside the fire, stoking the flame-licked logs with a red-tipped poker.

"You need not be alarmed, young one." He smiles and raises the smoldering end of the poker. "I want to discuss your progress." Fane sets the poker back in the iron rack on the floor and takes a step back to admire his blaze.

I seize his momentary distraction and shatter the silence in a way only she could hear. I close my eyes and plant my feet. With every fiber of my being, every nerve, every cell I funnel the rampant dread in my chest, boil it down and wrap it neatly in two words that cannot possibly find Stela fast enough.

He's here.

"Come." His voice booms and Fane waves me closer with an open hand. "We both know your lover is not far behind. And we have so much to discuss, the three of us."

"Then, shouldn't we wait? For Stela to—"

"Everyone material to this discussion is already in attendance," he says slyly. He storms down the few short steps into the living area and squeezes himself into the armchair. "Have a seat."

I take the longest possible route around the back of the couch and sit on the edge of the sofa's arm, as far from him as I can get while still obeying his demand. With an amused grin—tense at the corners of his lips—Fane tips his head and brushes an errant wrinkle from his emerald silk pants.

"Have you any interesting news to report?" he asks.

News, not discoveries or advances. A rush of anxiety sweeps sharply through me, like a hand constricting my heart. Stela hasn't sent me a verbal response, but her fear for me leaches through our bond. She's coming. She'll come.

"Nothing conclusive," I reply steadily.

His amusement fades quickly. "You have a sample of my blood," he states. Something in his tone, not quite an accusation. An insult, perhaps.

"I do." I cross my arms protectively, and for all my posturing I may as well roll out a red carpet for him. If it's answers he's after, he'll dig them out soon enough. "I'm afraid I have more questions now than I did when I started."

"That makes two of us," he says, leaning forward, flashing his too-white teeth. "Do you know that I find modern science absolutely fascinating?" Fane stands abruptly and stalks the living room purposefully. "Genes, chromosomes, sequencing…" he trails off suddenly, his eyes unfocused as though he's waiting for something, listening for someone.

"Science is deductive reasoning," I interject. "Not a treasure map."

He laughs hard and only once with a finger raised in warning. "None of that," he admonishes. "There is not room in this world for your ego and mine." His countenance appears affable again. He resumes his pacing, smacking the back of one hand in the palm of the other. This time he keeps his eyes on me, and their magnetism is undeniable. Fane slithers right past my defenses, and whether or not he can hear my thoughts hardly matters. He soothes me, deliberately infecting the air between us with forced calm that erodes my defenses brick by brick.

"I trust my blood was without parallel," he says.

It isn't a question, but it's the most research-related statement he's made thus far. Is that why he's here? To stop me from telling Stela the truth? He had to know I would see the similarities.

"We are rare, and we are worshipped," he says mostly to himself. There's a misplaced pride in his tone, as though his biology is his own creation. "Do you know *how* rare?"

I struggle to keep my thoughts clear with his damnable calm crawling all over me, and it takes longer than it should for me to realize I've been asked a question. "Yes. You said there were nine. Nine great houses."

"So we thought." He smiles again, too many teeth in that smile. He flexes his shoulder blades and they stand out on his back like wings. "The reason the Moroi are without rival, the reason we rule without contestation is truly quite simple." He stops short and turns on me. "I could end you right now and never give your death another thought."

His synthetic calm radiates in my bones—the same sensation as sinking into a warm bath—loosening my tongue. "Science has characterized that phenomenon. We call those individuals psychopaths." Completely matter-of-fact, an affront to my own ears. Deep inside me something screams, a part of my body immune to Fane. A warning to behave rumbles on my periphery, like flashes of heat lightning. And with the safety of distance, what is a storm but a show?

Fane guffaws. "Child. Are you suicidal?" He shakes his head incredulously and towers over me. Even his wrists, poking out of his sleeves, are wrapped with muscles thick as cable, and bands twice as wide protrude from his forearms.

He moves closer and sits on the sofa, his arm inches from my thigh. "I warned Stela away from you. Even after you passed my test, I remained unconvinced of your so-called loyalty."

"What test?" I twist on the arm of the sofa, and Fane cocks his head as though I couldn't have asked a more ignorant question. I know the answer already. Somehow, I've always known. I could feel Stela's hand guiding the whole evening, but I never had proof. To know that once again she was acting under orders only doubles my indignation.

"The only way to become what you were destined to be was to purge yourself of the past." He shrugs. "Stela found herself in a similar position the evening after I turned her."

My chest compresses and I nod absently to myself. The young man Stela loved when she was still human, her fencing instructor. A name she can't even recall anymore. How long until I forget the name of my first kill?

"James wasn't a test. He was a person, a father-to-be, a good nurse, and a friend of mine."

"In the end," he says, "it matters not who they are or how they lived. Only that you are and must feed." He reaches out and covers my thigh with his burning palm. "That is why I lead, Irina." The unexpected physical contact forces my eyes to his and I'm distantly aware that I've made a horrible mistake. The boyish face again, the troubled prince who toils in secret for the sake and safety of his clan.

"You had such promise." He twines my hair back around my ear, brushes his thumb down my jaw. "A fire that burns inside you, the likes of which I have not seen since your Maker. And she lost that conviction decades ago."

He takes his hand away and my body leans forward after him. The change in my center of gravity is just enough to shake me awake and I bolt upright on my feet.

"There was a time when Stela would have followed me to the depths of hell and back again, if such an adventure awaited." I take another step back. Fane watches me closely, and the reaching influence of his gaze is held between us like an outstretched hand.

"She is so secretive these days," he says. "Quieter even than you, young one. Well, that is not exactly true anymore, is it?"

My blood wakes from sedation, and either I've managed to inch my way backward and out of Fane's influence, or he has stopped affecting the room so that I can feel fear again.

"Stela was always the strongest of her kind," he rushes to say before I can ask him what he meant by his last comment. "I take great pride in her…abilities." Not enough to create her, possess her, and mold her in his image he has to brag about it too. A shiver of disgust rattles through me and somehow Fane is standing directly in front of me when it passes. He tilts my face up to his.

"Does she know the truth?" he asks. Fane cups my chin in the vise grip of his fingers and the pressure of his stare pierces my eyes. I can't turn away. I can't blink. A dangerous throb starts at the base of my skull with the promise of pain soon to follow, but all I feel is fury.

"You just couldn't get enough of her, could you?" I ask, my jaw barely moving. Fane arches his brows, amused. "You had to take her from her mother. Claim what was yours. Father her, turn her, bed her. It was all the same to you."

Fane barks his laughter in my face and seizes my jaw. He lifts me off the floor as easily a child retrieves a discarded toy. When we're at eye level with each other he brings his lips near to mine. "You are an ignorant fool, *Elizabeth*, if you think that I can be so easily derailed." Fane's grip tightens, and I know I'm going to lose my jaw if he doesn't drop me soon.

"STOP SHOUTING," he screams abruptly and glances suspiciously around the room.

It dawns on me quite suddenly that he isn't screaming at me, which isn't much of a comfort given his agitated and aggressive state. My name…God, he knows.

Fane turns back to me, still holding me up off my feet. His eyes are clear and bright again, calculating not paranoid. He pets the side of my face as I scrabble for a grip on his forearm, anything to take the weight off my crushed jaw. "Did you honestly think you could conceal this from me?" he asks. He shakes me once and my neck makes a sickening pop, pain radiates up the back of my head. "Hide the truth?" Fane releases me with a flick of his wrist that sends me sprawling on the steps in front of him. I push myself upright and an electric current shoots up my spine. Damage to L2 and L3, spinal compression.

I can't move my legs.

He crouches above me and bats my shielding arm aside. "Tell me Stela does not know," he says plaintively. "Tell me, and I will spare your lover's life."

The air of calm has withered and died, and my panic is a welcome reminder that I am in control, free from his influence. I nearly call out to Stela but keep my thoughts to myself. It would be safer if she just stayed away, though if I asked it of her she wouldn't listen. We're going to die down here. A real death this time.

"Stela doesn't know," I say in the steadiest voice I can manage. But I'm not certain I know what I'm affirming. I don't believe the truth of Stela's conception would shake him this much.

"Liar," he says with smile and disappears behind me, up the steps.

The feeling returns to my toes. I wriggle them in my boots but I'm not sure how much longer I can placate him. I've sustained more than my share of injuries while sparring with Bård, but he never damaged my spine and he always fed me a blood bag immediately after to hurry along the healing process.

"Such loyalty to one who has consistently manipulated you," he says from behind me. His footsteps shake the floor and I try to lift myself up into the sleeping quarters so that I can see him. Fane grabs me under my left arm and drags me up the steps, as though I'm a doll he's simply tired of playing with. He flings me toward the bed and I slide across the floor and into the bed frame. The disks in my back are healing far too slowly, feeling returns to my calves as needle-sharp pinpricks. The pain is considerable, but the klaxon resounding in my brain is hunger. A bone-deep, reason-shattering hunger.

Fane sits beside my head on the edge of the mattress, when I notice that he's retrieved the hunting knife Stela keeps on the nightstand. Fane seems to calm himself, and he takes note of the bedpost beside his arm, the one I shoved Stela against. He smiles to himself as though he can picture that fight perfectly—perhaps he can—and nudges the splintered wood with his elbow.

"Something I have often wondered, Elizabeth," he says and hoists me up on the bed by my collar. "Did Stela ask you if she could share your memories with me?" I stare at him stupidly. "All those stolen moments from your nights. Your reflection in the mirror as you painted your face, hiding from Erebus in the freight tunnels, the little bread crumbs she fed me to sate my curiosity about you. Did she ask your permission?"

Fane faces me and taps Stela's hunting blade on his knee. I regard him from the corner of my eye. He purses his lips, flicks the soft pale hair away from his eyes. "I thought not," he says.

Would she do that to me? Did she pry into my mind without a word? Or is this just another of his smoke screens?

Fane stands. "She betrayed you," he says and tilts my chin up with the tip of the knife. "She used you, Elizabeth." He drags the blade down my throat and holds it against my jugular. "Perhaps it is not too late to be redeemed, young one." He stares imploringly into my eyes, and the effect is as though he has placed a dozen hands all over my body. Hands that plead and pull, and long to embrace. The heat of his stare is extraordinary, burning my body from the inside out. "One small…" he looks over my body, "sacrifice, and you could belong to me."

The scream of my hunger is constant, and the smell of Fane is thick in my throat. Maddening to be this close to him and starved at the same time. If I could get the knife…

"Frankly," I say, and the voice does not belong to me at all. "I would sooner die in the sewer at the mouth of your dogs."

Fane laughs again. And I don't know why I would bait the terrifying man who holds a knife to my throat. I didn't plan on saying anything at all.

Fane's eyes fix upon mine as he grabs a fistful of my hair to expose my neck to his blade, and as he does a familiar song fills my blood. Stela is in the tunnel. I hear her frantic footfall as the blade breaks the skin and a pearl of blood blooms from the superficial wound. *Please stay away. Stela, please.* But as soon as I ask it of her, Fane turns away from the drop of blood spilling down my neck and stares expectantly toward the hatch just in time for Stela's boots to smack against the floor.

The look on her face…

A furious snarl twists Stela's beautiful lips. I barely recognize her. There's no sign of my lover in the monster in front of me, just a coiled spine, two trembling white fists, fangs bared and a scream that builds upon itself—deafening, terrifying—made all the more gruesome by Fane's delighted laughter.

The room is suddenly sweltering, as though a fire has spilled across the room, unnoticed in the commotion. The heat rolls over my body in blistering waves. Stela threatens something in her native tongue and then Fane is removed from my line of sight. Stela launches herself at her Maker, and they fall to the ground on the far side of the bed.

X

Put Asunder

Andrew stands with his hands cupped behind his back. His fingers tremble as he stares out at the glittering city beyond his office window, no doubt committing the night-washed landscape to memory. I stand beside him at a respectable distance, attempting to do the same.

We will all have to leave this remarkable city and it amazes me how deeply that sentiment runs as grim acceptance takes hold. Chicago has blossomed before my eyes, from a harbor, to a town, to a thriving metropolis rotten to the core. The sleek buildings and horrendous traffic, the constant noise and pervasive crime. I started a new life here. I had purpose, no matter my role. It was here I found Elizabeth sitting alone in a hospital waiting room.

Perhaps the true value of a place cannot be fully realized until you lose it.

"You'll never make it past the city limits," Andrew says. His eyes made solid white from the reflected light of a thousand glowing windows spread out at his feet. Andrew turns and scoops his neglected glass of scotch off the desk behind us.

"I know. I still have to try."

Andrew downs the remainder of his drink and cradles the slick glass close in his thick fingers. I lean against the window but keep my eyes to myself. My sunglasses sit neatly on the edge of his desk. I believe the face should unencumbered—especially the eyes—if one intends to strike a bargain.

"You can't honestly believe he'll let you go." With a nervous smile Andrew turns in my direction. "And why would I jeopardize my life, the safety of my family to help you?"

"Andrew, you have only two choices. You can refuse and die at my hand now. Or you can trust me, do as I ask, and take your chances."

Andrew sets the high ball on the desk and misses the edge entirely. The glass hits the rug below with a thud, and rolls beneath his chair.

"In your bid for freedom I'm a dead man either way." He is seething, red in the face and verging on belligerent. Whether his mood is purely fear-based or compounded by the scotch, I cannot say. Drunk, obviously, but not wrong.

"If you agree to aid us, I promise you, before we depart the city I will remove any trace of treason from your memory." I have only rearranged the memories of someone once—Derek Carrington the night Elizabeth was shot. Whether I can replicate my initial success remains to be seen, but why worry the man?

I retrieve the glass to return it the bar in the corner. I hesitate over the crystal decanter, curious if another finger of liquid courage would do much to sway Andrew. In the end I return to our stalemate empty-handed. The drink will kill him soon enough. He must know this. His body carries a distinctly sweet odor: too much sugar in the blood.

"And if I refuse you, Kathryn?" He crosses his arms over his swollen belly.

"As I said, refuse and I will leave your body here for Rachel to find in the morning."

I lean back against the paper-strewn desk, my hands folded neatly in my lap. Andrew leers at me, his bloodshot eyes sizing me up from my bare neck to the parted black shirt and down my tweed slacks, as if struggling to remember whether his fear of me is justified.

"I have access to all of Mr. Radu's accounts, Andrew. I can finance my departure with or without your help."

"Then why come here at all?" He asks, puffing his chest. For a man of such financial brilliance, he can be astoundingly short-sighted. "You've got it all figured out. There's no need to enlist me in your coup."

Fiercely gripping the back of his chair Andrew holds himself upright. I put my hand over his. "Andrew, if I rob Mr. Radu on your watch, it will hardly matter whether you helped me or not. Someone will be made to pay with their life, and you will be the obvious choice for instant gratification. An example will be made of you for the benefit of the rest of my family, and what could be done to them should they follow my lead or your incompetence."

"Besides," I pat his hand and stand up, thrusting a pen at his chest. "My ward Natalie's account is the only one Mr. Radu knows nothing about. When I disappear he will most certainly call on you. But if you have no recollection of this conversation or any assistance rendered he cannot follow the money."

Andrew fumbles with the pen and teeters unsteadily above his desk. I shuffle the necessary documents into a tidy stack and guide his gently swaying body into the leather chair. Andrew gazes emptily up at me, holds his breath. I lean closer, my lips beside his ear.

"Think of your wife, Andrew. Think of your beautiful Christine." I retrieve the family photograph from the corner of his desk and hold the gilded frame in front of him. "What would the loss of you do to them? What would it force Christine to become?" He takes the photo reverently in his hands, traces his daughter's face with his finger. "Is she ready for all this? I offer you a few more years to continue your work. A few more years to explain the...intricacies of this company to your heir."

Andrew releases his trapped breath and returns the photograph to his desk. I kneel down, swivel his seat toward me, and stare openly into his tear-clouded eyes.

"I am still your best chance of survival, Andrew." I clutch his dry hand in mine. "And if you help me, I will do everything in power to ensure that when Mr. Radu comes calling, you are nothing more than a loyal servant and frustrating dead end."

He looks down at my hand and covers it with his. "You could do one better and make me forget you completely." His shoulders shake and the two of us share a rare laugh. I pat his leg and stand up when the moment passes.

"A clever deception requires a modicum of truth, Mr. Opes. I fear you are stuck with my memory."

Andrew returns to the paperwork in front of him with renewed interest. "Quite right," he says and waves me away while he starts to read.

I walk around the side of his desk and drop into an open chair. The clock on the wall ticks the seconds away. Time has never held much value to me. There has been so much of it, and surely there would always be more. But sitting here in Andrew's darkened office, the passage of time carries new weight. Each second is one moment closer to the inevitable. Will we escape? Will Fane incinerate us both before we step as far as the freight tunnels? The uncertainty thrills an old part of me. But the adventure is overshadowed by unwelcome apprehension—a boundless concern for the safety of another. I have led a long life and have the stamina for a dozen more, but what would eternity mean without Elizabeth?

My mobile vibrates in my blazer pocket, as though my darling girl caught wind of the shift in my thoughts. Elizabeth's message is a simple request asking that I hurry home. I shut my eyes and seek her out only to find a new partition raised between our minds, and one that I did not erect…

"Is something the matter?" Andrew has stopped signing, his glasses slipping down his nose.

"Nothing at all," I say and tuck the phone back into my breast pocket. Andrew hesitates with the pen poised above the paper, and I place my sunglasses back on my face where they belong. He mumbles to himself and resumes.

The mobile was an odd choice. Why would she communicate with me that way? The more my thoughts drift to Elizabeth, the stronger my concern. Something has unsettled her, but she leaves no door open in her mind. All I can glean is a malingering melancholy, a whiff of distress and the stench of disinfectant.

"The passports will take time," he says, flipping over a fresh page.

"How long?"

"At least a week, Kathryn. And that would be a miracle."

"Have you a contact that could create them sooner?"

"Not if you want a convincing cover identity for…" he retrieves the aliases from a discarded page, "Katherine and Natalie Isles." He smiles to himself and taps the paper with his pen. "You know, I've always liked that name. Natalie."

"So has my ward."

The rhythmic brush of his hasty signature becomes as aggravating as the ticking clock, and minutes drain to hours. I sit politely in the thickening dark and watch the night sky. Andrew files and sorts, types half a dozen cryptically worded emails to his more sordid contacts, responds to several text messages all with a seamless ease that leaves me mildly impressed.

"What else do you require?" I ask as Andrew encloses the paperwork in a manila envelope. He leans back in his seat with the sigh of a man who has just completed a marathon.

"Now we wait," he says. "I will contact you when the particulars are in order. Updating the name on the trust belonging to Ms. Dum—changing the name to Mrs. Isles will be simple enough. The passports, as I said, are another matter."

I rise to my feet and extend my hand. Andrew watches me closely, suspicious of my intentions now that most of the legwork has been completed. He stands and takes my hand in both his sweaty palms, clearly puzzling over what he wants to say.

"Who will they send to replace you?" he asks in a soft and shaky voice.

"I would imagine Ms. Dilay Sadik will take my place." I could lie, comfort him, but I doubt he would appreciate the surprise after the scare Lydia gave him during her first visit to this office.

"Kathryn…" he clears his throat and relinquishes my hand, having held it a beat too long. Andrew bobs forward on his toes, eyes downcast. I see the doting father before me, the concerned husband. "Don't ever come back here," he says, but that is not what he holds in his heart.

"I know, Andrew." I suppress a smile and straighten my jacket. "As much as it pains me to admit it, I shall miss working with you too." The vein beside his eyebrow beats beneath the skin, and the corner of his mouth quirks upward. "Until next time."

I make it only as far as the door before he stops me.

"Kathryn, how will you make me forget all this?"

I do smile at him now, opening the door to the hall. "Without bloodshed or injury, Andy. You have my word."

He nods to himself and turns back to the window, rolling his shoulders.

As I wait for the elevator, I take in the clean lines and glinting marble of the lobby with the nostalgic pride of a retiree. I never considered that this building, this company exists not only because Fane willed it, but because I labored to make that wish a reality. How marvelous to think that long after I have left this city, business here will continue as usual with new acquisitions secured and yet unnamed partnerships.

Part of me had hoped to find Rachel with her fiery red hair hiding her face as she peeked at her cell phone, manning the reception desk, but she left hours ago. She has been my favorite administrator, unwavering in the courtesy she extended toward me and occasionally crossing the line into kindness. An intelligent woman—far too good for Andrew—who understands more of my nature than she has ever been told.

"A pleasure as always," I say to no one in particular as I board the elevator.

When I reach the parking garage, I check my mobile again. Two hours without another word from Elizabeth beyond her first vague message. A quiet foreboding drifts on the crisp night air and not a hundred feet away I hear the gentle patter of lonely footsteps. My senses alight, and beneath the stench of stale exhaust and dried oil so indicative of car parks I detect the musk and sweat of another late-night visitor. A paralegal or junior associate of some kind from the sound of his modest shoes.

He's here.

I wheel around, half expecting to find Elizabeth behind me. The stark clarity of her voice is astounding, it lingers in the awful silence that follows like an empty echo. I wait with closed eyes as though clarification is forthcoming—as though any is required—but there is only fear and I cannot tell whether the anxiety is hers or mine.

"'Scuse me," the young paralegal mumbles. He sidesteps my frozen body, headed for the elevator. Quite of its own accord, my right hand darts out to haul him back by his hair. He screams for all he's worth and I let him. One of us should be screaming. The gel in his hair flakes around my fingers, dusts the tips of my eyelashes as his spine snaps in my arms and I rip his throat open with my teeth.

The arterial spray is regrettable, spotting the pavement in a wide arc before my lips can seal his wound. Garnet blossoms of blood soak through the front of his pale dress shirt, smear against my shoes and pants. I drink to the bottom of this random passerby in the camera-monitored garage of a building where I keep close ties, and the longer I hold the body to my mouth the clearer Elizabeth's fright becomes.

I wipe my lips on his shoulder and drag the body back to my car. My plated vehicle, which will have to go. I hit the trunk release and drop him inside, head over feet. Once behind the steering wheel, I shut my eyes and push all the calm that I possess out of myself and trust that it will find Elizabeth as readily as my whisper.

Say nothing. Stall for time.

* * *

The garage above the lair is deceptively quiet. I leave my car running and without a second thought dart down into the tunnels.

Not a single impression from Fane all this long evening. Only the ebb and flow of Elizabeth's mounting dread, which beats in my breast at an alarming pace. There is pain, regret, a choking sorrow that turns my stomach, and none of it is mine.

As I bear down the freight tunnel Erebus rushes out of the darkness and matches my stride. His howl rings off the weeping walls, ripples in the few dank pools of runoff, but his battle cry goes unanswered by his pack. He doubles his pace and disappears around the bend as I punch the keycode into the hatch that guards the main entrance.

Please stay away, Stela. Please.

Elizabeth's whisper carries everything she has left, threatening the considerable pace of my crawl through the candlelit corridor above our room. Her love for me is everywhere, and her terrible fear inescapable. I throw myself down through the hatch and hit the ground below with an echoing thud.

There is no mistaking this sight. Her tousled hair, the way she braces herself on her arms to take the weight off her back, the blood oozing down her neck, my hunting knife held to her skin, and Fane's bellowing laughter. My body contorts into a pounce as Elizabeth volleys what strength she has regained to kick away from him.

A fury like nothing I have ever known engulfs me from head to toe. The room is sweltering and I spare a glance at Elizabeth's horrified face only to realize that the screams I hear are my own.

In our mother tongue I tell my Lord that this is the moment of his death and lunge at his torso. Our bodies crash on the far side of the bed, fists and feet beginning their assault before we land.

Fane grabs me by the throat and hurls me head first into the opposing wall. The windowscape screens shred as my body drops to the floor. I struggle to stand and as Fane closes in on me, still laughing, realize my left ankle is bent at an unnatural angle. In my periphery Elizabeth has already hobbled away from the bed in search of something. I slam my foot against the ground to straighten my twisted bones.

"After all that I have given you Stela, you bring *this* into my house?" Fane snatches me off the ground by my hair and rears back to launch my head into the newly exposed cement wall.

"Don't touch her!" Elizabeth screams, fire poker in hand. She slams it into Fane's temple when he turns. The wrought iron handle hangs behind his shoulder, the curled prong lodged in his skull. He smiles at me as he wrests the prong loose and turns on Elizabeth. He keeps me held behind him as he focuses on his assailant and I climb up his arm to tear my hair free or tear it out completely. My scalp splits a moment too late and Fane sends Elizabeth flying toward the bed with one swing of the poker.

"Elizabeth, run!" I curl my legs up to my chest and kick away from him. Fane drops me of his own accord and towers over my bleeding body.

"Yes, *Elizabeth*. Run," he commands calmly. He leans down over me with a sneer. "It is so much more rewarding when they run."

My body blazes from the inside out and my vision tunnels so that all I can see is his delighted face. I launch myself off the floor and tear at his throat with my teeth.

"Honestly, Stela. At a time like this?" Fane jerks my arm out of its socket and detaches me. His blood is barely a trickle down my throat as he seizes my leg and whips me over the sofa and into the corner of the hearth. Elizabeth hoists herself off the floor and screams my name, a thick piece of splintered bedpost sticking out of her back.

Where is everyone? Why has no one come to bear witness to our execution? They must hear us. My body lies inert on the floor, the taste of blood thick on my tongue. I struggle to find my bearings but my arms will not support my weight. My ribs have splintered into my lungs.

"Stela," Fane mocks Elizabeth in a high-pitched voice, and I turn to see her yanking the shard of wood from her back. Fane, stained by my blood, stalks toward her. "Does she not disappoint you?" he asks her, shaking his head. "Is this your savior, child?"

I roll my body to the side and with all my silent might I beg Elizabeth to save herself. She does not respond, but brandishes the blood-smeared scrap of wood like a sword.

"Love," Fane sneers, "has lessened her." He spares a contemptuous look in my general direction just as I manage to lift my chest off the floor. "Such a warrior once. A child after my own heart," he says in a soft and remote tone.

Distantly, there is a scuffle. Then a banshee's wail fills the air. The second Fane turns to inspect the cause Erebus bursts through the service entrance beside the bathroom. He is a blur of black until he collides with Fane, sinking his teeth into Fane's midsection and wrestling him to his knees with a savage thrash of his head. A spray of blood spatters across Elizabeth's face, and as quickly as the scuffle began it stops. Fane pries Erebus' mouth open and away from his gaping wound, then slams him hard against the floor. But Erebus has not finished and sets to right himself immediately, fortified by Fane's powerful blood. Fane kicks the hound into the open bathroom and slams the door closed. The wound on his side is much deeper than my feeble attempt at his throat, the blood dripping down his silk pants.

"You will be next, old man!" he screams.

I hoist myself up off the floor as Fane wrenches the wood from Elizabeth's grasp. Newly armed, he hooks his foot behind her calf and shoves her sternum so forcefully it cracks. He crouches over her sprawled body with the shard positioned over her heart.

"You know, a stake through the heart will not kill you," he says, driving the point into her breast. "But you will wish for death by the time I finish."

My eyes are locked on the blood streaming down his side. Already the wound has begun to sew itself shut, but the gash was considerable. The thirst seizes me body and soul, consuming my reason. Beyond pain, beyond fear, there is only his pulse. Even Elizabeth's broken cries are lost.

In an instant I am above him. Fane has always been stronger, but he has lost a considerable amount of blood. I cannot pull the shard from his hand, but I can pull the point away from Elizabeth. The relief is enough and Elizabeth joins the struggle, gripping my hand in hers and together we bury the shard in his swiftly closing wound just above his hip.

Fane does not cry out. He slams his fist into my temple, the side of my face as I close my mouth over the gushing, ravaged flesh and rob him of all he has left. Elizabeth, pinned beneath us both, wiggles herself loose as he rears back to tear at my hair. Two considerable handfuls are all he can take and the pulling stops. Fane continues to strike wherever he can but the blows come slowly, his swings wild and growing weaker by the moment. I look up at him when sight returns to my swollen left eye and see that Elizabeth has ripped into his throat. His blood weeps down her neck and chest, her hands hooked into his shoulders like two small and fragile claws. Even his back has begun to bleed from her nails. I take another mouthful and my ribs begin to right themselves, snapping together. I extricate myself to ensure he does not swing at my love again. Let Elizabeth have her fill of him—she's earned her kill.

"You only…delay…the inevitable," he whispers, eyes locked on mine as I sit up. "This…will not stand."

A god among beasts. A shell of a man.

Fane unravels in Elizabeth's mouth, and the room fills with the crack of her bones mending as his bones snap under her fingers. Vengeance should be enough, but my rage only grows as Elizabeth heals, as though I had forgotten how beautiful she is. He wanted to take her from me. He wanted to destroy her. My vision clouds over, blood-red and seething.

The gurgling stops and Elizabeth gasps, throwing her head back gloriously. Still heavy in the swoon, she falls back against me and I prop her up against the footboard. Fane's blue eyes are nearly white, only pinpricks of black iris remain and the faded yellow ring that surrounds them. Even bested he smiles at me, his neck slack on his shoulders, his mouth moving with inaudible threats.

"I worshipped you once." The voice is mine but beneath it is a tremulous baritone. My whole body has begun to spasm and quake, and the terrible heat inside of me grows. Fane's youthful grin wanes, and if fear is something he can feel, he does now.

Elizabeth has stirred from her sated swoon. She speaks to me, lovely words that wither in the heat. She pulls me back by the collar, but I cannot be moved. She touches my face, my shoulders, is she standing? She kisses my cheek and drags me to standing, begs me to follow her. But the longer I stare into Fane's empty eyes the farther away from her I drift. My blood is molten in my veins, throbbing in my temples as though threatening to erupt.

Fane tips backward, catches himself on his palm with the last of his strength. "You are mine, my dove," he mouths. "You were *always* mine."

Somehow his words are warning and flint all in one. "No." I kneel in front of him, and Elizabeth tries to hoist me back up, a litany of pleas falling from her beautiful lips. "Not anymore, my Lord."

It begins with a spark, a flash of white behind my eyes and a glimmer of recognition passes over Fane's face. His features twist into snarl and he claws at his bare chest. The blaze in my body pulls all that frightening heat radiating off me back beneath my skin, up my spine where it nests in my skull. Fane's head drops back, his mouth opens in a scream that never arrives. Flames lick the roof of his mouth, burn the backs of his eyes until they blacken, shrink, and shrivel in his head. The body thrashes against the ground, the lungs collapse upon themselves as the flames eat through the front of him. I rise to my feet once more with fire dancing in my black eyes.

"Stela…" Elizabeth whispers, horrified. "We have to go. Now." She bravely positions herself between my body and the curling corpse at our feet. I shut my eyes before the flames claim her too. "Please," she begs, pressing her mouth over mine in a kiss neither of us can remember how to shape. She is shaking fiercely. "That's enough."

The air grows caustic with thick gray plumes of smoke and ash. Bone grit dusts my darling's face and hair as the bed skirt ignites. Fane's carcass smolders, filled with hot coals where organs should be, and the flames spread across the rug beneath him. Erebus howls wildly from the bathroom, heaving himself against the bathroom door.

"Take the service entrance, quick as you can," I say and push Elizabeth toward the narrow shaft intended for the hounds. "Erebus and I will be right behind you." Elizabeth hovers, crouched in the opening for several fraught seconds before she disappears on all fours, headed for the freight tunnels.

The flames have taken the bed and spilled out across the lacquered hardwood floor. Erebus bursts through the bathroom door before I can reach it. He races past me and up the smooth dirt shaft, kicking clumps of rock and clay into my face. Smoke fills the chamber, inhibiting my vision, and I follow the sounds of Erebus until my hands land on cool packed earth and Elizabeth wrenches me to my feet.

The worlds tilts on its axis and time grinds to a halt. Elizabeth and I can only stare at each other, our faces smeared with blood and dirt and ash. I crush her trembling body against mine and run my hands along her back, her stomach, checking for wounds I might have missed in the chaos. Elizabeth assures me she has healed but does not pull away. She clings to me in a boneless way I have not felt since before she was turned.

Erebus nudges our thighs apart with his grimy muzzle. A whine whistles through his nose as he rakes his front paws through the packed dirt. Now is not the time. I release Elizabeth as Erebus begins to tug at the split seam of my pant leg. The three of us begin to run, Erebus nipping at my pants as I drag Elizabeth behind me by the wrist.

"Please tell me you have your keys," I say, twisting back to regard Elizabeth from over my shoulder.

Elizabeth squints, both of us close behind Erebus who has taken it upon himself to be our escort through the tunnels. "I left them on the dashboard," she says.

The lightbulbs down here are mounted behind iron grates, and they glow in yellow clouds of smoke. Erebus barks some sixty feet ahead of us, perched beneath the ladder that leads up to the garage. Above our heads and down around our feet the air vents issue acrid smoke. Elizabeth and I stand beneath the lowest rung of the ladder and stare down into the face of our only cohort.

"Should we take him with us?" she asks, her fist knotted in my tattered shirttail. Erebus growls in her face.

"He would slaughter half the city if we did," I say. "He knows he cannot follow."

Elizabeth drops to her knees in the dirt and wraps her arms around Erebus's stout neck. The hound lowers his muzzle down over her shoulder protectively and tolerates the affection. I pull her back up and she stands beside me, pointedly silent. Erebus rises to all fours and butts my hand with the top of his head. I scratch behind his ears, his neck, and look into his eyes.

"Run." I hold his stare and push the command deeper than my words can travel. The second I release him Erebus is gone with a lonely howl, barreling down into the murky darkness.

Elizabeth ascends the ladder ahead of me and I wait in the tunnel for sounds of life. Swords drawn from scabbards, the clamor of revenge, the scurry of survival, something, anything. But all is quiet underground. No way to know for certain what path the fire cut through the lair, how quickly it spread to neighboring rooms, or if the several feet of concrete between suites was enough to confine the flames. The smoke billowing from the air vents suggests otherwise. The others must be awake. They sensed his death as surely as I did. With one hand wrapped around the bottom of the ladder I consider turning back for my siblings, but nothing I do now matters. Saving their lives would hardly make us even, given what I have taken away.

"Forgive me, Brother."

From above, haloed in the sterile light of the garage, Elizabeth calls down into the tunnel clearly panicked. I climb the ladder for what I know will be the last time. My every ally has become my foe.

"C'mon. Come here." Elizabeth drags me out the hatch by the collar and wastes not a second. She sprints toward her Bentley, pausing briefly to consider my vehicle, which is still running.

"Body in the trunk," I explain, pushing her toward the passenger door.

"And apparently, you're driving," she says, as I push her down into the cabin and slam the door. Elizabeth has already started the engine when I drop behind the wheel, the stereo blaring with her awful music: sad songs by neurotic people. She switches it off, and the silence proves to be that much worse.

We barrel out into the brightening night. Elizabeth and I say nothing on the drive. When we stop at a red light ten miles out, she darts over the center console to make sure we are not being followed. She holds that pose long after the car has begun to move again, and when she finally falls back into her soft leather seat all the fight has left her body. With empty eyes Elizabeth watches the streets flash by, her temple pressed against the side window. I reach across the divide and hold her hand. She hums softly to herself, perhaps to us both, the same lullaby I used on Erebus when Macha birthed her litter. The pups come unbidden to my mind, flashes of singed fur and pink mouths open wide in torment. I push the thought down and grip the steering wheel with bloody hands.

* * *

When we park, the sun is just visible between the shield of skyscrapers. Elizabeth has to be led the several blocks from where our car is hidden in a public lot. These streets are never deserted at this hour and that is precisely the point. Covered in ash and blood, our clothing torn, we garner more than our fair share of concerned glances, but as is true with any major city, even the most inquisitive stranger quickly looks away.

The bottom three floors of this building are gallery and showroom, with extravagant living quarters stacked atop one another and reaching for the sky. The penthouse is not our target destination, but a small, immaculate flat on the south corner. We bypass the doorman by way of a service elevator and have to take the stairs after that for ten flights. Thankfully, we are the only two beings on the walk up, though I note each camera we pass.

I deposit Elizabeth against the wall beside the door marked "226E" and slide the bronze address plaque back for the spare key tucked behind its face. Humans are so hopelessly obvious, and it never fails to astound me. I pull her inside behind me and deadbolt the door.

"Where are we?" she asks, stepping into the open floorplan. She sounds half asleep. I step around her and flick on two table lamps that flank a gray tweed sofa.

"A well-kept secret," I say, making the rounds to check behind each door just in case.

"Don't do that, Stela."

Her weariness borders on hostility, and I lean back against the black marble island in the kitchen and take note of the fact that she has not strayed one foot further into the apartment. The skin around her eyes is red and ragged, swollen though she has not cried. There are flecks of caked blood and grit in her hair, charcoal-like smudges streaming down her face. She is wise to be cautious of unfamiliar surroundings, prepared to take her frustrations out on me if I keep evading. And yet, I have not seen a sight as beautiful as Elizabeth exhausted and alive.

"My dear Mr. Opes keeps a separate space for his extramarital activities," I explain.

Elizabeth hums, appeased for the time being, and steps toward the generous windows in front of her. She is gentle with her body and moves with the deliberate gait of someone compensating for injury, but I do not sense pain. I come to stand beside her and peer at the brightening landscape. Thankfully the rising sun does not face this side of the tower, but the surrounding glass and steel glint all the same. Though I yearn to reach out and touch her, I sense it would not be welcome. She clung to me in the freight tunnels but has since had time to reflect.

What must I have looked like to her, lording over Fane's burning body?

Since the moment we met, I have harbored an unexplainable entitlement where Elizabeth was concerned. Nothing could keep me from her. Not Fane's law, or her mother Claire and certainly not James. Yet standing here beside the glass, watching the shadows shorten and Elizabeth stare out across her beloved city, I cannot find the courage to brush her hand. She holds her limbs close to her body, shoulders turned away and hunched inward.

"I need a shower," she says without emotion.

"Of course." I take a step back, my hand hovering over her shoulder blade. "The bathroom is just here."

Elizabeth stumbles over the beige rug behind me, and I lead her to the uninviting washroom. Stark white walls, white porcelain cleaned recently with bleach. The shower curtain is only a frosted plastic liner, and the towels hanging on silver hooks look starched. Elizabeth locks the hollow wooden door, sealing us both inside. I start the water running in the tub, fretting over the temperature as though Elizabeth will forget the horrors she has seen tonight as soon as she scrubs herself clean. Elizabeth's clothes fall in soft piles around her feet, and I keep my hand under the running water, my back turned away.

"Thanks," she whispers and touches my shoulder briefly. Elizabeth steps around me cautiously, sinking into the warm water. She does not look at me but focuses instead on her blood-caked nails and the swirls of red and black rising off her body. I slide the shower curtain closed and turn to leave.

"Where are you going?" she asks in a small frightened voice. I turn around to find her dirt-streaked face peering up at me.

"To find a change of clothes."

"Can you just..." Elizabeth's wet hair pours across her shoulder, and the soot from Fane's body runs in black lines down her neck. I did not require her needs be vocalized when she was human and the same is true now. I sit beside the tub as she tugs the curtain closed again.

The sounds of her body tell me everything I need to know. A generous spreading of liquid soap, repeated three times before she shelves the bottle. The draining of the tub, the faucet running on full blast. The grating sandpaper sounds of the loofah against her skin, the soles of her feet, even her face. She ends with a scalding shower.

When the water switches off, Elizabeth stands behind the curtain and an eerie stillness settles over the cramped bathroom. I retrieve a towel from the hook and offer it to her.

"Your turn," she sniffles, scrubbing her face dry.

I have never been self-conscious about my body, clothed or unclothed, but Elizabeth's apprehension and vulnerability is infectious. I make quick work of my soiled garments and step into a shower of now-icy water. The cold is sobering. I scrub myself from head to toe and listen to Elizabeth towel-drying her long dark hair. A familiar sound at once domestic and comforting in its normalcy.

When I push back the curtain Elizabeth waits with a towel, less shy. She wraps it around my shoulders as I step out onto the tile floor. She rubs my arms as if trying to warm me up, a hint of a smile on her lips though the eyes are still exhausted and far away. My resolve crumbles and I pull her against me. At first, she stands in my embrace as though captive, but gradually her arms encircle my waist. She drops her head on my shoulder and we stand together or for some time, holding each other close.

Washed and dressed, we slip into the gray silk sheets on the platform bed. The loft is uncomfortably bright even with the curtains drawn, the pervasive glare of the city slipping around the edges. We lie facing one another, resting on our pillows and stare at each other. The strap of Andrew's white-ribbed undershirt slips off my shoulder. Elizabeth has commandeered one of his white dress shirts, her thin wrists swallowed by the billowing open cuffs. We were both grateful when we stumbled upon Rachel's undergarments, tucked neatly in the chest of drawers. Wearing Andrew's briefs would have been one insult too many.

"I have to tell you something," she whispers, shifting closer on the bed until our knees touch. "About you and Fane." Worry darkens her fretful face. For all the horror she has faced, I am still her only concern. My sense of unworthiness is enough to make me wish my siblings survived the blaze, if only to get what I deserve from them.

"I know." I catch her hand and bring her knuckles to my lips.

"I don't think you do, Stela." She leans up on her elbow and sighs heavily, looking at everything except me. I brush her cheek softly.

"I know, my darling."

Elizabeth shuffles and remains upright. I use my eyes to tell her what I cannot say out loud, what I desperately hope she will not voice. She looks into my eyes and squeezes my hand, nodding to herself. She parts her lips, licks them with a dry tongue—a thousand questions flit across her face, and I can only hope she will have mercy on me for one night.

"Have you always known?" she asks.

"I had not even entertained the possibility before tonight."

I grow distracted with more practical concerns. Hardwood floors everywhere, even in the kitchen which seems a careless choice. What would we do if the building caught on fire? The lower floors? How would we escape this room? And if a burglar broke through the front door, would Elizabeth have qualms about killing him? And how would we dispose of the body? I gather the sheets up around my chest, feeling exposed. The bed is too low and we are vulnerable out in the open among the masses, which is to say nothing of the very real retribution we will undoubtedly face from our own kind.

"Did you hear it from me?" she asks. "My thoughts?"

Elizabeth's delicate voice shakes me from my fortification troubles. I sweep her long chestnut curls back over her shoulder and permit myself a moment to appreciate her beauty. She blames herself for all this.

"I could not wield fire unless I was born to this life, as Fane was," I say carefully, testing the past tense. "I felt the inferno moving through my veins. Warm and vengeful. Silent all my life until roused and when it happened, I knew that the flames had been there all along." I take her hand. "Your thoughts gave nothing of my nature away." At this, Elizabeth brightens a little and lies back down as a wave of weariness overtakes me.

"How did you know?" I ask, but what I want to know is how could she have known before me? Five centuries of life…Why would a wealthy Lord take pity on a poor child from an unnamed village? Let alone raise that child as his ward? Why did it never occur to me to ask?

Elizabeth is wary of this question. She chews the corner of her mouth, carefully arranging her thoughts. True, she has always been more curious than I, but this discovery—so private in nature—is a connection I should have made long ago.

"I found similarities in your blood and Fane's. A unique color and similar platelet count, distinctions only the two of you shared." She twists toward me with newfound comfort, slipping so easily into scientific distraction. "Then I considered your light tolerance, your fair features, and I remembered seeing your mother in your dreams and she—"

"Enough, my love." I brush my thumb across the back of her hand. "A conversation for another evening."

She stretches out on her back and focuses on the high ceiling. Grateful, I press a chaste kiss against her temple and lie down beside her, my hand resting on her belly.

Elizabeth is fast asleep in less than three minutes. I bury my face in her hair. When I untangle my limbs Elizabeth turns over on her side, one sleeping hand spreading out against the bed as her body seeks to recover mine. She protests quietly, flexes her legs, and sleep soothes her features once more.

Elizabeth jerks against the bed, fingers knotted into fists, and I turn toward her to smother the nightmare I knew would arrive. I speak to her quietly and stroke her forehead until her body unfurls. In sleep, my mind seeks her out, drawn like a moth to flame into any of her dreams. Elizabeth does the same with me, and in the evening when we wake it is often difficult to determine which dreams were hers or mine. I have become better at barring her entry to keep my nightmares to myself, and I believed this was just another muscle that could be strengthened over time. Now it seems the ability was always mine and I was merely learning to control it. After all, Fane's thoughts and dreams were private affairs and I was never invited to share them. Nor was anyone else as far as I know.

The sun streams in from beneath the curtains in blistering swaths that cut across the floor, thin beams clogged with dust particles that drift in the light breeze from the air vents. I check to ensure that Elizabeth sleeps and part the curtains. The morning blinds me, sunlight glinting off every window, bouncing off cars that inch through the infernal workday rush. The light permeates my eyelids, painting the inside of my skull. I blink against the onslaught and take a seat on the sofa, my body ensconced in a halo of light. I sit quietly and watch the morning mature, the first morning that Fane has missed in more than a thousand years, and I wonder if the sun has registered his absence.

A familiar burn warms the back of my eyes. Anger comes readily and has for all my life. I understand that emotion, its worth. But stationed on the sofa I cannot reach my rage. Instead I think of the fact that Fane will never enjoy another sunrise, and when I tire of that useless thought, I try in vain to reconstruct my dead mother's face. Whatever this lingering emotion is called—certainly akin to melancholy—I want no part of it. So, I welcome the searing ache of a new dawn bleeding into day, flinch away only when Elizabeth stirs and return the moment she is subdued.

* * *

For two nights Elizabeth and I maintain our distance. We walk widely around each other in the small flat, speaking occasionally while our unvoiced tensions shiver in the air. What will become of us? What have we done? Soon we will need to hunt and what will we do then? Can we risk a drop-off to Derek Carrington? At the very least he will want to know where the rest of our brood is hiding. On the other hand, a trail of bodies is sure to be noticed eventually. And what will we do about clothing? Rachel has only a handful of garments in the closet, the waist and bust too generous for either of us, and the legs noticeably short on me. Elizabeth finds this concern about clean outfits absurd and stated rather pointedly that the flat has a laundry behind the door I had mistaken for a pantry. But how I was to know? Wardrobe was Lydia's department and I have never given much thought to what I wear.

On the morning of the second full day aboveground I sent an email to Mr. Opes. Nothing to indicate where I was staying as I knew his wife was in town and the flat would be of little use to him until she went to visit her sisters in Connecticut. My brief request for an update on the progress of our travel documents went unanswered.

Elizabeth woke that night to my arms around her waist despite my having spent another sleepless day on the sofa. She read the exhaustion in my face as easily as though I had just smothered a yawn. She said she had seen my eyes this way before—dull and vacant—when I had kept a close watch over her home as Mr. Collins stalked her from his car. I blamed the flat—too exposed—and my hypervigilance as I considered from where the next attack would come for my inability to rest.

We are each alone in our grief. Elizabeth with her nightmares of the fight, the certainty that Fane would kill us both. I with my guilt for the attack she weathered, for leaving my family to burn and for what I will never ask Elizabeth to understand, for slaughtering Fane. He was many things. Never simply good, nor purely evil, and though it would be impossible for her to accept, Fane was completely within his rights as the Moroi of our household. He gave me this life, he bore me to life eternal, and after centuries of guidance he is gone. Where is my place in this world if not in service to him? The despair of what I did to him and what he did to Elizabeth are inextricable. And the pain...

the physical pain his absence from this earth causes me…I do not pray, but I would pray if it meant that Elizabeth would never have to know this anguish.

"Has he ever taken this long to respond?" she asks, drawing a floral print silk robe around her. Elizabeth pushes back the curtains to appreciate the freshly fallen night. She sits beside me on the sofa with her legs tucked underneath her. I refresh my inbox for the fifth time in less than hour and send yet another text message to Andrew's phone.

"No. But I rarely contact him on weekends."

Elizabeth smiles halfheartedly and shrugs. "Maybe Mr. Opes takes his Sabbath day very seriously."

"I thought the Sabbath was Saturday?"

"Sunday for WASPs," she says.

I groan and lean back against the sofa. Elizabeth runs a hand down my spine. She rubs between my shoulder blades and I lean forward to grant her better access.

"You can't keep doing this," she says gently, the full force of her gaze on my face.

I laugh dryly and straighten up. "Fret over things beyond my control?"

Elizabeth spares a sad little smirk and brushes my cheek with her thumb. "You have to sleep, Stela."

"I know." I kiss her palm.

Elizabeth stretches her legs and places both feet on the floor. "I know why you're afraid to rest."

"There is only one way in or out of this flat, and I—"

"Don't do that. Don't distract with a half-truth," she replied wearily. She shakes her head and turns toward the spectacular view beyond the windows. "You're going to dream of him, Stela. Whether you sleep now or crash in five days. You will see his face." She trails off as her onyx eyes alight along the jagged rooftops. "In the meantime," she continues briskly, "your restlessness weakens you and jeopardizes us both. You know this."

When the woman is right, what can be said? I put my arm around her shoulders and pull her close. Elizabeth curls against me, both of us content to enjoy the simple sensations of each other.

"What do you do all day when you're awake?" she asks, resting her temple on my shoulder.

"Admire the view," I say, and she moves to lean away from me. "And think of my family." Elizabeth stays close but refuses to let me skirt the topic any longer. "When I have exhausted all worst-case scenarios, I stare at my reflection for hours on end."

"You're nothing like him."

A bitter smile spread across my lips. "I thought you said no more half-truths, my darling."

Elizabeth takes my hand. "That was the whole problem, Stela. His constant critique. You were never similar enough to him. Don't forget that now." She kisses me softly, the top of her robe parting as she leans against me. She holds me by the shoulders, forcing me to break away and look at her. "I don't see him here," she says, her tone plain and her eyes staring deeply into mine. "I only see you."

I suppose it is perfectly normal to seek our heritage, to hunt for inheritance that goes deeper than blood. When I look at Elizabeth, I see attributes of Claire, and those angles that offer no glimpse of her mother fit the descriptions she has given me of her late father. She is the undisputed fruit of their unhappy union. Why then does my hair color seem to be the only visible genetic similarity I share with Fane?

Elizabeth hooks her finger in the strap of my shirt and tugs. "You'll feel better in real clothes," she says, releasing the fabric which hangs off my shoulder.

"Nothing fits," I reply, sitting back sullenly.

Elizabeth chuckles and slides her fingers back through my hair, pulling it lightly with an exhausted grunt. "You're depressed." Her lips ghost along my hairline, across my forehead. "Everything will be better tomorrow."

"Be serious," I scoff. "Depression is a human constraint."

Elizabeth laughs openly and tilts her head. "How long have you been wearing those clothes?"

"Two days. Hardly a record, definitely not a symptom."

"Why haven't you changed?"

"What would be the point?" I ask.

She taps the tip of my nose with her finger. "Exactly."

Elizabeth hops off the sofa and tightens her satin belt.

"Where are you going?" I ask without giving chase.

"To run you a bath," she calls back over her shoulder. "And Stela," she says, only her head visible around the edge of the bathroom door, "go pick out some clean clothes. Andrew has a robe in the closet."

Elizabeth closes the door behind her and I rise on legs numbed by fatigue. How a bath will solve the issue of Andrew's radio silence is beyond me. But I do as I am told, and Elizabeth is waiting in the bath when I arrive. Small tea candles illuminate the back wall of the tub, dripping warm wax down the basin. She asks me not to turn on the lights and watches as I undress, flames dancing in her eyes. Here, in the flickering shadows with Elizabeth waiting, it almost feels like coming home. She pulls me down into the water and holds my body flush against her, my back pressed to her front.

"I'm not afraid of you," she whispers, cupping the scalding water in the bowl of her hand and smoothing it down my arms. The surface of the water ripples with her every move as our bodies warm back to living temperatures.

"You are," I reply, nodding gravely.

"I'm afraid of what you can do, Stela. What I saw down in the freight tunnels. Something I still have no sound scientific explanation for, but that is not the same thing."

Something stirs against my spine, followed by a low growl. I lean forward, looking back Elizabeth curiously.

"Sorry," she says, pulling me back into place. "Just my stomach." Her head thumps against the tiled wall, and she sighs wearily. "I'm starving. Woke up famished. Went to bed that way, actually."

"Your body never makes that noise."

Elizabeth shrugs behind me. She goes back to running handfuls of water down my chest and arms.

"Did feeding from Fane ever leave you ravenous?" she said.

"Quite the opposite. It made me feel as though I would never need to hunt again. Of course, the hunger always returns. Yours is a day early, my darling."

She hums and moves her hands over my body. "Different bodies, different responses," she says casually. As if to reiterate her point, Elizabeth's stomach groans a second time and she laughs.

"I swear to you, I have not heard that sound since before you were turned."

"Shh. Stela, you're killing the mood."

"The mood? Your stomach is going to give our position away if you—" I turn to face her and my good humor disappears. It is written all over her face, etched into her skin held tight against her bones. I should have noticed…she is starving. Elizabeth does not shirk away from my gaze, she turns me toward her and rests her forehead on my collarbone. Her fingers hooked beneath my shoulder blades. I lift her face by the chin and those dark eyes threaten to swallow her sallow face.

"Please," she says. Her eyes focused on my neck, she leans forward with parted lips and rests her open mouth on my throat but does not extend her fangs.

As though I would deny her anything.

"Sparingly, my love." I cling to her shoulders and place my hand gently on the cradle of her head. Her fangs descend almost timidly, but the flesh relents all the same. Then comes the rush, my blood an ocean in my veins and crashing down her throat. Her touch becomes familiar, ardent, hands pulling me closer as I unravel. The swoon carries me away with her like water down a drain.

* * *

"Are you sure this is wise?" she asks for the eleventh time this evening. I shove the keys to her Bentley into my pants pocket—technically, Rachel's pocket—and shoulder out of the vehicle.

I bend down and tug the cuffs of each pant leg down around my ankles. The car keys bulge against my hipbone, the pockets too shallow to hold anything of significance. Space enough for a metro card, perhaps a lipstick. Hardly what I would consider utilitarian attire. Where on earth did Lydia procure our clothing?

Elizabeth links her hand with mine as we sidestep a black smear on the floor of the garage still protected by yellow crime scene tape. I forgot to mention the sloppy kill, but the way Elizabeth's eyes linger on the spray pattern tells me that an explanation is no longer required. She enters the elevator at my heels and intentionally positions herself between me and the blinking camera mounted in the corner. My protector.

"What happened to 'no news is good news'?" She turns toward me as the lift ascends, her arms crossed harshly.

"Dearest, you have never believed that." I smile at her and she rolls her eyes.

Elizabeth relents and focuses on the smooth steel doors in front of us.

We delayed our feeding schedule one full day in the hope that Andrew would reach out to me with an update about our passports and Elizabeth's money. None came. Not an email or a text or a bothersome phone call. He is many things, my Mr. Opes, a coward first and foremost. What he is not, however, is negligent.

Reflected in the steel doors, our image would strike fear into the hearts of absolutely no one. She with a peasant blouse covered in roses, and I with the only carnation-pink shirt Rachel has in her abbreviated weekend wardrobe. The inside of each cuff is adorned with pale pink polka dots of all things. If Fane's siblings fail to murder us, I shall take my own life to spare myself the embarrassment.

The higher the elevator climbs the stranger the sounds. The gentle whoosh of recycled air, the insistent peck of birds against the windows—all this is to be expected. What is missing: the electric chirp of printers, fingers striking against keyboards, the hum of distant conversation. When we reach the top floor, the phone can be heard ringing before the elevator doors have opened. The ding of our arrival is the only welcome we receive and Elizabeth does not disembark, but clutches my bicep to keep me beside her.

"Rachel…"

One hand on the phone as though she might move to answer the deafening ring at any moment. The other hand palm down against the desk, so purposeful. Her eyes, the color of green apples any other day are clouded with a milky film, and the only hint of color that remains—the only whiff of life left—is the ruby red streak of dried blood flaking on her neck.

Elizabeth hits the door release and then chooses the basement level, but I pull her by the wrist and into the lobby before the elevator can seal us inside. She speaks to me in whispers though I am sure we are the only living souls to be found on the top floor of Opes and Sons, and urges me not to disturb the physical evidence.

Rachel waits so patiently for our approach, obviously enthralled before she was drained. No signs of a struggle. Her features are smooth, untroubled, not even her eyes show signs of shock. Someone spent time on her, arranged her just so. Someone who knew I had a fondness for the genteel redhead and left her posed like a doll for me to find.

I step closer and sweep the hair away from her neck, moving carefully around the corpse. The skin above her jugular is marred by two perfectly round holes, the skin is barely bruised and the wounds are punctures not rips. For that I am grateful. She may have had horrendous taste in romantic companions, but Rachel was thoughtful, courteous to a fault. She was the only reason Fane never found out about Andrew's love nest, at least from me. It seemed a betrayal to shed light on Rachel's personal affairs. I let her brilliant red hair slip from my hand and turn to meet Elizabeth's panicked eyes.

"This girl deserved better," I lament, and close her eyelids with a brush of my fingers. Elizabeth is noticeably calmer without the distraction of a dead woman's gaze.

"We need to get out of here, Stela." She inches back toward the elevator. "For all we know the cops are already on their way."

"Do you ever have the feeling…" I step around the desk just in time for Rachel's head to thud dumbly against the keyboard, "you are exactly where you are supposed to be?"

"We don't have time for this."

"On the contrary, my darling. This is all the time we shall ever have."

Despite her protestations I slip around Elizabeth and down the marble corridor, but true to form she is close behind me cursing steadily. Handprints mar the frosted glass door to Andrew's office, small as a child's. Blood on the silver door handle—is it Rachel's or his?

The office is in ruins, and I would expect nothing less. Chairs knocked over on their arms, desk drawers busted into shards, papers shredded underfoot, but the blood is highly controlled. No greedy spray pattern here. Not a drop wasted. Elizabeth covers her mouth with both hands and sinks to ground beside the door. Abstractly, I want to commend her for not screaming.

Andrew's body is crucified to the far wall, a letter opener driven through each wrist, a third—Rachel's, if I am not mistaken—secures his crossed feet. A far less dignified end for Mr. Opes, but then, the worst is always reserved for traitors. The buttons of his shirt sprinkle the floor around him and his belly hangs bare and exposed. A deep ravine runs its length. Dimpled cellulite trims the gash in his gut so that if I tilt my head his whole body is a smile, with ribbons of viscera reaching for the ground.

The pageantry was all done post-mortem, no signs that he struggled once he was pinned to wall. A nasty gash in his throat tells me that torture was not necessary. I did not return in time to rid his memories of our plot, and his blood told his executioner all she needed to know.

He was a man, now a message written in my native tongue. I have not witnessed such cruelty in ages.

"Oh, sister mine…" I shake my head in disbelief. "You have been a busy girl."

Should I be amused by such violent hyperbole, or terrified? If the latter be true, I would never give Lydia the satisfaction of knowing she succeeded. Without doubt, the travel documents—assuming Andrew had the time to secure them—have been seized, and without his authorizing signature access to Elizabeth's funds are impossible. This is a declaration of war, and conflict depends upon confrontation. Lydia has gone to impressive lengths to ensure my engagement.

"What do we do?" Elizabeth asks, her voice brittle and wasted. I had almost forgotten she was here. What do we do? What can we do? There has only ever been one answer and now that answer is painted across the window of Mr. Opes' majestic skyline view, in the brush strokes of three steady fingers. The blood was used sparingly enough that the letters are clear.

Run.

As though we have the option.

XI

Random Variables In A Complex Equation

China plates with pale blue pagoda patterns are spread across the impostor bamboo mats. My mother had beautiful china—sold at auction by Opes and Sons—but those were guest dishes and in truth she only dusted them off for high holidays and wakes, always laid out on her finest linens.

This dining room reeks of Crate and Barrel, beautifully contrived finery without history.

A gold leaf rendering of the Buddha hangs on the far wall above round faux-stone candles. They've upset the Zen of the room with a Hijri Calendar printed on a black velvet scroll strung up beside the clock, a menorah in the center of the table instead of a candelabra. Clearly the aim is inclusion, but it is not successful. The whole beautiful family reaching over their plates for a second serving of ham—sinful in at least two of their conflicting ideologies—on a brisk Thanksgiving night.

My stomach gurgles and the taste of blood climbs up the back of my throat as the daughter, Kylie, pours a river of gravy over her buffet. She is the only member of the family keeping an eye on the brother.

She leans over his shoulder and tucks the paper napkin back into the neck of his superhero T-shirt.

Headlights blast between the slits of the privacy fence and I drop down beside the Japanese maple. The father looks out across the patio, wipes his lips with the back of his hand and returns his full attention to his lovely wife. College sweethearts—though I have no way of explaining my certainty—Ivy League graduates. The wife's hair is severely blond but professionally treated, and her hands—like mine—have never seen hard labor.

The way this couple speaks to one another, with their eyes locked and matching smiles, you would swear they were seated at the table alone. Their little boy chokes on a bite of ham and his sister Kylie pounds his back with a balled fist until he spits the meat into her cupped hand. His father tells him to chew with his mouth closed and focuses again on the mother. She says something about a deposition that was going to be a problem when they went back to work after the holiday.

When asked for her opinion on children, my mother gave the same response without fail: "Women should procreate only when they want nothing more from life than a child." I was an unplanned pregnancy and though Claire Dumas was not a religious person, she was a narcissist who believed that having an abortion would mean admitting she made a mistake. She was also aware that having me was the only way to keep my father around.

So, why did *they* have children? Two successful attorneys, clearly enamored of each other. Societal pressure and immortality? I take the confiscated envelope from my coat pocket and examine the names handwritten in elegant calligraphy. I don't have to open their mail to know what the letter will say. Elijah and Sarah Goldberg are cordially invited to witness the union of…whoever.

Sarah laughs at some private joke, her hand gently grasping Elijah's forearm. The strain of her amusement makes the muscles in her neck jump and my entire body hums when her carotid becomes visible beneath the skin.

My stomach somersaults and I lean back against the privacy fence until it passes, breathing through my mouth and willing my blood to quiet. The roil persists and I count the meals I've had since we left Andrew's condo. There was the young tourist asking for directions, six blocks from Opes and Sons. The bartender two nights after that. Stela doesn't know about her. And the benefactor of my navy-blue Windbreaker, a homeless woman peddling her wares from a shopping cart not three hours ago. Of course, if you count Stela herself, from whom I have fed every night since, that raises the total to six meals. She's the only thing that calms my stomach. The only thing that curbs this crippling hunger, and even then, it returns a few hours later.

Inside, the Goldberg children have started a game beneath the table, pinching each other's legs to see who will scream first. I would have thoroughly enjoyed having a sibling.

The blood drains down my gullet, the taste of the old woman sloshing back down to my belly. Exactly the same sensation as a stomach flu, which makes absolutely no sense. I wipe my face with my palm and the skin is damp and cold. Stela never perspires, and before draining Fane neither did I. Like the memory of my certain death at his hands is not punishment enough, his blood seems bound and determined to eat me from the inside out. I'm feeding constantly, but I can still sense him in my veins. Never mixing with any of my meals, his blood is a caustic, unstable poison.

I can barely sleep the urge to drink from Stela is so strong, if only for the few hours of peace her blood brings.

She suspects something.

We were both operating under the assumption that Fane's blood doubled my appetite, but now I'm not so sure. I had these symptoms before we killed him, though to a lesser degree. Anyway, the hunger isn't what worries me. It's the sinking sensation I get after I've fed from anyone but Stela. The way the blood bubbles up in my throat, begging to be purged. For the first time since I was turned, my body aches.

What I wouldn't give to ask Darius about my ailment. Perhaps he was a little crazy, but a wealth of knowledge all the same. With our luck Lydia was the only member of Stela's family that was spared in the fire.

Lydia…

She's the whole reason we're stuck in this hell. Every time I close my eyes, I see her handiwork. The porcelain gleam of Rachel's dead eyes, the wet slap that, despite my protests, Andrew's intestines made when Stela pried his body off the wall. The family photo of Andrew with his wife and his daughter Christine. The frame was angled to face the door, red fingerprints visible on the glass. I couldn't look away from their smiling faces. A professional photograph, but the happiness was real.

Stela will be back by now, having inveigled her way into the pockets of several unsuspecting gentleman. She'll be tearing through the maintenance room we've commandeered in the middle of the Blue

Line, screaming my name and imagining the worst. I can't think of a single lie to explain my absence. The moment Stela closed the steel service door I was up on my feet and dressing for an unscheduled hunt. I left as quickly as I could and grabbed the first lone figure I came across—the homeless woman. I crush the Goldberg's wedding invitation in my hand and drop it in a shallow puddle of melted snow.

"If you intend to give me the slip…"

The corner of my mouth curls up. I hadn't sensed her approach. These days my blood is constantly rushing, irrespective of Stela's proximity. However, other senses have been heightened: smell, for one, and our strange prescient empathy. Her footsteps are soundless as she sidles up beside me in a faded tweed blazer three sizes too large.

"Do us both a favor. Be less predictable, my darling." Stela nudges me with her shoulder, but her mood is miles away from playful. Her face betrays nothing. Smooth brow, distracted eyes taking in the familial scene unfolding in the dining room.

"Never intended to give you the slip," I say and take a step toward the patio. Elijah and Sarah are sealing the leftovers with plastic wrap while the children quietly finish their dessert.

"Elizabeth, if I can find you, so can they."

We haven't talked about the others and that is not my fault. Stela only acknowledged Lydia's survival while standing in front of Andrew's corpse. After that, the subject was closed. She didn't want to discuss the possibility that her siblings escaped, or that in all likelihood they were combing every corner of the city in search of us. She didn't want to talk about leaving Chicago. We left Andrew's office and we haven't gone back or to his apartment in the financial district. We ditched my Bentley in the parking garage and boarded the El. I still don't know how Stela found the maintenance room halfway down the tracks, or why she thought it a safe place to hide when just like the apartment there's only one door.

There are so many things we don't talk about. Mandates she's given, rules that I've made. We don't need words to know, to feel or understand. But the human part of me still aches for dialogue.

"Why did you come here?" she asks. "Again."

I smile softly as the Goldberg's son trips over the corner of the rug and dumps a mug of cocoa on the floor. His mother picks him up, reprimands him for running. Jeremiah. That's his name.

I shake my head. "I honestly don't know."

Stela steps up behind me and wraps her arms around my waist. She pulls me back against her. I hadn't noticed that I was inching closer to the sliding glass door. The daughter, Kylie, mops up her brother's spilled drink. Together the children disappear around the corner and settle in the living room in front of the television.

"Would it bring you peace to kill them?" Stela asks, her lips just beneath my ear.

"No." I watch the glow of their living room for shadows, knowing I've lost sight of them for the evening. "But thanks for asking."

Stela sighs, presses a gentle kiss against my neck. I hear her tongue skim across her lips, and her embrace tightens. "You fed," she says coldly. Denial would be pointless, and she's too angry to press the subject here out in the open. Her fingers lace through mine, her hand noticeably warmer than mine as she tugs me toward the gate. I let her pull me backward across the darkened lawn as a brisk November breeze ruffles the grass and savor the sight of my empty kitchen. Somehow, I'm certain that this is the last time I'll see my childhood home. Stela knows it too, and she gives me the honor of locking the tricky gate behind me.

We walk to the end of the alley and cross the street. The traffic calmed hours ago, everyone safe at home with their families, gorging themselves on turkey. The lights are on in every living room window, children and parents, aunts and uncles visible through the blinds. Stela moves silently beside me, immune to the spirit of the evening.

The platform is deserted, except for one man curled on a bench along the wall. The train arrives all the same, squealing to a stop and opening its doors for precisely no one. Even the train car is empty, and after a few seconds the doors wheeze and close. Stela waits at the edge of the platform, ready to drop down to the tracks once the train disembarks.

"Elizabeth..."

Her voice reaches me from afar. The sound of my name is empty, as if from the bottom of a well. Between my ears, in my veins resounds the steady thump of a heartbeat. It pounds in my blood like a drum. The man on the bench turns toward the wall, asleep, his torso covered by a green wool blanket, military issue. A bottle drops from his slumbering fist. Whiskey pools around my heels...

Stela hurls me back against the wall. The front of my blouse is a troubling shade of red, and my fingers come away from my lips smeared carmine. The man is screaming, and the subway tunnel seems to carry those cries to the bowels of the earth. Stela bends above him, pries his hands away from his ragged throat and a spurt of bright blood stains the sleeve of her jacket. One look from Stela and the man stills, his blood gushing in a steady stream from the gaping hole in his neck. She stares into his eyes as she opens her own wrist and presses her wound to his.

I rush across the platform and drop down to the tracks, pushing myself up against the wall before he regains consciousness. First, he gurgles, and then he coughs, babbling incoherently at Stela who soothes him into silence.

"You were attacked," she says gently.

"I was?" His dazed indifference a testament to Stela's thrall.

"You need a hospital."

I slip down the wall and crouch in the dirt. From above, I hear the shuffle of fabric as Stela helps him fold his blanket. She feigns ignorance when he presses her for a description of his attacker. He'll never get that memory back. Her eyes will keep that small part of him. I listen to the sound of his unsteady feet on the stairs, his dizzy lumbering until Stela drops down beside me.

"Get up."

She pries me off the ground with the full power of her glare, urges me closer. My vision darkens as she draws me near, despite the ample lighting. The closer I get to Stela the darker the world around us grows, but she stands out like a beacon, a lighthouse in the storm of her own ire. The blood I've stolen moves back up my throat and my legs tremble.

Stela sneers and seizes me by the wrist. She drags me behind her down the tracks, headed for the maintenance room. Blood pools in my captured hand, my wrist cracks loudly, but I grit my teeth and stay quiet. She has every right to be furious with me, and the pressure of her hand is reassuring, a tether to keep me grounded as my body revolts and sickens. I shuffle behind her like a disobedient child.

Stela relinquishes my wrist and heaves the recessed steel door open with her shoulder. An ugly shriek of metal scraping against concrete is all that welcomes us home. I recoil but Stela turns in the darkened door and yanks me inside by the front of my soiled jacket. The door screams again as she forces it shut, grinding its rusted hinges back into place, and I fall to my knees at the sound with both hands clamped over my sensitive ears.

The darkness down here is absolute. Not a sliver of light once she seals us inside. Slowly I let my hands fall away and place my palms against the cement floor. In this blackness there are only varying shades, not solid lines. As sensitive as we are to light, we still require it to see clearly. But my ears attune to my surroundings, fill in the blanks.

A constant buzz hums in the air, the walls all lined with electrical panels and levers that never sleep. The shivering electricity buffets our bodies, twitches across the floor, and I can sense Stela's position in the room like a rock splitting a stream. If I were deaf and blind, I would know her. The floral scent of her. I would taste the sweetness of her blood from the other side of the world. My mouth waters. I try to swallow this relentless craving.

"Have you any idea how reckless…" Stela paces when she's furious, especially when she's powerless. Between her jagged steps, the cutting motions of her hands, and the incessant buzz of the wiring I can only grasp fragments of her lecture. "We are two people, Elizabeth. Not one. If you cannot protect your own…"

Despite the deliberate placement of my hands on the floor, the room beings to spin as I crouch on all fours. My body temperature plummets and for the second time tonight a drop of sweat beads on the tip of my nose. I hear that droplet ping against the concrete. I try to lift my palm to mop my face but my left arm buckles. My organs shiver against my ribs, my whole body clenched as though mid-seize. "This is not the first time you have fed outside of your schedule, and if you think that I—"

"Condensation…"

Stela wheels around, seeking out my voice in the dark. "What did you say?"

I push myself up to my knees, wavering. My head whirls and I use every ounce of focus I can conjure to find the outline of Stela's face hovering above me in the dark. Her eyes are waiting for me and our surroundings brighten when our sights align.

"It isn't sweat."

Stela's hands cup my clammy cheeks. "Your body is like ice," she says, horrified. Stela's touch is feverishly warm, her palm pressed to my forehead. I cling to every brush of her skin. I move into her touch and when she pulls away to examine her own dampened hands my body reels. The room tilts on its axis and Stela reaches for me as I collapse on my side. I try to make sense of her questions. I try to reason my symptoms out with her, but I open my mouth and the blood of two victims rushes back up my throat. Stela holds me by the shoulders as I wretch, my muscles straining against her as everything I've ingested in the last six hours splatters on the floor.

Stela says my name, gently, at first and then she's screaming. I spit up the last of my meal and grope blindly for her forearm, climb to her elbow as she embraces me with my head tucked beneath her chin. "I'm sick, Stela."

A deeper darkness envelopes me, at least three hours too early but welcome nonetheless. The heavy calm of sleep descends making Stela's desperate grip on my body fade into a soft embrace. My eyes drift closed and the world slips away, carrying Stela's panicked cries with it.

* * *

In the cramped room dust hangs suspended, silhouetted by a single column of stark light. Nothing disrupts it. No movement of any kind, and the fear that Stela has finally left me strangles my heart.

"Lie still," she says. "Get your bearings."

Her voice pierces the thick fog swirling around my brain. Stela doesn't reach for me, but from the pillow of my threadbare coat I can see the heels of her boots three feet from my head, her ankles crossed. She's sitting in the corner between two electrical panels—the weight of her glare all too detectable—intentionally removed from the single stream of light cast by the flashlight.

My body is colder than the cement beneath me and I'm groggy for the first time since before I was turned, hungrier than I've ever been in my life. The hunger is worrisome, the skin around my legs and ribs is as constricted as a bandage. I lift a tremulous hand to the skin around my eyes, my cheekbones and jaw. My features are too sharp, too thin. Stela remains where she is.

"How long was I out?" I croak. Stela shifts her legs, uncrosses her ankles. My limbs are heavy with fatigue. The simple act of leaning up on one arm is exhausting. My panic mounts as I realize that I'm aware of every ache in my body—the strain of sleeping on a hard surface, a scratchy throat from my violent retching.

"Forty-three hours," she says at last. Her tone is clinical, as deliberate as her position on the floor out of sight. I heave myself into a seated position and try to concentrate on her face, but I cannot sense her eyes on me.

"Must have forgotten to set my alarm."

Stela remains silent, unprovoked, and the weak smile on my lips fades. Why won't she look at me?

"What is the last thing you remember?" she asks, the same weary tone of a nurse on the last hour of her shift. I shake out my jacket and pull it around my shoulders but there is no body heat to trap inside. Strigoi don't feel the cold.

"I threw up."

Silence.

The would-be doctor inside me takes over. "A rapid drop in body temperature, followed by intense vertigo which resulted in nausea." My fingers probe the space between my pronounced ribs. Tiny pinpricks of light dancing in my vision. Blood rushing through the vessels in the eyes. Dizziness, loss of elasticity in the skin, dry throat and mouth, fatigue—all signs of dehydration. My fear subsides with a diagnosis and my stomach fills the strained quiet with a loud rumble.

"Have you been watching me the whole time?" I rub my hands together briskly, blowing breaths of chilled air between them.

"Where else would I be?" she asks softly. Her pale hand stretches out from the shadows.

I shuffle to her, and Stela guides me into her embrace. She crosses her arms around my front as I settle back against her torso, stealing the few scraps of warmth she's managed to safeguard despite being a day late for her feed. Stela was never as cold to the touch as I am.

"I didn't think we could get sick," I marvel. Stela doesn't respond. She pulls her arms tighter around me, and the huff of her frustrated breath warms the side of my neck momentarily. I can still hear the knife's edge of her panicked screams before I lost consciousness, traces of fear linger in her touch.

"You're angry with me."

"Never, my love." She strokes the side of my face with the back of her finger.

"You're quiet."

"Contemplative," she says.

"Stela…" This is not a fight I want to have for the hundredth time. She knows more than she's saying, so she says as little as she can to avoid lying. Secrets are the only real threat we face from each other, and they've nearly done us in more than once.

Stela helps me to my feet. "We should hunt," she says wearily. I have to hold on to her shoulder to keep my balance. The floor keeps slipping out from under me. "You must be famished. I know I am."

She busies herself with tidying my appearance, straightening my wrinkled top, zipping my weathered coat and combing her fingers through my tangled hair. Her eyes skirt the edges of my face, and an unspoken worry hides behind them. There is something soft and frightened about her, but she is trying to alchemize that fear into a sturdy metal. I lay my hands over hers and she pulls away, dusting off her pants and straightening her clothes. We both pretend we don't notice.

A train thunders through the tunnel outside, shaking the cement walls. I can't block out the noise and cup my hands over my sensitive ears, but even my weak pulse thumping in my wrist grates my nerves. I haven't been this raw since I was first turned. The experience seems similar to what I witnessed working in the ER, helping patients who thought their withdrawals might kill them. Just the scrape of the rusted door against the floor is a nail in my temple and I don't let Stela open it completely. I clutch her arm and bury my face between her shoulder blades.

"I can't, Stela. I can't go out there like this," I confess, trembling against her. She stills, the muscles in her back tense. I expect to be shoved aside any moment. Stela turns her head to the side and appraises me from the corner of her eye.

"Dearest, we must eat. Please, do not make me force you." Not a threat, but an earnest plea. Suddenly I can't get close enough to her. My hands glide down to her hips, fingers tugging at the tucked edges of her shirt to reach her skin. Stela's forehead thuds against the rusted steel door, still cracked open, and the yellow light of the subway tunnel wraps around us both.

"Elizabeth." Definitely a warning this time. I turn her around slowly and assail every inch of her exposed neck. Stela just stands there. Even the spot beneath her ear is immune to me—a first. Her scent is strong there, stronger still where her hairline meets the back of her neck. I nose beneath that curtain of perfect blond hair and Stela shoves against my sternum, wheeling me back on my heels.

"Stop," she says. Her eyes finally meet mine, her jaw flexed. Her chest is heaving, and not in a good way.

"You're afraid of me." My realization made all the more ridiculous by the fact that Stela has to catch me before I stumble back into a wall. She looks away and doesn't bother to deny it. The muscles in her throat twitch. "I wasn't going to feed from you." Was I? "I just... wanted you. Wanted to be close to you."

She laughs, a dry and harsh sound, and studiously avoids further eye contact. Her body is on high alert, and from the ridges in her upper lip I know her fangs have drawn. She moves into the shadow cast by the door, though with the light from the tunnel flooding our pitiful hovel I can see her perfectly. I wish I couldn't. I wish I could sleep for two more days and forget this moment, because I can't deny that I have asked for more than my fair share of her blood.

"Have I..." But the words won't come. Have I taken advantage of you? Abused your generosity? Disrespected your body? Am I like *him*?

Stela knows, whether I finish the question or not. She watches my face fall and reaches out to hold my chin in her steady hand.

"Forgive me, my love." She brings our noses together, and I sense her apprehension. "These are trying times," she says. "You surprised me."

"I *surprised* you?" I take a step forward. Stela takes a step back. She straightens to her full height, her features neutral. "Stela, we've never been able to keep our hands off each other." Anger takes a backseat to my swelling humiliation.

"Elizabeth," she sighs, "we have to hunt. We can discuss this later."

I shoulder past her and nearly rip the door off its hinges with a strength I can't explain in my current state.

"You're the boss."

Stela is smart enough to spot a backhanded comment and wise enough to know when to ignore it.

"Shall we?" she asks, her hand an olive branch. I stalk off down the tunnel without taking it, and Stela remains a step behind me.

* * *

I have no defense against the elements. The wind is relentlessly razor-sharp, ripping straight through me. The icy rain pelts our faces, though Stela doesn't seem to mind. We move down to the lower levels, the seedy underbelly of Clark Street to hunt, with the steady roar of traffic pounding overhead.

The service roads look like the abandoned sets of a postapocalyptic thriller, and tonight I find myself courting disaster. Massive floods brought on by global warming, nuclear attack, the outbreak of a viral pandemic. I yearn for an epic catastrophe to level the playing field between hunter and prey. A reckoning for humankind that would send them sprawling into the night, unprotected, ripe for the picking. No thought of cameras or police. No concern of where or how to dispose of a kill. Just chaos and all the camouflage it yields.

What has become of me?

Little by little the human attachments fade, the moral hang-ups, so gradual I barely noticed, like every one of my victims took a piece of my humanity with them.

"Up ahead," she says. "Fifty paces west."

I've already heard him, shuffling through damp newspaper and debris. All alone. His joints crack with every step. Slow movements, careful with his body, he knows his limits. Elderly, but not feeble. He's been living like this for too long, relegated to the fringe of society.

Aren't we all?

Stela moves into position beside me, the two of us branching out like hyenas to flank our prey. We don't converse but there is an understanding. Stela will take the right and I will stay to the left in the shadows. The wall beside us opens to a small thruway, a footpath with no formal lighting. The walls are wet with runoff from the highway, the rain glistening in the light of a modest fire. Our mark is so close I can smell the singed wool of his fingerless gloves. Just the one gentleman, which is odd. Stela prefers to ambush pairs, one quick hit, both our appetites sated and then we disappear. She slithers back against the wall and motions me on with a nod, but I remain at the entrance of the path. She is late for her feed, seems only right to let her eat first.

I rather enjoy hunting down here. The warped yellow light, the putrid stench of decay. On the lower levels it's always three in the morning, even at midday. Everyone here is displaced, forgotten. In a place like this you can forget there was ever any other way to live.

Stela's voice moves through my mind, urging me onward. I don't understand her haste. She's a meticulous hunter and we can't share a single warm body.

"You take him," I whisper. "I'll get the next one."

"Move on your target, now," she orders. Stela glances over her shoulder. She's been doing that a lot lately. Waiting for an attack. Lydia's gruesome performance at Opes and Sons has unnerved her more than she would ever admit, especially to me.

The firelight makes it impossible to hide my approach completely.

"Excuse me, sir?" I say softly. My voice carries more than I'd like. The old man looks in my direction with cataract-clotted eyes. "Could I sit with you for a while?" He squints at me, neither inviting me closer nor willing me away. "I'm freezing." I pull at the edges of my busted jacket and that is not part of the act.

Stela's footsteps reach my ears as I crouch down beside the small fire. She's hovering at the mouth of the footpath, angling for a better view.

The old man licks his dry lips, furrows his shaggy brows, but remains seated with his palms above the flickering flames. He is not a father or a son. He is no one's brother or uncle. Not anymore. Not down here. Not to me.

He doesn't ask my name or introduce himself. We don't flirt or comment on the weather or current affairs. I stretch my hands out close to the fire and savor the warmth.

My companion smells of sweat and his odor wraps around my head unappetizingly. I consider taking my leave, asking Stela to finish him off. His matted beard will be impossible to avoid. Will it stick in my teeth? My stomach pitches so violently I think I'll be sick all over again. But the thirst is there, through it all, demanding to be quenched even as my body warns me that this man will not go down smoothly.

The old man can sense my eyes on him even if he can't see clearly. He stares square in my face as I inch closer. "You're new," he says, pulling his knee tight underneath him and away from me.

"How'd you know?" Surely my stained attire didn't give me away.

"Too friendly with strangers," he says drolly. "Unarmed." He chews on the inside of his mouth and spits thick rust-colored gunk into the hissing flames.

I stare down at the end of the walkway where Stela waits in the wings.

"Not entirely." I smile, fangs drawn.

His name is Lee. He hasn't been the same since he lost his dog, Jack—a terrier mix with folded ears and a bristly coat. The dog was clipped by a cab last winter. Jack had been tugging Lee back out of a busy intersection when it happened. Lee had lost both his parents to morphine, six months apart, before his twelfth birthday. He was an electrician in another life, an unremarkable score of years during which he enjoyed the love of two devoted women. The first of which couldn't talk him out of joining the army, though she tried. The second couldn't eclipse the true love of his life. He was just twenty years old the first time he smoked opium in a Vietnamese brothel. Twenty-one years old the day he met heroin. In this moment, with one hand fisted in my hair and the other twisted in the front of my jacket Lee wants to make it perfectly clear that he was never a junkie. He got clean, several times. He tried goddammit.

Lee is a fighter, opinionated, no crazier than the world we live in, a bitter mouthful to the end. The final acrid drop of him oozes between my lips and sits sharply on my tongue. Lee slumps face first into the fire the second I release him, bits of his spidery beard fizzling in the heat and drifting up into the night.

Stela is close behind as I stand up—leery—and the second my knees lock my body pitches forward. The pain is searing, like my stomach is a bag of hot knives. Stela hoists me up by the armpits and drags me back out of the thoroughfare. My body temperature plummets to new depths and it's nothing to do with the weather. She pulls me toward the mid-level of Clark Street with one arm hooked under my breasts and the other clamped over my mouth to muffle my screams.

I have been shot, stabbed, sliced, nearly exsanguinated, speared, clubbed and generally knocked around. I, like Lee, have buried two parents, lived with the weight of my regrets, lumbered beneath the burden of my own bad choices. I have been humiliated and homeless. But never have I felt as helpless as I do now, with Stela's soothing voice in my ear, her grip around my jaw as my insides burn and threaten to incinerate me from the inside out. Without Stela's arms around me, my body would split at the seams.

We don't make it to the speeding traffic of Clark Street proper. A young man—early twenties, with hard eyes—spies Stela dragging me away from the scene of my most recent murder. He asks if I'm all right. Stela drops me, wheels around on him with murder in her eyes. The young man takes a large step back, flicks a collapsible baton open with his wrist. She barely blocks the wide-arc swing, catching the weighted tip in her hand. Every bone in that beautiful hand shatters. Stela wrests the weapon away with her good hand and breaks his knee, poor man. I'd appreciate his gallantry more if he hadn't injured her. Stela tears his throat open right in the middle of the service road, in full view of any car that turns to take the underground. She follows him down as he sprawls out on his back, his leg twisted grotesquely and drinks until she can wiggle the fingers of her busted hand again. Greedy mouthfuls spill down her chin, drip to her neck as she tightens her grip on his throat like she means to wring him dry.

"Stela…" I whisper in a small, hoarse voice. I can't move. Curled on my side, watching the scene play out to its inevitable conclusion, it's everything I can do not to start screaming again. The pain is radiating in my molars, piercing the soles of my feet like needles. Still she drinks.

Stela feeds past the point of death, until the skin of her victim is ashen and his lips are perfectly white. She pulls away with a growl, sprawling on her side. I try to move closer to her, I try to chastise her for chasing his death too closely but my mouth fills with blood. I manage to crawl on all fours to a barred sewer grate before emptying my stomach completely. The blood splatters down into the stagnant water below, and this bout of sickness is not as effortless as the first. My torso seizes, my legs lock beneath my chest as I wretch. I waste Lee until I fall face first into iron sewer grate and I swear I can hear Erebus howling beneath the city.

Her victim's death doesn't slow her for long. Stela flips me over and pulls my head into her lap. She tries to rouse me. I'm certain I'll be sick again as Stela props me up against her. Nothing is real but the pain in my abdomen, the fiery fist that was once my stomach.

The pain eases at the sound of Stela's skin splitting between her teeth. She presses her torn wrist to my lips. I turn away with what strength I have left and find her calm black eyes waiting for me. *Feed.*

Stela strokes the back of my head now cradled in her healed palm and my tongue swipes her weeping wound. "Come now, my darling," she says, her irritation showing. The wound has healed but the taste of Stela is something I cannot resist for long. Her skin opens under my fangs and she sighs as the swoon moves through her, her forehead pressed in the crook of my neck, her hair spilling across my cheeks.

The blood drains down my throat and coats my spasming stomach. With every drop my grip on her elbow tightens and soon the pain fades and there is only this: the taste of Stela, the tangle of her fingers in my hair as she slumps forward. Her body yields to me in every way, urging me closer. When she turns my chin to look into her eyes, I see my own face reflected in their black depths, I hear my name though her lips are slack, and deep inside my chest a budding warmth starts behind my lungs. The warmth turns to heat, webbing around my ribs, moving up to curl itself around my brain. The call of my name grows sharper in my mind as Stela's free hand drops from my face, and a dangerous yellow ring encircles her black pupils—boiling the fresh blood in my belly.

When my jaw fails to unhinge I tear her flesh from my teeth, but I can't look away from her eyes. Stela growls menacingly and turns on her side away from me. She cradles her wounded wrist against her chest like a broken wing, her chest heaving.

"I'm sorry," I say. She could have killed me. She almost did. My lungs are singed, and the roof of my mouth tastes like ash. "Stela, please, look at me. I didn't mean—"

"Nor I," she whispers. Delicate and frail, her voice stuns me. It retains the breathy cadence as she turns over on her back, eyes shut tight against the fire burning in them. "I seem to be struggling to control my newest defense mechanism."

I lean over her, run my fingers through her hair, and when her eyes open cautiously the yellow iris is gone. "Forgive me," she says, cupping my face in her hands. She rubs her thumb affectionately over the swell of my bottom lip and licks the pad of her finger clean.

"I hurt you..." It barely seems possible. Our bodies respond violently to injury. I could have killed her. She defended herself, albeit unconsciously.

"We have to move," she says. She smooths her fingers over my cheeks, eyes unfocused, darting around our exposed position.

"Lift the grate," she orders, hands on her hips to hide the wavering stance. I do as I'm told, I lift the manhole cover up as Stela roots through the pockets of the young man, now cold. She twirls his keys on her finger and shoves them into the pocket of her dirty pants. He's carrying a wad of cash in his billfold, and Stela pitches the cards and ID into the sewer. She can't lift the body, but she doesn't ask for my help, and I don't offer. She wouldn't be pleased to know that her frailty is obvious. She gathers one ankle in each hand and has to shove the body over the ground, head first into the muck.

I close the grate to cover our tracks. She allows me to wrap an arm around her waist, to hold her up. For the first time in days, I'm not tired. My body feels foreign—heavy, but spry. We have to disappear.

Stela deposits the young man's keys in my palm. "Lived alone. Not far. West Adams Street." And with those words, Stela's eyelids close for the evening. Her body falling slack in my embrace.

If hailing a cab is tough in this city, then convincing a cabbie to drop you and your thoroughly incapacitated counterpart off in a questionable neighborhood in the middle of the night is to move mountains. Money talks, and Stela has a pocketful of dirty bills.

I keep my window cracked and have to rely on scent to pinpoint the newly vacated property. Stela won't wake until tomorrow evening, and she forgot to mention the street number before she expired. Her mark's scent lingers on her lips, tangled in her hair, making it possible to sniff out his modest worker cottage on a street of little else.

The driver is hesitant to stop, quicker still to reach over the backseat with an open hand. I shove a crumpled hundred into his sweaty palm and keep hold of him until he turns on me—stricken, ready to fight—and meets my glare. It's dark in the back of the cab, but the streetlight makes it possible for him to find my face. I lean into the light and burrow my way into his eyes.

"You were never here. You never saw us." The cab driver nods, vacant and dumb, and parlor trick aside, I'm surprised by the venom in my voice. Stela's strength running through my veins.

I gather her into my arms as the cab speeds off, letting the wind slam the door shut on the backseat. There are eyes on us, I'm certain of them as I take Stela around the back of the house. They follow our path over the sidewalk, down between two buildings, over the frozen grass until the night swallows us whole.

The furnishings leave much to be desired: spartan, indicative of a bachelor, reeking of youth. There's a plaid sofa. A brown recliner in the corner. Two blue milk crates act as a coffee table. One standing lamp. The kitchen sink is stacked with crusty dishes, dried noodles mummified in three white bowls. Half a pizza open and uncovered on the two-burner stove.

I deposit Stela on the couch, draw the front window's warped blinds and move in the dark to make our surroundings more presentable. I end up throwing nearly everything away in four trash bags. I scrub the sink—I just can't tolerate filth.

I retire to the armchair, ankles crossed on the edge of a milk crate, and watch Stela's placid face. She is ghostly pale, one leg flung over the edge of the sofa with the toe of her boot resting on the floor. The leg she usually kicks over my hips when we sleep.

My eyes trail over her sprawled limbs, crawl across her torso to find the exposed skin of her throat, and as though the line of my sight is felt even now, her throat bobs as she swallows. She draws her chin down to her chest, and just like that, in the soft purple light of the early morning hours, my appetite returns.

* * *

Her hand twitches and I react a moment too slowly. Stela seizes my bicep in her crushing grip and I'm relieved to note her strength has returned. A flutter of eyelids and then her affirming gaze. Stela regains consciousness and glances anxiously around the unfamiliar room. She rips the IV bag from my hands and sits up on the stained sofa, draining the O Negative to the last drop. She discards the crumpled plastic without a word and reaches for the second pouch in my lap. Once the second serving has been emptied Stela brushes the hair out of her eyes and leans back on the couch, her arms spread gracefully across the back. She could make a throne of a cardboard box. Her black eyes settle on my face. She doesn't invite me closer. I can't say I blame her. I stay on the edge of the couch, staring back at her, bracing myself.

"Where did you get them?" she asks, waving the last wrinkled blood bag in her hand.

"I risked a trip to the ER," I say, sensing her disapproval. "Not a hospital I've visited before. And one I don't care to visit again." It was like something out of a horror movie. Fresh blood on the tiles, on the curtained partitions. Three patients admitted with lacerated carotids, all pronounced dead on arrival. The family is never so careless with their prey. Such a show had to be intentional, a power move like the mutilated body of Andrew Opes. Stela should know, but she needs to regain her strength first.

"Were you seen?"

"In and out in ten minutes tops, I promise." That was the fastest hospital visit of my life, made all the easier by the rank stench of human beings. I can smell the same odor seeping from Stela's mouth, mixing with her own lovely scent, tainting her. My stomach rolls.

"You didn't wake up," I say, eyes fixated on the moldy beige carpet. "Night came and you were asleep. I spoke to you. Smacked you once. I didn't know what else to do, Stela."

Stela remains intensely quiet. She rakes a fingernail around the chipped edges of a dried splotch of marinara adhered to the upholstery. Every living thing casts a shadow, leaves some trace after its gone. A stain, a smell, yesterday's dishes crusting in the sink.

"That must have alarmed you," she says distractedly. She leans forward with her elbows on her knees, her hands clasped.

Alarmed? It was horrifying not being able to wake her. Was she *alarmed* when I slept for nearly two days? I hadn't even considered that Stela and I had a similar scare. I was thinking of my mother's body at the foot of the stairs. That despite all my training, my first instinct was to shake her awake. Who's to say that didn't exacerbate her injuries? As though any of that matters now…

Stela reaches for my hand, squeezes it firmly as though to banish the dread that drove me to the hospital this evening. I felt so alone without her by my side, so powerless, so sure that I had finally taken too much. I didn't even stop to drain a mark of my own, and I only brought back enough blood for her. Despite my growing hunger, just the thought of drinking from a blood bag, how cold and dead the blood would be, makes my stomach clench.

"How are you feeling?" she asks softly, tilting her knees in my direction. She brushes my forehead with cool fingers.

"Better." Somewhat. The lethargy has returned, but not as pronounced as before I fed from Stela.

She smiles crookedly, swipes a thumb below my eye. She doesn't believe me.

"You look tired, my darling."

"I was worried."

Stela parts her lips, looks away and swallows roughly. She leans back on the sofa. I know she's nervous. Her body tells me everything her mind withholds.

"You know, don't you?"

"Hmm?" she mumbles, snapping back to attention. Stela makes a valiant effort to maintain her blank expression, but her heartbeat tells a different story. Her pulse kept the same pace when she would catch me talking with Lydia.

"Stela..." Her face hardens, her features dark and sharp. "What's wrong with me?" I'm not sure I want the answer. But I am sure that she knows much more than she's letting on. She always does.

Stela stares back at me without a word.

"You've seen this before? My symptoms?" Side effects, maybe? Mutation? There's an ugly word. But what are Strigoi if not a mutation? Even now I can hear mice scurrying across buckled floorboards in the attic of the shotgun house across the street, and I mastered the ability to control the range and volume of my hearing months ago. You have to, the endless creaking of the world will drive you crazy.

Stela's eyes remain locked on mine. Her expression has softened. She takes my wrists and strokes my skin with her thumbs.

"Not exactly," she says. Normally, this is the part where I egg her on, but her sad smile gives me pause. "I witnessed something similar, once, ages ago."

"Please, Stela. Don't be coy. Just tell me."

Stela stands and paces. "Fane..." she says, testing the waters, but I will not give a dead man the satisfaction of flinching at his name. "You read my journals," she continues, "Fane exhibited similar symptoms after he turned me. Fed from me. My mortal blood made him violently ill."

I nod to help her along. We're no closer to an answer. "Fane was a Moroi, Stela. Born a monster. I wasn't. You turned me into a Strigoi."

"Precisely."

"Precisely what? I fed from blood collection bags for nearly a year without sickness. I wasn't tired. My sense of smell, my hearing has never been as sharp as it is now. It's driving me crazy, and the hunger... is worse now than it's ever been." I will not get angry with her. "Is Fane's blood doing this?"

"In a sense." Her eyes plead for me to understand, but I can't. And then I realize why. She doesn't want to be the one to tell me. But who else is there?

I throw my hands up in defeat and slump back against the couch. Stela sinks to her knees, between my legs. I run my hand back through her hair, reveling in the scent of her, and she runs her hands up my thighs. The frustration thrumming in my temple quiets as she lifts the edge of my shirt and brushes her lips over my navel. Stela meets my stare, stroking my obliques with long fingers.

"I love you," she says with heartbreaking solemnity. "More than my own life. Tell me you know that." She's the closest to tears I've ever seen her. I reach out to cup the side of her face.

"Stela—"

Stela digs two fingers into my abdomen, just south of my navel. The shock renders me speechless. I push at her shoulders, squirm away from the incredible pressure and wedge myself deeper into the cushions at my back. I scream, but she clenches her jaw and stares impassively back at me, pressing deeper. A flutter ripples through me, lower than my stomach. Stela recoils and the second her fingers quit their assault I stand up, shoving her as I go, as hard as I possibly can. Stela goes sprawling into the small entryway and sits up, fangs bared.

I cover my stomach protectively as the discomfort evaporates. Beneath my fingers, it happens again. A ripple, foreign, faint. I lift up my shirt and stare down at my body, willing the muscles to twitch. Stela picks herself up off the floor and crosses to me, an unspoken apology curtaining her eyes, and she flattens her palm over the bruise she made that has already begun to heal. There's no mistaking the sensation this time. If I had trouble deciphering the movement within, I would still see the truth in Stela's face. She keeps her hand on my body for a fourth and fifth weak kick.

"No." It's not possible.

"Elizabeth…" Stela exercises every ounce of thrall she has over me, staring deeply into my eyes, taking hold of my hips. But the balm of my name falling from my Maker's lips falls on deaf ears.

"No." I knock her hands away roughly.

"Dearest, please, listen to me." She speaks softly, and I hate her for it.

"You knew!"

Stela rears back an inch as though slapped.

"You fucking knew and you said nothing?"

"What was I supposed to say, Elizabeth?" Now we're inches apart and we're both screaming. Stela's fingers curl into hooks and my hands shake at my sides, my nails pressing so deeply into my palms the flesh splits.

Stela clears her throat, her eyes sad and wide. "This is not something…" She shakes her head. "I have only ever read about it. There was no way to be certain, until you fell ill in the maintenance room."

"You slept for nearly two days," she says, as though I'd forgotten, as though she wishes she could. "She whispered to me then, something more and less than words, begging for blood. I was as incredulous as you are now, my darling. It was not possible. Perhaps, because I refused to listen the child began to speak of other things. Not—" Stela huffs, kicks at the carpet. "Not merely with words, nor simple images. They were memories, you see. Distinct impressions of how she came to be, why you were sick. Slowly, I started to believe. But I needed proof."

I shove past Stela, circling the room, stalking her statuesque form. Itching for a fight. "So, you took me on a second hunt to see if I'd get sick again?" And I was. This isn't real. It can't be true. "You didn't think to read me in on your little experiment?"

My fangs haven't retracted since our shouting match began—though Stela has resumed her inside voice—and I'm salivating uncontrollably. Stela remains collected, but she keeps her eyes on me, following my every move around the small living room.

"There was no reason to frighten you unless I was absolutely certain. And now I am."

Certain. The word hits me like a truck. My legs start to tremble, the faintness of starvation creeping up on me. My fangs recede. Stela takes a tentative step in my direction.

"Stay where you are." I warn her, halting her advance mid-stride.

"The Moroi are very rare, my love," she whispers. "Our people have not seen a new regent in more than a millennium."

She can't see my shaking my head. "You're wrong, Stela."

"The children are volatile when young," she continues, speaking to herself. "Their thirst is prodigious."

"Don't say that word again." Violence radiates through my entire being.

"Fane's heir should be the responsibility of his coven, because the child—"

"*What did I just say?*"

Her head snaps up, and she stares blankly back at me, eyes unfocused. Lost to her thoughts. "Procreation is feared among our kind," she says. "With good reason." She actually smiles, a million miles away from me now. "Fane tried many times over the years, with Lydia and me. But the Moroi are incapable of reproducing. He could only taint what was already inside you."

My blood goes cold. There is no whisper, no words. Memories. Dozens of them flood my mind. It's as though I'm remembering some repressed truth. Some of the memories are mine. Others are impossible, formed *inside* my body. I see James, alive and laughing, curled on Stela's side of the bed. The two of us talking quietly late into the night, safe in my bedroom, in the brownstone, the last time he stayed over. Then cells, mine and his, merging, splitting. Stopped.

Frozen in time, suspended in my body. Two weeks after conception? Three before I was turned? So small, so insignificant. A stowaway from another life. Quite dead.

Until I drank from Fane.

Stela watches the realization wash over me.

She told me on the night I was reborn that she could see me living a life with James. Starting a family. I told her then, I wanted none of it. I could not picture any life without her in it. I refused that life and walked willingly into the darkness with Stela.

"She will need a family," she says calmly. "A brood. It would be impossible for you and me to keep her fed."

"*It!*" I scream. Stela jumps to her feet, her body poised and ready for an attack. "It, Stela. Not *her*. Not *the child*. It."

Stela tilts her head, then narrows her eyes. "She has not spoken to you, has she?"

"This isn't happening." I shiver when Stela takes a step closer. I can taste her blood with perfect clarity. "I don't accept this. It's ridiculous." I shake my head and storm across the living room for the black jacket I commandeered in the ER. "I won't accept it."

"Where are you going?"

"To fix this."

Darius gave me the highly abridged version long before the fire consumed the whole of his library, and possibly him with it. The parents of a Moroi never live. There was a father named Leonis who had the foresight to present his newborn Moroi with a coven of his own. The boy prince, Cyrus, grew into adulthood rapidly and ultimately slaughtered Leonis, the father who escaped his thirst, and absorbed what remained of Leonis' clan. That, as they say, was the way of it.

Stela stops my exit with a hand on the front door.

"Get out of my way," I growl. I can smell her fear, and the scent alone makes me dizzy with thirst.

"Hear me, my love." Her voice betrays nothing but dreary resignation. "It is done."

"Bullshit. A lot has changed in the last thousand years, Stela. I still have options."

She dips her chin. "Elizabeth, you are not a fool. Where do you think the lethargy comes from? A body as strong as yours. You must have a theory."

I grab her by the collar, try to heave her away from the door. Stela won't budge.

"You know exactly where it comes from," she says. She runs her fingers through my hair, as though this is any other night, as if I'm not seconds away from opening her throat with my teeth. "She is feeding from you, Elizabeth. Taking all but enough to keep you alive."

I shove her back into the door. "It."

"Call *it* what you like." She straightens, rises to her full height. "If you taint your blood with mortals, *it* will rid your body of sustenance." My fingers loosen their grip, fall away from her shirt. "If you starve yourself, *it* will drain you dry."

"You're forgetting the third option," I say calmly.

Stela rolls her eyes to the ceiling.

My stomach flutters again, a single sentient motion. I jump back as though I can escape. A warmth starts low in my abdomen, pleasant at first. My temperature climbs, the same way it did every morning in our suite when Stela and I would warm ourselves by the fire. But the sensation spreads, down my legs, up my spine, a great heat building at the back of my eyes.

Stela stares at me somberly, her eyes on my belly, hands hovering as if to help. She looks up at me, hopeless, terrified. She's not doing this… I drop my coat to my feet, take a step away from the door. The heat fades quickly, as though it was never there.

"I don't want this," I whisper, my whole body shaking. Stela calls my name, opening her arms.

"I know," she says. I lean into her embrace willingly, and Stela closes her arms around my shoulders. My body trembles, and despite Stela's soothing voice in my ear, immune to her charms. I'm so hungry and she's so dangerously close. We drop down to the cracked tile in the entryway and Stela rocks me gently in her arms. "Neither do I."

XII

Needs Must

As I have tried to tell Elizabeth, if there is a trick to surviving eternity, it is to live completely in the moment.

Easier said than done.

I have made the moment a daily practice, but in truth the only being I have ever known who embodied this philosophy was Fane. The irony is, I would not be in this situation were it not for his attempts to gain some level of control over Elizabeth. And yet, I have never needed his counsel more than I do now.

These are things I do not say to my darling girl.

Instead I wish her a good evening, I ask how she feels, I remind her to feed. I urge her to feed from me. Elizabeth in turn says nothing. Goethe once wrote, "Give more and more, and always more, and then you cannot miss by very much." I no longer believe that to be true. I have missed by quite a margin.

Her body stirs from slumber—soon she will awaken. If only I could keep her in this stasis, alive but unresponsive, at peace in dreams, until I find a way out of this situation. If only the burden were mine, this affliction Fane always intended for Lydia or me. But the end result would be the same, no matter who carries the next Moroi. And Elizabeth, I remind myself, is no damsel in distress.

The soft purple of the evening spreads across her face as she entangles herself deeper into the sheets and rolls over on her back. I absolutely abhor this hovel we have stolen, with its threadbare sheets and mildew stench, black mold in the corners of the shower.

The bedroom is on the second floor. It was not my idea to keep the bed up here. A hollow fiberboard door opens directly onto the stairs, which means the only escape route is the bedroom window—in full view of the street. Too easy to flush us out up here, control our path and capture or kill us. One full-sized mattress on the floor, a box spring but no frame. The mattress reeks of body odor, and frankly, I am surprised Elizabeth did not douse the bed with bleach before collapsing. She is so tired these days.

When she feeds from me, I have to restrain her, also not my idea. Her consideration for my wellbeing is touching, but I have taken every precaution. I am hunting for three now.

No Strigoi I have known has ever carried a child. That is not to say that my role in her pregnancy is unclear. There is a second record of births, a sacred text which Darius copied into a tower of scrolls. I would give anything for an evening in the library, alone with my reclusive brother to consult those texts and pick his brain. Lydia would be jealous of Elizabeth, but ultimately, she would learn to accept it. She would dote on her, spoil her with finery, construct a nursery from nothing. Crogher would be elated in his own unobtrusive way. Bård would be vigilantly attentive. In fact, if I had Crogher and Bård to hunt with me, Elizabeth would never go hungry. Erebus would lie at her feet, day and night, to keep watch.

I miss my family.

All I have in the world is curled on her side, facing the peeling wall. Awake, though she remains still. Unreachable, despite being within arm's length of me. I do not regret my actions. I would burn my siblings to a cinder a second time if it guaranteed Elizabeth's safety. The problem is, I have ensured nothing and something else is coming. The three dead bodies Elizabeth stumbled across in the ER were only the overture.

I awoke with a start in early dusk this evening. Fleetingly, I thought Lydia had discovered our location, or worse, that Bård had survived. I sensed the footfall of an old one, within the city limits for certain.

Years ago, Fane's brethren turned on his bloody crusade, deeming him too ruthless in his pursuit of the unnamed Strigoi. They were only too happy to see him off to a new continent. But it was silly of me to hope that his death would go unnoticed, unavenged. Fane was their equal, and it was always only a matter of time before the cavalry arrived.

I should have woken Elizabeth immediately. Made a run for it. But where would we go? With Andrew Opes dead, I cannot risk forging his name to withdraw a single penny from Fane's considerable estate, and as it stands the city officials here are still receiving their monthly stipends. Elizabeth and I have no way of bribing our way into the heart of a new town. When we leave Chicago, we will have to survive as we did in the old country. In those days we purchased loyalty with brute force and fear, promised entire villages eternity, enthralled them to us and inevitably abandoned them in the dead of night. We left those villages as silent as a plague and spread into the next territory. We were the monsters of legend, campfire stories.

In her condition, upheaval is hardly an option. We need a fertile and familiar hunting ground. At the rate I am feeding, camouflage would be impossible in a strange environment.

"Could you do that somewhere else?" she asks, her forearm draped across her eyes.

"What, dearest?"

"Your brooding will wake the neighbors, Stela." She rolls over with a sigh.

"I do not brood." I try to keep a smile from my lips but fail. Elizabeth chuckles and inches into my arms. The soft bump of her belly presses against my hipbone. A fortnight has passed since that terrible night Elizabeth found out about the child, and she has just begun to show. The delivery date is drawing near, faster than either of us expected. Fane's blood must have sped the gestation along, but by how much? No text I have read exactly detailed a Strigoi pregnancy. What was recorded was the moment of birth, with brief reference to conception but no dates. What I do know—and this mostly from lore—is that birth follows soon after the pregnancy becomes obvious.

Elizabeth has not mentioned the change in her appearance, and therefore, neither have I. She dresses now in sweatshirts she found in the closet. She wears them to bed.

Evenings are her most agreeable time. The early hours between twilight and moonrise. Those hours have always been ours, filled with banter or passion depending on the mood. The latter is regrettably, mutually rare as of late.

"Were you with me this morning?" she asks, running her fingers through my hair.

"In your dream?"

She nods, tracing the line of my collarbone, avoiding my eyes.

"No." Ah, the succinct, uncomplicated truth.

"I wasn't in yours either."

I did see Elizabeth in my dream, but it was only a reflection, not the woman herself. A version of the very first nightmare we shared.

I was transported to Claire's bedroom, just outside the door. There were soft sounds coming from that bedroom. I opened the door, expecting to be greeted by the malodorous stench of impending death. Instead, the air was dusted with talc. There was no sick bed, but a white bassinet. Elizabeth stood before the crib, cast her eyes over her shoulder at me. She smiled and turned toward me. The shadows, the weariness under her eyes were gone. She was radiant and strong, her smile glowed. There was no pillow in her hands with which to smother her ailing mother, but in her arms was a bundle wrapped in a swaddling cloth. I could just see a sprinkling of blond hair under that cloth, the curled shell of one perfect ear, the bud of a nose pressed to Elizabeth's chest. "There you are," Elizabeth said, stroking the infant's cheek. She ran her thumb under the babe's chin and the child twisted in her arms. Its dimpled chin stained with Elizabeth's blood. "We've been waiting for you."

"Where are you?" Elizabeth asks, leaning up on arm.

"Right here," I reply, settling a hand on her hip. "With you."

She kisses me chastely. "What were you thinking about?"

"You."

"Liar." Elizabeth smiles in her far-off way but does not press the matter. Her smile lingers until a ripple of movement through her abdomen steals her good mood. The child is awake.

At once, Elizabeth perches on the edge of the bed. There is nothing I can do but draw up the sheet and watch her go. Surprisingly she lingers and strips off her red sweatshirt. She rubs her hands over the slight swell of her belly, stares down at herself.

"How did you know?" she asks, turning her face to the moonlight. "The sex, I mean."

Elizabeth never calls it "the child," "the baby," She has never referred to it as "she."

"I cannot say for certain…" I begin, waiting for Elizabeth to grow defensive and cut me off. She plants her hands on her hips instead, and stares at me expectantly. "I think she told me."

I wait for the vehement dismissal, the usual outrage over my insinuation that the infant is not only cognizant but communicative.

Elizabeth smooths her hand over her belly. She sighs, tries a thin-lipped smile that is more a grimace.

"I'm gonna shower," she says and pads toward the washroom.

I hear the weak stream of water hit the fiberglass shower stall and close my eyes. I try to picture the face of our pursuers, but the harder I focus my attention on them the more impenetrable the darkness around them becomes. Whatever hunter has been sent to investigate Fane's murder is no amateur. That knowledge alone offers some insight. An old one, most certainly. But a Moroi? That would mean the presence of an entire clan as a regent never travels without their food source.

I rummage through yesterday's clothes for the blood bag I brought to bed this morning. I find it curled and twisted in my pants leg, drained to the dregs. Elizabeth's fatigue seems to be catching. My muscles have weight, my vision and hearing are dulled. My whole body sluggish, shrinking in on itself, ribs jutting out, my skin ashen.

"Stela," she calls from the shower.

"Dearest?"

"Get in here."

That is not a request. I drag my fingers back through my bedraggled hair and join her in the washroom.

A plume of steam greets me, the harsh white lights above the sink giving form to the heat. Condensation runs down the mirror in jagged lines, slicing my reflection to pieces. I rest the small of my back against the sink and think of my old washroom. The cool shale walls, the generous tub, our bed resting just beyond the door—beckoning us back. Elizabeth pushes the plastic shower curtain back, cranes her soapy head in my direction.

"Don't loiter. It's creepy." She extends a wet palm.

"As you wish." I take her hand and allow her to pull me under the sluggish trickle of blessedly hot water.

Elizabeth, sensing my troubled thoughts, grasps me gently by the chin and stares deeply into my eyes. "You look tired." She pushes my body ahead of her and massages my scalp with her fingers, soft soap bubbles running down her thin arms. I could deny it, but I remain quiet and enjoy the attention of her hands on my body.

She pulls me against her by the hips and whips her wet hair over one shoulder, cradling the back of my skull as she brings my face to her neck. We stand very still with the water pounding on my back and spilling down her front. I breathe her in and the scent is reminiscent of her, but unmistakably altered. A note out of place, sweet despite the astringent soap on her body. Elizabeth's fingers skate across my shoulders, down my spine. Her touch is soft, inquisitive, probing for injury and weakness.

"Go on," she urges, returning her hand to the back of my head. Pushing my face nearer to her bare throat.

"No." I push her back with a hand on her sternum. That is a mistake. Elizabeth wrenches the offending limb behind my back and uses the weight of my own body against me. The action sends her back against the wall, and I follow after pinning in her place.

"Don't do that," she warns. Her voice low, deliberate, teetering on threat.

"Do what?" I can only lift my face inches from her skin without breaking her hold, which would undoubtedly lead to a much larger disagreement. Elizabeth secures her slick grip and my elbow protests the sharp angle as she raises my hand to the middle of my back. She is not often forceful with me. She fears her capacity for violence.

"The hero thing."

I am not two words into my protest when her grip disappears and her hands wrap around my neck. Her eyes are sharp with aggression that is not entirely her own, and I cannot look away from them. She holds me there, her lips parted, nose pressed against mine. "You're exhausted," she says, pressing her lips to mine cautiously. "Starved. I can see it all over you." She speaks the words directly into my mouth. "Take a little," she demands with deadly calm. "Just to get you going."

"Elizabeth—"

She drags me forward, the back of her head and the top of my knees thumping against the wall. Something breaks in that half a second, something shatters. A barrier in both our minds lifted, a line crossed. Her tongue is split—her own doing—and dancing over mine. My hand curls around her neck, to push her away, to stop the assault of her blood upon my senses. She moans and I feel the small sound roll through my fingers.

I have a memory of swimming in the Danube when I was still mortal and very young. The water was brisk, murky, it stung my eyes. But beneath the surface the whole world was quiet, removed, and I had the shimmer of the sun as it broke through the ripples to light my way through the dark. Kissing Elizabeth, her body against mine, is not like breaking through the surface for that first breath. The rush of wind in my ears, blood pounding in my temples. No, feeling Elizabeth open to me, wrap around me, urge me on, the pressure of her palm on my hand as she steers it down her torso, is exactly the sensation of being submerged. Those first few strokes underwater when my lungs were full and there was only the dank, uncharted territory ahead. When it felt like I could keep swimming forever.

We drown ourselves in each other, and when I am lost to the noises she makes, the sounds she pulls from me, and the force of her grip in my hair, when I am only an inch from the surface myself—gasping, reaching—she cranes her head to the side and my teeth latch onto her neck without a second thought to her hunger, to the child's.

Her blood is richer now, thicker, it does not blossom readily to the surface. It has to be dragged, as if the child inside of her controls these tides, reins in the flood. The taste—smooth, sweet, like Fane's—is different enough to be disconcerting.

"No more," she whispers, two shaking hands on my shoulders. My fangs retract instantly, my body bowed around her, and I watch the puncture wounds shrink and seal. New pink skin dotting her throat, just beside two milky scars. Scars I gave her, wounds I made in another life.

"Sorry," I say, running my thumb over the freshly thatched punctures. I watch her face, wait for her to push me back into the now-cold water spraying out against the floor. Elizabeth rests with her eyes pressed shut, her head thrown back. Her tongue darts out to wet her lips.

"Don't apologize." She shakes her head, eyes parting in that drowsy way that makes my heart race. "You needed to feed." She straightens and reaches around me to shut off the shower. The pipes shudder in the walls. "We needed that," she amends in a quiet, thoughtful voice.

Elizabeth steps out first, wrapping the towel around her torso, avoiding the mirror. She hands me a towel. I watch her watching me. Her eyes admiring in a comfortable, entitled way. I missed that look.

"How do you feel?" she probes.

"Better. Thank you."

"You don't need to thank me, Stela." She runs her fingertips down my arm, shoulder to wrist. "Thank *you*," she says with downcast eyes. I do not require a window into her soul to sense the scope of her gratitude. I am deplorably undeserving of it.

"Elizabeth, it was never my intention…" to deny you, avoid you, yet that is exactly what I have done.

"It's been hard. I know. For both of us. Sometimes I forget that you're in this too. That isn't easy for me to remember when—"

"I know." Would that I did. Perhaps I would be better equipped to give her what she needs. To comfort her. I have so many limitations. Elizabeth stares unabashedly into my eyes, and her gentleness makes me all the more wretched.

"I need you," she says, plainly, calmly, devoid of blame, though I deserve it. She has been feeding so much. Her insatiable hunger unsettled me, made me leery of her affections. Worse, it made me forget who we are together, what binds us. I did not want to hurt her, push or punish her. We are so much more than this.

"So do I, dearest."

Elizabeth presses against my arm and ghosts her lips along my shoulder. The tender moment is brief, her eyes flick up at the dripping mirror, run once along her poorly concealed abdomen, and she turns away with a downturned gaze, shoulders slumped and heavy. I take in my own reflection, the gray bags beneath my eyes, the dart of each blue vein and my fist sends the mirror spiraling to the floor in shards. A dozen slivers of my face stare up at me from the ground, and Elizabeth's surprise reaches my ears from the adjoining room.

As I dress I cannot meet those understanding eyes, but I feel her body close by, hovering within reach. She pads barefoot to the open door, surveys the damage and the corners of her mouth curl in fond exasperation.

* * *

Hunting has never been a chore, but Elizabeth holds an increasingly strong tether on my thoughts. How much of that is her own doing is difficult to judge. I get anxious the longer we are parted, though not for my own wellbeing. There is a new voice in my head, low, beneath the pounding blood of the passersby. A voice that urges haste.

Can Elizabeth hear you, child? Does she sense your influence? Understated, yes, and carefully controlled.

There are nights when I almost believe that steadying voice. Evenings and early mornings when my mind fills with peace and I catch myself thinking: She will be fine. Elizabeth will be just fine.

Do I mean to harm the child? Could I end her life as I ended Fane's? If she stared up at me with his blue eyes and Elizabeth's chestnut hair? If by some magic she opened her mouth and my ridiculous laugh spilled from her lips, what would I do then? And would Elizabeth be alive to hear it too?

I push the thoughts aside and focus on the hunt. The city sings to me on the darkened platform stairs. The clap of heels on wet cement, the brush of coats. Cars hurl past, feet slap through oily puddles. Pedestrians buffet around each other, colliding on occasion in the pre-holiday traffic, bowed down with brightly colored bags. When Elizabeth and I are finally forced to leave I will miss this place.

In the midst of this crush, a light finds me. Faint at first, I have to halt on the sidewalk to follow the sound of her pulse. I shut out the bustle of the city and narrow my focus on a single footfall, only vaguely familiar.

On the corner of Halsted Street and Belmont Avenue, surrounded by an entourage of enthusiastic young women, I see her. She shakes the hair from her eyes, which is no longer the ghastly platinum and purple streaks of her rebellious youth, but the rich honey tone she inherited from her mother. Gone is the white powder makeup, the black liquid liner that concealed her soft hazel eyes. She has traded fishnet stockings for leather leggings, her multitude of gaudy rings for brightly painted nails, finely cut diamonds in each ear.

Christine Opes. Sole heir of Andrew Opes and future—far future—president of Opes and Sons, her family's vast financial empire, is being dragged across the intersection by the cuff of her lovely cashmere sweater.

Ms. Opes' companions are exuberant, slightly inebriated and huddled closely as they rush up the block. She is more lovely than I imagined, despite her current look. For the first time since his death, I mourn Andrew. Not for what I lost, or my wasted plans, or Elizabeth's inaccessible funds. Andrew belonged to Christine in the truest sense, and I can read her pain in the slump of her shoulders, the clench of her jaw. My Elizabeth wore the same expression the night I came to claim her at her mother's grave.

I follow them to Sheffield Avenue, where they halt at the tail end of a winding queue wrapped around The Vic. I stand surveying at a safe distance waiting for another glimpse of her face. I can see plainly that she is here against her will, so why do her so-called friends take no notice of her mood?

I am pulled into her orbit. Christine is a student at one of the finest universities in the world, years to go before she graduates. Still, I stare at her like a savior reborn, as though at any moment she will dismiss her present company to take the reins of her father's empire—to sort through the bureaucratic nonsense and restore Opes and Sons to Strigoi control. My legacy secured and Elizabeth's modest wealth reinstated with her signature.

"What time does the show get out?" she asks, rubbing her bottom lip with her thumbnail. Her question lingers unanswered as a shiny silver flask is uncovered and passed around her circle. She dismisses the offer, repeats her question as three phones raise to snap a photo of this moment from varying angles. The effervescent group talks over her, around her, posing for pictures, the glare of the flash twinkling against their glittery tops.

I step outside a group photo and keep close to the wall, my blood roaring in my ears. I never meant to get this close, and I could reach out and touch her if I dared. Christine grows irritated, snatches the flask from a friend who has held it just a beat too long. She wipes her lips, closes her eyes, channels her patience. Beside me a beautiful young man with a mighty beard has two tickets in his back pocket. Elizabeth would enjoy him. I slide one ticket free and read the call times.

"Seriously guys," she says, "I need to check on my mom." Christine is gently teased. She only just got back, they say. All she does is study. Live a little, and so on.

Who are these venomous creatures? And would Ms. Opes mind terribly if I dispatched of the lot?

I touch the shoulder of her soft sweater against my better judgment and lean close to her ear. "Eleven-thirty."

Predictably, Christine turns around. Inexplicably, I remain where I stand. She mouths a silent thank you, flashes a weak, troubled smile and focuses on her cohorts once more.

"Guys, I'm sorry. I'm really not feeling it tonight."

"Chris," whines a tall, impeccably dressed girl, "this is exactly what you need." The tall one takes Christine lightly by the shoulders, gives her a playful shake and a stern once-over. "Your mom told me to get you out of the house." The tall one senses my stare, peers over the top of Christine's head and promptly loses her train of thought in my eyes.

"Yeah. Maybe you're right…" Christine says with a sigh. When her friend fails to respond, Christine follows her line of sight. I turn my gaze to the pavement. Christine takes a small step outside her insulated circle, dips her head. I meet her eyes briefly and catch a glimmer of recognition.

I move to step around her, but Christine stops me with a hand on my arm. "Kathryn, right?" To pull myself away would only pique her interest. I linger, gradually turn back around. She has the eagerness of one clinging to memories of happier times. "We—you were one of my dad's clients."

"I was."

"We met once. You were in his office with another woman. I forget her name."

I smile, decidedly too pleased someone else finds Lydia as forgettable as I do. "She was an intern."

"You knew my dad," she says and it is a question and revelation all in one. Tears well in the corners of her eyes. Did she see the remains? I dearly hope not. Would that I could have spared Elizabeth that gruesome scene. I lay my hand over Christine's and give her the only gift I have to offer. She looks into my eyes, opens to my stare and receives a rush of calm. Her hand goes limp in mine, her eyes wide and dazed. A small grin washes over her sad face.

"I am truly sorry for your loss, Ms. Opes."

Christine nods dreamily. The tall one, growing concerned, comes close behind and tugs Christine back by her sweater. I release Christine's smooth hand but hold my gaze steady as she wobbles backward, filling her mind with peace until she blinks.

From a respectful distance I watch the line inch through the open doors as the concert hall swallows the queue. One by one Christine's brood slips inside, the tall one still holding Christine by the sleeve. Christine hesitates in the door, pushed from behind by a crush of excited concertgoers. She stares out across the darkened street, sweeps the pavement with her eyes and disappears.

"I thought she was taller."

The hair on the back of my neck stands on end. I straighten up from my crouch behind a parked car and keep my eyes on the door, willing Christine deeper inside the building and out of harm's way. I keep my features calm as her body nears to mine, wholly unafraid, blood boiling with rage. A smell like rotted leather fills the air.

"When last you saw Christine, she was wearing boots with five-inch soles."

"She was what age then?" she asks, conversationally.

"Eighteen."

"And what is she now?"

"Nineteen, nearly twenty."

Lydia's lips part in a humorless chuckle as her profile slides into my periphery.

"Hardly seems fair." She casts a perfect lock of black hair back over her shoulder. This reveals a patch of scorched scalp beneath. "The fate of an empire depends on one so young."

I sigh and lean back against the parked Buick, my elbow resting casually on top of the cabin. "Am I to believe that one who took so much from Ms. Opes would trouble herself about the poor girl's lot now?" A hardened pink scar gnarls her ear like a piece of coral, sweeps up over her cheekbone and engulfs one lidless black eye. She senses my eyes on her and turns to face me. The left side of her head is smooth, hairless, covered in scar tissue that folds and twists like the petals of a carnation. Burns and amputation are the only injuries that take a while to heal on Strigoi. "You look well, Sister."

Lydia laughs, her head thrown back, a hand on my bicep. The pressure of her grip and the stealth of her approach assure me that her injuries are only skin deep. Lydia waves a hand at her burns. "You should have seen Andrew's face when I came calling, Stela. He was dead of fright before I laid a finger on him."

I step away from her touch and she preens at my obvious discomfort. "You laid much more than a finger on that man."

Lydia matches my step. "You laid much more than a finger on our Lord." She lets her words do the work, presses forward, stalking me with a bemused smile. "And on your brothers, and on me."

I stand my ground. She is so close the white fuzz on her bald patch of scalp can be counted. "And you mean to what? Even the score?"

Lydia spins away, graceful as a dancer. Her still-perfect mouth bowed with a smile. "You will die soon enough," she assures. "The Inquisitor will see to that. Justice will be served." She tilts her head. "Justice for Fane, at any rate."

She walks away from me, completely unconcerned about an attack, headed for the train platform. "If I ever learned anything from you, dear sister, it is that there are far worse fates than death."

"You flatter me," I say, closing in on her back as she doubles her pace.

Lydia throws a sneer over her shoulder. "Our own ineffable Stela," she laughs. "Tell me, how can you think of hunting at a time like this? And so recklessly."

Instead of marching up the platform steps she ducks into an alley, leading us out of public view. Her body dissolves into the shadows some twenty feet ahead of me, but her laughter rings off bricks and pavement. I keep still, my fists clenched, and listen for her footfall.

"A new corpse every night for nearly two weeks Stela," she tsks, "like a bread crumb. Your arrogance suggests you want to be captured."

"And here you are, or were." I keep my eyes trained on the blackness, peeling back the shadows. "Did you commit to stalking me these last few weeks only to run from the altercation now?"

She chose this location, specifically. Her voice echoes everywhere at once, covers the tread of her nimble feet. I never gave Lydia enough credit for her prowess. She is the quietest hunter I know. My eyes widen, sucking in the light, but only her disembodied voice remains.

"Typical Stela, so certain she is both heroine and victim." Her voice runs down my spine like a familiar hand. I sense her lips at my ear. "To think you have always believed hubris was *my* flaw."

Cold certainty fills me with dread. She is baiting me. Keeping me here to toy with me, away from Elizabeth. The city swells, a cacophony of noise between my ears, and despite Lydia's shadowboxing laughter I hear the heel of her boot make contact with the ground.

With one sweep of my arm I have my meddlesome little sister pinned between my body and a brick wall. She writhes, two scarred hands wrapping around my forearm to ease the pressure on her throat.

"If you lay one hand on Elizabeth, Lydia, I swear what you did to Andrew will be merciful by comparison."

Lydia lunges forward against my forearm, her face only inches from mine. "Do you honestly think I could be the one to put Elizabeth down?" she asks. I trade my arm for a hand and close my fingers around her throat. Her only response is to fall slack, looking almost bored but for the sadness in her eyes. "The only crime Elizabeth is guilty of is loving you," she growls, breathlessly. "We both know her fate was sealed the night you met."

I pull her back and slam her into the wall.

"Come now, Stela. What would Bård say if he saw us fighting?"

Her question does exactly as she intends. My fury dissipates like smoke, replaced by a mix of dread and hope. Lydia grins.

"My brother lives?"

A moment's hesitation was her goal, and the instant my focus wavers Lydia brings her arm down against my elbow so swiftly that my knees follow my arm to the ground. When I look up Lydia is lingering at the mouth of the alley. "Save your strength, Stela," she warns in her most playful tone. "They are coming for you."

* * *

"Elizabeth?"

No answer.

The house is dark and an eerie chill rushes up to greet me as I bolt the front door. An uninhabited silence fills the depressing entryway, but there are no signs of forced entry or evidence of a struggle. I sweep the first floor in a panic, flinging doors, checking under and behind every available hiding place. I find neither monster nor my beloved.

I do not call her name again. I should not have called out the first time. I take the stairs two at time to the second level. The bedclothes are rumpled and the light is on in the empty bathroom. A stiff breeze whips around my ankles and I fully expect to see Bård's charred body climbing in through the open window. But all is quiet apart from the billowing curtains dancing in the wind. I reach up to close the window and stop when I hear the steady beat of Elizabeth's heart. My own blood quickens.

I heave myself out the window and from there the roof is well within reach. I hoist myself up and find Elizabeth seated cross-legged on an old quilt, her head dipped to the side as though straining to hear a whisper. I hear nothing apart from her pulse and the occasional passing car, the whistle of the strong breeze through branches.

"Dearest?"

Elizabeth starts, covering her heart with her hand. "Jesus, Stela. You scared the hell out of me." She smiles drowsily and pats the blanket beside her.

The clouds have cleared and the crisp night sky is a smooth expanse of indigo speckled with stars that Elizabeth traces with her eyes. She learned the constellations from Lydia.

"I was just thinking about her," Elizabeth says, quite unprompted.

"Thinking of whom?" I ask, though I know very well.

"Lydia," she replies with a sardonic smile.

"Cassiopeia is her favorite," she says, tracing the thunderbolt shape of the constellation. "It points the way to Andromeda. The closest major galaxy to the Milky Way, and the brightest. So many worlds." Her eyes remained fixed to some distant star, some unreachable unknown. "Sometimes, the thought of the sheer possibilities in the universe is just…" She dips her head, listening intently with clouded features. How I wish we could return to simpler times, when the only voice in her head was that of her mother's ghost.

There is something sedate about her tonight. She runs her pale, bony hands over her protruding abdomen—her belly has not swollen dramatically, but the rest of her has shrunk—and I realize she looks cold.

"Something happened tonight," she says assuredly. She does not ask me a question and I wonder if she already knows, if the child knows. No wall I raise is strong enough to block this child's sight. Perhaps the infant has ingested too much of my blood for such tricks. She has Fane's keen insight and Elizabeth's blatant disregard for privacy.

"Nothing of note," I say with a shrug.

Elizabeth leans closer, presses her chin to my shoulder. "Don't lie to me before I've fed, Stela," she warns. She nudges my earlobe with her nose and returns to her meditative posture, one hand on each knee, with her palms to the heavens. "You're hiding something, and not just what frightened you this evening. I don't understand this compulsion to compartmentalize information." She sighs, looks back up at the stars. "When has it ever helped us?"

I take a deep breath and exhale wearily. Elizabeth pulls me into her arms. With surprising strength she maneuvers my body between her legs and wraps her arms around me. Her brute strength is calming. Elizabeth now is not Elizabeth Dumas, the beguiling twenty-something with a chip on her shoulder and a scowl as charming as her smile. I would do well to remember that. Lydia's words come unbidden to my mind.

We both know her fate was sealed the night she met you.

Elizabeth once said that given the opportunity to relive this dance from the beginning, she was not sure she would choose any differently. But was the choice ever hers to make? I chose to stroll into that dark waiting room. I met her eyes and gave her my true name. It was my thrall to assert, my blood to give. How much say did she have in her fate? Was everything that has happened to her set in motion by *my* whims?

"Stela don't make me glean the truth from your blood," she whispers. "That's cheating." She places a soft kiss to my neck, her lips lingering above my jugular.

"Do you love me?" I have never seen a reason to ask—it seemed so obvious. For a long while I did not wish to hear the words from her. The pain of losing her was too real.

Elizabeth gapes at me, pulling herself up straight and untangling our arms so she can watch my expression. She appears braced for a punchline and seeing that I am serious she grows grave. "More than my own life."

"Never say that again."

She laughs quietly, presses her forehead to my temple. "I love you, Stela. With every heavily fortified cell in my indestructible body. Better?"

"Yes." I turn into her arms, draw them back up around me. "Thank you."

"Not exactly the response I was hoping for, but you're welcome."

We sit comfortably together for a while. She holds me close, and against my spine I sense the child roll and stretch with a foot pressed to the small of my back. Elizabeth groans in a way I know only too well. They are both restless with hunger.

"I saw Christine Opes this evening." Good news first.

Elizabeth presses her cheek against the side of my head. "Is she everything you hoped?"

"So far, all that I hoped and more."

"Has she taken over her father's company?"

"She is years away from such an undertaking," I admit.

"But you made contact?" She keeps her voice low, even, but there is something behind her question. Nothing as trivial as jealousy. Hope, perhaps.

"We had little time for introductions. Lydia made an appearance."

"Did she hurt you?" Her hands skim my obliques, dart up and down my arms, inspecting my body for injury. I pull myself upright and brush her hands aside.

"Her intention was to intimidate, not to maim."

"She's not the reason you're afraid."

"No, though I am sure she wishes otherwise."

"Stela…"

I pace the lip of the roof. "She wanted me to know that I can be found."

"Did she threaten you? Or me?"

"She did not need to threaten. The threat comes from elsewhere."

Elizabeth falls deathly still, scanning the horizon for unseen assailants. "I know." She nods. "I've felt their presence." Elizabeth smiles sadly over her shoulder and holds her swollen belly in her hands. Something in the movement of her fingers strikes me, the way she rakes her nails over the stretched fabric of her shirt. The clenched jaw. Elizabeth is not protecting the child from harm, but probing, tracing lines around limbs with her hands.

An image flashes behind my eyes, whether from her or the child I cannot say. My dearest standing barefoot in the dirty kitchen with a carving knife clutched in her trembling hand. The image disappears in an instant.

"Who is after us, Stela?" she asks calmly.

I resume my place beside her and pull her anxious hand into my lap, away from the baby. "They are blocking me. The presence is familiar, but that is not surprising. I have a great many cousins, you know."

"They must be strong if you're without a guess."

I kiss her knuckles. I do have a guess, but why worry her for nothing? "I am not the force you think I am, angel. Though for both our sakes, I wish you were right in your overestimation of my gifts."

"You're stronger than you think you are, Stela." Elizabeth jerks and leans back reluctantly, her hands on the ground behind her. A move to take the pressure off her midsection. The infant stirs.

"Come, you must feed." I offer her my hand, but Elizabeth stares intently at the offending lump of her belly. "The hour grows early."

"Soon, I promise." Her eyes stay fixed on the stars above. I notice that the calming breath she takes rises like steam in the chilled night air. She has been noticeably warmer to the touch these last few days.

"We have to disappear," she says.

I fear our window for escape has long since closed, and we cannot travel with Elizabeth feeding at this rate. The bodies of our victims would be too easy to follow. Lydia has made that clear. There would be no time to learn the lay of a new city, the camera-dead zones, the sewage systems, the waterways, the city dumps. What money I have managed to save from the pockets of my victims would be drained quickly. Elizabeth must know this, because she drops the subject.

"You are weary." I stroke the back of her neck, and Elizabeth falls forward with an elbow on each knee. I rub circles into the top of her spine and she leans into my touch. Her eyes stay fixed on the dim glow of the horizon.

"I'm going to watch the sun rise." There is an edge to her voice.

"Dearest—"

"I want to see it, Stela."

"The sunlight weakens you…" I get no further. Elizabeth turns on me with eyes smoldering like coals, and the warm predawn hues can only be blamed for so much. She does not argue. She holds that contemptuous look, dragging her nails once more along her abdomen, daring me to contest her wishes again. "Will you feed before dawn?" I ask, bargaining.

She shakes her head. "After," she assures. "The morning will drain you too. It'll be less painful to watch on a full stomach."

"*My* stomach is not what concerns me."

"I'll be fine, Stela." She squeezes my thigh. She sounds so sure of herself. "Trust me."

She commands, and I acquiesce, such is the nature of our relationship. I sit beside her, near the edge of the roof, and watch the evening blossom into day.

I have a memory of Elizabeth alive, when Mr. Collins was still stalking her every move and I was stalking him. She came out of her brownstone one morning and pointed her face toward the sky. The sun spilled down her neck and hair, alighting every inch of her in gold. Just before she released the door and stepped down to the street, she smiled. I fancied that look of serene contentment had something to do with me.

Elizabeth's eyelids flutter, like a newborn babe, testing the brightness, flirting with it. Her black eyes appear before me, ringed with light, crinkled at the corners from her smile. She takes my hand, turns her head, and faces the sunrise without flinching, fortified from the inside out, by the strength and resilience of her progeny.

* * *

Evening has barely touched the sky when my eyes open and I am instantly aware of an unexpected vacancy in the bed. My mind has only a split second to revisit the horrible image I gleaned from Elizabeth the previous night. But before I can toss aside the sheets and rush to the kitchen downstairs and pry a carving knife from Elizabeth's hand, a shadow falls across the bed.

Elizabeth stands beside the open window, her eyes widened in alarm.

I sit up and lean against the cold wall. Elizabeth watches me closely. A hundred unspoken questions swirl in the early evening air, the least of which is how she managed to wake up before I did. The other questions seem too dangerous to voice.

Slowly the light gives way to night, and her most recent nightmare comes back to me in pieces. Elizabeth joins me on the bed. She places her warm palm on my chest, and I brush her hand with my own tepid fingers. Elizabeth dreamed of me standing on a cliff above the seashore. She called out to me, and I turned with something precious in my arms. My little cohort was not more than two years old, fair-haired with eyes that burned brighter than the sun. Ruxandra. She was as familiar in my arms as though I had held her on my hip for all my life. The child reached her small hand toward Elizabeth and then we woke up.

"Why would you choose that name?" I ask. No question seems safe, but I really must know. I clearly remember the night Elizabeth asked for my human name, before Fane turned me. I never once imagined she would remember let alone recycle it in such a way.

Elizabeth looks at me but her eyes are vacant. She stares deeply at me, unseeing, searching for some deception or clue. "I didn't," she says, quiet and low as though the walls themselves have ears. She stares down at her belly, her hands hover but do not touch.

XIII

Transverse

Six weeks. No morning sickness or bloating. No unusual cravings apart from my intolerance to human blood. No discernible weight gain, more a pooling of weight in my midsection, a thinning out of everything else. Minimal cramping. Quickening detected around week two, as near as I can guess and thanks to Stela's none too gentle probing.

Six weeks…

The nightmares are often more than I can handle. Vivid yet illusive, and rife with overwhelming dread, hate, blind rage on more than one occasion. Most evenings, I dream that my swollen belly is rippling and then the movement stops. A small handprint appears, then another. I stroke the palm of one hand through my skin and watch the imprint close around my fingertip with talons instead of nails. The next day a new dream follows like an apology, sickeningly sweet. A warm soft body curled between Stela and me, a baby's wet chortle. Sometimes, no Stela at all. Just a small face staring up into mine, tranquil, happy, with eerily familiar eyes.

I can smell everything. The musty mouse droppings in the attic. Discarded Christmas trees wilting on curbs. The mildew deep in the drain. The coming snow. And always Stela, the scent of her skin, her blood. She drowns everything else out. It's maddening, just sharing a roof with her. The thirst never stops.

I wanted an ultrasound. Stela assured me that was a ridiculous idea, the equivalent of taking a pet shark to a veterinarian. Maybe it would be funny if it wasn't all so upsetting. I've been under house arrest ever since. I'm not sure who she's protecting anymore. Me, or the baby?

I don't know when that happened either. When *it* became the baby. That was no conscious decision on my part. Last evening, Stela was rubbing my distended belly, humming the same tune she uses to pull me out of my nightmares. The baby started to kick and I almost called her by name. Ruxandra bubbled up my throat and died on my tongue, unspoken.

Stela doesn't trust me. Not to leave the house. Not to be alone. She has little choice in the latter. It's nothing she's said. She doesn't have to say a word. I've seen that look before, the sidelong glance. It was the same look she spared me when I was mortal asking too many questions. A wary, silent stare.

Things are progressing quickly now. The baby's movements are more pronounced. She kicks when we dream, or when I sit still for too long. Strong enough to make me ache, and that makes me curious about labor. Will there be pain? Will there be complications? And would I intervene if there were? Would Stela?

For the third evening in a row I've woken up in the kitchen with my hand on the utensil drawer. The setting sun fills the room with blinding orange light. I release the drawer handle and run a hand over my belly. Ruxandra responds with a *thump-thump-thump* against my palm. A weak smile touches my lips, stretches my mouth like a smothered yawn and wilts away into nothing.

I leave the cutlery and whatever impulse led my sleeping body downstairs and stand at the back door watching the sky darken.

Upstairs, Stela shifts between the sheets. She'll wake in a panic. I take one last look at the fading day and retreat upstairs. I don't want Stela to wake alone. I don't want her to find me in the kitchen, though I'm not sure why. Perhaps because she would ask what I was doing down there, and in asking insinuate that she knows.

I don't belong to myself these days.

I haven't belonged to myself for a while.

I sit on the corner of the bed and wait for the last threads of sleep to release Stela. Her pale foot, cold from blood loss, peeks out and rests against my bare thigh. Stela sighs when physical contact has been reestablished. It's an honest, uncomplicated sound.

Stela says an old one has arrived on our shores, a scouting party—though she can't say how many. I can only operate on what I know. From what I've read for myself in Darius' library, I'm expecting something more like a tribunal. The Strigoi are not bound by human law, but we are all governed by Moroi. Some infractions transcend familial autonomy. The unsanctioned murder of named Strigoi is forbidden, as is failure to comply with the whims of the Moroi. The murder of a Moroi—unprecedented.

Sometimes, I can almost hear a whisper of warning. A message in the air like a telegraph. It isn't Stela. I know her voice, her whisper, she resonates inside my mind as clearly as my own thoughts. What I don't understand is why Ruxandra relies on these little nudges instead of whatever strange method she uses to communicate with Stela. Maybe I'm unable to listen. Unwilling. I'm sure it's a fair mix of both.

She's sensitive to stress. When I try to focus on the face of my pursuers, when I panic about some all-powerful evil hot on my trail, or Lydia scouring the city block by block, the child casts a web of calm around my mind so thick I lose my train of thought entirely.

"Have you slept at all?" Stela asks, propped up on her pillow. The sheet is pulled tight across her chest, her arms crossed.

"I did."

It's all I do as of late. Eat, sleep, dream, wake.

"You left the bed," she says.

Why does it sound like an accusation? "I woke up early again. Went downstairs to watch the sun set over the backyard."

Little half-truths, scurrying between us. Deflection, protection, maybe I'm just carving out some small sense of privacy. We're both guilty of that.

Stela ruffles her tangled hair and twines it back behind her ears. The motion sends her scent spiraling through the air, and I have to focus very hard on her face. The scent permeates my skin, seeps into the walls of my nose, and an all too familiar hunger seizes my stomach. She burns the back of my throat. Her presence scorches my insides, makes me itch.

My pain must show, because with an apologetic smile Stela pulls the blanket tightly around her body. I hate myself for it. I despise this new thirst as deeply as I did in the beginning. Worse in a way, because Stela is mine—she's not some stranger. Feeding from her is beyond wonderful, and acutely painful every time her breathy plea begs me to stop. I would gladly kill James and my mother a hundred times over if I could spare her my voracious appetite.

Stela shifts her legs over the side of the bed and hangs there, bent over her knees, bracing herself for the day. She looks terrible. Gray smudges beneath her eyes, spine too pronounced. Her white skin is even paler, and dull. I watch it happen every morning, before her shower. I watch her ribcage heave and pretend for her sake that I don't pity her. I can't help it. Stela looks fragile now, younger and older at the same time.

Maybe that's why I say it.

"It won't be long now."

Stela turns her head, face obscured by loose strings of hair. "How…" she doesn't finish. "Are you certain?"

"As certain as I can be without an ultrasound." It isn't a ploy to get her to take me to a hospital. Not this time. More a promise to us both that the end is in sight. Whatever that means. Then there will be a baby, another Moroi, which is hardly what this world needs. She will still have to eat. At least the burden of hunting will be one we share. We've been lucky a couple times and dinner has been delivered to our door. The previous tenant's sister and the landlord dropped by to check on him. Stela buried the bodies out back. They won't be the last…

"I'll make a list of supplies. You should pick them up tonight when you go."

"A list?" Stela is incredulous. "Clothespins, bottles for blood, cloth diapers made from organic and responsibly sourced materials?"

"Don't be cute, Stela." Try as I might, I can't sound half as angry with her as I want to when she's making jabs at my generation. Her laughter makes me smile. "Gauze, gloves, lubricant…" Stela's smile falters, as though she's never considered her own role as midwife before this moment.

"Of course, my dearest. Draw up the particulars. I will see to it."

I move first, grabbing clothes from the floor of the open closet, and Stela takes that as her cue to escape to the bathroom.

Once dressed, I take a seat on the sofa downstairs and face the inevitable, armed with paper and a pen.

* * *

Slowly but surely, Stela has begun to accumulate a wardrobe of sorts. She's still new to dressing herself. Sizing is a skill she has yet to master. Her pants are all an inch too long, or two inches too short. Most of them require a belt to keep them up. She pushes up the sleeves on everything she wears, as the cuffs of her shirts hit her above the wrist or flow freely around her fingers.

Sweaters she can do because they're so forgiving. She wears them most evenings. She's careful with her feeds, practiced to the point that there is rarely a drop of blood to be washed from her attire. Dressing herself is a freedom Stela hasn't had since before Lydia was turned. Maybe longer.

Stela finds me on the sofa when she descends the stairs, clad in a soft navy sweater with a pale peach collar peeking out around her neck. The pants are courtesy of our departed host, a dark pair of straight cut khakis with creases at the seams to suggest they've never been worn and loafers to match. Stela halts at the foot of the steps when she sees my soft smile, and scowls.

"What?"

"Nothing. You look good. Handsome."

"Have you the list?" she asks, dropping a kiss on the top of my head as she settles down beside me.

"Right here."

Her face is serene, expressionless, but the silence that falls upon the room is far from peaceful. She sets the legal pad down slowly.

"How soon after delivery will I be able to tolerate human blood again?"

Stela stares only at the list, her hands folded on her knee. She doesn't know.

I pick up my pen, jot a quick note. "Then we should add a few blood bags to the list."

"Yes," she answers distantly. "You will be ravenous after, I imagine." She keeps her face forward.

"Stela," I whisper, trailing the back of my hand down her jaw. She stands up abruptly, grabs a jacket from its hook in the hall.

"I will wake early tomorrow," she says, pushing her long arms through her sleeves. "It is too late to hunt, dispose of the body and procure these items tonight."

She's stalling. She keeps her eyes turned to the floor, hesitating for a brief moment, torn between whatever it is she wants to say and leaving before an argument ensues. I tear the page from the legal pad and fold it neatly.

"I don't think that's a good idea." I hold the list out for her.

"Do you plan to deliver tonight?"

Her unchecked hostility surprises us both. I feel her eyes on me as I curl the paper in my palm.

"You don't get to blame me for this, Stela."

"Dearest, I would never—"

"You just did." Our eyes meet and Stela has the decency to look abashed.

"Tomorrow, I swear it."

I shake my head. "Tonight. We don't get to be afraid now. Our window has closed. This is happening, Stela. Whether we're ready, whether we want it or not. No one gets a choice."

Stela's straightens. She is undoubtedly brave. More than willing to gamble with her own life, but never with mine. Who can blame her? The last time she did I died in her arms, and the scars on my neck serve as a constant reminder of what she nearly lost.

I'll always be that girl to Stela. Naked and screaming in her bed, trapped in the iron jaws of death. This labor could kill me. I know that. Darius had the account of Fane's birth in the library. Whether his mother died bringing him into this world, or shortly thereafter from his insatiable hunger seems beside the point. I know the odds, I know I want this child out of me, and I've never felt stronger in my life. I've never felt further from the human I once was.

"When I return home, you will give me a detailed overview of the obstetrics ward of your former hospital," she says firmly. She turns to leave through the kitchen. "I trust you are familiar with the layout, and with your direction I will be in and out before anyone can register my presence."

"Tomorrow." I nod, and Stela is gone, her exit punctuated by the slamming door.

* * *

What I wouldn't give for one hour alone in the Vault. I've been thinking of that forgotten place a lot lately, the derelict chairs, the soft vellum spines and gleaming brass plaques. But these reminisces always lead back to one distinct memory: standing before the glass podium under the family's coat of arms. A whisper reached for me from the empty case built to house the history of the Moroi. The abridged family history, as Fane called it, would answer my pressing questions about delivery. It was spared in the fire, of course, but only because another branch of the family has it for now. Cousins in Spain, he said. Might as well have burned along with Fane for all the good that does me.

"Take a left here," I tell the cabbie through the plexiglass partition.

I walked as far into the city as I dared before hailing a cab, warm in Stela's lovely wool coat and a soft charcoal sweater. I would have walked the whole way to the hospital if I wasn't worried about being followed. The train would have been more convenient, but something told me to stay away from enclosed spaces. Sitting behind my human driver is torture enough. The tainted stench of his all-too-mortal blood permeates my clothing, curls in my hair and twists my stomach into knots.

The hospital looms into view, exactly as I left it. The small square windows are dark on the lower floors, but as we turn toward the back of the building every inch of glass glows along the emergency wing. From the curb I hear the electric whoosh of the receiving doors and smell the sweaty stench of human illness. I cup a hand over my mouth and purge all the air from my lungs. Ruxandra presses against my spine and goes still.

"You got it from here?" The cab driver asks, his red-rimmed eyes checking in with me in the rearview mirror. I keep my eyes away from him, faintly touched by his concern. I slide my sunglasses on before I reassure him.

"I'll be fine. Thank you."

He stares curiously at my dark lenses. "Twenty-one-fifty." He flicks the partition open and I pull a wad of loose bills from my pocket, placing thirty dollars in blood-spattered bills into his hand.

"Keep the change."

I regret the tip as soon as he pulls away from the curb. We need to conserve our considerably limited funds. Stela robs all her kills, but people just don't carry cash anymore.

My money troubles are quickly lost to a sea of roaring voices as I step through the emergency doors. So many sounds at once. The pounding of footsteps on tile, the screech of gurneys, the anguish of the unwell and the thunderous voices of their advocates. X-rays, CAT scans, MRIs. I tuck a hand inside my coat above Ruxandra's tightly coiled body. I've never spoken to her, but I shut my eyes and beg. She has to control herself for both our sakes, she has to block whatever stimuli she can.

"Miss?" With a raised hand a young woman in green scrubs comes toward me and the deafening din dissipates. The admissions nurse lingers in front of me as my sight clears.

"Do you need a wheelchair?" she asks. What a beautiful creature. Smooth skin, a light dusting of copper freckles across her pale cheeks. My first instinct is to grab her by the wrist and drag her into the nearest maintenance closet, which is odd because my hunger is separate from this compulsion. Draining this young woman would only sicken me, and yet the desire is as strong as ever.

"No. Thank you." I step toward her and take a page from Stela's playbook as I wipe a finger beneath my sunglasses. She doesn't know I can't cry. "I'll be fine," I whisper. She spares me a sympathetic smile and steps aside, one comforting hand on my shoulder as I breeze past. Her nights are filled with grieving family members.

I hover outside the locker room on the first floor waiting for it to empty, listening to the soft swish of scrubs and the weary laughter of exhausted doctors. I feign a call with my cell phone pressed to my ear, picking up the tail end of a conversation each time one doctor leaves and another one enters. I recognize a few of the faces, two surgeons from oncology, and one from cardiology. They don't recognize me. I am just another distracted visitor idling in the hallway. The secret to moving unseen in a clutch of people is to be both hyperaware of everyone around you and intentionally oblivious to what does not directly concern you. The Strigoi have perfected this strategy.

The last of the banter dies down in the locker room. A young nurse makes her exit, and a steel door rattles on its hinges.

I shoulder through the door into the locker room I've used a thousand times before. I'm not nearly as practiced at moving unnoticed as Stela is, so a bit of camouflage can't hurt. I find scrubs to fit quickly enough, and a backpack that will suit my needs.

I change as quickly as I always have, with an eye on the door. The cool, starched cotton pulls at my legs familiarly. Before I tug the top down over my torso, I run my hand over the bulge of my stomach. It seems less than it should be, though how could I be sure of anything with this pregnancy? As if sensing my concern, Ruxandra lands a swift kick to my palm.

She's right. We don't have time for this. I throw my clothes into the backpack and slip the bundle over my shoulder.

Obstetrics is on the third floor, and though the elevator will take me there quickly I'm still leery of enclosed spaces. I take the stairs, mounting them two at time. Ruxandra is tiring fast. She needs blood—she always needs blood.

"Almost there," I say, reaching for the door handle. I'm not sure which of us is more ravenous. Ruxandra curls in on herself, presses against my bladder.

I slip onto the obstetrics ward, quiet at this time of night. Two lone figures stand with their eyes glued to the dim nursery glass. A scruffy young man in a soft flannel shirt with his arm looped around his mother's shoulders. Beyond the glass partition I hear the breathy sounds of more than a dozen infants cozy in their cradles. I walk quickly down the corridor, but I scan these slumbering new faces. In the corner of the nursery sits a woman I once knew, a good nurse, comforting a newborn with colic. The young father takes note of my stolen scrubs as I pass and flashes me a grateful smile, pressing his cheek to the top of his mother's head. I keep my eyes on my feet after that.

The supply closet is beside the nurses' station. Only two bodies bent at their computers, both with their backs to me. The rest are working the floor. No one takes notice of me as I steal inside the supply room.

It's not as familiar as I hoped, but then I was never an obstetrics nurse. Every item is tucked away in clear bins no one thought to label. I find a trash bag easily enough. My haste makes me clumsy, though I don't know that the sound carries to anyone without my exceptional hearing. Slowly, my bag fills as I stumble upon the items we need: sterile pads, gloves, postpartum pads, cord clamps, antiseptic.

My midnight raid stalls when I reach for a receiving blanket. Plain white cotton with blue and pink stripes. The room closes in on me. Ruxandra twists, half starved. There's no space to think in this glorified closet. I shove the blanket deep into the trash bag and set off in search of baby clothes.

Somewhere on the ward a door settles shut and the blood in my veins begins to itch. I dump a pile of diapers into the bag and drop my backpack on the floor. I know this new sound, so alien compared to the chirps and beeps of the hospital.

The graceful footsteps of a Strigoi.

I take Stela's coat out of the pack and put it back on. There's no time to dress in street clothes. I shove the trash bag into the backpack and tighten the straps in case I have to run. The footsteps stop at the end of the hall, poised beside the exit door. In front of the nurses' station another figure looms, a black spot in my mind's eye, motionless. I doubt the nurses have even registered the presence among them. We're boxed in.

What follows is nothing like the smothering peace that floods my system when Ruxandra senses my fear. My hand reaches out, grips a sealed scalpel which I conceal in my pocket. My nostrils flare, my neck cranes back and I taste the air. The blood of my pursuers—sweet, so very close. I brace myself beside the door as the swoon takes control of me. Their sluggish heartbeats throb in my temple and when I open my eyes the whole of the world fits neatly into a single decision: rush the stairs or break for the elevators?

I tentatively open the door and cross the threshold. At the end of the hall a lone figure retreats around the corner. If I took the elevator, we would have an audience and we're too hungry to care about collateral damage. My hand tightens around the scalpel, flicking the plastic sheath off the blade. Behind me one of the night nurses finally registers the stranger in front of her, and she tells my assailant—who has moved into position to take me from behind—that visiting hours are over.

I keep my eyes trained on the exit sign above the door to the stairs and the genteel voice at my back is like a knife to my heart. Bård apologizes to the nurse and steps onto the elevator instead. Under normal circumstances I'd have no hope to outrun him, but this is my hospital and I know it well. The elevator will take him to the main lobby, and by the time he reaches the far side of the building I'll be gone.

As soon as my hand closes over the door handle, a second shadow falls across my feet. If there was ever any doubt who it belonged to, the playful chuckle in my ear chases all the uncertainty from my mind.

"I missed you too," Lydia whispers as I tangle my fist in the front of her leather jacket and swing her into the stairwell ahead of me. Her body thuds against the cinderblock wall. She teeters at the edge of the stairs, and in the blinding light bouncing off the white walls her gnarled pink scars gleam in a horrifying contrast to the rest of her lovely skin.

She's righted in an instant and launches herself forward in a halfhearted assault. I see her momentary hesitation before it happens, her reluctance to cause me harm. Her arms reach out to embrace me, not to crush. My body barrels into hers, sending us both crashing down the first flight of stairs, sprawled across the landing. My backpack lands beside her in the corner.

Lydia reaches for my arm, fingers tight around my wrist as I bring my elbow up against her chin. She's tipping back to the ground when the scalpel slips beneath her collarbone and ruptures the subclavian artery. My mouth is on the wound before her head hits the concrete.

Lydia rips at my hair, kicks her legs out from under me, shreds the back of Stela's coat with her perfectly manicured claws as a torrent of strength rushes down my throat. She makes a sound deep in her chest, and in my ravenous stupor I hear her plead with me. Lydia's hands fall limply to the floor, her light fading and leaving a cool husk behind. When her fingers relax palm up in front of my face, I try to stop myself. I pull myself back but my hands are still wrapped in the front of her once lovely blouse. I need more from her.

I need to know about the fire. I see the flames spreading through the tunnels. The heat is incredible, the scent of Fane's charred remains heavy in the caustic air. She must have been the first one in the suite after we left because I know the weight of Fane's blackened bones in her arms. And though she was gravely injured, though she loved—loves—Fane immeasurably, I watch Lydia claw up the walls and back into the tunnel…to save Bård. The anguish on his face when he cradled her smoldering body to him.

I rip my mouth away from her and cover the trickling wound with my hand. Lydia stares at me in silent shock as I cut my finger to seal her wound. She manages to move one hand and lays it gently over mine. To my surprise I realize she's willing me away.

"Elizabeth…" she croaks, her voice a dry rustle. She's never used my real name before. I hold her scarred face in my hands and press my lips to the gnarled shell of her once-perfect ear. I sob tearlessly. But Lydia isn't interested in my apology. Her hand slips between our bodies as she trails her fingers across my body.

"We. Are not. Alone."

Lydia presses her hand to my chest, using what strength she has to push me away. I don't understand what she means. Does she know I'm expecting? Can she hear the baby too? Does she mean Bård is with her? I can hear his nimble tread combing the halls below us. Her palm falls to my belly again, not to push but to protect. Her black eyes are grave, mouth twisted in a pained grimace. She watches me closely and sighs when the realization hits me. Their happy hunting party is a trio. The face of the third member is lost to the wind, barely an outline. I wouldn't have noticed if Lydia hadn't told me. Why would she tell me?

"Can you stand?" I hoist her up in my arms without waiting for a reply and her head drops against my shoulder. She pulls at my scrubs, as though tugging herself upright and I loosen my grip. Lydia immediately crumples to her knees. She smacks my hand away when I reach for her again.

"Elizabeth, go," she pleads. The scar that curls around her left eye doesn't allow the skin to stretch, but her right eye is wide with fright.

When Stela saw Rachel's exsanguinated body propped behind her desk in the lobby of Opes and Sons she said this girl deserved better. Maybe the monster that killed her deserves better too. "I won't leave you like this. Lydia I—"

"Run!" she yells with what little strength she has left. The same message she scrawled across Andrew Opes' office windows, painted in his blood. My God...was it a warning or a threat?

I kneel down in front of her and cover the scars on her face with my hand. The tissue is healing at an incredible rate, but only by human standards. I kiss the corner of her mouth. Lydia smirks up at me, in that eerily knowing and cheerful way of hers as I bend down to retrieve my discarded backpack.

"Congratulations," she whispers, and then begins to laugh frantically. I hear her echoing guffaw long after the steel door to the first floor closes behind me.

Bård is the least of my worries now. He skids to a stop in front of the stairwell I've just left as I barrel down the back hallway, headed for an exit on the south side. Whatever his orders, Lydia is wounded, weak and for all their shared contempt Bård is still her Maker. He won't leave her defenseless and exposed.

My phantom captor waits for me in the parking lot. A woman, of that I can be certain. I have never wanted to make someone's acquaintance less. I sense her through the walls, following my progress down the hall to cut me off the moment I emerge. There's nowhere else to go. I push through a fire exit and triple my speed, markedly aware of my inhuman pace in a populated area yet completely unable to care. There isn't time to worry about spectators or contemplate another cab. I would be overtaken before the door closed.

I assault the asphalt beneath my feet, both hands closed around my belly, preternaturally aware of the hands reaching for my back. My pursuer matches me stride for stride. She doesn't tell me to stop. She doesn't worry I'll escape either, but it's hard to say how I know that. I jump a hedge line at the edge of the parking lot and her feet echo right behind mine. I do the only thing I can think of, and head straight into the heart of the city.

The silver facades of sleeping skyscrapers whiz silently by and I check my reflection only once for a glimpse of this persistent hunter, but the path we're cutting through the late-night crowds has pushed innocent bystanders up against the glass. I note half a dozen raised cell phones up ahead recording our chase to share with the world, and I take a chance and turn down the first alley I see rather than risk Internet celebrity.

The footfalls behind me slow but they don't stop. As the alley opens to another teeming sidewalk I realize why. My only warning is a hearty grunt and I look over my shoulder to see a Dumpster sailing through the air. Doors flapping, trash whipping up into the sky, it skids against the brick of the building to my right in a shower of sparks. Pushing my body beyond unimagined limits, I watch the Dumpster reach the apex of my hunter's toss. The huge metal cube quivers and barrels to the ground—directly in my path. The movements are instinctive, fluid. The asphalt is gone from underneath me before I decide to jump and my right hand makes contact with the grimy top of the receptacle as it crashes to the ground, spraying putrid confetti across the sidewalk. Momentum throws me into the driver's side door of a parked Volkswagen. There are a handful of awed onlookers as I pry myself from the indentation I've made.

I don't wait for applause. My pace picks back up as though I never broke my stride, and the strangest part is how natural it feels: my hair whipping at my face, the rhythm of my feet, the utter ease of speed. Like every muscle in my body has been waiting for this opportunity, an overdue stretch after a long day behind a desk. I've never felt so alive, so powerful.

Gradually, the crowds thin and the streets grow dark in the now-sparse traffic lights. The only footfall I'm aware of is my own. I slip my hands beneath my scrubs and hold my belly, humming lightly to Ruxandra the way Stela does when she refuses to be still. She is fine. A light kick flutters against my fingers, and with that small reassurance my mad dash slows to a staggering crawl.

Around me the city is sparse and foreign. I look up at the intersection expecting to find Lockland Avenue. This is ridiculous. Where the hell are we? I spin in a slow circle, absorbing my surroundings, listening to the tumult of the city. I close my eyes and take a breath, tasting the air on my tongue and waiting for my instincts to catch up with me. As though summoned by my distress, a small silhouette appears at the top of the block, standing in the middle of the street exactly as I am.

"Stela?"

She doesn't move. Even at this distance I sense her anger in my bones, her fear. I reach my hand out like the act itself will bring her to my side. The figure turns and vanishes down another unmarked street to the right. I start running again, not without trepidation. It doesn't feel like a trap, but a well-crafted manipulation never does.

Stela told me once that before I was made Fane had come to her wearing my face. She'd been fooled into believing that I'd somehow managed to track her down and follow her into the freight tunnels. My powerful, beautiful Stela so grossly deceived by her jealous creator.

When I reach the spot where she'd stood the air around me grows warmer and just up ahead, a block to the east, she stands under a swaying traffic light blinking yellow. Stela stares at me, waiting, impatient, and vanishes once more.

I am not an optimist or particularly trusting. But one thing I've come to accept reluctantly is that Ruxandra's instincts far surpass my own, even in utero, and she couldn't be more relaxed than she is right now. Gorged on fresh Strigoi blood, she presses heavily against my hips, alert but complacent. I do trust her will to survive. She has often manipulated my mind to suit her moods.

"What do we do?" I ask, my chest heaving in preparation for a fight. Eyes darting from one derelict building to the next. And just as they had in the hospital's supply closet, with a renewed sense of calm my legs start moving without me, giving chase to the specter of Stela.

Every corner I round is the same, a lingering warmth waiting to embrace me in the exact spot Stela occupied, like a reward. The longer I follow, the deeper it reaches. I'm not surprised when the neglected construction bleeds into housing. Somehow, I knew that Stela was leading me home.

The back door is open when I reach the yard. I take a moment outside to listen, to ensure I wasn't followed. To ensure I'm not walking into a trap. Every light in the house is aglow, no shadows moving along the narrow windows. As I approach the kitchen door, I see that not only is it open, the door hangs on its last hinge. Somewhere inside, Stela waits, her anger and terror ebbing. The only sound worth listening to is her jagged pulse.

"Stela?" I struggle to right the kitchen door and manage to drag it nearly closed. "Where are you?" Only her blood answers. The lamp in the living room smolders on the carpet, a naked bulb melting the fibers with its heat. The blue milk crates have been smashed, and the armchair with its busted back rests tilted on its side.

They're here. They have her.

"Answer me!" I rush to the staircase, my hand on the rail. But she isn't up there. Slowly, I turn on my heels, intensely aware of the energy around me and the familiar electricity of impending peril. I would rather face a dozen assassins armed and waiting than this, anything but her pain.

Stela is collapsed in the corner of the living room behind the sofa. She is seething, wide-eyed and wild. She starts to pant, spoiling for a fight, an all-too-clear warning.

"Stela?" I inch toward her. The hair on the back of my neck stands on end. "Are you hurt?"

She tips her head forward, shoulders trembling and hair obscuring her face. The trembling becomes shaking and her laughter shatters the silence. It's a laugh I've never heard before, menacing, almost cruel. I keep my distance as she exhausts herself, and she stops as suddenly as she began. She whips the hair out of her eyes and stares at me. I calculate my odds of reaching the front door before she does. Stela flings herself to her feet by throwing both fists back against the drywall.

"Do you have any idea how frightened I was?" she asks coolly, still fighting to calm herself. "You were nowhere to be found…"

I don't defend my actions. She wouldn't be able to hear the logic right now anyway. "I'm sorry."

That damn laugh rattles out of her again, made all the more chilling by her clenched jaw. "You are nothing of the sort." She leans forward and there isn't enough space in this house for her rage.

"I'm safe, Stela." I stare into her cold, black, empty eyes. "I'm here now." I reach out to smooth the grimace from her lovely face. Stela seizes me by the wrist and pins me against the split drywall.

"Elizabeth," she whispers harshly, her lips to my ear. My hands hover at her waist but don't touch. "If you ever scare me like that again—"

"I know."

"No," she says, pulling back. "You have no idea." She runs her fingers down the claw marks Lydia made on my clothing. Her palm closes around my cheek, pulling me forward. Not since our first kiss have I felt a rush quite like this. Stela's tongue pushes past my lips. The taste of Lydia still lingers in my mouth.

"Did you kill her?" she asks, unable to mask her delight at the prospect. She steps back to to appraise me.

"She's alive." My answer is lost in Stela's hair as she checks me over. She slips the backpack from my shoulders and flings it onto the couch. I hold her by the waist for what comes next and more than anything I want to revel in her body, but it seems it's been years since life was that simple. "So is Bård."

Stela staggers back as though struck, and though it's the last thing I want, I let go of her. "Did he hurt you? If he laid a hand on you, I swear—"

"Stela, stop." She's enraged, desperate for a fight. I take her hand in mine. "They showed up at the hospital. I already had what I needed. I didn't see his face. I heard his voice, I sensed him. From what I saw in Lydia's blood, he suffered few injuries in the fire. Burns on his chest and arms from smothering the flames that caught her hair and clothes."

"What exactly did you sense, Elizabeth?"

"From him?" I ask. Stela nods, and in a rare instance she looks as young and vulnerable as I imagine the day she was turned. "Surprise, I suppose. Like I was an uninvited guest he was forced to entertain. Hostility, of course, but he held it in check. He was a man on a mission. They all were."

"All?" she says, staring at me hotly.

I take a step away from her. "They weren't alone. Someone was with them, waiting for me in the parking lot. I didn't get a look at her face. She was much older than you. Older than Bård. Fast. Highly trained. Objective and calm, given the circumstances. Easily the most intimidating presence I've encountered, apart from Fane."

"How did you escape?"

"I ran. Lydia warned me first, then I ran."

"How *sisterly* of her," she sneers.

"Stela… I know you're furious with me. I could feel it the second you found me. I hoped you'd have calmed down enough to listen before we got home."

"What are you talking about?" she snaps. She's stopped pacing around the room, her hands hanging at her sides still curled into claws but no longer clenched.

"On the walk home. I hoped you'd have mellowed out a bit before we got back but…" I wave a hand around the destruction of our pathetic living room. "Clearly, you didn't."

"Mellowed out? I went out for a feed and came home to an empty house!" She's beside me in a single motion, staring me down. "Do you have any idea the thoughts I entertained? You were gone, taken. You left me. And all that I could sense from you was panic. Your frantic heartbeat echoed in my chest, Elizabeth."

"No, I know. I meant, after you came looking for me." My hands spread out to hold her shoulders, but I leave them there lingering in her space, to walk into my embrace or step away again.

Stela leans forward. "I came home. You were not here," she says softly. "The furniture bore the brunt of my frustration."

"But I saw you."

"Dearest, I—," she stops short. "After, this," she twirls a finger in the air, "I collapsed."

"You found me, Stela. Or I found you. I was lost. And when I opened my eyes you were there. I followed you home. You had to have seen me, Stela. You were looking right at me."

"Hmm." She nods to herself, satisfied.

"That's it? That's all you've got?"

"I thought you meant, in the physical sense, Elizabeth. I misunderstood." My puzzled expression lingers as she begins to tidy the mess she's made.

"Hey, Stela. Some of us haven't been Strigoi for five centuries. Explain." She stands wearily, and dumps a handful of our crushed coffee table into the waste bin. "You were, or you weren't with me?"

"I was quite literally right over there." She points to the split wall. "You followed *your* blood home."

"Oh…I'm hallucinating again?"

"What? No, my love. You will never be lost to me, nor I to you. We are tethered to each other, Elizabeth. Bound by our blood. It will always lead you back to me. Once I calmed down and cleared my head, my blood would have done the same. I would have found you." Stela presses a soft kiss below my ear.

"Girlfriend GPS. Got it." Stela shakes her head bemusedly, setting the overturned armchair upright. "Any other super handy strengths you've neglected to mention?"

"Such as?"

"Oh, I don't know." I shrug, tugging her down beside me on the couch. She doesn't move to embrace me, so the anger isn't completely spent. "Dumpster hurling, the long jump?"

"Elizabeth, can we save the teasing for tomorrow? I am truly in no mood."

"Sorry."

Stela lifts her arm in unspoken acceptance and pulls me against her. For a while we sit quietly, side by side, her thumb rubs soothing circles against my bicep. The unquiet of the city around us is both a distraction and a threat. My mind struggles to make sense of it all.

"Tell me what happened. Start at the beginning. What time did you leave?"

Stela is quiet, receptive. She listens closely as I recount the evening's adventure.

"Lydia's blood showed me memories of the fire. This proves my theory that blood memories can be channeled and controlled by a turned Strigoi, barring the very real possibility that the skill is one more temporary muscle this pregnancy has given to me. It's difficult to explain but extracting those memories of the fire felt as effortless as hurtling through the crowded city streets. Just a part of myself that had gone unused but had been present all along."

I fall into a meditative silence, mulling over the scope of our abilities. What are our limits? My concentration breaks when Stela places a protective hand over my belly, exactly as Lydia did only a few short hours ago.

"Was it The Lady?" I ask.

Stela answers with a sardonic smile.

"Who then? Who chased me? I know you have someone in mind, Stela."

Her eyes fall heavily on the flimsy front door. "If Her Grace had given chase you would not have cleared the parking lot. I can only venture a guess, having not seen your pursuer myself. When you first arrived, I sensed something familiar. A faint scent, perhaps. Then it was gone."

She shifts uncomfortably beside me, her leg twitches. She distracts herself with my discarded backpack, riffling through the sterile packets. When she discovers the receiving blanket she stops, brings her hand around to the side of my head and presses my cheek to her collarbone.

"Antonia," I whisper, and Stela brushes my lips with her finger. "The Lady's eldest..."

"Hush now, my darling," she says, and taps my chin gently. "Our names hold great power. You know this better than most." I stay curled against her side and sense Stela's anxiety as she watches headlights cut across the closed blinds and then disappear. After a brief eternity she says: "More than likely, it was she."

"You're afraid of her."

Stela huffs. "I am afraid for your safety. There is a difference."

"I can take care of myself."

"Yes, I know you can." There's a smile hidden in those words.

"Will she..." I pull back to watch her expression. Stela is a skilled liar but she gives herself away in what she avoids. I cannot bring myself to ask the odds that either of us survive this. "Will they hurt her?"

She almost slips and speaks Antonia's name aloud. "Hurt the child?" she nearly laughs. "Hardly."

"How can you be so sure?"

"Dearest, of the three of us, Ruxandra is the least likely to be harmed. On the contrary, her birth may well be a cause for celebration. A new regent for this era. An heir to Fane, if her human paternity is not cause for disqualification. She is powerful. She grows more powerful each day."

"Then why are we hiding?"

Stela withdraws, leans forward on her knees. "Your pregnancy does not absolve us of our guilt. Fane is dead. His siblings care little for our motivations. And once she is born, we are dispensable."

"He deserved to die."

Stela nods. "In your opinion. In mine. But all the Moroi will see is the threat of uprising their own fledglings pose. The very crusade that all but toppled Fane the first time. The point of his bloody retaliation against the unnamed Strigoi. I would not be surprised if my actions spark a second war, Elizabeth. The life of every Strigoi may be in jeopardy."

"Don't be so melodramatic. They need us for food, if nothing else. Besides, The Lady was not in favor of Fane's first war. She could be sympathetic to our situation." She glares at me in disbelief. "We can't run forever. They know we're close."

"They do," she says wearily. "After tonight they know what they only suspected. You are with child. Antonia will tell her mistress if Lydia has not already."

I don't believe that Lydia warned me only to rat me out later. Something in her eyes when she pressed her palm against my stomach. "She laughed about it."

"Who laughed?"

"Lydia. When she congratulated me, she was laughing."

"You fail to see the humor in your expectancy?"

"I fail to see the humor in plenty of things."

Stela has the good sense not to agree. "I believe she spared your life, Elizabeth. As much as it pains me to admit, she does care for you. May I speak plainly?"

I nod, close her hand in mine.

"If Lydia was laughing, it was because her actions do not matter. Whether the Inquisitor condemns us to die or pardons us, our fate is sealed."

"Ruxandra's wellbeing will be the Moroi's first priority. If we are permitted to live, we will be captives until the child finishes us off. Fast work if we are denied the right to hunt, which we almost certainly will be." She watches the horror steal across my face.

"We need to leave," I whisper, my head in my hands.

Stela laughs dryly. "Shall I call a cab, or do we have time for a shower?"

"I'm serious Stela."

"So am I," she says. "My darling, we need transportation, money, a steady food source."

"We don't have time to map everything out. It's about survival."

"Ah, but this is all the time we will ever have." Stela shrugs, stretches her legs. "Our enemy is organized and well-funded. They expect us to make a break for it, and that will be our undoing. We will leave Chicago, but not tonight."

She's right. They're watching the hospitals, we know that much for certain. Lydia and Bård have joined the hunt, at least for the sake of appearances, and who better to anticipate our movements? Where are Darius and Crogher in all this? Did they survive?

"Elizabeth, we need to talk about food," she begins, carefully. "The only way we will be able to keep Ruxandra fed is by gifting our blood to mortals. By building the child a coven of her own."

I withdraw my hand. "I'm not doing that. I'm not condemning a human being to this life, Stela. I won't."

"*Condemning*," she whispers. "Is that what I have done to you?"

I didn't mean that.

I think to kneel in front of her, to comfort her somehow. But I remain where I am. If I relent, even a little, what will be asked of me? "Stela…" I am not a spiteful person. I am not ungrateful to her, and yet I can't think of a single soothing thing to say.

The early morning light is creeping between the pulled blinds. Stela can't even look at me.

"I do not apologize for loving you, Elizabeth. I will never be sorry for that."

"I'm not asking you to apologize, Stela. I'm asking you not to have me…do this…to someone else." She flinches. "It was my choice to follow you into this life."

Stela sneers. "Your choice was to carry my shadow in your heart for the rest of your days or join me in this hell." She stands slowly, headed for the stairs. She pauses at the landing. "For what it is worth, I never had a choice either." She mounts the stairs, her face turned up to the open door. "I loved you the moment we met."

* * *

"Stela!" The pressure brings me upright in bed, screaming in the mauve light of early evening. I kick the covers back with heavy, aching legs.

The sheets have been soaked through. The pressure builds, and my mind identifies it immediately.

"Stela. *Wake up*." I shout, rolling myself to the edge of the bed. My belly is unrecognizable, swollen and stretched. I heave myself upright and Ruxandra thrashes, but Stela slumbers on. "Please. Wake up," I whisper, doubling forward from the pressure.

The strength has all but left me. My hunger is a bone-deep ache and I crawl to the bathroom. Ruxandra is heavy against my front, fitful and urgent in her movements. I have no idea when I went into labor, how long she's been struggling without my help, or how much of my blood she's taken. The contraction stops when I reach the wall between the tub and the sink. I time the length between contractions, taking slow, deliberate breaths.

Four minutes, thirty-nine seconds.

Ruxandra kicks me in the liver and Stela wakes up to hear me howl.

"Elizabeth?" She scrambles out of the blankets.

"In. Here."

Stela flips the light switch in the bathroom.

"Contractions are—" I inhale sharply, and Stela takes my curled fists in her hands, strokes my wrists until my grip eases. "Four and half minutes apart."

"How long do they last?" she asks.

I laugh dryly in spite of my pain, and groan in relief as the pressure relents. "You'll—be the first—to know." Stela relaxes, moves to take a seat beside me.

"Don't sit down!" I jerk her arm, and she's up on her feet.

"What?" she asks. "What do you need?"

"Get the bag. Please." A rush of strength washes through me as the pain subsides. There isn't enough blood on this earth to sate me. "Downstairs. The backpack."

Stela leaves swiftly and returns with the backpack in one hand and a cooler in the other.

"What's that?" I tip my head toward the cooler, but I can smell it already. Stela shakes the container and the sound is unmistakable. "Blood," I whisper and offer her a weak smile. It's all the praise she needs.

"That was the reason I thought it wise to make two *separate* trips to the hospital," she teases.

I toss a wad of balled clothing at her. "Put the scrubs on."

"Why?" she asks, her eyes narrowed.

"Because it'll help me take you seriously."

Stela's lovely laugh fills the room with light as she does precisely what I ask. That's the thing about Stela: she always does what is asked.

"My love?" My voice quavers. "I'm sorry," I say, choking back a sob. "For what I said last night…you didn't condemn me to anything."

Stela strides over to me. Even in that awful teal color she is beautiful. But the cost of my love, of keeping me alive has taken its toll. Her sleep-rumpled hair has lost its shine, smudges of purple rest beneath both black eyes and her cheeks appear sunken. She kneels between my feet once more, resting her hands on my knees.

"My darling," she kisses the top of each knee, squeezing my trembling hands, "never apologize for what you have lost. Not to me. Not to anyone."

"I was trying to—"

"Make amends," she finishes with a pained smile. "Yes, I know." She massages my aching calves. "If I wanted a mindlessly demure companion, I would have chosen accordingly."

"I knew you liked my surly demeanor."

I grunt, curling in on myself as the contraction starts.

"Ah, there she is," Stela teases, hoisting me up to my feet. "Welcome back."

"Why am I standing?" The words leave me in a wasted rush. I lock my arms around her neck as she takes small, backward steps.

"I read somewhere that it helps to move."

I laugh harshly. "You're the doctor." What starts as a wink ends in a muffled cry of pain against her shoulder. I didn't know we could feel such pain. Then again, I can't remember the last time I was this starved. Stela wraps an arm around my waist and rubs my back with the other as we take a lazy lap across the cold bathroom tiles. She kneads my lower back as the contraction passes, her hands leaving my body only as long as it takes her to set the water running in the tub. I grip her shoulder tightly to keep upright. Before I can apologize, she maneuvers me gently down into the warm water.

"Oh," I moan, letting the sudden warmth relax the knots in my thighs and back. Stela drops on the floor beside the tub, stroking the side of my face and smiling indulgently.

The contractions begin again, sharper than before, lower. I reach for Stela's hand, breathing through the pain, and fight the urge to start pushing early. I clench my teeth to avoid crushing her hand. Stela tips forward, braces her free hand on the rim of the tub.

Running her hand up and down my back Stela speaks soft words of encouragement in my ear as my body contorts. The contraction lasts for a full minute, and the resting period between them is dwindling.

"What is it like?" she asks, awe in her voice.

My head thuds back against the tiled wall as the pain crests and then passes. "Like being torn in half."

Stela casts her eyes down to the water, saying nothing. My grip on her hand tightens ahead of schedule. This is a new pain, something like a tear, a burning sensation. Nothing I can categorize or explain.

"Relax," I say. "False alarm." The pain recedes but remains on the fringe of my awareness.

Stela nods and leaves my side to throw a clean towel on the floor. She strides into the bedroom and returns with two pillows. I watch her kneel beside the towel and unpack the birthing supplies I stole from the hospital. She holds the receiving blanket in her hands, rubs the material between her fingers and sets it aside. She bends down to adjust the pillows.

"You *did* read up on this, didn't you?"

Stela turns with her hands on her hips, arches her brow. "Did you think I would let you brave this alone?"

"I don't know what I thought," I admit, gratefully letting my eyes drift closed. The pain returns unannounced, and this time the sensation lingers. A deep, grating burn. Stela's presses her cool lips to my forehead.

"Elizabeth…" Stela's hand closes over my shoulder, and the anxiety in her voice forces my eyes open just in time to see a red, curling cloud of fresh blood bloom between my legs. The burn becomes a searing pain, climbing the column of my spine as Stela heaves me out of the tub. I can't get my breathing under control as she bends down and lays me gently on the towel. Her neck is so close. One volley of strength is all it would take.

Stela loses her composure, closing my legs in an effort to stop the hemorrhage. She flicks open a clean towel and wraps it around my torso, rubbing my ice-cold arms, watching my face. I know she's speaking to me, but the only sound filling that stark, sad space between us is the beating of her heart. Reading my mind, or perhaps, just knowing my expression, Stela pulls the cotton neckline of her teal scrubs aside and bares her neck to me.

The ache to feed is furious and at the sight of her pale throat the muscles in my arms and legs begin to twitch. I try to push her back by the shoulders, frightened by the severity of my hunger and the pain burning low in my abdomen. Stela shoves my hands aside, wrapping an arm around my shoulders. She forces me sit up as her free hand cradles the back of my head, pushing my mouth into place. Unconsciously my fangs descend through the soft flesh of my gums and into her waiting jugular.

The blood is quiet at first, rushing into my open mouth where a heavy sob of relief threatens the first deep drink. Stela's voice becomes clear, moving inside of me under the thick sweet taste. Memories of happier times appear, lying together in our lavish bed, taking time with each other, talking about my past and our shared future. A time before I understood the depths of my allegiance to Stela, before I truly realized the threat our coven of two was to Fane.

"Stop." The whisper reaches me in the heavy shadow of our darkened bed, and sounds more like a hiss from the crackling fire in the hearth, than a plea. I can smell the wood she used to build it, dried birch and oak.

"Elizabeth." Her arms encircle me, and there is no pain here. Just the welcomed weight of Stela's embrace, the brushing of our legs.

"Enough!" Stela's hands wrench me back by the shoulders and the first thing I see when my eyes open is the gnarled flesh of her beautiful neck ripped open and dangling savagely just above her clavicle. Stela falls back onto the tile, clutching the wound closed in a weak hand and struggling to focus on my face.

"I'm sorry." I lunge forward with renewed strength and close my hand over hers, doubling the pressure on her weeping injury. Stela rests heavily against the arm I brace around her waist, and gently I scoot our bodies across the tile to the small cooler she brought with her. The blood is cold, a meager consolation that will have to do for now. She cups her sticky hand around my cheek as I bring the collection bag to her lips.

Stela's wound clots with the first drink, and she can support her own weight with the second. By the time the bag is empty she's sitting upright on her own, wringing the plastic in her hands. Wordlessly, she reaches for another.

I've said before that feeding is sedative and stimulant in one. As the high of Stela's blood recedes, I see the danger of that combination in a new light and come crashing back to reality mid-contraction. Stela makes quick work of her second helping, tosses the bag over her shoulder and eases me back onto the sopping towel. Fearless, even for her. Quite unlike someone who was very nearly murdered. Her resilience is astounding.

Together, we count and keep track of the time. One minute becomes a minute and a half, becomes two full minutes, and somewhere along the way the burning sensation returns. So does the bleeding.

"Stela." I tighten the arm slung over her shoulders to force her to look at my face, not at the blood draining out of my body and webbing out over the floor. Reluctantly, she complies. "Something's wrong."

Her body bows protectively around my side. I wish I could keep her here, pressed close. I wish I could end this for her. "I need you to look and tell me what you see. Can you do that for me?"

The slow, patient timbre of my voice gives everything away and Stela's steely, determined expression slips into something heartbreakingly human. That small, single frown line appears between her brows as she nods absently, like a woman headed for the gallows. Stela holds my legs apart with a hand on each knee.

"What do you see?"

"Blood." She all but spits the word on the floor. Whether it's her appetite or her mounting concern for me, I can't be sure. I wager it's an unhelpful mix of both.

"Can you see the head, Stela?" Her scowl deepens, and her chin dips in thought. She's stopped breathing, but I can see the strength it takes for her to resist the instinct. Her hands tense from the force of her restraint.

"No." Monosyllabic responses are never a good sign with her.

"Okay, what else do you see? Besides blood."

"Nothing."

"Stela… Nothing is not an answer. There has to be something." She lowers her eyes, and I note the presence of her hand, the pressure of a probing touch.

"A hip, I think." The second tenuous push of her fingers is like gasoline to a flame. It takes every ounce of strength I possess not to scream.

"I think it's her back." Stela straightens up and instantly registers my pain. "Are you having another contraction?"

"The contraction hasn't stopped, Stela."

"Should you push?" She takes my hand, trying so very hard to help.

I choke back a scream and ride a wave of nausea which I haven't felt since my last human victim. The burning radiates to the tip of each finger and the soles of my feet. I focus my attention on the source, low in my pelvis, and suddenly a nightmare comes back to me. Claws just barely visible beneath the skin of my belly. Ruxandra will rip her way out if she has to. Burn her way out. She's already begun.

"Stela, listen to me carefully. The baby is horizontal."

"Yes," she says with a nod. "At least she appears that way to me."

In struggling to form my next coherent thought, Stela finishes it for us both. "You will not be able to deliver her this way."

"Exactly."

"Should I…what can I do?" Her brazen armor slips, and her arms fall helplessly to her sides. I turn my head and dry wretch.

"We have two options, but we're going to focus on the first." I wipe my dry mouth with the back of my hand, lift myself on my elbows despite the persistent pain. Stela is going to need reassurance. "You need to turn her around."

"How?"

"With your hands."

Stela all but jumps into action. Before she can begin, her reason and worry get the better of her. "Will it cause you pain?"

"Most likely. But not as much as option two, okay?"

She doesn't respond. She doesn't move. Her face is intentionally vacant, but her eyes broadcast her concern louder than words ever could. I place my hands palm down on the tiles and focus on the stillness of the house, the dreary chill, Stela's steadily climbing heartbeat.

Stela opens my knees and pushes her body between them. The pressure on my lower half is as great as catching an anvil with your pelvis. I grind the side of my tongue between my molars and savor the distraction of new pain.

Just as I feared, Stela's first steady push sends the burning everywhere at once. Behind my eyes, clawing up the back of my throat, ringing in my ears like a siren. Stela knows, her touch grows exploratory and seriously lacks conviction. The baby moves, largely, I suspect, on her own and not in any useful direction. Ruxandra curls in on herself, immensely displeased, and shrinks away from Stela.

"Dearest, I—"

"Try. Again."

And so she does, firmer this time, but without anything to grip. A foot would be something, an arm, but Stela is starting to suspect what I already know. Blood floods my mouth, seeping from the corner of my lips before I can swallow it back down. The last few drops of fortitude Stela spared me dribble down my cheek, but I don't feel sick anymore. In fact, I've lost all feeling in my legs.

"It's all right," I whisper. Stela continues undeterred, focused on the task. Her hand keeps slipping, pushing the baby up. "Stela, it's all right."

The pain is fading fast, and my vision has begun to darken around the edges. Blood drains out of my body. I'll lose consciousness soon. Stela's hands and forearms are crimson and dripping when she withdraws. She stares at them as though she's never witnessed such carnage.

I clear my throat and focus on the ceiling. Stela falls silent and even now I know her thoughts, they litter the air. She's waiting for a reprimand, convinced that this too is her fault. But this was always the only way, I see that now. Ruxandra tried to tell me.

"Go downstairs," I say, summoning all my strength to speak steadily, "there's a chef's knife in the drawer beside the fridge." How many evenings did I find myself standing at that drawer with my fingers on the handle? Why didn't I listen?

"No," Stela says, but I hear the waver in her voice. The word is a plea, not a refusal. Sadly, we don't have time for either.

"Bring it to me." The shadow in my vision has darkened around the edges, an inky tunnel, like staring up from the bottom of a well and just as cold.

"There has to be another way." Her crimson fingers grip both my knees, but I can't feel her.

"Stela…" I reach out my hand and she catches it quickly, bending over me to kiss my palm and hold it against her cheek. That I can feel. The sensation hasn't left my arms. "You have to hurry. I'm going to black out."

I've never believed in fate but there's something comforting about the concept. It's comforting to believe that all roads would have brought us here in the end, because if I can believe that then everything that has happened had a purpose. And if fate brought me to this moment, maybe it isn't an end at all.

Stela extricates herself and watches me closely, her nerves getting the better of her. Her chest heaves. She points a determined finger down at me. "Stay with me, Elizabeth." She's not asking. She's giving an order, and if there was ever any doubt that I belonged to her there isn't anymore. My name dances in the air above my body, bears down upon my chest, and finds a way through all the damnable silence to steal inside my heart. The blackness shrinks but doesn't fade. Still, I can see her face more clearly now, like the sun is shining down on me. I know my voice is there before I speak. I know it will be steady and strong, and exactly what she needs to leave my side.

"Always."

Stela retreats, her own blood loss slowing her steps. There isn't much time, and I'll be damned if I waste any more.

"Can you hear me?" The burning subsides, like something inside me was being pushed or twisted and then released. "Ruxandra," I whisper. The name falls comfortably from my mouth, familiar though I have never spoken it aloud. The name has weight, gravity all its own. It finds her. Everything stops, the burning is gone along with some of the pain. She moves inside me as though she's angling in for a secret. "Push against my hand."

Nothing happens. I drum my fingers over the taut, swollen skin of my abdomen and wait. "Ruxandra, I need to know where you are. Take your hand and push." She may not even know what a hand is, or what the word push means. She could be as startled to hear her name from my lips as I am.

I press down with my palm and her small body flutters. I release the pressure and notice Stela standing in the open door. The chef's knife shimmers against her thigh, clutched tightly in her right hand.

I push the heel of my hand down again and this time I'm met with resistance. A wave of relief rushes over me and slowly I raise myself upright. This brings Stela to my side in an instant, and I'm grateful for her assistance. Without a word she rests my shoulders back against the wall, adjusting my pillows to support me.

"Keep your hand pressed against my hand and bring it over your head." Ruxandra doesn't move straight away. I know she can hear my voice, but it seems to take time for her to absorb the meaning of each word. Inside, her tiny fist drags across the tattered tissue in which she is ensconced, giving me a clear picture of the internal damage as her balled fist travels from the base of my palm to the tip of my fingers. She pushes up against my hand once more, and then curls her limbs in tight.

"Give me the knife." I hold my hand out to Stela, open and expecting. I knew she wouldn't love the second option. She remains frozen at my side with the blade clenched in her lap.

"Let me." Her resolve is firm but she doesn't move. Ruxandra has stopped clawing her way out, but the reprieve won't last and I'm still losing blood.

"There's no shame in handing me the knife, Stela. If the tables were turned, I don't know what I would do."

"You would do exactly what needs to be done," she growls.

"Yes, I would." I lay my hand on hers and her grip loosens. She'll give it to me, but she would prefer it be taken by force. "Allow me do it now."

The knife is in my hand. "I'm going to scream," I tell her. "Don't let me stop." She nods in acknowledgment, but her eyes are glued to my belly and the small knot two inches from my navel where Ruxandra has raised her balled fist once again.

The blade is dull, chipped at the edges with small spots of rust gnawing at the tip. The blunt tip dimples my skin. Stela's hands twitch in her lap, and I know that in a moment she'll wrap her hand over mine and force the metal down. I don't wait for her. The strength of my scream surprises me. It's more life than I thought I had left. But the blade is buried now, moving deeply and regrettably slowly. Ruxandra draws her body close, her legs pulled up against her chest.

What blood I have left oozes from the wound, streaking down on all sides, coating my hands, covering the blade and obscuring the wound. The familiar dark closes in. Stela's hands are hovering around the incision, pulling the skin back. She's asking questions, I hear the shape of them, but the strangest clatter fills my head. My last death was such a silent, impartial thing. Everything now is sharp and urgent. A distinct sound reaches me as I lose my grip on the blade, gunshots or a series of fireworks, I can't tell which. Beneath the noise is a familiar song, hundreds of voices. What are they singing?

Stela snatches the knife and I see her wedge it between the walls of muscle and weeping vessels. She has something in her hands, a dripping bundle so deep a red as to be almost black. Stela claws it open with her nails, and the amniotic sack splatters to the floor.

She's not crying. Ruxandra doesn't make a single sound, but that awful commotion between my ears continues, louder and closer than before. A great joyous din, everywhere at once, deafening.

As the curtain closes over me, I sense Stela's body. She lifts my head, her fingers part my lips and the tepid plastic of a blood collection bag scrapes the tip of my tongue. Stela must have bitten it, because the blood pours freely into my slack mouth, down my throat. I try to speak. I try to ask her if she hears that terrible noise. One after another the bags are drained. Gradually, I see her shadow towering over me. I can feel my legs again, the pressure of Stela's fingers, insistent, clenching the back of my head. I hear my muscles slipping back into place and Stela's soothing encouragements. Her lips are noticeably warmer than my skin when she presses them against my brow, and soon I'm holding the bag in my own hands.

"The baby?"

"Is fine," she says. "Feed." Stela leans over for another bag, and in my newfound clarity I wait for all this human blood to make me sick, but it doesn't. Resting on the backpack beside me, wrapped in the cheap receiving blanket—now spotted with Stela's bloody fingerprints—is a swaddled Ruxandra, fitfully kicking her strong legs.

I hoist myself up, a hand falling instinctively to my waist, but there's nothing to hold in. The wound is closed. My abdomen is blood-smeared and concave from starvation, but otherwise recognizable.

Stela forcefully pushes another bag to my mouth and watches me eat as intently as she used to when I was newly made.

She reaches for a fifth bag, but I wave it off. I'm weak but I'll survive. "Did you clamp the umbilical cord?" I ask, unable to take my eyes off the wriggling infant in the corner.

"No need," Stela assures, baring her wrist to me. There is a faint pink ribbon of new and freshly mended skin.

"You fed her."

"She was famished." Stela shrugs, as though the child told her in plain English. No one speaks after that, we sit closely together, Stela's hand resting protectively on the top of my thigh. Distantly I realize that the noisy clatter of death has followed me back to this bloodied bathroom. Now awkward, stumbling steps and happy chatter on the streets outside. Real and alive.

"What day is it?" I ask.

Stela tears her gaze away from the child. "The first of January."

She reaches an arm around my shoulders, timidly at first. I welcome her embrace, the sudden crush of her arms around me and sigh contentedly when her familiar scent swims around my head. Delicious as always, but resistible once again. Stela kisses the top of my head, my ear, my cheek, moving slowly to my lips. I savor the taste of her, reveling in her touch now that the overwhelming urge to consume her has passed.

"Do you want her?" she asks in a low, grave voice.

Not: would you like to hold her?

I turn Stela by the chin and all the fear she's so desperate to hide is written plainly on her face. She loves her already. She loved Ruxandra the moment she felt her move inside me. Perhaps, even before that.

"Bring her to me."

Stela leaves my side only long enough to scoop Ruxandra off the floor and deposit her gently in the waiting cradle of my arms. Then she slumps back against the wall beside me, taking hold of Ruxandra's blanket-wrapped foot.

Ruxandra curls against me. Her eyes shut tight. Her head is capped with wild curls, blond hair burnished with gold and streaks of chestnut. Her sticky skin is pink and thin, veins can be seen on a small patch of cheek that Stela wiped clean. Her face is shaped like my mother's, but beyond her curls she hasn't inherited anything other than my chin. Not a hint of James.

I eye the open cooler hungrily. We can't risk another hospital heist until we shake our pursuers. We'll need to restock our supply of blood bags once we're outside the state. Stela can enthrall some unsuspecting mark and procure a vehicle easily enough, but then what?

Outside, the neighborhood is a riot of taxis and liquored-up pedestrians. People shouting over fences, bottle rockets, a stampede of feet echoing up into the cold, dark sky. The new year arrives in the dead of night, in the blistering cold, doused with champagne, greeted with a kiss, with promises and resolve strengthened by the presence of strangers and close friends.

With a contented sigh Stela rests her head wearily on my shoulder. Ruxandra wiggles a fist free, sucks her bottom lip into her mouth and opens her eyes.

Pale blue eyes. Alert, penetrating, and wholly unafraid.

Fane's eyes…

Stela smiles down at Ruxandra and kisses the side of my neck as a row of scalpel-sharp, perfectly formed teeth pierces my breast.

Bella Books, Inc.

Women. Books. Even Better Together.

P.O. Box 10543
Tallahassee, FL 32302

Phone: 800-729-4992
www.bellabooks.com